# And the Next Thing You Know...

## Chase Taylor Hackett

**LYRICAL PRESS**
Kensington Publishing Corp.
www.kensingtonbooks.com

Lyrical Press books are published by
Kensington Publishing Corp. 119 West 40th Street New York, NY 10018

First Electronic Edition:
eISBN-13: 978-1-5161-0446-8
eISBN-10: 1-5161-0446-3

First Print Edition:
ISBN-13: 978-1-5161-0447-5
ISBN-10: 1-5161-0447-1

Printed in the United States of America

*For Travis, without whom there would be no point.*

*Or dinner.*

# Chapter 1
## Running

*JEFFREY*

Thamp thamp thamp thamp thamp thamp thamp thamp.

That was my running shoes on the wet pavement of East 87th Street. Not fast, just trotting, just getting warmed up. I don't really hit my stride until I get to Central Park.

It was still mostly dark out. Even though it was a Saturday, I liked to get up and out this early, before the rest of the world. Not a lot of people out this time of day.

Except for this guy and his gigantic dirty-white poodle and a fifteen-foot leash, I swear.

*Yo, Pierre, gimme a break!*

It was like waiting for a freight train to go by—I jogged in place until I could get around them. Who knew poodles even came in that size? There ought to be a law. That thing was like a Shetland pony with a haircut.

Garbage truck. The garbage guys saw me practically every day and waved, like I was their buddy or something. I raised my head in a nod.

What a miserable morning. It was cold, it was drizzling. Wasn't this like the first day of spring or something? Typical. People always got all stupid about spring, but *this* was what spring really was—cold and wet.

Man, was I in a bad mood.

Got up in a bad mood.

Again.

It had been a stretch of bad moods lately. Seriously. Since like October. I suppose that means since Roger. Old boyfriend. Make of that what you will.

It didn't help that my apartment was half a construction zone. I had bought the apartment below me and I was doing a huge reno to turn the two apartments into one giant duplex. I mean, I was having *people* do the reno, e.g., architect, contractors, subcontractors. I'm a lawyer at a big New York firm; I wasn't swinging a hammer myself. The place would be fantastic when it was done, but until then...

As always, I turned left onto Fifth down to 85th Street—there's an entrance to the park at 85th.

I had to jog in place, waiting for the light before I could cross Fifth Ave. with a couple of other runners. I nodded. One woman wiped some soggy hair from her forehead (from the drizzle, not from sweating) and smiled—I didn't.

And that was about it for a social life for me on the run. Occasionally, very very occasionally, I'd see some hot guy who'd catch my attention. But even that had been a while. Maybe it was menopause. My thirtieth birthday was coming up. Was this the beginning of the end?

Oh God, maybe.

There was never much traffic at this early hour, and I didn't wait for the light to change. I jogged across toward the park entrance as soon as I could.

I had work stuff in my head. I realized I was making a list of crap I had to do. And then I started a second list of crap I could move off *my* list and on to somebody *else's* list of crap to do.

Across Fifth Ave. there's a short path that leads along through the park just above the 84th Street transverse, with the Metropolitan Museum off to my left. Then a sharp right onto the East Drive. That's where it happens. That's where I stop jogging and start running—and once I'm there, I'm in the zone and I'm not bothered by anything. The Guggenheim could be in flames, I wouldn't notice. It was just in the warm-up that my head kept churning.

My route: uptown past the reservoir, around and down the west side and then loop back up to the Met. It's about a five-mile circuit. I jog/cool-out on the way back to the apartment.

I was just across Fifth when my phone gave out with a text-ping. Fuckaduck. *Why do I bring the damned thing with me?* I asked myself. In case of a work emergency was the answer. This wasn't a work emergency. It was from my best friend Rebecca. She wanted me to help her help somebody move.

Like as if.

Don't get me wrong—I adored Rebecca, there wasn't anything I wouldn't do for her. Unless it was help her help somebody I didn't even know, move. In the rain.

I stopped jogging long enough to dictate my response.

"Not on your life."

I deleted my response.

I dictated again.

"Gosh comma wish I could period incredibly swamped period good luck with the move period." Send.

I put the phone away. It was time to get going.

It was like giving a horse his head. As soon as I let them, my legs stretched out over the pavement in long, perfect strides. The legs knew the pace.

Thamp thamp thamp thamp.

Work, construction, gigantic poodles, even ex-boyfriends—all melted away.

And I was gone.

# Chapter 2
## Moving In

*THEO*

"Christ-on-a-crosswalk! That hurt! Ow!" I was holding one end of my keyboard, wrapped in a blanket. The keyboard was in the blanket, not me. I was backing through the door to Rebecca's building, and somehow, between me and Becca, we'd just managed to smash the fingers of my left hand between the keyboard and the doorjamb. Actually, now I was holding the wrapped-up keyboard with one hand, while I waved the wounded one in the air, trying to shake off the pain. "You know, if you break my fingers, we can just forget about the keyboard altogether."

"Sor-ry!" said Beccs in exaggerated syllables, still holding her end of the keyboard. I blew on my now-bleeding knuckles to make them feel better. "Little Theo get an owie?" If that sounds like a tormenting big sister, that's because that's exactly what it was. My tormenting big sister.

I hate hate hate being called little and Becca knows it. I'm not very tall, I concede the point. That does not make me 'little.'

But Rebecca was helping me move, so I had to shut up about it. Not only was she helping me move, she was helping me move into *her* apartment to sleep on *her* couch—totally temporarily—but she was my sister, so she couldn't say no.

We'd managed to get the shittiest weather possible for this little move, too. Cold, rainy. It was supposed to be the first day of spring—on the calendar anyway—but in reality, it was just piss-miserable. But we had to do it today, it was the only day Beccs had free. (She has this total dregs job—she's a lawyer at a big ugly law firm.)

We'd already made a couple trips loading the elevator (Rebecca lived on the fifth floor) with the few boxes of clothes I had. This was *after* we'd moved everything down from my old flat-share—three flights, *no* elevator, and *no* help from my roommates, now *ex*-roommates. Becca had tried to rope in some friend of hers but he'd squirmed out of it. When I say it was 'some friend,' I mean it. *Some friend,* I thought.

Not that I had a lot of stuff because I didn't. I lived like a monk. The worst were the boxes of books (not a lot!), some boxes of scores (okay, those boogers were heavy), and the keyboard. Not much more than that. We'd filled the elevator and left the scores in the double-parked rental van for the next trip up.

Rebecca, in her pink track suit, leaned against the elevator wall, sighed, and she pushed some wet strawberry-blond from her forehead (it was drizzling). Becca's a big girl, but not as fit as I am, so it was taking a toll.

We rode in the elevator in silence. I'm not exactly famous for being the most sensitive person in the world, but even I had the general idea that this would be a good time to shut the hell up.

"So Theo," said Rebecca, once we were in the apartment, "here's what we're going to do. We're going to go back down to the van, and you're going to unload the boxes of scores into the lobby. While I watch. Then I'm going to drive the van back to the rental place while you bring the boxes upstairs. From here on in, the only thing I'm lifting is a glass of very cold Chablis."

"I'm not leaving my scores in the lobby! Somebody could steal them!"

"For the love of Mike, nobody but nobody is going to steal a box that weighs sixty pounds, not even in New York." We're from Iowa. We grew up on a farm even. I tell you this so you can get all your hick jokes out of the way now, since I've heard all the wisecracks about Mayberry already.

"I suppose," I said.

The boxes were precious to me, but I recognized not everyone found the same value in conductor scores of old musicals.

"Okay?" she continued. "By the time I come back, you'll be done. Right?" She was looking at me for a confirmation.

"I guess."

"I'll call for pizza on my way—there's money in the kitchen drawer if the guy gets here before me. So. Ready?"

"Ready."

And that's what we did.

So how did I get myself exiled from my flat-share, I hear you ask.

It just wasn't meant to be. For starters, they were always bitching about me and the keyboard being in the way. What was I supposed to do about that? I'm a songwriter, which they knew before they asked me to move in, so I needed the keyboard. I used headphones and everything, but was being silent enough for them? No. I was apparently supposed to dematerialize as well.

And on top of that, people tell me I can be a little bit spiky sometimes, and sometimes I say things which I usually mean to be mere constructive criticism, that others sometimes consider to be mean, and which are sometimes totally misconstrued as being unforgivably cruel. For example, one of my flatmates, Beth, had asked me to read her new play. Why would she ask me to read her play if she didn't want to hear the truth about it? And the truth about it was that it was an imitation of an imitation of a made-for-TV movie. Okay, harsh, I admit, but so is showbiz. It also seemed to me that if she really wanted to work in the theatre, she should maybe toughen up, instead of exploding into sobs the way she did in the face of the tiniest criticisms. And I told her that too.

After that, they *all* hated me for some reason because it was somehow *my* fault that I had made Beth cry, and she was now talking about moving back to Tennessee, which was obviously unfair, since I'd never said a *word* about Tennessee.

And then of course there was the whole rent thing.

People can be so petty.

So that's how I got myself voted off the island, or at least out of a really cheap, really really crowded apartment-share in Alphabet City.

I was reliving these happy moments while I lugged one incredibly heavy box after another from the elevator into Rebecca's apartment. When everything was done—meaning boxes were stacked in the corner—we finally sat down to our favorite pizza. Hamburger. (We're from Iowa—remember?) I was starving.

"So, Theo," she said midway through, "I have a surprise for you."

"A good surprise or a bad surprise?"

"A good surprise, for sure."

"You didn't get us tickets to a show, did you?" That would have been awesome, and I could really have used it right then, considering what I'd been through with the dipshit ex-flatmates and just how monumentally foul my life seemed to be going. I didn't expect *Hamilton,* or anything, but there were plenty of other things. Any show is better than not.

"Well, sorry, I didn't get you tickets to a show."

"If it's underwear, that would also be fantastic." I never had any money, and when I did, I never spent it on clothes. It was a part of the homo gene I'd missed. I was the worst-dressed gayboy in Manhattan, but the underwear situation was starting to get desperate.

Of course Rebecca didn't owe me anything. She was already letting me sleep on her couch, and she had also paid for the rental van to move my stuff because if I'd had any money I'd still be in the flat-share with the dipshits. And of course if it weren't for Rebecca's couch, I'd be on a bench in Central Park or something. Or more likely I'd be on a bus back to Iowa. Which would definitely be worse. So I didn't expect anything more from my sister. But she'd said she had a surprise, so—

"So? What's my big surprise then?"

"I got you a job."

"A job?! Like that's a good thing???"

"It is. Once you get paid, you can buy yourself all the underwear you want!" My head fell forward until it thumped on the table. "As long as you're sleeping on my couch, you'll have a job. Or it's back to the farm. This is not the Rebecca McPherson Unemployed Songwriters Retreat. I'm serious."

"Okay, fine," I said, still without picking up my head. "Doing what? Garbage collector?"

"Nothing so glamorous. I got you a job in my office."

My head came up abruptly.

"Your law firm?!" Ugh. "Fine." I was a brave boy, I could face my fate, no matter how gruesome. "Doing what?"

"You won't be practicing law just yet, if that's what you're thinking. One of the secretaries is getting a hip replacement, and you'll be covering for her."

"A secretary?"

"A secretary. Answer the phone, type, and be polite. You're good at two of those."

"Will I get a hot boss? Not that I would ever go out with some Republican stuffed shirt of a lawyer—"

"Hey! I'm a lawyer, too, remember?"

"Sorry. But a cute boss would at least be a distraction."

"Hate to disappoint you, poops, but no cute boss. You're working for Victoria Collins. She's also the partner in charge of associate assignments— meaning associates like me. She can have a huge effect on my career—good or not so good."

"I'll try not to sabotage you."

"You know how to be charming, I've even seen you do it, in short spurts. So make an effort. Maybe you could get me on the *Hiromi* case."

"What's that?"

"Big case, Japanese conglomerate, might be going to trial. Everybody wants on it."

"Oh."

"Anyway, sorry—Victoria is not remotely cute."

"Is there anything good about this job?"

"Let's see—it's not in Iowa, and there are no literal pigs involved, only figurative ones. How's that?" She had a point. "You should thank me."

"Did you tell them about the workshop?" I'm in a songwriters' workshop that meets every Monday at four. I was hoping for a deal-breaker here.

"Yes, and they'll live with you cutting out at three thirty on Mondays—"

"Damn." They *would* be flexible.

"—and you'll make up the time during the rest of the week."

"Fine."

"Oh, and one other thing, about this job I got you?"

"Yeah?"

*"I* got you the job. Where I work. What you do there reflects on me. Therefore, you will behave yourself."

"Yeah yeah yeah."

"I'm dead serious. There can be no tantrums at this job."

"Fine!" I admit, sometimes I had a hard time staying calm. Everyone said it was natural because I have this red hair—in contrast to Becca's strawberry blond, mine's like a forest fire. So instead of being easygoing like her, I was the redhead cliché with the crazy-ass temper.

But I swear, I only went ballistic with people who really deserved it.

"You are aware," I reminded her, "that that thing at the diner was totally not my fault."

"Oh absolutely, Theo. Absolutely." Sarcasm. From my own sister.

The reference was to a tiny little incident at my last awful day job—waiting behind the counter in a diner. I sort of went off on a jerk—who was also a customer. That the jerk soooooooooo had it coming didn't impress the manager, who was not exactly the sharpest note on the piano either. I was immediately asked to turn in my clip-on bow tie.

I'm not gonna lie—it was a great job to get fired from, and getting fired like that was—fan-fucking-tastic. I highly recommend it.

But Rebecca was pissed about it and said I was irresponsible, which I was/am, I admit. And of course the loss of a job and the concomitant loss of income meant that I couldn't quite pay the dipshit flatmates this month's rent on time—which was apparently the straw that broke the camel's water, and that's how they became my dipshit *ex*-flatmates, which necessitated the move here—to my sister's fold-out couch.

"Human Resources wants you ASAP," said Rebecca, "but when can you start?"

"Oh man. I was hoping Madison would ask me to go with him up to the Goodspeed Opera, but I don't know yet. Can you put it off a week?" Madison was my sort-of boyfriend, whose new musical was getting a development production at the Goodspeed in Connecticut—it's not really an opera house or not anymore, anyway. Madison wrote the book and lyrics for this show.

"I'll see. When will you know?"

"I'll talk to Madison."

"Good. Let me know. Soon."

"Maybe you should make it two weeks just to be safe? Or three?"

She gave me one of her big-sister looks, which I took to be a—

"No."

# Chapter 3
## When Things Started to Go to Hell

*JEFFREY*

I was in a hallway at the office, talking to another attorney, when I heard something from around the corner that made my blood freeze.

"Well, da-yam!"

That—in case you don't know—is a 'damn' that is so damned gay that it cannot be confined to a single syllable. I shuddered involuntarily.

I recognized both the voice and the strange locution.

How do I explain it? It was like finding a squirrel in your living room—probably harmless but it doesn't belong there.

I didn't bother to finish what I was saying to the other guy—I had to look around the corner and see for myself.

"Tommy!"

Tommy Radford was sitting at a secretary's desk at my firm. Where he definitely did not belong.

A., he worked at another firm; and

B., he was Roger's best friend—Roger, my ex-boyfriend. Which meant that Tommy should have been carefully filed away under Somebody-I-Never-Have-to-Deal-With-Again, no?

And yet.

Tommy never liked me, and I never liked Tommy. So what the hell was he doing at *my* firm? Did he just move over here to torment me? Spy on me? What?

"Tommy, what the hell?" I said by way of a greeting.

"Hey, Jeffrey." He smiled at me sweetly and folded his hands on his desk like a little girl. "How've you been?"

"I'm great. Never better. Why the hell are you here?"

"I work here, like it's any of your beeswax. I hopped firms and now I work for Mr. Kaminsky, among others. Have you met Mr. Kaminsky?"

"Of course I've met Mr.—! Since when?"

"You mean me, here? Since last week."

"Great. Great." I shook my head. "Congratulations." This was just like my life. "And I'm so glad for Mr. K."

"Don't you want to ask how he's doing?"

"Mr. K.?"

"No! Roger!"

"No. No, I definitely don't want to ask how Roger is doing."

"He's doing great!" said Tommy anyway. "You probably heard about him and Fletch?" I had. "And that he left Goodkin Berdann?" I hadn't. "And now he's taking some classes at NYU, he's teaching violin—it's that whole follow-your-bliss thing."

"Thanks for the update, but I don't care, I really don't."

We were talking about my ex, obviously. Roger, a lawyer, who had apparently given it up. He wasn't a very good lawyer, so it was a smart call.

"Speaking of bliss, you should see him and Fletch and just how happy they are together." This is why there are gun control laws. "I'll tell him you asked about him."

"I *didn't* ask, you twit."

"Let's try to be professional, Mr. Bornic." He was obviously just trying to piss me off, and he was just as obviously really good at it.

I had started out this Monday morning—like so many others—in a fairly bad mood. Discovering that Tommy Radford was now going to be underfoot, a constant, little pissy reminder of some of the many *reasons* I was in a permanently bad mood, did not help. Tommy would be here— what?—reporting back to Roger? And vice-versa? Did Roger send him over here? To keep me up-to-date on just how *wonderful* his life was without me?

I mean, seriously!!!

"Can I get you something, Jeffrey?" Tommy said, smiling.

"Yeah. You can get stuffed."

It was of course at *exactly* that moment Victoria Collins came out of Kaminsky's office—Victoria who was the partner who oversaw all the associates—I'm an associate—and who was quite influential in sorting out the associates who wanted to be partners—and boy-oh-boy did I want to be a partner. And she just heard me tell a brand-new secretary to get stuffed.

"Jeffrey?" was all she said. And she walked away.

It was official. I hated my life.

I hated Tommy Radford's life more. Somebody should do something about it.

I stomped down the hall, past the elevator bank to the stairs, and then down two flights to my floor. If my office door had been closed, I'd have kicked the thing open. Instead, I found Rebecca McPherson leaning over my desk, writing something on a Post-it.

I closed the door behind me.

"Did *you* know they hired Roger's best friend?" I practically yelled at her.

"No. What was his name, Tommy? Wasn't he at Goodkin—"

"He was! Yes indeed, he was! And now he's on 23!"

"He's a secretary? Here?" she said after a second.

"For Kaminsky."

"No! Really? Too funny. Because with Kaminsky running the *Hiromi* case, you could be dealing with Tommy constantly."

"I know, I know, and it's not funny at all."

"Anyway, I was just checking in." She crumpled the Post-it and tossed it into the recycling bin under my desk. "Have you seen the new trainer in the IT Department?"

"Oh please. You're fixing me up with somebody from IT now?"

"I didn't say a word about fixing you up. Yet."

"I avoid IT whenever I can. Those guys—what's up with them?" The IT Department was computer/tech/network support. It was where the geeks you didn't talk to in high school went when they grew up. Those guys made the paralegals look normal. I swear, every guy up there had something wrong with him.

"Don't be such a snob."

"Seriously? A., what makes you think I'd go out with a guy from IT?"

"You haven't seen this guy."

"B., there are *no* gay guys in the IT Department ever."

"Until now. Rumor is this one—"

"And C., what is it about me that makes you think I can't get dates without your help? Am I that hideous? I don't think so! I'm tall, blond, blue-eyed, *and* I make a ton of money. Of course, I've really let myself go—" I said, pinching my completely non-existent tummy fat.

"No, you're not ugly, and no you haven't let yourself go," she said with an eye-roll.

"No! That's right! I keep all that ridiculously expensive gym equipment in my spare room because I actually *use* it. Truth is—I'm totally hot."

"I know, I know. It's just that—you know—since Roger, you've been so—"

"I haven't either!" I knew what she was going to say. That I've been sort of out of it, that I've been distant, cold, crabby. Okay! I got dumped last fall, so cut me some slack! Dumped by my aforementioned ex-boyfriend. My far-too-frequently aforementioned ex-boyfriend, if you ask me. How was I supposed to get over Roger if that was all everybody wanted to talk about, huh? And now with Tommy hanging around.

And I *was* getting over it!

Totally!

And it did *not* make me a sexual charity-case, because I most decidedly wasn't.

"I don't need your help, you know. I get plenty of dates."

"You get plenty of hook-ups. You do *not* get plenty of dates. When was the last time you saw somebody for more than sex? Or more than once?"

"First of all, counselor, that's *my* choice. And furthermore, *re* second dates, I could ask you the same question."

"We're not talking about me."

"Terrific. Let's talk about me. I love talking about me. Know why? Because there's nothing wrong with me. I am perfect. Okay, I can be a bit of an asshole, but I am still eminently date-able."

"All true!"

"You were supposed to argue with me about the asshole thing."

"Yeah, yeah."

"Look. Do-not-do-not-do-not try to fix me up again. Please? Understood? It's just embarrassing for everyone."

"Okay! I won't fix you up. Except..."

"Except?"

"Well, there's maybe one guy I met at a City Bar thing—he's from a little boutique firm, I forget the name—and I may have already kinda talked to him about you, and I may have kinda sorta promised."

"Dispromise."

"He's super sweet with gorgeous eyes."

"Your idea of gorgeous and my idea of gorgeous are two very different gorgeouses."

"Even by your high standards, these eyes are gorgeous."

"If he's over forty, forget it."

"He's definitely not over forty. I don't think."

Deep breath.

"We'll fight about it when the time comes."

"Agreed. Argument adjourned," said Rebecca. "Plans for lunch?"

"No—*Un Deux Trois*?" Little French joint.

"I'll make the reservation."

"And hey, Rebecca? Now that we're not fighting—I need a favor. Kind of a huge favor?"

"Whaaaaat?" She drew the word out, long and wary.

"The work on my apartment—they have to cut a hole through to the floor below me?"

"Why you bought that apartment below you, I will never understand."

"Yeah, well, I did. And the schedule had them cutting through in a few weeks, but something changed, and now they want to cut through the floor this week."

"And?"

"And can I sleep on your couch while they do it? My apartment will be completely unlivable for a few days."

"Normally I'd say no problem, but my baby brother just got tossed out of his apartment, so sorry—no room at the inn."

"Oh, was that the move you wanted me to help with? Sorry, I—"

"If you couldn't, you couldn't. Don't sweat it."

"Sorry." One of those Rebecca things. Was it because she was from Iowa that she didn't even consider it as a possibility that I'd lied just to duck? "Next time."

"I'll call you when he moves out."

"He moved in with *you*?"

"Yup. So the couch is, sadly, *ocupado*. Wouldn't you be more comfortable in a hotel anyway?"

"There's some frigging thing in town, and I can't get a room in midtown anywhere. Darlene found me something in New Jersey."

"Sorry. Wish I could help. A sleepover might be fun."

"I thought so too."

"And you'd be lots easier than my brother. I love him like crazy, but he is an even bigger pain in the butt than you, and that's saying something."

"It is gratifying to know that I am the standard against which all other butt-pains are measured."

"Why don't you come over and we'll put *him* in a hotel. In New Jersey."

"He's that bad?"

"He's something. You'll meet him. Anyway, he's twenty-four and I haven't killed him yet, so I guess we'll survive. I'll see you at lunch. Now get back to work, you."

Deep breath. Definitely—get back to work.

Reminder: Keep looking for a hotel room. Damn.

Amend that.

Reminder: Tell *Darlene* to keep looking for a hotel room. (See how I work?)

I woke up my computer screen and rattled my password in.

Why do people send so much frigging e-mail, anyway?

# Text to Jeff

*I'm running late. I invited Theo.*
*Introduce yourself.*

*!!!*

# Text to Theo

*Running late. Be nice to Jeffrey.*

*I'm always nice.*

*Stop making me laugh—I'm in a meeting.*

*Who the f is Jeffrey?*

# Chapter 4
## The Blind Date that Wasn't

*JEFFREY*

*Café Un Deux Troix.* A noisy pseudo-French place, not fancy, around the corner on 44th Street. I told the fat, pseudo-French guy at the door that I was meeting someone, etc., just as I got the text from Rebecca.

"*Ah, oui,*" said the guy. "This way. The first of your party is already here. *La.*" He gestured across to the other side of the busy dining room—lunchtime in Midtown Manhattan, of course the place was full. And, *la,* sitting alone at the table in question: a guy.

I should just bolt.

I couldn't believe that after our conversation this morning, Rebecca had immediately turned around and set me up with yet another in her string of losers. I guess this was the one she promised—and the *last.* It had better be.

I could kill her anyway. And of course she's deliberately running late, to toss us two together. I'm sure she thinks she's being soooo crafty.

The guy had flaming red hair, and he was slumped down in his chair, staring at his phone. Charming.

So what had she said? I hadn't been paying that much attention, and now I couldn't remember. Was this the new IT Department guy who was supposed to be so hot? Or the lawyer from some puny "boutique" firm. Puny firm—they should just call it Barely Passed the Bar, LLP.

But he didn't really look like a lawyer, lousy or otherwise. And except for the slacker slouch he was working, he didn't really look IT either. A bunch of curly red hair. She had said something about cute—even gorgeous—and I had to hand it to her, this one was certainly pretty.

I don't do 'pretty.'

This kid's features were girlish, delicate, and absolutely nothing I would ever ever *ever* date. Since when did I go out with skinny little twerps??? Since never! What was Rebecca thinking?

I went out with manly guys, scruffy guys, guys with chests and chest hair, burly bastards, gym rats, guys with honest-to-god beards. Roger, in case you were wondering, was an exception, but even Roger wasn't as far out of my target demographic as this one.

This one looked like a hundred pounds of twink.

All of this shot through my head as I navigated between the tables of the dining room.

*Let him down easy,* I said to myself, moving sideways through the room. I'd had lots of practice blowing guys off. Usually I was so smooth at it, they felt flattered by the time I was done giving them the shove.

"Hi," I said from across the table with my darlingest smile, and I extended my hand. "I'm Jeffrey." He seemed perplexed, and then he finally took one hand off his phone, reached up and shook my hand from where he was sitting. Kids these days.

"Theo," he said. He went back to his phone. Theo? Seriously? How twee was that? I looked at him again. Of course he was Theo. You never saw such preciousness, with his long lashes looking down at his phone, ridiculously pale skin—and some freckles. And yeah, Rebecca was right—nice eyes. But not my type. Way not my type. Totally not sexy.

"I'm really glad to meet you," I tried again, pulled out the chair across from him and went to sit down. Problem: he was slunk so far down in his chair, his feet—in falling-apart sneakers—were *right there.* I gave him a look, raised my eyebrows and smiled an even more charming smile. The little creep sighed, I swear to God, before he sat up halfway.

"Thanks." I sat down and graciously shook out my napkin with my best prep-school manners. He didn't seem impressed. One of his sneakers actually had duct tape holding it together. Like I would date a guy in duct tape. "So nice of Rebecca to arrange this."

"She's running late," he said, extending his hand to show me his phone with her text.

"Yeah, I got something similar, in point of fact. But I have to tell you—Theo, is it?"

"The-o," he said, with super careful enunciation. I wanted to pick him up and throw him.

"I'm not sure what Rebecca told you about me—"

"Not a damned thing."

"Oh." He was no more enthusiastic about this than I was. "Okay. Well, I just want you to understand—this is nothing personal, and it's no reflection on *you* whatsoever—you're a really good-looking guy and under different circumstances, I'd be thrilled to go out with you—"

He set the phone down finally.

"Oh really?" he said.

"Absolutely! But I've just come off a pretty bad break-up," I said with a touch of melancholy in my voice, a carefully practiced sadness in the eyes, "and I'm simply not ready to jump into a relationship or dating or anything right now, okay? I know, I'm probably just too sensitive." There was a noise from the other side of the table—it was almost, not quite, a snort. "But please, no hard feelings, all right, Theo?"

"I'm sorry?"

"Don't take this the wrong way! You're clearly a great guy—fabulous really—and honestly, it's just a question of lousy timing. It's totally my loss."

"Wait. Did I do something to make you think I was hitting on you?"

"No! No, not at all. You've been—terrific! Perfect, really! And so understanding as well. I can tell, you're a sensitive guy, too. And I'm sure there's a fantastic man out there for you somewhere. I just didn't want you to have any expectations that this could lead to—"

"Which I naturally would have because…you're so…" he said with a vague gesture that seemed to indicate me from shoes to hairline, "…whatever."

"I just wanted to be sure—in case Rebecca had led you to think, that maybe something might—"

"Rebecca didn't say *anything* about you, okay? I'm just meeting her for lunch. I was totally surprised by her text. She told me to be nice to you. Fine. I have no clue who you are, and I don't care. I can absolutely promise you I have zero expectations of you, *but*—and I don't want you to take this the wrong way, because you're clearly a great guy—fabulous, really," he said pointedly, while I started to burn. *"But*—I have no interest in you. Absolutely none. I don't want to date you, I don't want a relationship with you, I don't want to talk to you. I don't even want you to get down on your knees and suck—my—dick. Okay?"

What the—???

"I hope that doesn't bruise your ego," he said smiling, "but I doubt anything could."

"Look, I'm sorry, there's obviously been a misunderstanding. I just assumed you and Rebecca had discussed that this was a set-up."

"A set-up?"

"Yes. Apparently sometimes a blind date can be just too blind."

"This is not a set-up. You suffer egomaniacal delusions, my friend."

"I'm telling you—*my friend*—she's been trying to set me up for months."

"Look—I know you told me your name, but I wasn't really listening. Jeff was it?"

"Jeffrey."

"Jeffrey. Of course. How could I forget? It fits you. So pompous."

"Hey. I wouldn't make fun of names. *Theo.*"

"The point is—*Jeffrey*—you might need Rebecca to fix you up with guys. I do not. I do just fine without any outside help."

"Let's get a few things straight. A., I don't *need* help getting dates, which, B., I have explained to Rebecca many times—and C., she obstinately arranges these things anyway."

"She would never, in a million years, try to set me up on a date."

"I'm pretty sure she has, little Theo."

He paused for a second, while his face got really red.

"If you call me that again, I swear to God I will cut your nuts off right here with this butter knife, you condescending prick."

Touchy.

"Okay, all right!" It was impossible *not* to roll my eyes. "Theo! I'm just telling you, she's trying to fix us up."

"First of all, nobody's fixing me up because I'm *in* a relationship, asshole—"

"What language to come from such a baby-faced—"

"So setting me up would be kind of stupid."

"Oh. Then why are you here?"

"And I would like to think that if she *did* actually try to fix me up, she would think more of me than to try to fix me up with an arrogant, constipated, piss-elegant, Armani-wearing lawyer—you *are* a lawyer?"

"Yeah I am! And the suit's Brioni."

"Believe me, nobody cares."

"You brought it up."

"And the other thing is, I can't believe she would be trying to set up her little brother. How sick is that?"

"You're Rebecca's little brother?"

"Yes! You moron! But you had to assume that the only reason I could possibly be sitting at your lunch table was to be offered up as some kind of appetizer for you! Because I must be begging my sister to fix me up on dates with a conceited, overbearing, pompous, lacrosse-stick-up-his-ass lawyer who's way too old anyway! In your dreams, Ace."

"Old?!"

"Old."

I couldn't believe the ball bearings on this kid. *I'm not even thirty!*

"I'm not even thirty!"

"So old."

"How old are you then, twelve?!"

"Twenty-four, but still too young for you, you zeke."

"What a piece of work."

"I am! You know what else I am? Outta here." And with that Theo threw his napkin on the table and stood up.

Oh for crying out loud, he was tiny. Five-foot-six maybe? And that's *with* the curls. I tried—and failed—to stop the laugh that burst out. His great dramatic gesture—his furious exit—was ridiculous, this itty-bitty redhead with the bright pink face.

He heard my half-laugh and his head snapped around at me. I thought for sure he was going to lose it completely. The only thing that stopped him from flinging himself across the table at me was—

"Hey, boys," said Rebecca, suddenly standing next to him. "Wanna hold it down a little?"

"Please tell me that you did not try to pimp me out to this narcissist loser."

"Listen here, you pipsqueak," I said, trying to keep my voice down. "I don't know who you are or who you think you're talking to—"

"Shut up, the pair of you."

Okay, it's not as if every head in the restaurant—and did I mention this was a really noisy place?—wasn't already turned in our direction, but now the overweight headwaiter guy was making his way through the tables as best he could, scooching his fat *derrière* between the tables sideways.

"Sit sit sit!" said Rebecca. To my surprise, little Theo obeyed like a cocker spaniel. She turned to the panting *garçon* with a smile. "I'm so sorry the boys got carried away for a moment. They promise to behave themselves."

He was too out of breath to respond—he just gave us a look before he started to make his way back to his post by the door, huffing his *pardons* left and right.

"Did you fix me up on a date with this geezer?" Theo demanded, as soon as she sat down.

"No!"

"Who's a geezer?!"

"Let me think—that would be *you,* grampa!"

"Stop!" said Rebecca forcefully. "Theo, I didn't set you up with anybody." She turned to me. "Jeffrey, is that really what you thought? I'd hook you up with my little brother?"

"I didn't know he was—!" I stopped myself before I was yelling again. "You know what? Forget it. I'm going to go." My turn to throw in the napkin. "Enjoy lunch with your—with this demon seed. I'll see you back at the office. I can buy my own lunch somewhere, and he doesn't look like he can." I kissed her on the cheek quickly.

"I can't believe you're being such a child," she said rolling her eyes.

"Me?!" I stopped myself again. This time the little pygmy marmoset definitely snorted.

"You're the one storming out of a restaurant."

"Which I'm not doing fast enough," I said. I turned to the little-shit brother and smiled. "So nice meeting you, Theo."

He smiled back at me for a second.

"Fuck off, dickwad."

# Chapter 5
## Live at the Apollo—Diner

*THEO*

Monday afternoons I had my songwriting workshop, and afterward a group of us always went to the Apollo Diner down the street.

The workshop—really quickly, it's a bunch of us who are writing or hope to write musical theatre. Some are lyricists, some are composers, and some, like me, do both. I won't drop names, but some seriously big shows and people have come out of this workshop.

We meet every Monday at 4:00. Somebody gets up and plays a song they've written, and then we all talk about what we heard. The good and the bad. You have to audition to get in, there's a two-year apprenticeship before you get into the main group, and yeah, it's a big deal to me that I get to spend my Monday afternoons in this workshop—even though you've never heard of it.

Swithin, Jasper, Jessica and I made up our little crowd that went to the diner after. Oh, and Tyler. It's easy to forget Tyler because he hardly ever says anything, but he always comes along. He works with a lyricist, but she doesn't come out with us—he does. And he doesn't speak.

Jasper and Jessica work together. Jasper quit smoking, but doesn't seem to believe it. He always has a pencil or something between his fingers. He's from Mississippi, very southern, very laid back, and very, very gay; Jessica is native Brooklyn and she's butch-er than the rest of us guys put together. They are a strange pair.

We all started together in the first-year group a couple years ago, along with forty-some other wannabe songwriters, and after two years we few, we happy few, were the only ones invited into the big group last fall.

The big group is where I met Madison. Madison had been in the workshop for a while, so he wasn't officially one of our crew, but I had been dragging him along, sort of an honorary member. Madison works with a composer, Carol, who sometimes hangs with us because we're so awesome.

These meetings at the Apollo—we partly dissed the songs we'd just heard (especially those from people who *aren't* in our little group), and partly we just traded theatre gossip.

On this particular Monday, Madison's composer Carol had performed a new song from their show. It had gone okay. I'd done a song too. It had gone like gangbusters.

As we got to the diner, Madison was avoiding the topic of how our respective songs had been received by lecturing Carol and me about our miserable Shakti—whatever they are. Madison, you see, was on some wacko path to enlightenment or Nirvana or something. I never paid much attention.

"Oh God, here we go," said Carol. "When he starts talking all this swami crappola, I'm done." I didn't have much patience for it, either.

"Hey!" shouted Swithin, as we approached. They had commandeered a couple tables and shoved them together. "You were brilliant!"

I beamed and smiled and the others applauded. Yeah, I know it wasn't exactly Sardi's, but there are worse things than getting an ovation in the Apollo Diner.

"Thank you, thank you," said Carol, confiscating the applause for herself and curtsying. "You're too kind."

Everyone laughed except for Madison who made a face like he was having a baby.

"You guys were great, too," said Swithin, "and Carol, you know how crazy I am about your voice—"

"Thanks, Swith," and she kissed him on the cheek as she went to sit down.

"But you!" Swith went on. "Man, you were a rock star!" He didn't mean Madison. He raised his hand for a high-five, then lowered it some because my five can only go so high. "That song—was the sweetest thing I'd ever heard."

Swithin was an oddity among us. Another composer/lyricist like me, but he came out of a folk music background. And California. His parents were both studio musicians out there. He was tall and lanky with straight blond hair that fell across his face, and I always thought he looked like this surfer-boy/pizza-delivery-guy fantasy.

Okay, I might make fun, but I really liked Swithin. And his songs were always good, if different. And different was also good. And he said all this great stuff about my song—what's not to like?

Madison and Carol had been in the workshop for a few years before us. Madison had had an off-Broadway show about what—five years ago?—that had been sort of a success and it still got occasional productions out in the regionals, and now he had this new show going into development at the Goodspeed Opera House. Which was huge. A developmental production there was no guarantee of anything, but it was a gigantic break, people in the business would see it, and it could lead anywhere. Any of the rest of us would have killed for the opportunity.

And he was my sort-of boyfriend, a status which probably needs to be explained, but I don't want to. Or can't.

He'd been really keen and I'd been cool, he kept at it, and I relented. And then all of a sudden he seemed to have something better to do.

What was the deal? I'm not very tall, but it's not like I'm repulsive or anything. Guys hit on me all the time. Like Madison had. Or that nut-job Rebecca invited to lunch, whatever *that* was about.

I mean, I wasn't ready to marry the guy. Madison, I mean, not the nut-job.

Of course maybe it was stress about Goodspeed. Or maybe it was the upcoming cabaret night.

One more thing, real quick—the songwriting workshop was putting together a cabaret night to showcase the best material that had come out of the room this past year. And none of Madison's songs had been chosen. Which meant that the workshop director, a guy with three Broadway shows (and one really terrible movie adaptation) to his name, had picked a bunch of songs over Madison's. It was no small slight.

"These things are completely political," was Madison's only comment.

Political. *Two* of my songs had been chosen, and I was hardly the most popular guy in the workshop, given how bitchy my comments usually were. But I let it slide.

Madison would *never* in a million years admit it, but I'm sure the whole thing stuck in his craw. Probably didn't help that I couldn't stop chortling about it.

Anyway, *that* might be the reason for Madison's sudden—diffidence. I should really try to do something about the chortling.

There, now I think you're up to date.

Back to the Apollo and my friends all applauding for me.

"You really outdid yourself, darling," said Jasper getting up to kiss me on both cheeks.

"Man, you have *got* to show me that wonky chord thingy in the middle of the bridge," said Swith.

"Yeah, what the hell was that?" said Jessica.

"A mistake!" I explained. "But after I played it, I really liked it, so I kept it."

"Frickin' brilliant." Jessica again.

Of course I was eating this up. It was maybe a *little* awkward that nobody was gushing about Mads and Carol's song and they were *right there.* But mostly I couldn't stop smiling.

"I really liked it," said Tyler very quietly. All heads turned to him and he blushed. Tyler spoke. This was a big deal.

"Thank you, Tyler."

"Madison was just lecturing us," said Carol, "about our blocked chakras, and boy, do I not need to hear any more about my kundalini!"

"He talks about your kundalini?" said Jasper, one hand over his mouth in feigned shock. Then he turned to Jessica and whispered loudly, "Isn't that the thing that gives a woman an orgasm?"

"Jaspeh," laughed Jessica—that's Brooklynese for Jasper—"you are such an idiot."

"Honest," I said, "when he first started going on about it, I thought he was talking about some fancy pasta we don't have in Iowa. Kundalini Alfredo or something."

"Laugh all you want, kids" and we did "but it doesn't bother those of us who are just a little more enlightened."

After we (both the less and the more enlightened) had trashed the other songs we'd heard that evening, we talked about the cabaret night that was coming up at Don't Tell Mama, a little club on 46th Street. Okay, I wasn't the only one from our group who had material picked for it—in fact we *all* had songs in it. All of us except Madison. Even Carol had something on the program she'd written with somebody—not Madison.

(I don't like to brag, but—for the sake of transparency and full disclosure and all, and just to be completely fair and honest with you, I should mention that I was the only one from our group who had *two* songs chosen for the program. Actually, come to think of it, I was the only one from the entire workshop to have *two* songs chosen for the program. The only one. Just me. Nobody else. Just sayin'.)

Madison, being the mature professional at the table (not to mention the one on the path to whatever), reacted exactly as you'd expect—he sulked like an eight-year-old the entire time we talked about the cabaret night. Then he graciously mumbled something about being sorry, he would really *try* to get to the performance but he couldn't promise because, well, Goodspeed, you know.

Is it bitchy of me to notice that he had just deflected the conversation back to himself?

"Really, darlings," Jasper said to Madison and Carol. "Really interesting song tonight."

"Thanks, Jasper," said Mads, pouting. He was obviously marking this down as too little/too late; and let's face it, everybody knew that 'interesting' was the universal code word for nice-try-but-it-didn't-really-work-now-did-it. "It's just a first draft, you know, I'm not sure why everyone took out after it the way they did."

"It's a terrific song, Madison," I said. I could afford to be nice, and besides. I had a plan. "But how does it work with the scene? I'm trying to remember—"

"Well, you haven't read what we've been working on. Tanner's ideas, really."

"Really?" I'd been hearing about this Tanner guy a *lot* lately. And that's the guy's *first* name, believe it or not.

"Tanner?" asked Swithin.

"He's directing."

"Ah," said everyone, nodding.

"Tanner and I have been working on the show pretty closely now for a couple weeks." Carol cleared her throat menacingly. "Carol, too, of course. But less. It's all going very quickly, but Tanner's been so inspiring—"

"Demanding, he means," said Carol.

"I'd love to see what you've got," I suggested. Hint.

"It's still very fluid." And Mads brought us up to date on the bright ideas good old Tanner had brought to their show. I was skeptical.

"That's a lot of changes. I'd love to see how you make that work." Hint hint.

"Tanner knows what he's doing," said Madison, answering my look. "Anyway we've got a read-through, sing-through planned for Wednesday. We'll know more after that."

From the above hints, you might have noticed that I was waiting for Madison to turn to me and say, 'Hey, you want to come up to Chester?'— where the Goodspeed Opera House is. 'Spend a few days, meet some important people?' That's why I was so coy with Rebecca about when I could start this stupid-ass day job at her office. I was waiting for Mads to ask. But he hadn't asked.

Did he just not want the distraction? Or was he being protective/jealous of his contacts? What?

Of course the number of times the word 'Tanner' had dropped into his conversation should have been a clue.

At the end of the evening, we stood on 57th Street in front of the diner, before we went different ways.

"So. Have a good time up at Goodspeed," I said, kissing him on the cheek. "Be brilliant."

"Hey, thanks. See you when I get back." And he turned to go.

Bastard.

Fine.

So we're not boyfriends. And I'm an idiot.

Fine.

I turned.

I stopped.

*Screw this,* I thought.

I turned around.

"Hey!" I yelled. He was like twenty feet away now. "Can I come up and see what you're working on? The read-through?"

"Um, it's for a very select group, Theo."

*A select group,* I thought. *Sounds like me.*

"Perfect—I'll see you Wednesday, you said?"

"Theo—"

I turned and headed toward the C train. I hadn't realized how miserable I'd been about this until now that it was done. Even if I had to invite myself.

I was going to the Goodspeed!

# E-mail to Jeffrey

**From:** McPherson, Rebecca
**Sent:** Wednesday, March 23, 8:15 a.m.
**Subject:** We Have a Vacancy

My little brother Theo—whom you've met—has informed me that he intends to go to Connecticut with his boyfriend for a few days.
So mi casa, su casa.

Or at least mi sofa. Theo tells me it's pretty comfortable.

# Chapter 6
## My First Sleepover

*JEFFREY*

"Hey, Rebecca," I said, dropping my gym bag of clothes on her living room floor, "it is really great that you're letting me stay here. I was not looking forward to commuting from the Fort Lee Econo Lodge."

"What does this mean for your birthday party? Will the hole-cutters be finished in time?"

"With the hole, yes. The stairs, no. So I have no idea what I'll do. Right now I'm thinking of skipping the whole thing."

"I'd be happy to throw you a party here, but we'd have to scale it back a bit."

"Last year did get a little out of hand. But I don't know how much I really feel like celebrating turning thirty."

"It's not so bad."

"And if I *don't* have a birthday party, does that mean that I *don't* turn thirty?"

"That how that works?"

"Seems like."

"Then again, do you really want a do-over on twenty-nine?"

"Good point." Twenty-nine had been the absolute worst. "I'll let you know what I decide."

"Seems a shame when your birthday falls on a Friday and everything."

"Yeah, but a gigantic hole in the middle of the living room floor? It's a sign. In the meantime, while I'm here, I'll buy you dinner. Every night. And you won't hear a peep out of me. I'll be quiet as a mouse. You'll hardly know I'm here."

"That will definitely make a change from Theo."

"What's his story?"

"What do you mean?" she said laughing a little.

"Do you let him out often without supervision?"

"He's not that bad."

"Maybe a leash for little Theo then?"

"Don't ever let him hear you call him that."

"It was about the second thing I said to him. He threatened to neuter me with a butter knife."

"And you'd deserve it. Don't be so condescending."

"Funny, that's the word Theo used, too."

"If you look at it from his point of view, his reaction is understandable. A guy he's never seen before sits down at his table and tries to break it to him as gently as possible that he doesn't stand a chance? I mean, c'mon."

"I suppose..."

"You just got off on the wrong foot. Feet. I admit he has a temper, he always has. He was always lots smaller than other kids, but nobody ever really messed with him—they were all terrified of his mouth. That and his big brothers."

"Are the brothers all like him?"

"Oh God, no! *Nobody's* like Theo. Rodney is about six-foot-two. Gilbert is six-one, but even bigger. Both football players—Gil played college ball even. And then there's Theo, of whom we are all extraordinarily protective, especially Gil, who's just a year older. No, we have always understood that Theobald wasn't really like any of us."

"Theobald? Not even Theodor?"

"Nope. Rodney, Gilbert and Theobald. Did I luck out or what?"

"Well, I hope he's having fun with his boyfriend."

"Madison. I get the idea that it's not going so well, but he doesn't talk about it."

"Well, I'm grateful that he has relinquished the sleeper couch."

"I should warn you that the environmentally conscious co-op board turns the heat way down at night. I don't notice so much in the bedroom, but Theo tells me it's freezing out here in the morning."

"I'm sure I'll be fine."

"I wear flannel pajamas."

"Seriously?

"No joke. It's just a suggestion."

"The things you learn about a person when they let you sleep over. I'll think about it." I never wore more than boxer-briefs to bed, and most often, not even those. I was not about to try to sleep in flannel pajamas.

"Anyway—you know where everything is. Help yourself to whatever you need."

"I even packed a towel," I said fumbling through my bag.

"The thoughtful houseguest."

"So. Dinner out or dinner in? Your call."

"Chinese—and definitely in."

"I was hoping you were going to say that. I've still got a couple hours' work to knock in."

"Me too. My friends back in Iowa think I live this fabulously glamorous life in New York. Every night a different man. Little do they know." She picked up the phone and speed-dialed. "Four nights a week, it's just me and General Tso."

# Chapter 7
## When the Train of Thought Pulls into the Wrong Station

*THEO*

The train lurched forward before I could even throw myself and my bag down into an empty seat in the practically empty car on this train I had only juuuuuuuust caught.

So—was this me, all excited to be heading off to the Goodspeed Opera House, ready to learn new things, meet new people, have an adventure and reconnect with my—whatever Madison was?

No. You missed that train ride. *That* was this morning. *This* train ride, my second for the day, was taking me *back* to New York only a few hours later on the last train to—New Haven. From there you can get a train to Grand Central. That's how much fun this trip was.

Breathless and sweating, I hadn't even had a chance to *think* about what had just happened that had got me here.

Which was probably a good thing, because if I *did* think about it, I'd scream.

Of course now I had nothing to do for the next two-and-a-half hours *but* to think about it. Let the screaming commence.

Madison was of course busy in rehearsals all day.

Fine. I expected that. I figured I'd sit in the back with him. No, he didn't want me around for his rehearsals, because he wanted it all fresh for me when I heard it in the run-through—like I hadn't heard most of this material before????

But okay, fine.

And then the run-through.

He wouldn't sit with me. He didn't even sit with Carol, his collaborator—I did. He had to sit with the director, Tanner. Tanner, who turned out to be incredibly good-looking—and very aware of it. And a complete fucktwit— and not aware of it at all.

Fine.

Okay, this week wasn't about me, it was for Madison and Carol, for their show, and making it the best show possible. I could subvert my ego for a day and just try to be helpful to Madison and his director, this ass-arrogant tool of a director with a permanent can't-fuck-this look on his face.

Madison barely even introduced me to the tool.

"This is Theo."

That's what I got.

I kinda thought he might have said something like 'this is my boyfriend Theo,' or even 'my boyfriend, Theo, who's a really talented songwriter, they're doing a couple of his songs next week at Don't Tell Mama, you should go.' I mean, wasn't that sort of the thing to do?

Okay, subvert the ego, right? This wasn't about me.

Fine.

But you'd think he was ashamed of me. A boy could get a complex! And it's not like Madison is exactly centerfold material himself. Older, pudgy. Whatever.

But that was all the introduction I got. This is Theo. He didn't even say 'and this is our director, Tanner.' I was just supposed to figure it out.

And of course Tanner, in all his self-absorbed loveliness, could have cared less.

Do I sound angry to you? Just wait, because it gets so much better. Because the real killer was *after* the run-through. We went to dinner—me and Madison. Romantic? No, just separate from the others, like he was still keeping me as far away from everyone else as possible.

Okay. Fine.

Now I had hardly said a thing about his show, which was—I'm not gonna lie—maybe not so good.

Of course you're thinking I was being my usual, super-critical, bitch-mouthed self. But I *wasn't,* and this time I mean it. I was absolutely on my best behavior, all Iowa farm-boy manners, I swear.

I'd said all the nice phony things people say, I'd said congratulations, I'd said what a terrific opportunity this was, and how great everyone seemed to be, how everybody should be so proud, and all the usual horse apples.

I didn't say any of the stuff I was thinking, and this in spite of the fact that—after the way the day had developed, being treated like total crap by Madison—I was just a wee bit edgy and not particularly in a mood to suck up to anybody, no matter what their showbiz credentials were, and who the hell was Tanner, *anyway*???

So. Dinner. Just the two of us. He talked about actors, some he liked, some he wanted to throttle. You know—actors. I agreed sympathetically, I nodded supportively. Finally, as we were about done, he said it.

"So?" said Madison.

"So?"

"So what did you think?" I mean, this was the reason I was here, right? To give another point of view, an objective eye.

In hindsight, I realize that he was asking with the full expectation that I was going to gush all over him and his precious Tanner. He thought I was going to lavish praise, assuring him that the show should transfer to Broadway immediately and if he didn't have a Tony *and* a Pulitzer (not to mention a penthouse) by spring, something was seriously wrong with the universe.

But I didn't know that at the time. No, at the *time,* I thought he actually respected my opinion. At the *time,* I thought he was asking me because he genuinely wanted to know what I thought.

My bad.

Thinking he wanted an objective, critical opinion, I gave it—or started to anyway.

The first twenty-five minutes, I explained, needed to be the first five. The two new songs (Tanner's ideas) weren't nearly as good as the songs they replaced. The whole thing felt slack and overwritten and had been in much better shape two months ago. There was a running gag (Tanner's invention) that wasn't funny the first time, let alone the third.

And I was only halfway through the first act.

Of course all through this, Mads was increasingly huffy and defensive and started every other sentence invoking the name of the divinely talented director. It was obvious he had a total boner for the guy.

Too bad for Madison because it was equally obvious that Tanner did not have a boner for anybody but Tanner.

Now, could I have expressed my criticisms a little more tactfully? I don't know, maybe.

Okay, probably.

*But.* I wasn't used to being treated like somebody's embarrassing cousin who doesn't speak English, and I really really didn't feel much like looking out for anybody else's feelings when my own had been handled so shabbily. I'd been a goddamned cheerleader, I'd done everything but give out hand-jobs all afternoon, and look what it had got me.

By the time I'd got as far as the running gag that wasn't, however, old Madison was done listening. He started slurping on that stupid vape thing of his—which always looked so frigging Freudian, they should just make them dick-shaped if you asked me—until the cute little waiter-boy, who'd otherwise been playing eyesy-eyesy with me all night, had to come running over in a lather to ask Madison to stop.

And did I make eyes back at the flirty little waiter whose name was Eddie? No, I didn't. And let me tell you, flirty little waiters were way more my style than older, pudgy, vain, vaping lyricists.

"This is exactly why I didn't want you to come," said Mads, still surreptitiously sucking on that thing and exhaling into his napkin—he looked like an overweight dragon with a head cold.

"Then why did you invite me?!"

"You invited yourself!" Fucker. "And I can't, Theo, I literally can't. You and your terrible chakras. You've been oozing negativity ever since you got here. Everyone's felt it."

"Nobody's paid the tiniest bit of attention to me all day."

"With *your* attitude, are you surprised? I know it's bothering Tanner."

"Tanner doesn't even know I'm here. There's no way he said something."

"He didn't have to, I can sense these things."

"I see. Same-wavelength kind of thing? Sympatico?"

"He's very spiritual. And he wouldn't say anything because he thinks you're my guest—"

"Which I *am*—!"

"—but I can sense it."

"Soul mates, I can clearly see that."

"Go ahead and mock, Theo. I don't expect *you* to understand. In any case you still need to get a train back to New York tonight."

"Tonight?!"

I was totally stunned. I mean, what the fuck?

"I can't have you around me, not like this, not when I have so many people depending on me to be creative."

"What the hell time is it, that I'm going to get a train?"

"I'm sure they run all night."

Of course in this, as in so many, many things, Madison had his head fully up his ass. I had it on good authority—from Eddie, of course—that there was one last train, I would need to hurry, but if I missed it, Eddie told me, I could crash with him—which was sweet but I was hardly in the mood. He slipped me his phone number anyway, just in case. Madison didn't even notice.

Some little assistant stage manager, who had absolutely no idea what was going on, was roped into getting me and my blocked chakras to the train station at warp speed.

Now that I was sitting in this fucking train, which was freezing and fuck-me-running what *was* that *smell*???—only now did I realize: Mads had started to lose interest in me about three weeks ago; Mads had first got a glimpse of the ravishing Tanner about three weeks ago. Hmmm.

I'm sure that's just a coincidence, right? Yeah right.

And now Madison, spiritual and enlightened as he was, was making artistic decisions with his willy-wonka.

I know I'm only twenty-four. I know I don't have a bunch of Broadway shows on my resume (Tanner has exactly *one*—I checked—he was somebody's assistant, meaning gopher, and I'm pretty sure I know what he did to get *that* job), but in spite of my skimpy résumé, I can tell you this much: Madison's willy-wonka didn't know piss-squat about writing musical theatre—and neither did Tanner.

I just wished Mads had told me not to come.

I changed trains and stared out the windows at the darkness that was Connecticut until Grand Central. The crosstown shuttle got me to the 1 train to the Upper West, and back to Rebecca's apartment.

And one more thing? I was, by this time, fall-down-dead tired.

It would have been wonderful to have had a place of my own and a real bed to collapse into, considering how monumentally shitty I felt—but as it was, Rebecca's couch would have to do.

I let myself in super quiet, and set my bag down. I didn't want to wake Rebecca, and not just because it was a work night. More than anything I did *not* want to have to explain to anybody the humiliation of going all the way up there, wasting an entire day, only to be sent packing in the middle of the night. By my ostensible boyfriend. Of course Becca would be sympathetic. I just wasn't ready for sympathy.

I left the lights off, figuring the bathroom light would do, and I started across the dark living room on tippy-toe.

I met a series of surprises, all of them nasty.

The first surprise—discovered by my shin just below the kneecap— was that Rebecca had pulled the bed out for me. This was thoughtful, but weird, since I wasn't actually supposed to be here. It was also more than a little inconvenient because it hurt like screaming hell, and because I lost my balance and tumbled forward onto the pulled-out bed.

The second surprise was when I stretched my hands out to catch myself—and they landed not on the good old sleeper sofa, but on a body—on bare skin. Someone had apparently deposited a naked corpse in the middle of my bed in the middle of my sister's living room.

The third surprise—almost as disturbing as the first two—was to discover that I could scream like a little girl.

Don't judge. Until you have stumbled upon a dead body in the dark, you don't know, you just don't know.

All I can say is—this sort of thing does *not* happen in Iowa.

"Wooomph," said my cadaver.

Flailing with my arms trying to get up, and with strange noises still escaping me, I managed to push myself up off the corpse *and* the couch, and I then fell backwards, knocking over a lamp while I tried to catch my balance. The stiff chose this moment to speak with a decidedly not-dead baritone.

"What the fuck?" came from the talking dead.

You'd think if you'd gone to all the trouble of dying and coming back, you might be a little more articulate about the whole thing.

Of course I wasn't all that coherent myself, just making a lot of sounds without any consonants, while I scrambled back in a straight-up panic. I frantically thrashed around on the wall until I found the light switch and then—

There, on *my* bed, squinting and shielding his eyes, was the egomaniacal nut-job from lunch a few days ago.

And not dead.

And, as far as I could see, naked.

All I really wanted to do after this unbelievably crap-ass day was to curl up somewhere alone. In my own little corner in my own little chair. Not a lot to ask, was it? And honestly, I thought I had earned a little self-pity time. But no, even that was to be denied to me by this—this incredible dorkwad, who would no doubt assume that by falling over him in his sleep, I was coming on to him. The thought of that made me even angrier than I was, and, as you know, I was already seriously not happy long before my bare hands had come down on whatever part of this naked scumball they had come down on.

"You! Why you!? Of all people on earth who don't belong in my bed, why is it you who ends up there? And naked!!!"

"A., I'm not naked." And he threw the sheet back to show off his expensive undies, those boxer-brief things. "B., Rebecca—"

"Do you *have* to number your paragraphs?!"

"*B!*" he said just to piss me off—oh, like *that* was necessary— "Rebecca said I could stay here for a few days because, C., you're not supposed to be here."

At this point, Rebecca's bedroom door flew open.

"For the love of Mike!" she yelled. Understandable, since neither of us was bothering to lower his voice.

"You really do wear flannel pajamas," said the underwear guy about my sister's pink floor-length nightshirt, and he hastily pulled the sheet back over his stuff.

"Shut up, Jeffrey," said Rebecca apparently in no mood to discuss fashions. *Yeah, shut up, Jeffrey,* I thought. *And go the fuck away!* "Theo!" Rebecca turned to me. "What are *you* doing here?"

"Me?! You said I could stay here, remember? The question is—what's *he* doing here?"

"She said *I* could stay here," said Mr. Pomposity. "You're supposed to be with your boyfriend or something!"

"Shut up!" I said.

"Everybody, stop yelling!" said Rebecca. "Theo, seriously, are you okay? Something happen with Madison?"

"I don't want to talk about Madison," I said with a glance at the ex-corpse.

"Don't mind me," he said, hands in the air. "Pretend I'm not here."

"Oh if only!"

"Whatever," said Rebecca, interrupting us. "Theo, Jeffrey needs a place to stay for a couple days, and you're supposed to be in Connecticut, but you're not. So everybody, deal with it. Jeffrey, scooch over."

"No way!" I said, shrieking maybe a little. "I'm not sleeping with that! I can't believe I already touched his flabby body."

"Flabby?!"

"Theo!" said Rebecca. "How many couches do you see around here?"

"I'm not sleeping with him. I'll sleep with you."

"Forget it. If you'd rather, you can sleep on the floor for all I care."

"*I'm* not sleeping on the floor. Make *him* sleep on the floor!"

"No. He's a guest. Now grow up!"

"Ha!" said the shithead. I was just about to throw myself at him but Becca's hand was already on my shoulder, digging in.

My big sister grew up with all of us boys, whom she ruled by dint of her sheer appalling meanness.

You know that place right where your neck and shoulder meet, and if somebody pinches you really hard there, there's nothing you can do but say 'ow ow ow' until she lets go? We called it her Spock grip. It was a favorite of hers, and she used it now.

Ow ow ow.

"Stop being babies," she said letting me loose, "and go to bed."

"Hey, I'm not the one being a baby," said Jeff-*rey,* sounding exactly like a big baby if you asked *me.*

She flashed us both a mean big sister look, went back to her bedroom and slammed the door. I was still rubbing my neck.

"Fuck," I said.

"And people say millennials have no language skills."

"Right here, buddy," I said, pointing to my left butt cheek. "You can kiss me. Right. Here."

"And Theo—" said Rebecca sticking her head back. I stopped and turned back to her. "I'll talk to Human Resources, tell them you can come in for training on Friday."

"Oh, c'mon, Beccs. Can't we push it till Monday?"

"No. You have tomorrow to do whatever. No whining. Jeffrey, he's Victoria's new assistant, so be nice to him."

Fuck. I would start this new suckshit day job just that much sooner. One more reason to resent Madison.

"Victoria Collins?!" Jeff didn't seem too pleased with my new job. "You're kidding me."

"Nope."

"First Tommy, now this?"

"It's a hard knock life," I smiled and sneered. If it was bad news to this ignoramus that I was working for Victoria-whoever, then, hooray! I was working for Victoria! "Who's Tommy?"

"See?" said Jeff. "You cannot let those two meet! It could shift the entire twink center of gravity, it could bring down the whole solar system."

"Who's Tommy?" I knew already I was going to like this guy.

"But think, Rebecca! What if they have children!"

"G'night, boys," said Rebecca and closed her door again.

Mr. Armani was still just sitting there with his abs hanging out. Damn, the dickhead was really fit. You know, for his age. He leaned against the back of the couch and folded his hands behind his head. Well damn.

I looked up and he was smiling. Fuck!!! He'd totally caught me checking out his abs and stuff. That's *all* I needed.

"What kind of barbarian are *you* supposed to be?" I sneered. "Put a shirt on, Attila."

The Hun reached over, rummaged in his bag on the floor by the couch and pulled out an undershirt, the sleeveless kind, and he tugged it down over his head. Like that helped.

"I've got this side, okay?" he said—the side closest to the windows. And the bathroom. I didn't care.

"Fine. Just—*stay* on your side." I knocked my shoes off, one shoe against the other.

After I'd done the necessary bathroom stuff, and I was over on *my* side, I started stripping down to my underwear.

"And don't look, you letch."

"Believe me, I'm not looking," he said. He was facing the other way, but it creeped me anyway.

I turned out the lights and got very carefully into the sleeper, as far away from him as I could, and tried to get settled.

"If you so much as touch me, old man," I said, "I'll clock you with this lamp, I swear."

"What did you call me?"

"You heard me, perv."

Finally. The end of this godawful day. Just part of this godawful week. I was so tired I could almost cry. Fuck it, I *wanted* to cry.

I would admit this only because I was *so* tired and *so* miserable—

Most of the time I was perfectly fine with the whole Bohemian thing. Riding my bike past the three-piece suits. I was proud of it even. I wore my duct-taped shoe defiantly, daring people to make a judgment about me. But there were times, I'm not gonna lie. Sometimes the poverty, the constant worry about tiny amounts of money, desperately counting dollars, quarters, dimes. Walking blocks because the subway was too expensive. Washing one of my three pairs of remaining underwear in the bathroom sink, and wanting to break something when my finger somehow tears yet another rip in one. Showing up at people's apartments at six-thirty, hoping they might be eating dinner. Coming home and finding nothing in my tiny section of the fridge but one of those things of Kraft pre-grated cheese, and a tablespoon of mayo in the bottom of a jar—and calling it dinner.

Hi-ho, the glamorous life.

It hadn't been exactly fun getting kicked out of the flat-share, squalid and miserable as it was, getting ganged-up on by people I used to call friends, with lots of yelling; and then having to crash with my sister, which, in the war for survival in New York, felt like a pretty serious defeat. I was just a minor second away from having to Greyhound it back to Waterloo.

And then Madison exiling me from the entire State of Connecticut, and I swear to whatever that I am *never* setting foot in the state again, and now I end up having to share a sofa bed with this awful awful awful lawyer.

Fortunately, I don't normally cry. I grind my teeth instead. Right up until I kill someone.

And I obviously wasn't going to cry with this piss-ant over there anyway.

"So," said my new bedpartner, apparently wanting to have a little roomy-roomy pillow talk. "Your boyfriend's name is *Madison*?"

"Shut up," I said politely. I thought that would be the end of it.

"Seriously. And I thought *Theo* was precious."

"Seriously. Shut up."

Did he take the hint that time? Nope.

"Trouble in paradise?" he asked after a bit.

"Shut-up-shut-up-shut-up-shut-up-shut-up!" I screamed at him.

I plopped back down on the mattress, facing away from him still—and I swear I could feel the bed shaking a little. The dipstick was laughing at me. I picked up my left leg and kicked behind me like a mule—as hard as I could.

"Ow!"

I'd caught him on the calf. I could feel him sitting up. I half-expected him to hit me. Just let him try. After the day I'd had? I was *so* ready for a fight.

"Go for it, asshole, I dare ya," I said, glaring up at him.

And then we heard, muffled, from the bedroom:

"For the love of Mike!"

# Chapter 8
## There's Got to Be a Morning After

*JEFFREY*

Without opening my eyes, I knew it was light out already. I'd overslept. Damn, how'd that happen? There'd be no run this morning.

There was a pain right along the bottom of my rib cage—what the? Like a metal bar or something. Like from a hide-a-bed.

And then it all came rushing back. Rebecca's hide-a-bed. Someone had told her it was comfortable. Theo. The psychotic little brother with whom I was sharing this fold-out torture device. The psychotic little brother had lied.

And Jesus Christ it was cold in here.

I needed to pee. I started to get up, but realized I had a pretty serious tent pole going in the underwear. I hadn't thought to bring a robe, and I wasn't really keen on bumping into either Rebecca *or* the red dwarf with this thing proudly outlined in the thin fabric of my Diesels. I tried to gather up some of the bedding to wrap around me.

Of course even in his sleep the little homicidal maniac was a total pain. As I pulled gently, he clutched. I pulled again, he clutched more tightly. I pulled again with increasing force.

"Stop!" he said finally, without turning over.

"Dude, I need to take the blanket for a bit."

"No."

"Yes! I need it."

"I don't care."

"Look, it's morning, and I am not going to prance around your sister's apartment in front of the gayboy leprechaun with a morning hard-on. Let me have the blanket."

"Gross. And no," he said louder.

"Yes!" and I yanked harder—while the little spider monkey just held on tighter. I was really starting to hate this kid.

"Trust me," he said. "I'm not going to look. The last thing I want to see is a paunchy old lawyer with a boner." Yeah, yeah, paunchy. He'd seen me shirtless, he knew better.

"Okay, you win," I said. "Keep the blanket." Of course I could have just thrown caution to the wind, and counted on the fact that Rebecca's door would stay shut, and that Theo really had no interest in seeing what was to be seen—or even if he did, what did I care if he peeked? But by now it was a matter of pride, a question of principle. I couldn't let this spoiled little brat-boy have his way.

I let him enjoy the bedding a little longer, long enough to relax just a tiny bit, just enough, and—I yanked on the blanket, sheet, everything, as hard as I could, and—as calculated—they slipped right out of his freckled little hands and I had them. I started to wrap myself in glory and bedclothes.

"Yes!" I yelped, clutching victory in my hands.

Now, what I should have guessed—but hadn't—was that Theo had his own reason for not wanting to give up the bedding. While I shouted in triumph and Theo screamed in horror, I saw Theo's own, seriously impressive morning embarrassment poking up out of a ratty pair of tighty-whities.

I let out a huge laugh of surprise, just as we heard, from the bedroom: "Have you two lost your minds?"

"Don't come out here!" we yelled in unison, as poor Theo flipped over onto his stomach. Rebecca came storming out anyway, in her pink flannel night-dress thing, while Theo yelled an amazing string of threats, generously laced with obscenities. He might be from Iowa, but he could swear like a New Yorker. As for me, I couldn't stop laughing while I separated the sheet so Theo could at least keep the blanket, and we'd both be relatively decent in front of Rebecca.

"Look, I'm sorry, dude," I said to Theo, trying to stop laughing. "I didn't realize, or I would never—"

"You guys know what time it is?" Rebecca yelled over the top of all this, while she stood there, arms akimbo. Really. Akimbo. In a pink flannel pup tent, with bunnies, which did nothing to help me with my giggles. "What are you two doing???"

"Nothing!" I managed to get out. "Bedclothes malfunction! Sorry, Rebecca, it's all my fault." Theo was still threatening some really torturous disfigurements. "I'm-so-sorry-I'm-so-sorry-I'm-so-sorry!" I called to both of them, as I hightailed it to the bathroom in my toga.

# Text from Madison

*Hey.*

*Hey, u there?*

*I'll try again.*

*Hey, u there?*

*Fuck.*

*Off.*

*I'm sure you're pissed.*

*Did you figure that out on your own, or did Tanner explain it to you? Or did you just intuit what Tanner was thinking?*

*I guess I have that coming.*

*Ya think.*

*But I was saying something before, and now I've forgotten what it was.*

*Oh yeah, now I remember.*

*Fuck.*

*Off.*

*Hey—I just wanted to say I'm sry. I'm under a lot of pressure here.*

                                      *I got three words for you.*

                                             *Yeah yeah yeah.*

*People have huge expectations of me.*

                                                     *I don't.*

*I said I'm sorry.*

*Hey, u still there?*

*U still there?*

*Theo—talk to me.*

# Chapter 9
## Peace Offering

*JEFFREY*

I didn't get back to Rebecca's until after ten—just another twelve-hour day at the office.

What I do. I'm a litigation attorney, who somehow got pigeonholed as an advertising claims lawyer, which was never my ambition.

Ad claims law is when you see an ad on TV that says this antacid works twice as fast as this other antacid. The manufacturer of the other antacid resents the piss out of this—but instead of sitting at home, repressing his anger and getting an ulcer, he calls us. And we sue the lying bastards, throwing all the scientific evidence we have at them to prove beyond the usual reasonable doubt that our client's antacid is actually faster than theirs. It may be slightly more nuanced than that, but you get the idea.

Is it important? Is it meaningful? Is it making the world a better place? Okay, maybe not. It's a job. Yes, I'd like to do other kinds of litigation, but then I'm not the boss, now, am I? Not yet, anyway.

So that's what my twelve-hour day had been, split between an absorbent paper towel and a fabric softener, but I still had to deal with my new housemates and my charming new bedfellow.

When I came in, Rebecca and Theo had already pulled the couch out into a bed and were lounging thereon, leaning against the couch back and watching some sci-fi thing. Rebecca was in her ludicrous pink flannel nightgown. She had to have brought that thing from Iowa—there's no way you could buy that in Manhattan.

"Hey roomies," I said, all chipper. "Glad you guys are up and I don't have to wake anybody. Or trip over anybody." I said the last bit pointedly at Theo—who ignored me.

"Hey, Jeffrey," said Rebecca, using the remote to pause the show. She even had fuzzy pink slippers to complete the ensemble.

"Sorry about this morning—both of you."

"Is he still staying here?" asked Theo, with barely a glance in my direction. By contrast, Theo's pale white feet sported nothing but some freckles.

"You know he is, we talked about it an hour ago. Get over yourself." In acknowledgement, Theo picked up the remote and restarted the show. "I got you an order of eggplant parmigiana, if you're hungry."

"Thanks, I ate."

Theo was in a dingy tee shirt and gray sweatpants. At least the sweatpants didn't have holes in them—which was more than I could say for the tee shirt. I plopped my briefcase down on the counter, and held up the pair of big brown bags from Bloomingdales I'd carried in with me.

"Look, I went out shopping at lunch—" Rebecca took the remote control away from Theo, muted the alien explosion that was ripping through the spaceship, and put the remote on the side table carefully out of Theo's reach. Theo stared sullenly at the silent TV. I tried again. "So that there will be no repeat of this morning, I went out at lunch and bought myself this."

I pulled a bathrobe out of the first bag—but I have to tell you, this thing was no ordinary robe. Velour, and it had to be the absolute height to which velour could ever aspire. 'Lush' didn't begin. The stuff was like three inches thick, I swear, imported from Turkey. Incredibly luxurious. There was a hood even. It was also maybe the world's most expensive bathrobe, but who cares? It was dark blue, to set off my eyes. As soon as I saw it—and felt it—I had to have it.

"Oh. My. God!" said Rebecca with awe, as she felt the robe in her hand. "I want! You've got to feel this, Theo." Theo had apparently decided he didn't have to. He didn't even turn his head.

Okay, this next part needs some explaining, but I can't really explain it. I was shopping, I was thrilled about the robe, I turned around and looked at the rack—and I *did* feel really bad about yanking the blankets off and exposing Theo's hoo-ha to the world, and the next thing you know—

"Here." I handed over the second shopping bag. "I hope you like it, Theo. Because—I really *am* sorry, and I really *didn't* mean for that to happen this morning and I shouldn't have laughed."

The bag only got as far as Rebecca because Theo wasn't having any of it. Rebecca looked inside, and started to pull out the identical robe. Only it was much smaller of course, and green—a really pretty dark green, I thought.

"I'm sorry and I mean it." Theo's eyes had finally been pulled away to look at the robe. "I hope you don't mind the color—it was all they had in your size." *N.b.,* I didn't make a single crack about his size, and I so easily could have.

"Christ-on-a-crossword-puzzle," said Theo slowly, finally feeling the deep velour. "For me?" He looked up at me. I nodded. "Give it to me. I gotta try this." And he hopped off the bed and pulled on the robe. Then he took the robe off again, pulled the pit-stained tee shirt off over his head, and pulled the robe on again. Then he turned around and pulled off the sweatpants he was wearing, before he closed the robe and turned back around.

"Whoa—are you butt naked under there?" I asked, laughing.

"I just wanted to see what it felt like and put that picture right out of your head, you troll."

Such gratitude.

"On behalf of all of Iowa," said Rebecca, "I would like to apologize for my brother's manners. This is not how he was brought up, I assure you."

"Thank you, Jeff."

"You're welcome, and it's Jeffrey."

"The color couldn't be better if you'd designed it for him," said Rebecca.

I wasn't sure what she meant, and I glanced over at Theo. And then, I suppose for the first time, I really looked at Theo. Because she was right. Had I thought about it, which I certainly hadn't, I'd have told you Theo's eyes were blue, but they were actually this strange blue-green and they really popped green with the dark green robe. With his pale skin and red hair...Rebecca was right.

Theo, of course, was already at the mirror on the bathroom door, to see if what she'd said was true. *You vain little thing, you.*

It occurred to me this was also the first time I'd ever seen Theo really smile.

"I'm glad you like it."

"Okay," said Rebecca. "Truce made. I'm going to trust you two to behave and go to bed without bloodshed. Theo, don't stay up all night."

"I know, I know."

"Tomorrow's his first day at the firm."

"Congrats. Good luck with Victoria."

"Yeah yeah whatever."

"I think it's all training tomorrow. Anyway, g'night." She kissed her brother. "G'night," and she kissed me.

I looked over at Theo.

"Don't even think about it," he said. Like I was thinking about! Dream on, little boy.

"Don't start," I said. I would be the grown-up.

While still in the robe, he turned away and started pulling his gray sweatpants back on—sweatpants that were way too big on him. Then, as he was cinching up the drawstring of these way too-big sweatpants around his tiny-tiny waist—wait, on the pocket, was that a Princeton logo? Rebecca hadn't mentioned Theo went to—wait a sec.

"Are those—my—sweatpants?"

"Yessireebob."

"You went through my stuff and pulled out a pair of my sweatpants for yourself?"

"Had to. I have to do something to protect myself, before I wake up screaming 'rape' in the middle of the night."

"Think you're that irresistible, do you? That I'll lose all control, driven mad by your provocative sexuality?"

"It can happen." In the robe and sweatpants, he padded into the bathroom looking very like the little prince he usually acted like.

"I'm sure you must experience that all the time," I said, following him as far as the bathroom door, "with your irresistible charm."

"Only just this morning you were ripping the bedding away so you could get at me."

"You know that's not—and I apologized!!! Lots!!!"

"Doesn't change anything." The toothbrush full of Crest went into his mouth.

"Yeah, you're totally right. I just couldn't keep my hands to myself, faced with the vision of masculine virility that you are."

"Fuck off." At least I'm pretty sure that's what he said underneath the mouthful of foam.

"Let me tell you," I explained, "you know who I think is hot? Mark Ruffalo is hot. Matt Damon? Jake Gyllenhaal? Mad hot. Shaun White? Hmm, not so much. But you're welcome to the sweatpants."

He spat.

"Just don't get any ideas." He rinsed, wiped his mouth and pushed past me. I guessed it was my turn for the bathroom.

Theo was settling into bed and he turned the light out—just as I was coming out of the bathroom. Into darkness. Nice, Theo.

I got into bed—in the dark—careful not to get anywhere near Theo's precious little boy-buns. My eyes started to adjust. Street lights threw some light onto the ceiling, which I was staring at.

"I'm really sorry about this morning," I said, finally. "I didn't mean for that to happen."

He didn't respond, and I figured he was either asleep or pretending to be which was as good as. I rolled over—away from him, you can be sure. I don't know how long the silence lasted. I'd started to drift off when something almost pulled me awake—but maybe I dreamt it.

"Thanks," he said softly.

Yeah, I know. I must have dreamt it.

# Chapter 10
## Orientation, but Not that Kind—Okay, Yeah, that Kind Too

*TOMMY*

I'd been at this effing job for two weeks at Parker O'Neill—with practically no training—working for this total bastard litigator. Which I was doing because no one else would. *And* because they offered me an outrageous amount of money to do it. I even had the brazil-nuts to say it wasn't enough, and they, believe it or not, offered me more. I had to say 'yes' after that, didn't I? And as long as the total bastard litigator was happy, no one seemed to mind. So. I was the most overpaid little office boy in the entire world.

Guinness people: Please note.

I had started working at a law firm a few years ago because my best friend in the entire world, Roger, was a baby lawyer and I couldn't think of anything better to do, so I lied my way into a job at the firm where he worked, Goodkin Berdann & Dunkel. And then my best friend in the entire world reconnected with an old boyfriend and decided he couldn't stand being a baby lawyer another minute. Love will apparently do that to a person.

Somewhere in that brief narrative Jeffrey Bornic came and went, but not significantly.

What mattered was that my best friend in the entire world abandoned me at Goodkin Berdann, just left me standing at the elevator bank, forsaken and bereft, weeping quietly and waving a lace hanky.

Or something like that.

And then I heard about *this* gig over here at Parker O'Neill, with the jumbo hazard-pay if you could handle this total bastard litigator, and I figured what the hells. How bad could he be? Pretty bad, it turns out, but if you don't give a whoopy-ding-dong, and I so don't, it's all just water off a duck *à l'orange*. We work perfectly together, Mr. Kaminsky and I.

He yells, I yawn.

But this particular morning Mr. K. was forced to fend for himself while I sat, being oriented. Or orientated, but you have to be really stupid to say orientated.

Jocelyn, the head of secretarial services, was walking us newbies through the ins and outs of payroll, personnel and other such blather.

The 'us' in question consisted of me and another new guy-secretary, Theo, who just started today. Incredible red hair—which usually means it came out of a box, but I was pretty sure his was real—which was certainly not something I could say about Jocelyn's highlights. I could only hope she did that herself—it would be a crime if she'd *paid* somebody for that.

Back to Theo. He was shorter than me even, and way pretty. He hadn't said much, but I was good and sure he shopped in the same department I did, if you know what I mean.

"Before we finish up here," said Jocelyn, "we should talk a little about your specific assignments. Tommy, you've been working for Mr. Kaminsky for a couple weeks already, and I'm sure he's got you in knots."

"Just a bit."

"And he has this benefit coming up. How's that going?"

"That's pretty much all we're doing these days."

"That'll change. If the case against Hiromi Industries takes off the way it's expected to—watch out. He'll be running the case—with an army of associates."

"Oh goody."

"But I have to say this, Tommy—in the two weeks you've been here, I haven't heard a peep out of Mr. K., and I can't *remember* the last time that happened. That guy—what a scooch-a-menz." I swear that's what she said. "Know what that means?" Two shaking heads. "Pain in the ass. If you can really keep him happy, you're aces in my book."

"I'll try."

"Theo," she said turning to the red curls, "your primary responsibility is working for Victoria. She's a senior partner, with a considerable practice, but on top of that, she's in charge of the associates, handles their reviews, case assignments, even terminations. You will inevitably be privy to some extremely sensitive information and documents. It's imperative you understand that we depend on your discretion. What goes on at your desk has to stay at your desk, *capiche?*"

"Yeah, sure."

"The assignments for the *Hiromi* case I just mentioned are an example. I understand a lot of attorneys want on that case. People's jobs and careers are involved."

"Hey—I can keep a secret."

"Glad to hear."

There was a quick knock, the door to the training room opened and a gorgeous head popped in.

"Hey, you ready for me?" said the gorgeous head.

Oh yes, please.

"Enrique, c'mon in," said Joss. "Theo, Tommy, this is Enrique, he's from the IT Department, and he'll train you on some software specific to the firm."

I can't let Enrique pass without comment. Beautiful curly black hair, matching dark eyes and a body—this was one computer geek who knocked in some serious hours in the gym. Arms, chest, thighs—all were built up and dressed in clothes carefully chosen to be exquisitely just a smidge too small. With an artfully maintained three-day stubble. Thankyoujesus.

This was going to be oh-so much more fun than Jocelyn.

"Okay," she said, "I'll leave you guys to get further orientated—" What did I tell you about orientated? "After Enrique, lunch. Tommy, you can show Theo where the cafeteria is?"

Theo and I moved to computer desks and Enrique—as much as I could listen to him while I was quietly obsessing over his collar bones and that little depression below the Adam's apple, which seemed to hold a strange fascination for me—and Enrique told us all about saving docs and client numbers and litigation folders and metadata and lockboxes and so on and so forth. If poor Theo was overwhelmed—and he plainly was, biting his lower lip like a little orphan boy lost in the woods—he certainly got extra attention from Enrique to help him out. Enrique seemed pretty smitten with pretty Theo and was all too eager to lean over him to use Theo's mouse, purely for demonstrative purposes, I'm sure.

"Oh, you flipped your mouse," said Enrique.

"I'm left-handed, yeah."

Enrique struggled bravely with Theo's mouse, no doubt breathing lightly into Theo's ear. The guy was smooth.

"I'm left-handed, too," I offered. Me, the left-handed plate of chopped liver.

For his part, Theo, even with this guy's beautiful arm around his shoulder, was oblivious to the attentions. Alas, poor Enrique was destined to disappointment from that quarter.

Of course, if he needed succor, I knew right where he could find it.

When the hour was up, Theo and I adjourned to the firm cafeteria for turkey tetrazzini.

"The food here's not that bad, considering. The attorneys eat it, so they can't let it get too crappy. Maybe avoid the fish."

"Good to know."

"So—what did you think of that guy from IT? Totally hot, which I didn't expect."

"Good-looking guy, for sure."

*"And* gay."

"Ya think?"

"Theo, he did everything but grope your butt."

"If you say so."

"He thinks you're cute."

"Yeah, well, no law against thinking."

"Really? Not interested?"

"Not the tiniest, sorry."

Takes all kinds, I guess.

I paused in my mixed vegetable medley and considered this alien creature across from me.

"So tell me, young Theo. You're really from Iowa? That's an actual place?"

"It is an actual place, full of cornfields and cattle and hogs. And me."

"And you came to New York seeking fame and fortune—as another Stephen Sondheim."

"There will *never* be another Stephen Sondheim so don't even joke, but yeah. Oh, here," and he started rummaging in his backpack. He pulled out a small stack of advertising postcards. "A couple of my songs are going to be in this showcase."

I read the postcard—a place called Don't Tell Mama. I'm pretty sure I'd been there. Little gay-ish cabaret in the middle of Restaurant Row.

"Featuring the songs of," I read out loud, "somebody, somebody, somebody else, *Theo McPherson!*" He bowed his head a little. "That is so cool! Can I come?"

"Of course you can come!"

"You must have been a very odd bird growing up among the overalls and pitchforks and Grant Woods, no?"

"I guess so. My sister tells this story—I don't remember this at all—but apparently I came home from school one day, threw myself on the couch with the back of my hand to my forehead like some silent movie star, and announced, 'I am *never* going back to that school again!'"

"Ha! And what happened?"

"I don't remember it but I'm sure they just told me to change my clothes and do my chores. It was a farm, there were always chores. Hogs have to be fed, watered and cleaned up after—every day, summer, winter, Christmas. You probably stood out as a kid as well, I imagine. The butterfly of the nursery school."

"I did! I was fantastic. Just ask Roger. Roger's my best friend since literally the beginning of time. I, of course, thought I was completely normal, but Roger says that I was a bit *outré* even in kindergarten. Growing up, my dad used to give me these boy toys—footballs, baseballs, you know—crap I was *never* going to touch. He was always trying to butch me up. One year he gave me a baseball glove, and then he was soooo crabby when I bedazzled it."

"I can't imagine you playing baseball."

"Well of course I couldn't, but with that glove I *looked* amazing. Anyway, it accomplished what I wanted. I not only *didn't* have to try out for Little League—whoopee!—I was *forbidden* to. *And* it pissed him off."

"Win-win."

"For me, anyway. Maybe not so great for my jock-father. One year he got me this giant G.I. Joe—it was like a Ken-doll, with uniforms. I didn't know *what* to do with poor Joe and his macho self until it occurred to me—with a seam ripper and some safety pins, you could refit Barbie costumes for him."

"That's awesome!" laughed Theo. "Wait, didn't G.I. Joe have like a little scruffy beard?"

"I know! Hot—right? I was *miles* ahead of Conchita Wurst. Anyway, I was just helping Joe do his duty. Like the posters said—be all you can be!"

"G.I. Josie joins the Marines!" laughed Theo.

"The few, the proud, the *fabulous*! Ooooh-rah!" I said, but unlike the Marines, I threw one hand over my head as I said it. "I always think that works a lot better with the hand. I don't know why the Marines don't do it that way."

"Ooooh-rah!" we said together, hands up high, laughing.

"Good lord." Suddenly Jeffrey Bornic was standing at our table—and all the sunlight and happiness was sucked right out of the room. "It's a twink convention."

"I'm not a twink," said the two twinks simultaneously.

"You two, it's like bumping into the scary twins from *The Shining.*"

I looked at Theo, whose eyes were as bright as lighthouses.

"Halloween!" we screamed together discreetly.

"Jinx, you owe me a Diet Coke," I added.

"The pair of you, please stop speaking in unison, before I call a priest."

"And we're both left-handed," I volunteered, and he made a cross in the air.

"I suppose it was inevitable you two would find each other."

"Shut up, Jeff," said Theo turning back to his lunch. Kid apparently had no fear of attorneys.

"Whoa," I said. "So how do you guys...?"

"Theo is my best friend's annoying little brother," said Jeffrey. "I've known him since he was a child—not very long."

"Hardy-har-har," said Theo, demonstrating his maturity.

"You remember my best friend Roger?" I explained. "Jeff is the guy Roger dumped."

"He didn't dump me, we came to the mutual—"

"Don't even try, Jeffrey, don't even try."

"Whatever," said Jeffrey.

"Oh my God, Tommy, you've got to fill me in on the details."

"Well, since you asked—!"

"Yeah, or not, too," interrupted Jeffrey before I could get another word out. How rude. I took another breath, prefatory to telling the whole story *anyway,* but Jeff knocked it right out of my head by saying, "Theo and I have also been sleeping together for a while."

Well that would explain—no, actually, that wouldn't explain anything. I looked at Theo.

"We're sharing my sister's sleeper couch," he clarified, with a peevish look to the tall blond.

"True," said Jeffrey. "But, in point of fact, I *have* seen Theo's..." and here he made a vague gesture with one index finger in the general direction of Theo's lap.

"Shut! Up!" said Theo, not too quietly.

"I have just one thing to say," said Jeffrey, and he whispered. "So pink."

I realize in retrospect that I probably shouldn't have laughed.

"Shut-up-shut-up-shut-up!" yelled Theo. And he actually picked up a french fry and flung it at Jeffrey, about as hard as you can fling a french fry anyway. (I know, turkey with pasta, *and* fries. Oh to be seventeen, or however old this kid wasn't.) The fry in question bounced off the chest of Jeff's pink dress shirt and fell to the table.

It's probably not necessary for me to explain that a food fight in the cafeteria of a more or less stodgy corporate law firm was considered more or less 'not done.' Least not on your first day.

"Did you just throw that french fry at me?" asked Jeffrey, incredulously, if somewhat stupidly.

"You're lucky it wasn't the cherry cobbler!"

Jeffrey picked up the offending fry—and ate it.

"Theo," I intervened cautiously, "you're going to find out just how 'temp' the word 'temp,' can be."

And sure enough who should suddenly be standing there at Jeffrey's elbow, but our old friend (and immediate supervisor) Jocelyn.

"Theo, can you step down to my office for a moment?"

And I figured that was that. Too bad, because this job could have been a hoot with feisty Theo around.

But you know, sometimes in life, people surprise you. Take Jeffrey Bornic. I'd known the guy for a while, but I'd never seen him do anything that wasn't completely self-interested. Until now. He turned to Jocelyn, all blue-eyed charm.

"Joss, I'm sorry, this is totally my fault. Theo and I go way back—because of Rebecca, you know—and we sometimes horse around like brothers. I'm so sorry. Please, as a favor to me?"—and he did one of those puppy dog looks with the worried forehead—"please don't hold this against Theo. Just forget this, and I promise it won't happen again."

Who would have guessed that Jeffrey Bornic even *had* a puppy dog look in his repertoire? Well he did, and he was crushing it. You could watch Jocelyn melt under those sky-blues of his.

"Well, okay, Jeffrey. If you say so."

"You are the *best!*"

She's also admin. and he's an atty. and I had learned that the difference made a *lot* of difference at a law firm.

"Thank you, Jeffrey," I said when Jocelyn had gone. The Bornic took that as an invitation. He pulled up a chair, sat down and stared at Theo, apparently expecting some hint of gratitude from the Iowa delegation—which was *so* not happening. Theo seemed perfectly content with his fork and his tetrazzini, and he smiled at Jeffrey while he chewed.

Ever the peacemaker, I tried again.

"Theo was just telling me about his showcase," and I gave Jeffrey a postcard from Theo's stack. "You probably knew about this already?"

"No," said Jeffrey, and looked at the card. Theo reached over and took the card from Jeffrey's hand and put it back on top of the others. "Rebecca told me you wrote songs," Jeffrey said, and he picked up the postcard again. "Are they any good?"

"They're brilliant, but I'm sure you wouldn't understand them," and he took the card from Jeffrey's hand and put it back on the pile. Again.

What was the deal with these two?

"Look," said Jeffrey, "I'm trying to be nice, okay? I didn't *have* to save your ass with Jocelyn, but I did, didn't I? I'm not all bad."

"I'm supposed to be grateful because you kept me from getting fired from this stupid day job that I don't want anyway? Gee, thanks Jeff."

"Hey guys." It was Enrique from IT. Our hottie trainer. Sigh. My God those eyes, those eyelashes. "I hope I was okay today. I'm still really new at this."

Before I could tell him he was fabulous and ask if he had anything else he wanted to teach me—Jeffrey was on his feet doing his best welcome-to-the-castle smile.

"I don't think we've met." Jeffie extended his princely hand. "Jeffrey Bornic, Litigation."

"Hi. Enrique, Tech Systems Trainer." He shook Jeffrey's hand, but he wasn't much interested. Now, loathe as I might be to admit it, Jeffrey Bornic was not a bad looking guy, but Enrique had a noticeable preference and that preference was for lip-biting, lost-in-the-woods redheaded boys, and his focus turned immediately back in that direction. "I hope that wasn't information overload, Theo. I saw your eyes glaze over a couple times."

"It's fine," said Theo. "I'm sure I'll get the whole doc system once I've worked on it for a bit."

"How about you, Tommy? I know it can be a lot, and I sort of gave you the whole thing all at once."

"Sometimes that's just how I like it."

It just came out of my mouth, like I was possessed, I swear. The devil made me say it, clearly. I thought Theo might shoot Dr Pepper out his nose; hunky hunky Enrique threw back his head and gave a manly laugh, which was incredibly sexy; and Jeffrey Bornic, a boy born to give dirty looks, flashed me one of his dirtiest.

"You okay?" Enrique asked Theo solicitously, one warm, masculine hand, lightly dusted with dark hair, resting on Theo's shoulder. This guy was good.

It took Theo a couple seconds for his coughing to subside before he nodded and took another sip. It was amazing to see the colors that kid's face could get. He too gave me a bit of a stink face; I shrugged in my innocence.

"Enrique, I don't think I've seen you around before," Jeffrey intervened, trying to pull the conversation back in his direction.

"I just started. These two were my first victims."

"You were fine, Enrique, really," I said.

*If only you'd take your shirt off now and then.*

"Well, I'm sure you'll have questions."

I definitely did. Like 'How's dinner and a movie sound?' Or 'Just how big *is* your hard drive?'

"Call me when something comes up, okay, Theo?" Enrique smiled to Theo and—I'm not making this up, I swear—he winked at him. "Or you can always come find me in IT."

Any woman would have busted Enrique's gorgeous ass for harassment long before things got this far, but Theo still didn't seem to notice that he was the object of any special attentions.

And although I might have felt bad because Enrique didn't wink at me, poor Jeffrey Bornic was left standing on the side of the road, looking like Claudette Colbert had just shown him how to hitchhike. Guess he didn't get ignored very often.

Enrique gave Theo's shoulder a squeeze and he walked away to go stand in the line of duty. Or at least in the line for the turkey tetrazzini.

Jeffrey and I watched him go, enjoying Enrique's khaki-encased backside.

"Kinda makes your teeth ache, doesn't it?" I said.

"Who—was—that?" said Jeffrey sitting back down at the table.

"That's Enrique the computer trainer," said Theo. "Keep up."

"Wow. They don't make nerds like they used to. I haven't seen him before."

"He's new, in IT," said Theo.

And Jeffrey Bornic, the hotshot, ambitious, smart-as-a-whipsnake lawyer-boy, got *the* all-time stupidest look on his face.

"What?" said Theo.

"The new guy in IT?" And he smote his forehead. You don't often see someone actually smite his forehead, but Jeffrey Bornic, with an audible smack, smote for all he was worth. *"That's* the new guy from IT!"

"What?" asked Theo, laughing.

"Rebecca was going to set me up with the new guy from the IT department—'But nooooo,' I said. 'There are no gay guys in IT,' I said. 'Why would *I* ever go out with somebody from IT?' I said. And instead I went to lunch, and I thought *you* were—oh man!"

"You could have had a date with—that," I gestured toward Enrique, still negotiating for his side dishes.

"Tell me about it," said Jeffrey wistfully.

"Of all sad words on tongue or pen..." I said, while together Jeffrey and I contemplated the sharp bitterness of fate—and the breadth of Enrique's shoulders. Sigh.

"And you got to meet *me* instead," Theo smiled.

"Lucky me."

"Problem is, Jeffrey, the trainer seems to be rather besotted. Our Theo has quite captured his fancy."

"That's a lie," said Theo, tucking into the above-referenced cherry cobbler. "I didn't go anywhere near his fancy."

"We need to face the hard truth, Jeffrey, that you and I were totally ignored, while the hottie Enrique wunk at young Theo."

"Wunk?"

"Past tense of wink," I explained.

"He's too tall anyway," said Theo. "Too macho, too—whatever. All those muscles—not really my thing."

Jeffrey and I, who didn't have any objections either to macho or muscles, looked dismayed at Theo—who went on blithely enjoying the cobbler.

Jeffrey scooted his chair back and stood.

"Later, Jeff," said Theo, without looking up.

And Jeffrey sat back down.

"My name is Jeffrey actually," said Jeffrey actually.

"I can't call you Jeffrey," said Theo. "It's too pompous, too overstuffed, too much like you. And that awful pink shirt. You had that made for you, didn't you." He tugged at Jeffrey's monogrammed cuff. "Your initials are J.A.B.?"

"Uh, yeah, Jeffrey Anthony—"

"Jab. Suits you. I'll call you Jeff."

"Roger called him Jeff," I said delicately, hoping to help.

"Thank you, Tommy, for reminding us all."

"Is *that* why I can't call you Jeff?" Theo seemed to find this wildly unjust. "Because the guy who *dumped* you called you Jeff?"

*"Everyone* calls me Jeffrey. What's the big deal?"

"I know. Why don't I just call you 'unbelievable fucktard'? Unless some ex-boyfriend's already got dibs on that one?"

Before I could stop myself, I was sputtering.

Jeffrey looked to me in head-shaking astonishment.

"Enjoy your lunch, boys," and he started off toward the steam tables—but he didn't get far.

He stopped, he turned, he came back.

He picked up a postcard from Theo's pile one more time, and walked away.

I wasn't entirely sure what I had just witnessed, but it was far more interesting than I had imagined lunch was going to be, and I'm not even *talking* about Enrique.

Theo.

Don't get me wrong, I wasn't lusting after the little pistachio-nut bundt cake, not in the least. But I was impressed as hell. I think of myself as sort of ballsy, kinda out there, you know? But I was totally outclassed by Theo.

Think about it—he had started a food fight in the firm cafeteria, he had utterly slammed a soon-to-be-partner, and, on top of everything else—he totally got away with it. On his first day.

And it was only one thirty.

"Theo, I really hope this songwriting thing works out for you," I said.

"Thanks."

"Because you sure aren't going to last long around here."

# Chapter 11
## Hush Up!

*JEFFREY*

I'm not exactly sure what I expected, but it wasn't this. I mean, I knew it wasn't going to be the Met Gala, but I guess I hadn't quite expected just how much of a dive Don't Tell Mama was going to be. What the hell kind of name was that for a club, anyway?

There was a blackboard outside proclaiming "Tonight! Songwriters' Showcase!" Below that was chalked the roster of entertainment for the rest of the week—a bunch of names I'd never heard of and you've never heard of either—*but* on *Saturday,* no less than Judy Garland *and* Liza Minnelli would be appearing live on stage together. As they apparently did each and every Saturday. Someone should tell the *Times.*

Anyway, you get an idea what kind of place this was.

And me in a Tom Ford suit.

Inside there was a dining room—a typical brownstone-basement restaurant you see in Manhattan, exposed brick, a bar along one wall. I said I was there for the songwriters showcase, and the bartender just nodded over to a curtained doorway. I pushed through the curtains.

"You with someone?"

It was this weirdly androgynous, weirdly tall waiter/waitress/maître d'/ person in black stretch pants and ballet flats, and the question came out of nowhere, like an accusation. It took me a second.

"No."

She/he glanced at my suit, arched an eyebrow—and then shrugged. "Twelve dollar cover."

I paid. She grabbed a menu.

"Follow me." I followed her (and despite conflicting indicia, I'm sticking with that pronoun from here on). It was a long narrow room with a stage at the far end. A banquette dotted with little round tables ran along each side of the room, and down the middle there was another row of small tables and chairs. The hostess plopped me down on the side banquette about a third of the way back. Aside from me, there were only a few other banquette-tables occupied—but there was a large group that had the center tables from the stage nearly to the back—and there, toward the rear of the group, Theo seemed to be the center of attention. And, just to make things worse, Tommy was sitting next to him, yammering away. *Figures,* I thought. He waved and hopped right over to my table—Tommy, I mean, certainly not Theo—before I even sat down.

The hostess came over to us. She looked at Tommy, looked back at me.

"You work fast," she said. "Must be the suit."

"Cranberry juice and soda," I said in response.

"There's a two-drink minimum," she explained. "Cranberry juice and soda isn't one."

"Charge me for the vodka, I don't care."

Theo had seen me, but seemed intent on ignoring me. Whatever.

"I'll have his vodka," volunteered Tommy. "And tonic," he added smiling, and the waitress was gone. "So, Jeffrey Bornic." Tommy put one elbow on the table, put his chin on it, and leaned forward like he was getting the dish from one of his girlfriends.

Were Tommy and I buds now???

"What are *you* doing here?" Tommy wanted to know.

"I just came to be nice."

"My aunt Fanny."

"Okay, don't believe me, it's none of your business anyway, and why do you even care?"

"Because honestly I always thought you were about the dullest person on earth. And yet—here you are, rich young whiz-kid lawyer-boy in a seedy gay cabaret, dressed to the nines at a table for one. Now *that's* interesting."

"Don't get your hopes up. You'd be amazed how boring I can be."

"And yet—here you are. And?"

"And what? I just came to be nice. There's no story here!"

I noticed that Theo had started to glance in my direction. Fairly annoyed glances, too.

"Really?" said Tommy, doubtfully.

"I swear. I have no hidden agenda, I have no rotten fruit to throw, nothing. I come in peace."

"You and Michael Rennie."

"If you say so."

I glanced over and Theo was looking at me again. He had moved up the scale a couple notches from annoyed to furious.

"So Theo wrote one of the songs?"

"Two," said Tommy. "One in the first half and one in the second." He pushed one of the programs on the table at me.

"Figures. I was hoping not to have to stay for the whole thing."

"I feel compelled to point out that checking your cell phone during the performance is considered very bad form."

"I did that *once!*" I said. "*Once!* Did Roger tell you *everything* I did wrong?"

Just then I saw Theo get up.

The only way you could get from his side of the big row of tables over to our side was to walk all the way down to the stage and around, which is what Theo did, and now he was headed in our direction. Man, he was seething.

"Look out," said Tommy. "Incoming."

"What are *you* doing here?"

"Hey, can't a guy just come and be a nice guy?"

"You can't and you aren't."

"Have a seat, Theo."

"No."

"Rebecca couldn't be here, so I thought it was the least—and after all, we *have* been sleeping together all week—"

He sat down.

"Hey!" he whispered furiously. "Madison does *not* need to know that."

"Madison is here?" I sat up and started sorting through the big table to see if I could pick him out. I *had* to see the famous Madison.

"He is," answered Tommy. "And no offense or anything, Theo, I know I just met the guy, but is he being a bit of an ass or what?"

"Yeah he is being. When it's not all about him, he gets a little—edgy."

"Which one is he?" I asked Tommy, knowing he'd tell me.

"Up at the very end."

"The blond beach boy?" I turned to Theo. "Nice. He's really cute!"

"I know, right?" said Tommy. "But that's not the one. The one with the goatee."

I looked to the long table again. It was like Brooklyn over there.

"Tommy, they all have goatees, even the women."

Tommy puffed his cheeks out, making a fat face. I glanced over again. The chubby one? That guy? No way.

"You're kidding me, right?" I checked with Theo, who looked like a boiler about to blow.

"So not kidding," said Tommy.

"The fat one with the little beard where his chin would be if he had one?"

"He's not fat!"

"Yup, him," said Tommy.

"What's it to you, anyway?" asked Theo, eyebrows scrunched together and ready for battle.

"It's just that you've been giving *me* crap since day one about being old and flabby—"

"That's only because you act like you're Channing fucking Tatum—"

"—and this whole time you've been sleeping with that?"

"Obviously not, since this whole time I've been *'sleeping'* with you," he said with air quotes.

"You're going out with *that* slacker?" It didn't make sense.

"Seriously," Tommy chimed in. "Madison is definitely updating." Updating? We both looked at Tommy. "When you go out with somebody way better looking than you."

I turned back to Theo.

"How old *is* the guy?"

"He's thirty-two, not that it's any of your business."

"Wow. Are you sure? Looks older. Have you seen his driver's license?"

"Okay, thirty-five, and shut up!"

"Is he still like Gen X? Because he looks more like Gen XL. Can we talk about the pudge?"

"He's incredibly talented and his career is really taking off!"

"So's his hair."

"That is so like you, you only see the surface of things. You see the pudge and the hairline and you think you know him. Let me tell you, he's smart, he knows gobs of shows and he can be really funny sometimes, he's into all these really cool eastern religions and—"

I could tell he was trying not to scream, and it occurred to me that I probably shouldn't have baited him this far. I *had* come to be supportive, after all, and instead—

"Hey look, Theo, let's not do this—I'm sor—"

"This showcase," he said very quietly and very intensely, interrupting me mid-apology. Wait, I was apologizing? "I know this whole thing doesn't look like much to you, but it's really important to me—"

"Everyone keeps telling me that—"

"So don't ruin it!"

He was starting to lose it, and getting louder. Behind him a couple heads glanced over at us.

"Look, please," he said quietly. "Go. Do not stay here. I don't want you here."

"I'm not going to go." Of course this was the last place on the planet I wanted to be, but now it was another one of those principle-of-the-thing things. I couldn't give in, even if I wanted to. If Theo wanted me gone, then I was bolted to that banquette. "I went to all the trouble to find this place, come here, I paid the stupid cover, and you know what else? It's a free country."

Theo looked me fiercely in the eyes for a couple seconds before he spoke.

"I hate you so much."

"I'm still not leaving."

"Fine," he said, clearly unhappy. Obviously little Theo was very used to getting his own way. Too bad about little Theo.

A different waitress—in a gigantic wig and a bowling costume, for no reason that I could guess—was suddenly there.

"One cranberry soda, no vodka. One vodka-tonic, with a side order of—vodka," she said sorting the three glasses out from the crowd on her tray. "And here's your Dr Pepper, hon." She gave a big motherly smile to Theo, set another glass down, and went. Theo was so involved in his outrage that his eyes never moved from glaring at me.

"Fine," he said again.

"Fine," I said.

"Fine-then-here's-the-deal. You can stay, but you may not speak about my songs. Not to me, not to anyone. If you love them, if you hate them, you keep it to yourself. Not a single word, understand?"

"Okay, I guess I can handle a non-disclosure. Where do I sign?"

Someone had sat down in front of an upright piano that had obviously survived the Great Depression—and probably the Civil War Draft Riots. The lights, such as they were, started to dim, and the good-looking beach boy next to Fat Madison called over in the world's loudest stage whisper:

"Theo!"

Theo stood up, picked up his drink and turned to go.

"Hey Theo?" I said.

"What!" he snapped back at me.

"Break a leg."

Theo took a slurp on the straw of his Dr Pepper.

"You look ridiculous in that suit."

I looked at Tommy for support.

"Just think what he'd have said if you'd brought him flowers."

Theo didn't have time to get back to his side of the long string of tables, so he grabbed an empty chair on this side of the Great Divide and sat with his back to us. The piano player got going then, and so did the evening. Our hostess-person was on stage, introducing the first song from notes on 3x5 cards—and we were off. I'll admit I didn't really get most of it. It was a weird mix of songs from musicals still being written. There was even one really bad hip-hop number. But Theo's songs were actually good—and it was a huge relief to be able to say that, because what would I have said if his songs totally stank? Of course I'd just promised not to say anything, either way, but I was still really happy that his songs were good, and they seemed to go really well with the little audience.

His first song was a guy singing how frustrated he was because he wanted to write a love song about his girlfriend and couldn't—and it was actually funny. It got so silly, by the end we were all doubled-over laughing.

And in the second half, a girl came out and sang this ballad about how she wanted people to look at her and see that she was special, and not just a typist. It was a really pretty tune, and it sat on the girl's voice beautifully—and it was such a modest little wish, it broke your heart.

So it was a double-win for Theo. I actually felt—you know—kinda proud of him. Which was stupid because none of this had anything to do with me.

When the show was over, there was a huge party over at the songwriters' table. I sat in my booth with Tommy—we agreed that Theo's songs were the best of the evening. We waited for things to calm down a little at the other table before we went over to add our congratulations to the great heap of gushing compliments they were hurling at each other.

Seriously, that was my intention when I slid out of the banquette. I knew it was a gross violation of the gag order he'd imposed, but I was just going to go over and say something nice. I stood behind Theo's chair for a bit—he knew I was there—and I waited for a chance to say something.

"Theo—" I said leaning down when he finally paused in his conversation with the guy on his left—and he immediately launched into an even louder conversation with the girl on his right. Seriously ticked me off, which I'm sure was his intention. When the same thing happened after my second try, I changed tactics.

*You want to be an asshole? Fantastic.* I'd had three years at Princeton Law learning nothing but how to be an asshole—and I graduated top of my class. *Welcome to the majors, Iowa.*

Across the table Tommy was shamelessly flirting with the hot surfer-looking-guy. *Too bad about you, Tommy,* I thought, as I reached over Theo and across the table and shoved my hand in front of the beach boy's face.

"Hi," I said, "I don't think we've met. I'm Jeffrey."

"Swithin," said the surfer a little uncertainly as he shook my hand. Did he really say Swithin? That's right, his name was in the program.

"I've heard *so* much about you," I said, lying. I was loud enough to be heard over the noise of the group. I was leaning across Theo, and certainly *he* could hear me, which was the whole point. "Congratulations on your song tonight! It went really well, don't you think?"

"Hey thanks, man."

Next to Tommy there was a very fey guy in his thirties, with a straw between his fingers like a cigarette.

"Hi, I'm Jeffrey," I said.

"Well hello, Jeffrey!" said the fey one enthusiastically. At least *somebody* was glad to see me. "Jaspuh. How nice to meet you, darling."

*Well hush my mouth. Jas-puh.* I didn't know which was sillier, the name or the deep-south accent.

"You had a song on the program tonight, too, didn't you? It was really great!" I had no idea which song it was and couldn't care anyway.

"Well aren't you suddenly the most interesting person in the room, handsome. But the song was only half mine—you must meet my collaborator, Jessica."

"Hi-how-ah-ya," said a dark woman speaking heavy Brooklyn, pumping my hand like a politician.

"A real thrill to meet you, after everything Theo's told me," I said, giving Theo's shoulder a squeeze. Good lord, that shoulder was like granite. Perfect. Well, it was time to stop dicking around and get to the point. I turned toward the upper end of the group with just a big ol' grin on my face.

"And *you* have to be Madison," I said to the slob with the awful little goatee and a sour look on his face. "I've definitely heard a *lot* about *you*," I said. "Just tons. Tons and tons."

"Jeff—" said Theo, finally, trying to turn around to me. *Now* he wanted to talk to me. *You had your chance, little one,* I thought to myself, and I kept right on going.

"Tons."

"Jeff—"

"What a shame *you* didn't have a song on the program tonight."

"I've got a show at Goodspeed in a developmental—"

"Theo told me all about it!" Actually I had gotten the details from Rebecca, and okay, yeah, maybe I'd asked her. "And how sweet it was of Theo to go all the way up there to help you out with your show." Judging from the large round eyes in the faces at the table, and the fact that all conversation around me had stopped, I gathered pretty much everybody here had also heard some version of the saga of Goodspeed.

"Jeff—" tried Theo again, but now it was Madison who was barreling on over the top of him.

"It's a very big deal," he tried to impress upon me, "and there's a tremendous amount of pressure—"

"I'm sure," I interrupted. "Just as well you didn't have a song on the program tonight, then. I guess they only picked the best writers to include." Swithin snorted. "But you just keep plugging away, Madison, and I'm sure even you'll get your chance someday." Jasper turned his head into Jessica's shoulder, and his body was shaking up and down.

"Jeff—!" said Theo really really loud trying to get up but my hands were on his shoulders keeping him in the chair.

This next part was a stroke of genius that just came to me in the moment.

There were probably sixty people at this long table and easily half were turned watching us at the upper end.

I leaned down and gave Theo a little hug from behind—

"I'm gonna run, honey," I said, still being careful to pitch my voice so everyone could hear me. "But you stay and have fun with your friends." I looked around to the others, still with my hands on Theo. "So nice meeting you all. And *you*," I said, giving Theo another big, affectionate squeeze, "I am so *proud* of you!" and I leaned down and gave him a quick kiss. He was too stunned to react. "I'll see you when you get home, Tiger," I said with a light caress of his cheek before I turned and headed for the curtained door.

Behind me I could hear Jasper gasp, and then Tommy cut loose with a screech of a laugh — and a chair scraped sharply against the floor. Theo had stood up, I guessed. But he didn't run after me ranting, and he didn't chuck the chair at the back of my head, which was what I fully expected.

"Lovely place you've got here," I said to the hostess/emcee as I paid the bar tab for me and Tommy, meaning Tommy.

"You got the Dr Pepper, too?"

"Oh hell yes."

There was only one drawback to the way this evening had gone—I couldn't be there to see Theo's reaction, or to hear how he explained me to Madison, *et al.*

Even so, as I sat in a taxi taking me back to Rebecca's, I could *not* stop smiling.

# Chapter 12
## Rude Awakening

*THEO*

The apartment was dark when I got in. Jeff was already asleep on the sofa bed. That miserable little reptile.

And why wasn't he wearing a tee shirt? I thought he was going to wear tee shirts and shorts to bed now.

"Hey!" I said, kicking the bed. He didn't budge. So I went around the other side of the bed. "Hey!" From there, I could kick *him*. "Hey!"

"What the—Jesus!" He sat up. I snapped on the lamp, and he shielded his eyes.

"You!" I said, still kicking. "You turd-ball! You scum-wad!"

"Stop kicking me!"

"No!"

He grabbed my ankle, which I should have seen coming, but I didn't, and because I didn't, when I went to pull my foot back to kick him again, I couldn't. I lost my balance, and I didn't have an extra foot with which to catch my balance and—*bam*—my ass hit the floor but hard. Butt hard.

"Let go of my foot!" He had both hands on my ankle and I couldn't yank it away from him.

"Are you going to stop kicking me?" he yelled back.

"No!"

"Well then…"

The overhead light came on, and there was Rebecca.

"What is *wrong* with you guys?"

"It's *his* fault," I said from the floor, pointing, in case there was any confusion.

*"My* fault?"

*"You* started it."

"For the love of—"

"I was sound asleep, in point of fact, until you kicked me!"

"Which you deserved, and you know it!" I was still on the floor, and he was still holding my foot—so I pulled my other foot up so I could kick him with that one."What did *I* do?" He pushed both feet off the bed.

"What did *you* do? 'I'll see you at home, *Tiger,*'" I mimicked back at him.

"Oh yeah, that." He was smiling, maybe even snickering to himself. At least I could stand up. Man my right hip was going to have giganto bruise.

"You—ass-hat!" I stood back up, rubbing my sore butt.

"What is all this about???"

"This nimrod was at my showcase tonight!"

"Oh yeah!" she said, remembering, and still sleepy. "How'd that go?"

"It went pretty well, actually," I said, pleased, before I remembered the half-naked jackass sitting up in my bed. "But *he* was there!"

"What were *you* doing there?" asked Rebecca.

"Why does everybody keep asking me that? I went to be nice!"

"No, seriously, Jeffrey, why were you there?"

"Temporary insanity, apparently! But I went there to be supportive. Honest."

"Seriously?"

"Clearly the biggest mistake in my life. *This* is what I get for being a nice guy."

"Don't listen to him," said Theo. "This slimeball kissed me in front of everybody."

"You what?"

"Okay, that was a joke, I admit. Maybe I shouldn't have acted like your boyfriend in front of your boyfriend."

"Why?" Rebecca started to laugh.

"Because he was behaving like a little bitch!"

"Don't you call me a little bitch—" and I reared up my foot and kicked him again and then—ow ow ow—Mr. Spock had somehow sneaked up behind me. Man, I hated that!

"If you don't want to be called a little bitch," said the dick, "then don't *act* like a little bitch."

Rebecca let me go finally. Damn.

"Don't let him talk to me like that!" I appealed to Rebecca.

"He has a point, Theo."

"He had no business being there at all!!!"

"You're right," said Jeff. "I had absolutely no reason for being there, nothing to gain. Which is why you're *supposed* to say nice things, *e.g.*, 'thank you for coming, Jeffrey, how generous of you to give up your evening,' stuff like that."

"Theo?" said Rebecca.

"I can't believe you're taking his side!" The injustice of it all! My traitorous sister.

"I'm not on anybody's side! I'm Switzerland. I'm on the side of going to bed. You two –figure out how to share a couch without screaming in the middle of the night. If not—*you* can check into that motel in New Jersey."

"Ha!"

"And *you*—can get on the next westbound Greyhound, okay? I'm serious. Grow the hell up!"

"Ha!"

"That goes for *both* of you!"

"Ha!" I said back.

I glared at Jeff, snapped up my things and stomped to the bathroom to change. *It's so not fair,* I thought, *that Rebecca invited this guy here when I was already here.* When I came back, teeth brushed and everything, the lamp on my side was still on. *She could have asked me first before she gave my bed away.* At least I didn't have to break my neck in the dark, while I went around the foot of the bed to get over to my side. *And the way this clown tried to insinuate himself among my friends!* I pulled back the bedding. *Crud-sucking sleazeball.* I got under the sheet and blanket—in his, now my, sweatpants for safety's sake—and clicked off the lamp. *"I've heard so much about you"—such a scuzzwad!*

I was still lying in the dark, grinding my teeth on all this, when Jeff spoke out of the darkness.

"I really liked your songs, you know."

"You what?!" I spun around and was sitting up, my fist completely ready to punch him in the head. He was on his side, facing away from me.

"I mean it." In the general glow of city light that came in from the window, I could see the reflection in his eyes as he looked up at me. "I really liked your songs. Your two songs were easily the best of the evening."

"Really? You're not messing?"

"I'm not!" He rolled over onto his back. "I know I've been a dick. But seriously, I mean this. I tried to tell you earlier, but you wouldn't listen."

"When?"

"At the table, afterwards."

"Oh."

I lay back down.

"Your first song was actually funny—none of the others were. And the second one—that girl broke my heart. She was also really good." I was on my side, and I could see the silhouette of his face against the window.

"Yeah, isn't she? I lucked out there."

He sat up and looked down at me. I could still see the streetlight in his eyes in the darkness.

"There was that terrific line about people whispering, what was it?"

I leaned against the back of the couch and pulled my legs up.

"They'll whisper and they'll wonder, as they watch me walk away," I said, quoting my own song.

"See—that's so good."

"Thanks. I've always really liked that line too."

"And I'll tell you it was a huge relief that your songs were good. I mean, what would I have said if they'd totally shat?"

"Shat? Is that like supposed to be—past tense of—shit?"

"Past participle in this case, but yeah. So I was totally relieved that I could tell you I genuinely liked your songs. There—I said something nice. No snark, I promise. Okay?"

"Okay. I know I can be a bit much, too, sometimes. Not that I'm apologizing, because I'm not. You totally deserve to get knocked down when you're being an arrogant bozo. And if you ever take that I'm-so-much-smarter-than-you attitude with me again, I'll clobber you again."

"Yeah, I can be a bit of a prat."

"Prat?"

"I guess that's like prep-school for ass."

"I've heard it before."

"So—we're okay? *Pax?*" I just looked at him. I mean, who really says this stuff? "Sorry, that's 'peace' in Latin."

"I know what it means, phlegmwad. But why do you have to say it in frigging Latin?"

"What have you got against Latin? *E pluribus unum* and *carpe diem*?"

"You know what I say? *Carpe scrotum,* before I kick you in the balls for being such a jag-off—oh sorry, that's American for wanker. Why Latin, you affected dipwad! Christ-on-a-Croissan'wich, where do they teach you this shit—excuse me—shat? Dartmouth?"

"Someone's been googling my bio."

"Or Choate?"

"Both, actually," he said. "And don't think I'm going to apologize because I went to decent schools instead of some one-room schoolhouse in Buttcrack, Idaho!"

"That's Buttcrack, *Iowa* to *you,* shithead! You see, exactly this kind of crap—it's points of fact and pax and prat—you always sound like such a—"

"Don't make me come out there!" came from the bedroom.

Jeff looked at me, smiling, and then, really quietly—

"I got you in trouble," he sing-songed at me, like a little kid you wanted to hit. Really hard. He settled back down in bed and rolled over on his side away from me, like usual.

I leaned over him in the dark and whispered.

"Did you do that deliberately?"

"G'night, Theo." There was just enough light from the window to see his smirk in the darkness.

I settled down in bed, facing away from him, furious. Like usual.

"G'night, you—prat-hole."

# Chapter 13
## Coffee and…

*TOMMY*

I wasn't waiting in front of my usual Starbucks for very long when I saw Theo coming around the corner in the morning crowds.

"Hey you," I said.

"Hey. So show me this famous ex of yours."

We had agreed to meet here before work, so he could get a glimpse of my incredibly good-looking ex-boyfriend who was the cutest barista-boy ever. Javier and I were still sort of friends, so it wasn't awkward. Okay, so it wasn't *really* awkward anyway.

We went inside. I suppose it is the condition of Starbuckses everywhere that the shops are too small and too crowded. I'm sure that if this place had an occupancy card on the wall, it would show that the premises were safe for about half as many people as were standing in this vague sort of line curving around the store.

I basically hated Starbucks. I'm not sure why I kept going there.

Of course there was the reason of my ex and ta-da! There he was.

"So?"

"The barista, behind the counter," I indicated with the subtlest of eyebrow gestures.

"Seriously? Dark hair, blue eyes?"

"My Latin lover, my Javi."

"Cute! Still have feelings?"

"No, not really. It never really worked. He had been involved with somebody—which explained why he had ignored me for so long—and when I got him he still wasn't really ready for any kind of a *thing* yet. I wasn't really looking for anything serious either, so we enjoyed it, and then we walked away from it. It was totally mooch, and we're still friendly."

"He doesn't spit in your cappuccino?"

"No," I said with a wistful sigh. "Not anymore."

"He's gorgeous, Tommy."

"Yeah, he is. And the sex was great. But of course I have my memories. And one forty-seven-minute-twelve-second iPhone movie that is totally *hot*."

"For when the memories fade."

"Exactly." The line at Starbucks would test the patience of a tree sloth.

"So are you looking at anybody else yet?"

"Not really. Okay-well-maybe."

"Really? Good for you."

"So," I said, the apex of discretion. "Tell me. What's Swithin's story?"

"Swithin?"

"Yeah, the lanky surfer boy. I mean, he looks pretty straight, but I thought I'd ask."

"Gee. I don't know."

"He's sort of dreamy cute. In his way."

"Swithin? Yeah, I guess."

Okay, Swithin was this guy at Theo's cabaret night. I met him, we talked a bit. He was tall and thin, had really long legs in a pair of those super-skinny jeans you see on rocker-boys, and straight blond hair that fell across his face. Normally I would find the hair totally irritating as fuck. But somehow on him…he used his hair like a veil, like Veronica Lake if you've ever heard of Veronica Lake. He could lean his head one way and disappear behind it, or lean it the other way and reveal these bright blue eyes, that always seemed to have just heard something funny.

As I said, that hair-gimmick on any other guy would just make me want to slap him, but on this one, it was adorbs.

"I've known Swithin for a couple years, but I don't know if I've ever heard him mention dating or a girlfriend or boyfriend or anything. He seems pretty straight, but I don't know. It *is* a musical theatre workshop, after all. I'm sorry I'm not more helpful."

"Hey, not your responsibility. Your songs were really good, by the way. Jeffrey and I agreed about that."

"Jeff is an ass. But thanks, I appreciate it."

"Next customer," asked my personal nemesis, the cashier. Her name, I had learned in my time with Javi, was Myrtle, believe it or not. Even stranger than that? It suited her.

Need I say more?

Of course not, but I will. She was maybe five-feet-nothing tall, and she wore a ton and a half of make-up, which was about a half ton too much. She had never liked me, and then I started dating Javi, and then she *loathed* me. Instead of writing my name on the cup, she used to write really rude things about me for Javi. He of course just laughed. I mean, he also read them out loud for the whole shop, but then he laughed.

These last few weeks since Javi and I split? She has had nothing but smiles for me. Maybe I should find a new coffee place with less history.

"Hi, Tommy," Myrtle grinned, the last of the Borgias, preparing to empty the contents of her signet ring into my cardboard cup. She tapped her fingernails along the top of her register, nails that were of a length that could only be called preternatural. Do you think they let her get on an airplane with those things? Each nail was an astonishing purple, and bore the image of a tiny Easter egg.

"Hi, Myrtle," I said. "I'll have a tall cinnamon dolce latte, with a shot of caramel, please. And ring his up on mine too, please." I gestured to Theo.

"You don't have to do that," objected Theo.

"Of course I don't *have* to, but you just started this job, you haven't been paid yet, and one of your shoes is held together with duct tape. You can buy mine someday when you've had a paycheck."

"Okay, thanks. Skinny latte, please."

She rang his up.

"Name?"

"Theo."

I paid and we stepped aside to wait.

"I'll see what I can find out about Swithin," said Theo, once we had maneuvered ourselves vaguely in the direction of the pick-up counter.

"Don't. It's too embarrassing and so junior high."

"I'll be discreet. Remember me? Keeper of all kinds of secrets."

"So you and Madison are—?" I said, shifting the subject, "What exactly?"

"I don't know. I told you how I'd gone up to Chester and he was a total jerk and I came back. Then he made this special trip down yesterday—in the middle of his rehearsals—to see the cabaret. Now obviously there were a lot of people there with songs on the program, not just me, but I have to think he came down to see me."

"And?"

"You know the rest. I was a bitch to him because nobody can treat me the way he did. And then Jeff did *his* whole asshole thing—"

"Sorry, Theo, but I thought I'd die, trying not to laugh—"

"Yeah, like you tried really hard—"

"C'mon, did you see Madison's face? It was like something from Molière. Anyway, did you explain to Madison? That it was just a joke?"

"No! Why should I? What's it to him if I'm seeing somebody?"

"Which you're not."

"Of course not. Jeff?" Theo shuddered slightly. "But Mads is the one who can't introduce me as his boyfriend, who sends me off on a train in the middle of the night because he can't stand to have me around."

"Fair point."

"So fuck him."

"And he still thinks you and Jeffrey…"

"Let him think.

"Cappucino for Tommy," called my old boyfriend.

"Hey, cutie, how's it goin'?" I said, retrieving the cup.

"Good, you?"

"Good. Busy, but good."

"I'm glad." And he turned his beautiful eyes onto the next order. Okay, yeah, I admit it—it twinged a little.

I was still thinking about that when Javi called out again.

"Skinny latte for—" and he started to laugh. "For Tommy's skanky new boyfriend???"

Theo looked at me, confused, although I could see dark clouds forming on that forehead. I turned to Javi for an explanation.

"That's what it says," he said still chuckling and turning the cup so I could read it. Myrtle of course.

"You don't *have* to read them! You're only encouraging her. Anyway, he's not."

"I'm not," said Theo.

"Not skanky?" asked Javi, those blue eyes twinkling.

"Not boyfriends!" said the *Shining* twins.

"You could do lots worse," said Javi looking at Theo. "Take it from me."

Ohhhhhhhhhhhhhhhh that was so sweet. I gave Javi a sad smile. Lord love me, he was pretty. And he grabbed an empty cup and went back to work.

Twinge, twinge.

Theo retrieved his latte, and we turned toward the counter with all the other stuff.

"So what are you going to do about Madison? Let him go or—"

As we turned, there was this tall oaf—in a really expensive pinstripe suit—who was squarely in the way. The pinstripes looked down at us.

"Hey, if it isn't Twinks United!"

The law firm was just a block and a half away, it was no big coincidence that we should bump into somebody from the office, but I was still surprised, and still not quite used to seeing Jeffrey outside of his relationship/non-relationship with Roger.

"Jeffrey—you startled me. And I'm sure I was just on the brink of saying something pithy."

"Well, don't get pithy with me."

"Ha!"

Theo looked like he wanted to ignore Jeffrey, but I saw the little smile he had to smother.

"Jeffrey made a funny!" I said. "I am sooooo stealing that."

"Hey Theo," said Jeffrey, "I'm glad I bumped into you. I was going to try to track you down at your desk. You're really into musicals, right?"

"Duh. Ye-ah. You *were* at the cabaret last night, weren't you?"

"Yeah, I was. I told you, I *liked* your songs. Really. Anyway, seriously, I wanted to ask you if you've seen this show *Hamilton* everyone's going on and on about."

"No. Madison and I were supposed to go—back when you could still get tickets—but—anyway, it didn't happen. And of course now tickets are like a bazillion dollars and a kidney."

"Well I just got two tickets from a client—freebies. Would you like to come?"

I nearly choked on my cappuccino.

"You got tickets to *Hamilton*? *Free*?" said Theo with disbelief.

"Well, I still have both kidneys. At least I *think* I have both, but..."

"I bet you could eBay those for like a year's salary."

"Really? What's the going rate for kidneys these days?"

"I mean the tickets, you dolt."

"Oh, yeah. I guess I could sell them, but honest—I'd rather see the show. So no interest then?"

"No! I mean, yes! But I can't possibly pay for it."

"Well then, I guess I'll have to give you the ticket."

"When is it?"

"Tomorrow night."

I stood by and watched in wonder, my eyes moving from face to face like it was a tennis match, but no one was grunting. Meanwhile, crabby and annoyed New York people were trying to get around us in every direction.

"Seriously?" said Theo. "This isn't going to be some stupid trick that you think is going to be screamingly funny but isn't—is it?"

"I'm serious. I don't have the tickets yet or I'd show them to you."

"Okay. Tomorrow night."

"Cool. I'm going to go get in line for a latte. You boys better get to work—you're going to be late."

I had absolutely no idea what I'd just witnessed. Jeffrey Bornic seemed once again to be doing something nice for somebody who wasn't Jeffrey Bornic. You could have knocked me over with a featherweight.

While I stood there, awash in uncertainty, reality swimming before my eyes, there were two truths of which I was certain. The first was this:

Clients did not give their lawyers presents—if a client paid his exorbitant bill without bitching too much, that was considered gift enough.

And the second?

While there might be a God, there might be a devil, and there might even be a Santa Claus and a Tooth Fairy, I was pretty damned sure —

There was no such thing as a free ticket to *Hamilton.*

# Chapter 14
## Afterwards

*Jeffrey*

You've probably figured out that I didn't actually get free tickets to *Hamilton*. I lied. It wasn't easy to get tickets—period—even if you were willing to shell out huge sums of money for them, which is exactly what I'd done. I managed to get my hands on two tickets to *Hamilton* for an undisclosed amount and an internal organ to be named later. Why?

Beats the hell out of me.

I'd sat there with my hand on the mouse for a long time. I clicked on the buy-these-tickets-button, and a little window popped up—like my conscience—saying, "Are you *sure* you want to buy?"

I looked at the *Yes* and *No* options. I left the mouse hovering there for about forty minutes while I invented a thousand ways to rephrase the question *"What are you thinking, you dumbfuck?"* I finally came to the conclusion that this made no sense. It was totally stupid. What would *anyone* think of me? I was just making myself ridiculous. Okay, I'd never tell anyone what the tickets cost me, but who in their right mind would pay that much? I was definitely *not* going to buy the damned tickets. For sure not. Absolutely not. And—having made that firm and unequivocal decision—my index finger spazzed all on its own.

I had just bought two astronomically expensive tickets to a show I didn't give a flying rat's ass about.

I guess I still felt like I needed to make up for something with Theo. And because his songs were good and it was clear he wasn't a talentless loser and he really cared about this stuff. And because I knew he'd get a kick out of it. And because I had crates of money, even when I was pouring thousands and thousands into an apartment where I could no longer actually live, so what did I care? Or maybe I just wanted to see what awesomely cool hipsters the founding fathers actually were.

For whatever idiot reason, I had just bought the two most expensive theatre tickets in the history of all mankind.

Of course, afterwards, the obvious question was: Was all that money for two not particularly good orchestra seats really worth it?

Okay, frankly, for *that* much money? If Jesus Christ had been in the show and if he had stepped down off the stage in the middle of the second act to get on his knees and give me head—while Aretha Franklin sang backup—it wouldn't have been worth *that* much money.

It was a *musical,* for fucksake. It was not a trip to Mars. It was not a Stanley Cup game. It was a bunch of rappers in powdered wigs.

If you're looking for more details about the show, I am sorry to disappoint. I spent most of the time watching guess-who. Which sounds totally pathetic, but I have never seen anyone enjoy anything so much. He actually shook with excitement, and at intermission he just rattled non-stop, texting like crazy at the same time, those pretty features of his face so animated, his face beaming. He was like an eight-year-old on Christmas morning, without the crying.

So. Was it worth it? Well you know, yeah, maybe it sort of almost was.

After the show, I'd planned to take Theo to Joe Allen's. It's just down the street from the theatre, it's nice, the food is decent, they have posters on the wall of musicals so obscure that probably even Theo wouldn't recognize them, and it's the only place I know where you can regularly see celebrities—which I also thought the little farm-boy would get a charge out of.

But it wasn't to be.

Instead of going to the nice, nearby restaurant with decent food and Bradley Cooper at the next table, Theo insisted we had to go to some diner on 57th Street. So I got us a cab and we went to this bright, noisy greasy spoon. As soon as we walked through the door, I realized why we were there. Halfway back was a table of waving faces—the ones I'd met at Theo's cabaret.

When did he arrange all this then?

Theo fairly galloped to greet them and plopped himself in the chair at the end that they'd saved for him. While I still stood by the door.

At least there was no Madison. That I could see anyway.

So, feeling like yesterday's mashed potatoes, and pretty seriously pissed off, I went over to the table to which I hadn't actually been invited, and sat next to the beach boy with the unlikely name.

"'Sup?" he said from behind a veil of blond bangs. I smiled, and extended my hand.

"Jeffrey."

"Swithin. We met at Don't Tell Mama."

"I wasn't sure anyone remembered."

"Are you kidding? That was the best! Madison turned purple."

"I thought I'd bust a gut!" said the Brooklyn woman. She nodded at the guy next to her who was elegantly smoking a breadstick. "Jaspeh peed a little."

"I'm so glad."

That was me, always with the high jinks. Regular life of the party, that Bornic boy.

Theo was at the other end of the table and in full flight, raving about the show. His excitement distracted me for a moment from my general annoyance with the way this evening had turned. I was glad I was able to do this thing for him that he could never have done on his own. But why was I in this awful diner?

The others threw out questions and opinions, all talking at once. A couple of them had seen the show downtown, and the rest of them knew it, if only from the CD. It didn't matter if they'd seen it or not—they all seemed to have an opinion about it.

After a few minutes of this, it was clear that I was utterly superfluous. I was not exactly accustomed to being a wallflower. I was more of a quarterback type than a benchwarmer.

I weighed my options. I could sit there, being quietly ignored. That was an easy 'no.'

I could take charge, the way I had at the cabaret. *Or* –

I could go find a more fun crowd than *this* one. If I wasn't wanted at this party, I could find another. I obviously wouldn't be missed.

Having no idea where I was going, I pulled a bill out of my wallet to pay for a Diet Coke I hadn't touched and tossed it on the table. The bill, not the soda.

"Night, boys," I said (although one of them was the Brooklyn woman). Theo looked up at me from the far end of the table, his brow furrowed. He seemed surprised.

Surprised that I was leaving or surprised that I was even there?

I wasn't really sure what I had expected out of this evening. Maybe I didn't expect anything. I don't know.

But whatever those non-existent expectations were, this certainly didn't measure up.

# Chapter 15
## Afterwards II

*THEO*

Jeff was leaving? That somehow didn't seem right.

Did I want that? Yeah, maybe, but—no, not really. I sort of knew that I'd been ignoring him, but not consciously. At least I didn't *think* I was doing it consciously. None of that made any sense.

Look—I know I can be a bitch, and I'm fine with that, but I didn't want to be *that* much of a bitch. I certainly didn't want to be an *ungrateful* bitch. He could have scalped the ticket for some serious bucks. He could have taken anybody. And he took me. I should say something.

I pushed my chair back, but I didn't get up.

"You need to talk to him," said Swithin.

"Do I?" I was suddenly chicken.

"Darling, don't just sit there. Go!" Mississippi had spoken. I got up, hustled out of the diner and looked east, and then west. Damn, his legs are so long, he was almost to Broadway already.

"Wait!" I yelled after him, running to catch up. "Hey. Are you—mad about something?"

"No. Why should I be mad?"

"I don't know, but you seem bent about *something*."

"Not in the least. I'm totally good. Never better."

"Fine. Don't tell me. I'm not going to dig. Thank you for the ticket. I know I've said that already, but I can say it again. Thanks, I don't know if you can appreciate just how much that meant to me."

"Good. I'm glad."

"I hope you didn't hate it."

"I didn't hate it."

"Good. I'm glad." *See how stupidly arrogant that sounds, you smug fuck?*

"You better get back inside. Your little circle-jerk in there will miss you."

"See, now what's *that* about, huh? Kind of a bent-douchebag thing to say, doncha think?"

He looked at me, dropped his head and shook it, and took a deep breath.

"I don't know *what* that's about. I'm sorry, forget I said it. I'm just in a mood, so I'm going to go. Have fun."

He turned and stalked off, arm raised for the next taxi, and almost immediately there was one pulling over. I brooded my way back to the Apollo.

I'd done something wrong, something dumb, but for the life of me, I couldn't figure out what.

"Hey," said Jessica as I sat back down at the table. "Is he okay, your boyfriend?"

"Definitely not my boyfriend. And he says he's fine."

"Didn't look too fine to me, darling," said Jasper.

"I know, right?" I said. "But you know what? I'm not his babysitter. If he's cranked about something, he can tell me what it is, but I'm not going to try to guess."

"No? You can't guess?" said Jasper. "Anyone here have any ideas? Hmm? Anyone? Hands?" Everyone raised a hand.

"Fine. You're all so smart—what???"

"Are you two...whatever?" asked Swithin.

"No!" I said. "We can hardly stand each other." Glances were exchanged around the table. "What???"

"So," said Jessica, "yeh tellin' us that this good-lookin' guy got all dressed up to take you to the biggest hit show since Thespis stepped out of the chorus to do a solo, and all because—he can't stand you?"

"Well, yeahhhhhhhhh." I could feel my face scrunching up.

"Really, darling, and all just for the sheer love of musical theatre then?" was Jasper's follow-up.

"Ehhhhhh—I'm not sure he'd ever *seen* a musical before. I didn't ask." I guess I *might* have asked him. I could be such a jerk.

"He dropped some serious bucks on those tickets," said Swithin.

"He said they were freebies from a client."

"It's a nice lie, darling, but just so you know, it's still a lie."

"First rule of show biz," said Jessica. "Never give away tickets to a hit, and boy is that show a hit."

"I mean—" I tried to explain. "I saw my ticket, and it said five-forty-nine. Which made me cringe, but he said not to worry about it."

"When did he get these tickets?" asked Jessica.

"Yesterday."

"Scalped," said Swithin. "Way more than five-forty-nine."

"You know," said Jessica, "if he just bought them yesterday, I bet he paid two grand, maybe more."

"For the pair?" I couldn't believe this.

"Apiece," said everyone at the table.

Fuck me.

"But you know," I argued, "he's not like us. He has bushels of money. It doesn't really mean anything to him." Even I knew I was trying to talk myself into something. "Besides, he's sort of an ass."

"He's sort of an ass—in a really nice suit," said Jasper.

"If you like suits," I said.

"Nice looking," said Swithin.

"Nice? He's gaw-jus!" seconded Jessica.

"And that sort of an ass took you out to a really expensive show." We'd worked our way back around to Jasper. "Darling, if you don't want that beautiful man, throw him my way."

"I think the sort of an ass is kinda pissed," said Swithin from his end of the table.

"Why?" I asked not feeling well at all. "Did he say something?"

"No." Swith picked up a bill from the table. "But look how he paid for his Diet Coke."

"Is that a hundred?" asked Jessica.

Fuck me.

"You acted like he wasn't even here," said Tyler quietly. You probably didn't know Tyler was at the table because he never speaks. Well he spoke. Yeah, even *Tyler* was impressed by just how awful I was. And then he added, even more quietly, "He thought this was a date."

Fuck me fuck me.

"Darling Theo, you brought a rich, good-looking beau in a Dolce suit to the Apollo Diner. To hang out with *us*. And you can't begin to guess why he might be in a tizz."

Fuck me fuck me fuck me fuck me fuck me.

# Chapter 16
## Son of Afterwards

*JEFFREY*

I hadn't done *that* in a while. In the aftermath of the whole Roger thing, I was a bit of a slut, having nameless sex every other night, if not every night. That was months ago.

But now, here I was, coming out of the Playpen on Eighth Ave., having taken advantage of the lovely Buddies Basement they advertise in neon outside. It's so dark down there, you can't see how disgusting you know it is, and the booths are barely big enough to do what you're there to do. At least it didn't take me long.

*What* is *that on my pant leg?* I wondered, as I glanced down, waiting at the corner. God damn it. Of course I knew what was on my pant leg, and it wasn't mine.

How, when I did the guy from behind, did he manage to get jizz on *my* pant leg? I mean, he had to have been aiming to do that, right? What kind of a kink is *that?*

Taxi!

God, I was in a vile mood.

First this stupidly overpriced musical. Then Theo and his pathetic friends. I was such a chump.

And what possessed me to go to that lousy sex shop???

It's just because Theo pissed me off so damned much. He says *I'm* arrogant. Ha! What a spoiled little brat he is. You can tell—Rebecca and his brothers have been looking out for him his whole life, he's never had to worry about a thing, so he has no sense of responsibility—which is why he has that impossible temper because he knows he can get away with it, somebody else will always clean up after him.

And heaven help you if he doesn't get his way!

Forget him.

So what happened tonight? It certainly hadn't been my intention when I left the diner to end up in a cab at a stoplight, steaming mad, with some nameless guy's splooge on my D&G pants.

I could scream.

At Rebecca's, I let myself in very quietly—so as not to wake the sleeping prince—but the ungrateful little wretch wasn't home yet.

He and Fat Madison were probably somewhere watching *The Sound of Music* and jacking each other off.

No wait. Madison was in Connecticut or something. Good. Let him stay there.

I tossed back a quick shot of Rebecca's vodka. Add booze to the long list of things I owed Rebecca McPherson—even if she *was* the one who had inflicted Theo on me.

Theo. Theo and Madison. Fuck, I mean, if they're happy, what did I care? Totally none of my business.

*But!!!*

*But.*

Hateful as Theo could be, that thing with Madison was just wrong. Theo was awful, but he should have been able to do better than *that*.

*And* the guy apparently treated him like crap too! What was *that* about?!

I didn't normally drink, but my hands were shaking. I was a frigging mess. Hands I hadn't even washed yet. I was revolting. I threw back another vodka, and I headed into the bathroom, pulling off my clothes as I went.

And then I stood under a hot shower for a long time, for a long, long time.

# Chapter 17
## The Never-Ending Afterwards

*THEO*

After the diner, we had gone out for beers at a bar somebody knew. It was too loud, I didn't really feel like partying, and I would regret all of this in the morning when it was time to go to that awful law firm.

Fuck, I regretted it, even as I was sitting on that barstool.

So I sat there between Swithin and Jasper, feeling like I'd somehow screwed everything up. The evening had been so much fun—and now it wasn't. I certainly didn't mean for that. I'd loved the show and now I was just miserable.

I knew I'd done something stupid, something I'd done because I was just too naïve or dumb or something, because I'm just this socially backward farm-kid. Or because, in my astonishing self-absorption, I had missed some clue somewhere that anybody else *wouldn't* have missed. Anyone else would have known how to behave. Anyone else would have understood and said, *well, in that case, da-da-dee da-da-da.* Only *I* didn't know, and I guessed I'd somehow behaved rather shabbily, and I didn't mean to. And I hated being stupid, and apparently I had been stupid.

But then—you know—apologies are hard, even when you *know* what you're apologizing for. So I wasn't in any hurry to run home and bump into old Jeff under the sheets so I could say I was sorry—for whatever it might be. And admitting that I didn't even know what I'd done wrong? *That* wasn't going to happen, now was it. Certainly not to Jeff.

After some serious contemplation of my 7-Up, I'd finally decided there was no way that Jeff could have thought this was a date. Was there? I mean, I don't care what those guys said, Jeff didn't even like me. Did he? He certainly didn't *act* like he liked me.

So why would he take me out on a date?

And even so, it wasn't *my* fault if he thought it was a date. *I* didn't say that it was. *He* didn't say that it was. If he *had* said it was a date, I'd have straightened him out. I'd have told him to forget about it. I'd have told him to kiss my flying buttress. I'd have told him—I wasn't the answer to anybody's midlife crisis.

Oooh. Now I wished he *had* asked me, if only so I could have said that. I should remember that line. That would really frost his birthday cake.

Or how about this one: I really like my dad, don't need another.

He'd die. I needed to remember that one as well.

"Theo, darling," said Jasper, gracefully knocking the ash off his swizzle stick, "I *know* you're not listening to a word of my terribly enlightening discussion of the distinctions between musical comedy and operetta, so tell me *what* has brought that perfectly insipid smile to your face?"

"I should go, guys," I said, and reached for my wallet.

"Don't worry," said Swith. "I think I can cover your 7-Up tab."

I was still working through my it-definitely-wasn't-a-date argument with myself—an argument I was handily winning, by the way—when I got up to Rebecca's.

If there was any confusion on Jeff's part about what this evening had been or hadn't been or was supposed to have been, it was clearly and totally in no way my fault.

That's what I was thinking when I slipped my key into the lock as carefully as I could, so I wouldn't wake him, and I just as carefully closed the door behind me. I used the light from my phone to get around the bed to get to the bathroom, because Christ-on-a-crosstown-bus, I had to pee. After I'd brushed my teeth, I tiptoed out, made my way just as carefully around the foot of the bed, and changed into my new sweatpants.

"You don't have to be so quiet," said Jeff behind me. "I'm awake."

"Sorry. I was trying not to wake you."

"You didn't."

"Oh." I used the phone to get back around to my side of the couch and got in. With my back to Jeff, like always. "Hey. Are you sure you're not mad at me about something?"

He didn't answer at first. He took a deep breath and he let it out slowly.

"No. Absolutely not. I mean, yes, I'm sure and no, I'm not mad. At you, anyway."

"I'm sorry if I didn't—"

"Look," he said, turning on his back. "You were great. It's all good. No worries, okay? I didn't take you to the theatre because I wanted you to feel like you owed me or because I wanted you to fawn over me with gratitude or because I wanted *anything* from you. Because I didn't. I don't. Want anything from you, I mean." He paused for a second, like he was reluctant to say the rest. "I asked you because I thought you'd like it."

"And I did!" I rolled over to look at him. With my head on the pillow next to his, I could see his face outlined against the windows—he was staring up. There was that glint of light reflecting in his eyes again. "Really, thank you," I whispered. "It was a fantastic night, and I really *am* grateful, and I'm really sorry if I didn't make that clear earlier." In silhouette like this, as close as I was, I could even see his eyelashes. "I know I can be sort of self-absorbed—"

"Not you, never."

"Fine. I was trying to apologize. I'm sorry if I should have been more grateful—"

"Completely not necessary."

"You're sure?"

"Absolutely."

"Okay then."

You know, Jessica was right. He wasn't half-bad looking. Maybe "gaw-jus" was a bit of an overstatement, but he wasn't half-bad.

In the dark, anyway.

"It's late. You guys go out somewhere?"

"Yeah, for a bit. Did you come straight back here? It's almost three. That's a long time not to sleep."

"No, I went out."

"Oh good. I hope you had fun."

"I did. I found a guy whose name I didn't bother to ask, and I fucked his brains out."

"What?"

"You heard me."

I sat up.

"You're totally messing with me, right?"

"Wrong. In the morning I'll show you the jerk's jizm on the leg of my pants."

"Shut up."

"I've been trying to work it out. Maybe you can explain it—I mean, picture this—he's bent over and I'm behind him, and somehow he still managed to point his thing around and—"

"Shut up!"

"Maybe the guy's double-jointed."

"Shut-up-shut-up-shut-up!"

"See? You can't figure it out either, can you? It's like the Kennedy assassination—the magic cumshot that hits the governor of Texas and then turns—"

"Get out!"

"I know what you're thinking. There was a second shooter."

"Get-out-get-out-get-out!" I yelled, scrambling up until I was sitting against the wall on the back of the sofa, my feet on the bed.

"What?"

"Get out of my bed, you filthy slut!"

"What's *wrong* with you?"

"I'm not sleeping with you, not while you're covered in—whatever."

"I showered."

"I don't care. God knows what you've picked up."

"I showered really well."

"Get out!"

"Theo, my friend, since the day we met, you've had this strange misconception that I'm somebody you can tell what to do."

"I'm serious!"

"So am I! Go to sleep!"

Rebecca's voice came muffled from beyond the bedroom door.

"One night, just one night, I'm begging you."

"Well," I said quieter, "get over there, waaaaaaaay over there, on the far edge of the bed. As far away from me as you possibly can." I could see that he rolled over on his side on the very edge of the mattress.

"Happy?" he asked.

"No!" I let myself back down onto the bed. "You're disgusting, you know that, don't you." I lay down on my side facing away from him, on the very edge of my side of the bed. "Just when I start to think, maybe you're not a *total* douchebag—you're a total douchebag!"

He let it go a minute or so before he spoke again.

"G'night, Theo."

I'd die before I'd answer him.

Douchebag.

\* \* \* \*

When I opened my eyes, it was still dark. I could hear Jeff moving around. It was the first time I had woken up even a little when Jeff got up to run. As usual, it was freezing in the apartment in the morning, and I bundled myself up in the warm blankets Jeff had left behind.

The light in the bathroom was on, and Jeff had left the bathroom door partly open so he could see to get ready. I cracked my eyes. Without lifting my head from the pillow, I watched him move about in his running clothes. I'd never noticed, but he had nice legs. His thighs were like right at eye-level. Tough to miss. He wore longer, baggy shorts to bed, but the ones he had on now were skimpy little things. In the light from the bathroom, I could see the little blond leg hairs on his thighs as he moved back and forth getting ready. I had to admit it—Jeff had really hot legs.

And then of course I remembered that he'd used those really hot legs to screw a complete stranger someplace disgusting.

*He* was disgusting.

I rolled over and buried my head in the pillow.

Douchebag douchebag douchebag.

# Text from Madison

*Hey.*

*Hey.*

*I'm sorry. I was a dick.*

> *You said that before. Speaking of dicks, had a chance to suck Tanner's yet?*

*Don't be juvenile.*

> *Why shouldn't I be? It's what I am, remember? Juvenile—meaning youthful. You remember that? Youth? Think back, Mads.*

> *Think waaaaaaaaaaaaaaay back.*

*So how was your date?*

> *?*

*I heard you had this big date last night. So how was it?*

> *Who told you?*

*Let me check. I got texts from*

*Swithin*

*Jasper*

*Jessica*

*LOL*

*And some guy named Tyler. Who's Tyler.*

*LMFAO!*

*Seriously. Who's Tyler?*

*Date was fabulous. You remember Jeff. Good looking blond? He took me to Hamilton, and then we went out for afters.*

*Hamilton? I thought Jasper was just yanking me.*

*Nope. You want to get yanked, ask Tanner.*

*Grow up.*

# Chapter 18
## The Day after All Those Afterwardses

*THEO*

There—in the middle of my morning. Madison. Of course I wasn't going to tell him that my "big date" had topped off his evening by topping off somebody else.

I'll admit that a part of me was enjoying Mads' attention—but mostly because I was enjoying being a bitch to him.

I guess I'd have been more thrilled about his attempt to patch things up if I wasn't so damn sure that it came out of a combination of guilty conscience and the growing realization that he was never ever going to get into Tanner's well-fitting blue jeans.

And I wasn't entirely sure I wanted to patch things up.

And I wasn't entirely sure why I wasn't sure.

In the meantime, I was here at the law firm, laboring for the greater glory of Messrs. Parker & O'Neill—neither of whom, Tommy told me, were still walking among us. In their absence, there was a passel of partners who divvied up the mountains of profits.

I worked for one such partner, Victoria, and a handful of baby associates who were only like my age or a smidge older. The Little 'Uns, I called them—and not a cute one in the bunch. As far as I could tell, associates were lawyers who dreamt of becoming partners someday, but mostly wouldn't. In the meantime, they did all the work. Jeff and Becca were associates.

The Little 'Uns only gave me their Uber receipts and late-night food orders to get reimbursed. The majority of my time at the desk was dedicated to Victoria. Victoria had decided that I was not only the *greatest* personal assistant a lawyer could ever have, I was also her favorite godchild or something. I swear she'd have adopted me if she could.

A legal question: Was it sexual harassment if a middle-aged woman pinched you on the cheek? Repeatedly?

Should be.

Tommy's desk was on the floor above me, where he worked for this guy who'd occasionally been known to chase his secretary around the desk—until Tommy anyway. Tommy got the job because they'd figured he probably wasn't Mr. Kaminsky's type.

Tommy's job was pretty hectic too, and Mr. K. was also big on the board of some not-for-profit that was like Lawyers for Peasants or something. Okay it wasn't really Lawyers for Peasants, but you get the idea. They did lawyerly things for poor people.

This worthwhile organization was now gearing up for a huge fundraiser at some ritzy hotel, and Tommy was up to his eyeballs in crap for that. Sounded like a nightmare. I'd already stayed late a couple times to help him out.

I was glad I had a friend in the office. The lawyers mostly creeped me out.

But I was a little surprised when Tommy turned up at my desk in the middle of this particular morning.

"I need your help."

"Sure—you need me to stay and collate again?"

"No, this is way bigger." There was an empty desk next to me—there used to be crowds more secretaries, back in the era of typewriters I guess, so there were lots of empty secretarial stations around. Tommy plopped down in the empty chair, looking pale and a little desperate.

"You okay?" I asked.

"No-kay."

"Talk to me, Tommy."

"I did something that I thought was a really good idea, but in the end, I may have screwed the Puccini but good. Here's the thing. This benefit at the Pierre? Before I got here, they'd hired some lounge pianist to play through the cocktail portion of the thing. And the pianist has now bailed. Some lame excuse about a death in the family or something. But my best friend Roger plays in a string quartet, they're still kind of attached to a law firm, Goodkin Berdann, so lots of people will know them. So I, being the gay one and the only one in the room with any taste, made the radical suggestion that they hire someone actually good and sort of classy instead of having some cheeseball knocking out Barry Manilow's greatest hits or whatevs, and they should get the Goodkin Berdann Quartet to replace the stinky lounge piano. Which they did."

"So far so good."

"Exactly. Just wait. The first violin, my friend Roger, is, you remember, Jeffrey's ex-boyfriend. I'm sure they haven't seen each other since Roger told him to get lost. Roger's boyfriend Fletch will be at this benefit too. And I just realized that Jeffrey RSVP'd. I mean of course he did. Why wouldn't he? Jeffrey loves schmoozing. I knew that. I just didn't think that far ahead."

"So you want me to—talk him out of going?"

"Will you at least warn him? I'll tell Roger because he *really* doesn't do surprises well. And if you tell Jeffrey, then he can come or he can cancel or whatever, but at least that way nobody's suddenly in the middle of something awkward."

"Wowie kazowie, what do you think is going to happen? Fisticuffs?"

"Not Roger, but Fletch? It's very possible."

"Cool!"

"If it were somebody else's party, I'd be right with you with a box of popcorn. But as it is—just tell Jeffrey, okay? Please?"

"I'll try."

"Thanks."

And he went.

But I had to think about this benefit thing.

Of course I wasn't invited to this little *soirée,* which seemed like an awful shame. Jeff the jerk was going. It would have been the perfect opportunity to see the guy who jilted Jeff the jerk. *And* to see the guy he jilted Jeff for.

What a pity I wouldn't be there.

Even better—it would be the perfect opportunity to see Jeff seeing the guy who jilted Jeff. *And* the guy he was jilted for.

And Tommy thought I would do something to make sure that this momentous and potentially extremely awesomely embarrassing meeting *didn't* take place?

Are you kidding me???

I might be twenty-four, but I never professed to be a particularly *mature* twenty-four.

The problem remained, however, that this potentially spectacularly humiliating event would transpire without my witnessing it, and where was the fun in that?

Now.

Sometimes there are temptations in life that are simply too great—and we all know what Oscar Wilde said about temptation—give in.

I flipped through my desk to find Victoria's invite to Tommy's little shindig, and I found the number for the RSVP. Damn, the tickets were super expensive. But it was for a good cause, right? I hesitated—for like a hot nanosecond. What would Oscar want me to do?

He'd want me to dial the phone. Which my fingers were already doing.

"Hi, I'm calling on behalf of Rebecca McPherson from Parker O'Neill. I believe she RSVP'd for the benefit next week, is that correct? Rebecca McPherson," I repeated slowly. "I thought so. She'd like to bring a guest after all. *Theo* McPherson." You can guess what the woman on the other end asked. "No, her brother, and it isn't either a funny name. Do you still have her credit card info on file? Great." Da-da-dee da-da-da. "Thanks, you too."

What a wonderful day this was turning out to be.

I typed my way cheerily through the rest of the morning, humming some Sondheim.

I was still smiling when I looked up from the computer to see Jeff the jerk in front of my workstation.

I had been glad to see Tommy. Jeff—not half so much.

"Hey," he said.

"What? You need something?"

"No, I was just checking in. Are we okay?"

"Sure. Why not. What are you talking about?"

I went back to typing. He came around and sat at the empty secretary's chair.

"Last night."

"Oh, you mean when you were such a douchebag?"

"Yeah. And I'm sorry."

"Oh speaking of being a douchebag, that reminds me." I pulled out my wallet and gave him his hundred dollar bill back. "This is yours. It was a douchebag kind of a thing to do."

"What? I thought I was being nice."

"No, you were being a passive-aggressive douchebag. 'I know, I'll throw a great big gesture on the table, because I'm sure nobody in this crowd of losers can afford to buy his own slice of cheesecake.' "

"That's not how it was at all."

"No?"

"No—well—I'll think about it—okay, maybe."

"See?"

"I'm trying to apologize!"

"Good. You should."

"It's just that I was so angry!"

I stopped typing and pounced.

"See! I knew you were pissed off, but you kept saying, no-I'm-fine-I'm-fine-never-better. Douchebag. So why were you so angry, DB?"

"I don't know! I've just been really angry for a while!" He lowered his voice. "And I wasn't particularly proud of myself last night." It was just at that point that Rebecca came up. Gosh I was popular today.

"Wow, it's just like home. Except no one's screaming."

"Yet," Jeff and I said at the same time.

"You agree on something! That's a first. How it going, working for Victoria?"

"She's crazy about me."

"I knew she would be. Can you put in a good word for me on the *Hiromi* case?"

"Ha. We'll see," I teased.

"I'm your sister!"

"*I* got him tickets to a show."

"You bastard!"

"Wow, I hadn't thought about influence-peddling as a sideline, but I could develop a whole new revenue stream here."

"At least a babbling brook," said Jeff.

"Hey! I'm your sister! That's supposed to count for something. Blood is thicker than bribery…or…whatever. Anyway, I just wanted to check up on you. You okay here?"

"Yeah, I think so. It's a job, but it beats loading heavy things onto trucks."

"I don't think you'd get that job," said Jeff.

"No?" I flexed my tiny bicep and laughed. "You sure?"

"I've got a conference call. I've gotta run." She kissed me on the cheek. "And don't forget—you have a date tonight."

"Me?" I asked.

"No! Jeff! Allen, remember? Bistro Saju?"

"There's no way you can get me out of this?"

"No! You'll like him. He has lovely eyes. Be there. Seven o'clock." And she ran off.

"Is this one of those blind dates you mistook me for? She really does that?"

"She really does."

"Bummer."

"Shoot me now." He went.

I sat for a second, before the words of Oscar Wilde popped once again into my head. I didn't waste another second before I was googling Bistro Saju.

You know for a day that didn't start out all that much fun, it had begun to offer so many possibilities!

# Chapter 19
## Another Try at a Blind Date

*JEFFREY*

"And how will that affect you, do you think?" I asked. Behind this polite, even charming inquiry, brow slightly furrowed in concern, lurked nothing but the greatest indifference.

*This is hell,* I thought. *Pure unmitigated hell.*

Allen, my companion for the evening (thank you so very much, Rebecca), was gesturing with a forkful of meatless Cobb salad, while telling me of the extraordinarily distressing political maneuverings within the marble halls of his little boutique firm.

They must have all of twelve employees, counting the receptionist. How much of a putsch could they really work up?

He was clearly distraught about the situation—some serious fallout would ensue, Allen assured me. I also thought it very strange he'd be telling these stories all over town. And the poor slob apparently trusted *me*. I know, go figure.

Since I didn't really know who any of these people were whose names he tossed around as though I should be deeply familiar with all of them, it was hard for me to care. Really really fucking hard.

"That's just it!" said my dinner companion, who had apparently misunderstood and thought the expression was *whining* and dining. "Who knows?"

I could see why Rebecca had recommended this guy because of his eyes. They were nice. A perfectly nice color brown, a nice shape, with nice longish lashes. Decidedly his best feature. Unfortunately the rest of him didn't quite measure up. He'd obviously been skipping the gym since about...always. He wasn't completely bald, but he would be soon enough—probably by the end of the week.

And he didn't make up for any of these physical shortfalls with a sparkling personality.

Bottom line was—pure unmitigated hell.

At least the food was good. I nearly always ordered the same thing here—rabbit braised in white wine and mustard.

So I sat there looking at this guy, doing my best to look like I was listening, and asking myself how it could be that my closest friend saw me as someone who would date *this*? Was it that she didn't know me very well after all? Or was she trying to tell me in a not-terribly-subtle way, that this was all I deserved and it was high time for me to lower my standards?

Well screw that.

And why had I agreed to this place? Rabbit or no rabbit, it was way too close to the office. Anybody could walk right in and see me sitting with this dud. My stock would tumble overnight.

"It must be exciting for you at least," I tried. "To be in the middle of it."

"Exciting?! Oh—my—*gawd!* It's terrible!" *If he gestures any more wildly with that fork,* I thought, *he's going to be slinging hard-boiled egg at me.* "The tension between the two sides of the office is awful. I hate every minute of it."

"Oh. But isn't this also a great opportunity for you?"

"What do you mean?"

"Play one side against the other—and then, when the war's over, push yourself through to the top of the heap. That sort of thing. Did you ever read Machiavelli's *The Prince*?"

"I could *never* do that!"

"I know, there's a lot of incredibly boring bits, but—"

"No! I mean—I could never—?"

"Use the situation to your advantage?"

"No! I mean, yes, I could never!" *I should really take that fork away from him before he hurts someone.*

"No, I guess you couldn't." Obviously Allen and I approached conflicts and crises differently. I mean, what was the point of other people's troubles if you couldn't take advantage of them?

"How's your...?" he waved his fork vaguely in the direction of my plate, too squeamish to name the dead animal in question.

"Delicious. Sure you don't want to try a bite?"

"I'm sorry—I told you—vegetarian."

"Don't apologize. I love vegetarians," I smiled. "I'm eating one right now."

It was about then that my eyes lost their interest in staring at Allen's comb-over and wandered across to the bar, where, seated with his back to us, was a guy. Smallish. With a mess of curly hair. Red curly hair. There were a dozen or so antique mirrors hung artistically above the bar, and my eyes moved up to those mirrors. In one of them—a pair of mocking eyes.

Thought I'd die.

I didn't want *anyone* to see me out with this geek, but absolutely the *last* person I wanted to see me out with this geek was Theo McPherson. I had put up with his taunting since I'd met him, and this was going to be catnip for him. I would hear about this for the rest of all eternity, or at least until I finally snapped his little neck in my bare hands.

It was in that moment of horrific, nightmarish embarrassment that I tried something desperate. I dropped my napkin, mumbled an excuse and dove under the table to look for it. Maybe Theo didn't see me? This was, of course, ludicrous. I couldn't stay under there forever, and I'd seen this in a movie or somewhere and it was totally stupid. I retrieved my napkin and sat up. *Grow up, Bornic.* Of course my eyes flashed over to the bar. Maybe he hadn't seen us, or at least hadn't seen me dive under the table.

He no longer had his back to us. He was now sitting there, turned around toward the dining room. Laughing. At me.

*When he comes to bed tonight,* I thought, *I will have a piece of piano wire under my pillow, and as soon as he drifts off...*

In the middle of this cheerful little homicidal reverie, I realized, with a deep shock of panic, that the object of my plan was no longer sitting at the bar—he was maneuvering between the tables on his way directly toward us. Even Allen paused in his blather as Theo stopped at the side of the table and he smiled—at Allen, then at me, then at Allen.

Fuckaduck.

"Hey guys, I'm so sorry I'm late," he said, grabbing an empty chair. "How's it goin'?"

"Good," I said. My voice seemed to have slid up somewhere in the range of eunuch. A growing dread spread through my entrails.

"Theo," said Theo, extending his hand to my date, whose name had gone completely out of my head.

"Allen," said the date, looking at me.

"Have you talked to him...about...?" Theo asked me, cryptically.

"About what?" asked Allen. "Jeffrey?" Allen looked at me for reassurance.

Poor Allen, the only person in the restaurant more scared than I was.

"No, I hadn't had the chance to mention...not just yet," I said to Theo, with more than a little misgiving.

"Well," Theo began, "we were thinking—hoping, really—" He laid his hand on my forearm. *Oh-my-stars-you-little-jerk. You're not.*

"Is this going to be weird?" The guy started waving desperately, trying to catch the waiter's eye. "Rebecca didn't say anything about anything weird."

"Well, she wouldn't, would she?" said Theo. "And really, I hope she doesn't need to know *all* the details. But," and Theo leaned in toward his prey, gently pulling Allen's waving hand—and fork—down to the table. In that moment I swear to you those pretty blue-green eyes were clearly the eyes of the spawn of Satan. He dropped his voice to the bottom of his range as he said—"Are you down for some—*fun*—Allen?"

Poor Allen. The deer caught in the headlights of an oncoming nuclear fireball. I had to bite my lips to keep from laughing out loud, watching little Theo play the creep.

When the frightened creature across from me came out of his trance, he looked slowly down at Theo's hand on his, said—

"Oh—my—*gawd*!"

—and he leapt from the table like it was on fire.

"Is that a 'no'?" I asked.

Allen threw his napkin down on top of his salad bowl. Dudgeon. High dudgeon. Extremely high, in point of fact.

"I really thought we had something, you know?" he said, hurt, gesturing between him and me. Thank the lord he'd put that fork down finally. He stalked off.

"I got the check," I called after him. I turned back to Theo. "I hope you're happy. You've probably made that poor man cry."

"Wouldn't be the first." If Theo was plagued by his conscience, you couldn't tell. He was contentedly tearing open a roll from the basket on the table. He leaned to the next table (mercifully unoccupied—would it have stopped him if it hadn't been?) and snagged a fork, skewered a really nice piece of rabbit loin from my plate, and made himself a little impromptu sandwich.

"Are you hungry, Theo? I can get the waiter."

"No, I'm good, thanks," he said around his *lapin à la moutarde—en sandwich.*

"Wine?"

He reached across and took my glass.

"Thanks."

It was easy enough to get the waiter's attention, since he was doing nothing but giving us the evil eye anyway.

"Could you please bring us another wine glass—and an extra plate, I guess?" I addressed the question mark to Theo, who shrugged and then nodded, still chewing. Not his fault, I thought. Blame it on Iowa. "And you can take these away," I gestured to the salad and other relics of the recently departed.

"This is really good," Theo said and took another bite of his sandwich.

"Glad you like it," I said. "It occurs to me that I ought to mention—in case it's an issue—you're eating rabbit."

His jaw froze mid-chew. He looked at me for a second in wide-eyed horror, and then started to make gagging noises. Like a cat retching up a hairball. He was going to barf right there. I looked around, saw a wine bucket and went for it. Theo pushed his chair back from the table, spread his knees and stared at the floor with another big round of heaving convulsions, and I shoved the champagne bucket between his feet.

"No no no no no no no no no!" said the waiter swooping down on us, "you can't do that here!"

Needless to say, the entire dining room was now thinking about nothing but our little table. Half of them were staring at us—in horror; and the other half were looking away—also in horror.

And at that moment, Theo looked up at me and then the waiter, swallowed his mouthful of rabbit—and smiled.

"Sorry. Just kidding."

I could have hit him with a chair.

For half a second his pretty smile and sparkling eyes even worked on the waiter. For just the tiniest instant, you could see the waiter thinking that the little dickhead was kinda cute—before he (the waiter) remembered just how much of a dickhead he (the dickhead) was, and he (the waiter) set the extra wine glass and plate down on the table in front of the dickhead with two hefty thumps of quiet server rage.

"Droll," he huffed over our heads as he turned and went. "Very droll."

Theo leaned to me.

"Did he really just say 'droll'?!" he whispered. "I've never heard anyone actually say 'droll' before. New York is just a city of wonders, isn't it?"

Smiling and shaking my head in amazement, I shoveled half of my rabbit onto his new plate.

"Sorry," he said gulping. "I haven't eaten. And this is *so* good."

"What are you doing here anyway? Stalking me?"

"I don't know—stalking is sort of a loaded word, don't you think?"

"So?"

"I came here, hoping to embarrass you in front of your date, of course."

"Of course."

"Anything to piss you off, Jeff."

"Well, you failed."

"He was sort of awful, wasn't he?"

"You have no idea."

"So after a bit, it became more of a rescue operation."

"Hey," I said, "I just realized—I suddenly have my evening free."

"You do, don't you? We could share a cab back to Rebecca's. That you would pay for, of course."

"Of course. Or we could…I don't know. It's Friday night. You want to—do something?"

"I have the shelter tomorrow."

"You have what?"

"I volunteer at an animal shelter."

"Oh. So…you want to do something?"

"Like what? And hey, I'm going to say it straight out, just to avoid any awkwardness later—I'm a really terrible bowler."

"I knew that about you somehow."

"So what do you wanna do?"

"The only thing I can think of—nah, never mind. Everyone on earth has seen the new *Star Wars* movie except me."

"You wanna?"

"You haven't seen it?"

"Is it still playing anywhere?"

Phones were consulted while we shared the rabbit, and dueling Siris agreed on one of those jumbo-plex places on 42nd Street.

"But we gotta motor, little one," I said as we headed to the door.

He froze in his tracks.

"Don't ever. Not ever. Okay?"

Little one. Got it.

"Sorry. But don't dawdle—there's a cab."

And we actually made it with time to spare. After I'd picked up the tickets, I turned to Theo.

"I'm going to go pee."

"You're on your own."

"Shut up and go get in line at the concession stand," I said pulling out my wallet. "Get us some popcorn we can share, and something to drink."

I gave him my Visa.

"Anything else?" he asked.

"Whatever you want."

"Okay, but I am not sharing a Diet Coke with two straws because that is just *too* gay."

"Agreed."

When I got back, he had just paid up.

"Thank God you're here. Help me carry."

A bucket of popcorn, two giant sodas, some Milk-Duds, Snowcaps, Twizzlers, Red Hots, Raisinettes and Jujubes. I had given my credit card to a fifth-grader.

He just grinned at me.

We found seats without much trouble because every other man, woman and child in North America had already seen the movie.

"You know Allen is going to report back to your sister."

"Yeah, I'd thought of that. I'll just blame you for everything."

"Figures. I *should* be totally peeved with you—but I'm just relieved."

"And what do you say?"

"Thank you, Theo."

"'Bout time. Think he'll blab it all over the legal industry? His big date with the hot young attorney who turned out to be a total pervy sicko?"

"Did you just say I'm young and hot?"

"In Allen's very limited worldview, possibly."

"Put the popcorn between us."

"Oh, yeah. Hey, is it just me or is it freezing in here?"

"Lean on me if you need to."

"Too gay."

"Suit yourself."

But as soon as the movie started, he leaned on me anyway—except for the exciting parts, when he leaned forward. And at the end in the big fight between Rey and the totally hot villain, Theo grabbed my forearm with both hands and squeezed till he left bruises.

But.

To be honest?

It was just fun. Way more fun than Allen anyway.

I mean, Theo was thoroughly irritating, a pebble in the shoe. And the way he looked up at me—like he was always making fun of me—just made me want to deck him. And he was way too little to punch. Excuse me, too short, not too little.

But yeah, he could be kinda fun to be around.

# Chapter 20
## Life in the Big City

*THEO*

Jeff got us a cab back to Rebecca's. He was really good at that—there were advantages to being that tall—but as we got to Columbus Circle, I leaned forward.

"You can just let us out here, please. We'll walk." I knew this would make Jeff's teeth grind—which was only *partly* my intention.

"Are you serious?" he asked. I really just wanted to walk. Irritating Jeff was a bonus.

"Yeah, it's a nice night. And warmer than that movie theatre!" I said, already climbing out of the cab. "Look, if you don't want, I'll get home on my own. *Or.* We could even walk through the park," I suggested.

"We could, but I'd rather keep my wallet today, thank you." He was paying the driver, so I guessed he was coming along.

"You're a big, manly guy, Jeff Bornic. Who would mess with you?"

"A big manly guy with a knife. We can walk up Central Park West, you'll get just as warm."

And so we did. A fair compromise, I figured.

"Thanks for the movie," I said. "That was really fun!"

"You had, of course, seen it before."

"Only twice. But it was great anyway. Did you have fun? *Can* you have fun?"

"Of course I can have fun. What's *that* supposed to mean?"

"Just that you're a teensy bit pompous."

"Something you've mentioned once or twice."

"I thought that might get in the way."

"I can have fun just fine, and I *did* have fun, thank you for asking."

"Okay then," I said. "I'm glad."

"I have *lots* of fun," he said defensively. "*E.g.,* sports. I like sports."

"Of course. Big professional sports fan."

"Yeah! Why not?"

"Football?"

"What have you got against football?"

"You're right! Professional football—what's not to love? Let's see, you have a bunch of wife-beating, dog-baiting, homophobic rapists who get paid gazillions to play a game."

"You're amazing."

"But by all means—buy another sweatshirt with an NFL logo on it and give those nice boys a little more of your money."

"Well the *good* news is, I won't be around to irritate you with my sports. I got a call from my contractor today. They say they'll be ready for me to move back into my apartment tomorrow. You'll have the couch all to yourself again."

"Oh." You'd think I'd be thrilled, but I wasn't entirely sure *how* I felt about this. "Too bad, just when we're starting to get along." He stopped and looked down at me for a second. "Why *are* we getting along?" I asked.

"No idea."

"Me either." We kept walking. "It won't last."

"Oh for sure not." We walked.

"It's just like you, you know," I said after a bit.

"What?"

"Now that we're finally *not* trying to kill each other, *now* is when you move out. I swear, if there's a contrary thing to do, you'll find it." He smiled at me, shook his head in what looked like disbelief, and he started walking again. "Wait a second," I yelled after him. "Are you laughing at me?" And I caught up to him.

"Dude, you laugh at me all day long."

"I don't either. And don't you dare dude me!"

"Just did," he said laughing.

As we turned onto Rebecca's street, there was a creepy skinny guy with a really big pit bull on a heavy chain leash.

"Hey beautiful," I said to the dog—certainly not to the ugly guy with a little scraggly beard and bad teeth—and I held out my hand to the dog to sniff. I love dogs, btw. The dog's ears went back and her tail started to wag, obviously happy to have found a friend. And that's when the jerk snatched the dog back hard—and the poor dog had this big prong collar on her.

"Stay t'fuck away from my dog," said the guy.

And I hated this guy, just like that. Somebody who keeps a big heavy chain on a dog with a prong collar and then yanks the dog around, just to make his puny little balls feel bigger. How loathsome was that.

"You know, if you trained her a little," I explained calmly, "she wouldn't need that awful collar. And no dog needs that chain for a leash."

"Bitch is strong."

"Stronger than you, for sure, but not stronger than a leather leash."

"Theo, c'mon," said Jeff.

"Whadda *you* know?" said the creep.

"I know what people say about little skinny guys who have these big macho dogs—the whole compensating thing. They usually say it's because of your tiny dick, but in your case—"

"The fuck dju just say?"

"—in your case, there are so many possible causes for your sense of inferiority—there's your looks, you were lousy in school, you're crap at sports, can't keep a girlfriend—really, so much to choose from."

"Theo, let's go now!" said Jeff and he had a hand on my arm.

"The fuck up—"

"Honestly, if you *don't* feel inferior, you just haven't been paying attention."

"Ya got a big fuckin' mout', ya little faggot." He turned to go.

"You're right. I'm queer. You can kiss me if you want," I said, giving him a little air-kiss and smiling prettily. "Right here." With my index finger I tapped my butt cheek.

"Fuck this." He reached up, looped the leash over the iron fence in front of the brownstone where we were, and he spit on the sidewalk.

"Charming," I said.

"Theo—"

"Did your mom teach you how to spit like that, all ladylike?"

And suddenly there was an incredibly strong arm around my waist, and Jeff had hoisted me up onto his shoulder like a grain sack while he backed quickly away, crossing to the other side of the street.

"There is no need for any trouble," Jeff was saying. "I apologize for my not very smart friend. I'm taking him home, this doesn't have to get any uglier. We are *so* sorry!"

I think I've mentioned that I have a bit of a temper. And I've admitted that I had been annoyed with the guy because I hated bullies, and I especially hated a jerk who bullied his dog. *And* he'd called me a faggot, which I always found a little, shall we say, off-putting.

But *now.* Ohmygod *now!*

*Now* I was slung over asshole Jeff's asshole shoulder, and I couldn't have cared less about the guy with the pit bull. *Now* I was in a blind, out-of-my-mind berserker-crazy, frothing-at-the-mouth rage at the monumental shithead who thought he could carry me around like so much dirty laundry. I kicked and screamed no end but I couldn't really land anything from up there.

I'd have bitten him, if I'd thought of it.

I don't know what all I was howling, most of it probably incoherent and lost amid my thrashing and kicking, not to mention the pounding blood-rush in my ears. All I wanted was to hurt Jeff. I was vaguely aware of a fair torrent of obscenities from the pit bull guy regarding our presumed sexual practices, which tapered off. I didn't taper, not the least bit. I was still raging like a wild animal. And the whole time Jeff kept telling me to shut up, and he kept pinching my thigh really hard when I didn't, and I couldn't make him stop pinching me, and I felt so helpless and humiliated, so the pinching was just one more thing to add to my already insane level of complete apoplectic crazy.

I was still trying to hurt him when he finally plopped me back on my feet a block or so away. He pushed me up against the brick wall behind me, but I was still raving, while Jeff was yelling at me, and he shook me hard but I still didn't stop.

"Theo! Theo! Shut! Up!" he yelled, out of breath, but I didn't shut up. "Theo!" He slammed me against the building behind me. "Will you stop!" I was stunned into silence.

Okay, he may have knocked the wind out of me for a second, but I was nowhere near done with him.

"Don't you *ever*—" I screamed, "don't *ever* do that again!"

"Ditto!" he screamed back, as red-faced as I must have been.

"I mean it!"

"So do I! Don't do what? Save your fucking neck? I promise!"

He turned around and started walking to the door—only now did I realize we were in front of Rebecca's building—but there was no way I was going to let him just dismiss me and walk away like that. That just pissed me off all over again. I wanted to punch his big smug face. I didn't care that he was twice my size, I didn't care if he kicked the tar out of me, I was totally ready, all I wanted to do was hit.

I grabbed his arm with both hands and threw my weight against it as hard I could to yank him back around to me.

"I'm serious!" I shrieked. "Don't ever—ever—pick me up like that—like I'm *nothing!* I'm not *nothing!*" No idea where that came from, but I was so furious, tears were pouring out and I couldn't wipe my eyes fast enough. I was so mad that I was crying and that just made me even crazier.

Jeff stood there, watching me be this hysterical thing, and he looked at me for a couple seconds, like he didn't know what to do with me.

"Theo—" he said finally. "Theo, that guy—did you *look* at him? One of those phone-things in his ear so he never misses a call? Pit bull on a chain? His tee shirt said 'fuck the five-oh.' He's a drug dealer! Did you even *notice* when he reached to hang the leash up—that he had a gun tucked in the back of his jeans? He was nobody to mess with!"

I stood there for a second. Did the guy really have a gun?

"You stupid little…" he said, and he turned and pushed his way through the door into Rebecca's building.

Fine. Walk away, you fucking fuckstick-fuck.

I was left on the sidewalk, my heart still pounding in my chest. It took a while before I could breathe without these little hitches. After a bit, I took a couple deep breaths, I pulled my striped tee shirt up to wipe my face one last time. I pushed the door open and went in the terrazzo lobby.

I was surprised to see that Jeff was waiting, leaning against the wall next to the elevator. When he saw me, he turned and hit the button and the door slid open. He stepped in, pressed the button for our floor. I stood in front of the elevator. As the door began to close, Jeff reached out and stopped it.

"Just get in the elevator, Theo."

I did.

We rode up to the fifth floor without another word.

We still weren't speaking when we pulled out the sofa bed together. We managed to get in and out of the bathroom, one of us always stepping back to let the other past. With the couch pulled out, there was only enough room around the foot of the bed for one person to get through. Inevitably we met there. I stepped back so that Jeff could get through, and then stepped even farther back so he wouldn't get close to me, and all without ever looking at each other. And of course when I came out of the bathroom in an undershirt and sweatpants and I needed to get *back* around the bed to my side, there *he* was trying to get across, so then *he* stepped back while I walked around, and I just wanted to stomp on his huge bare foot as I passed him. When I was ready, I got into bed, but I left the lamp on for Jeff, who was still setting out his running clothes for the morning. He finally got into his side of the bed.

"Ready?" I asked.

"Sure," he said.

I switched off the lamp, and tried to settle in, facing away from him as always. I was still so upset, there was no way I was going to sleep. I was tempted to do one of those mule kicks like I'd given him that first night. *It would be better if we fought it out,* I thought. *Better than this, lying here, hating each other.*

After a long time of grinding my teeth and not sleeping, I sat up and tried punching my pillow into shape. I dropped back down onto the bed.

"I didn't pick you up like that because I think you're nothing," he said. "I didn't do it to make you feel small." He was facing the window, not me. "I did it because I was scared to death something really bad was going to happen to you. Okay?"

Really?

I had to think about that. But still, I *hated* being picked up like that. I *hated* that he'd pushed me up against the wall. But somehow I was already about a jillionth as angry as I'd been.

I lay there in the dark for a while, with my fury melting away, feeling my jaw muscles relax, before he spoke again.

"And I really can't afford to become a witness to a violent crime," he explained. "Could have a seriously negative impact on my billable hours."

Impact, when he meant effect. That's the kind of guy he was.

Still, I knew he was trying to make a joke. He was trying. He didn't want me to be in bed so angry that I couldn't sleep. He didn't want me to feel hurt. But he knew neither of us could apologize—even though he obviously should.

Maybe I even smiled at his little lawyer joke about billable hours, but I also knew he couldn't see the smile, which was fine with me.

"Good night, Theo," he said.

I didn't say anything. I mean for a looooooooooong time I didn't say anything, I lay there looking at the darkness. It wasn't until I was certain he was asleep, when he started to snore a little—yeah, he snored but I had somehow gotten used to it—that I whispered.

"G'night, Jeff."

# Chapter 21
## The Last Morning

*JEFFREY*

I nearly always wake up without an alarm, and so it was on this particular morning. Without opening my eyes, I knew it was time to get up if I was going to run this morning. I felt that bar in the sofa bed against my ribs and I remembered where I was—and I realized that, for the first time since I'd been staying at Rebecca's, I wasn't absolutely freezing when I woke up. It was actually deliciously warm and comfortable. I started to stretch a little, enjoying it, but as soon as I moved, I knew why it was so nice and cozy. I cracked my eyes. I could see just enough in the darkness to take in the situation.

Theo's head was on my chest. His shoulder was nestled in my armpit, my right arm was around him, his was around me, his right leg thrown over mine. This should have been really weird and awkward, but it wasn't somehow. It felt—I don't know—safe. And so warm.

But I also knew it was crazy wrong.

It certainly wasn't good.

I had better get up.

If Theo woke up, it would be really embarrassing for everybody. Thank God we wore all these clothes to bed.

The problem was—I didn't want to get up. I didn't want to go running. I wanted to stay in bed and be all sleepy and warm, I wanted to drift back to sleep like this.

Even if it *was* with Theo. Theo. He was almost sweet. When he was asleep.

I closed my eyes and tried to enjoy the warmth and maybe drift off—but no matter how comfortable this was, the reality of a morning bladder could not be ignored.

I started to ease myself out from under Theo as gently as possible. I carefully lifted his arm.

He shifted, gripped me tighter, nestled in still closer, pressed his hips up against my thigh.

*Maybe he went to bed with a banana in his pocket,* I hoped.

I tried again, and, ever so slowly, gently, I moved to extricate my leg out from under his—banana—and I felt his muscles tense as he woke and realized.

I knew exactly what was going to happen next.

"What the—?" he said, already at the top of his voice.

"Shhhh. Go back to sleep," I whispered as I continued to pull myself out.

"You bastard!" he yelled. He was up and slapping at my head, while I tried to cover myself. "I *knew* you were going to perv out on me! I *told* you not to try to touch me, you miserable old pus pocket!"

"For the love of Mike, I'm begging you," called Rebecca wearily from the bedroom. "One night is all I ask.'"

# Text from Madison

*Stop ignoring my texts.*

> *I'm writing a song. What do you want?*

*At work?*

> *Duh. Now leave me alone.*

*I'm in the city.*

> *The new show at MOMA is supposed to be fantastic. Knock yourself out.*

*Meet me there?*

> *Of course not. Leave me alone.*

*How about lunch?*

> *You should take one of those boat tours. They're really cool. Did you know Manhattan is an ISLAND?!?!?!*

*I'll let you know when I'm back in the city.*

# Chapter 22
## It's for a Good Cause

*THEO*

If ever there was a time to put on your Sunday clothes, this was it. It was that benefit that had been making Tommy so crazy. Problem was, after I'd invited myself along as Becca's guest, I just didn't have much in the way of Sunday clothes to put on. In fact I was wearing the same dress shirt, pants, tie and sweater I'd worn to *Hamilton*. A sweater because I couldn't afford a jacket—and the shirt had a stain. There was nothing I could do about the gym shoes—complete with duct tape. I just hoped nobody looked down.

That was as swanky as I got.

Speaking of swanky, Rebecca and I got out of a cab in front of the Pierre—*ooh la la.* I have to say—Beccs looked amazing, all in black.

"You owe me for this, you know," she said.

"Don't you just charge the tickets off to the firm or something?"

"No, actually."

"I'll pay you back out of my first Broadway show, how's that?" Rebecca didn't think it nearly as funny as I did that I had RSVP'd myself as her plus-one.

"You have some nerve is all, especially after that stunt with my friend Allen—"

Rebecca also failed to see the humor when that little whiner Allen ran crying to her. She accosted me the first chance she got.

"Allen who?" I said. "I don't know what you're talking about."

"Funny, because Allen said everything was great with him and Jeff until this guy with bright red hair showed up—"

"Could have been anybody with—"

"Who wrecked everything—"

"While I'll admit that does *sound* like me, it's still circum—"

"Named Theo."

"Okay, fine! I *may* have been in the vicinity. And you should ask Jeff how great their date was going."

And *pop!* No warning, she just hit me in the head with a Kleenex box. Some people really need to manage their tempers better.

Anyway, back at the Pierre.

"I'm not even sure why you'd want to come to this thing," said Rebecca as we headed across the lobby. "*I* wouldn't be here if I thought I could get out of it. These things are generally incredibly boring."

"I have a feeling this one could be interesting." Of course I was thinking about what Tommy had told me, and the possibility of Jeff and this Fletch guy losing it. "I'm hoping it's going to be a riot."

Literally.

Tommy sat behind a table covered with a vast field of name tags, and I pounced on the chance to shift the attention.

"Hey, Tommy, how are you holding up?"

"Hey! I'm good!" he said, his eyes *really* wide, with a totally fake welcoming smile sort of rigor-mortised on his face. "Thank God for Red Bull, but I'm okay."

"Do you know my sister Rebecca?"

"We've met, I think," said Rebecca. "It's Tommy?"

"Tommy Radford. You're Rebecca, friend of Jeffrey Bornic, and I'm Roger Prescott's best friend, we met very briefly at Roger's once. Small world, isn't it?"

"Funny, isn't it?" I said, completing a line from a musical. Of course nobody got it. That was maybe the one thing about Madison. Mads got all my music theatre references.

Tommy fished our name tags out of the ems.

"And now you're working for Mr. Kaminsky," said Becca. "I'm so sorry."

"He's not that bad. Sort of."

"You're a better man than I am."

"Hey," said Tommy to me, tapping Jeff's name tag. "Did you talk to Jeffrey?"

"Um yeah, lots of times," I said, sort of dodging. Okay, straight-up dodging.

"Talk to him about what?" said Rebecca, suddenly the suspicious big sister.

"You promised!"

"Not technically."

"What?" said Rebecca, suddenly the scolding big sister.

"Nothing!" I said and instinctively took a step backward. I knew the swatting big sister was not far behind.

"Roger's here," said Tommy, ratting me out.

Rebecca turned to him.

"The music?" she said gesturing to the double doors and the strains of Haydn straining through. Tommy nodded. "Fletch?"

"Where Roger goes…"

"Oh God." She spun back to me. "And you were supposed to warn Jeffrey, so he could stay away?"

"Ehhhhhh, something like that," I said crinkling my face.

"Is Jeffrey here yet?" she asked Tommy.

"Actually—he's right behind you. Hi, Jeffrey."

"I am, in point of fact, here," he said, reaching over me to get his name tag from Tommy, "thank you for asking." He accidentally bonked me on the side of the head with his elbow as he reached, which—with the instincts of a lifelong little brother—I knew was no accident. I stepped casually back onto his toe and ground my heel for a bit, as effectively as I could with my sneakers.

"Hi Jeffrey," said Rebecca, oblivious, kissing him on the cheek while Jeffrey winced the tiniest bit as I shifted my weight on his shoe.

"And…" Jeff said, giving me a firm little push forward off his foot. "What are we talking about?"

"You," I said. "We know how you like to be the center of attention."

"Look who's talking!" said my dear sister, my dear, traitorous sister.

"Theo has something to tell you, Jeffrey," said Tommy. "Don't you, Theo?"

Jeff looked down his impossibly straight nose at me, one of his most arrogant looks. *Bet you won't be so smug when I tell you who's here,* I thought. I looked back up at him. Why did he have to be so damned tall? It was really irritating.

"Okay, fine," I said. Rebecca stood by expectantly. "Stand back, Buenos Aires," I shooed her a little. "I got this, okay?"

"Okay, I'll see you inside." And she went in. A swell of Haydn washed out as she opened the ballroom door. I pulled Jeff off to one side of the lobby so Tommy could get on with it.

"Uh-oh—look out," said Jeff.

"What?"

"It's your boyfriend."

Madison? I looked around. OMG it was Allen, walking directly toward us. Okay, I figured this was Jeff's deal, and I may have let myself slip behind Jeff as Allen got closer.

"Hi, Allen," said Jeff. Brazen. Jeff could be brazen.

Allen, for his part, went right past us without so much as turning an eyeball in our direction.

"You realize," said Jeff, reaching around to pull me out of hiding, "that Allen went out of his way just to walk past us and *not* say anything. Think he's still mad?"

"I think he hates you, Jeff."

"Me? I wouldn't stand too close to the edge of a subway platform if I were you. So—you had something to tell me."

"Ehhhhhh, yeah." I had hoped he'd forgotten. "It's actually a really funny story if you look at it the right way. You'll laugh when I tell you. Or someday maybe."

"What."

"The thing is, you hear that music? It's Haydn, I'm pretty sure."

"Like Haydn-seek?" Jeff smiled at his own little joke.

"Ha. Funny. Yeah, kinda. You could say that that's the You'll-Never-Guess-Who's-Haydn-in-Here *String—Quartet*." I emphasized the last two words, hoping he'd catch on. After all, how many string quartets did he know?

The light bulb over his head started to glimmer, and his smile began to dim. "Noooooo…it's not—"

"Ye-ah, it…sort of is. I understand the new b.f. is here too."

"Fletch?"

"Ye-ah. That guy."

"You knew this before, and you weren't going to tell me. You were just going to blindside me with it."

"That *was* pretty much the original plan, yeah—you know, catch you off-guard, watch you squirm uncomfortably, that sort of thing."

"You really *are* a little shit, aren't you?"

"Apparently. I admit it looks a little shabby just now, even to me."

"But—you know—it's okay." He pulled back his shoulders, ran a hand through his dark blond hair and took a breath. "It's not a big deal. I'm glad I got *this* much warning, but I'll be okay. C'mon. I'll show you my ex-boyfriend."

And he led the way in. I gave a thumbs-up to Tommy as we went by.

I'll admit I was impressed by Jeff's composure. He just wasn't intimidated by things. Brazen.

They were playing a waltz, Strauss, "Blue Danube," but people were completely ignoring the music. They were milling about, lining up at the bar, eating, drinking, talking, talking.

"They're very good," I whispered to Jeff—although no one else was bothering to whisper. I was speaking of the quartet, of course. Not these hateful people.

"I once told them they sounded like complaining cats."

"His quartet? And he dumped you anyway?" I said. "Imagine that." He got a point for composure, and lost two for music appreciation.

"Okay, I realize I made some mistakes with Roger."

"Can we sit?" I asked when they'd reached the end of the Danube. I clapped, but only a few others took the hint. "I hate looking up at you all the time."

There were little round tables with tall stools. I pulled him toward one and happily climbed up on the stool. They started a new piece, some campy Latin thing called "Tico Tico."

There were two guys in the quartet, and I had a feeling the thirty-something guy on the cello had probably never been Jeff's boyfriend, so the ex I was looking for had to be the first violin. Nice looking, for sure, about Jeff's age, really pretty complexion, gigantic brown eyes, with a big shock of brown curls that fell over his forehead.

I listened for a bit.

"So which one is Roger's new boyfriend?"

"Over there," he gestured with a nod. "Fletch. Fletcher Andrews. The languorous beauty leaning against the wall."

"You're kidding. That one?" There, leaning against the wall with a quiet smile and listening to the Ticos, was the single sexiest person I had ever seen *ever*. Even taller than Jeff. Blond, piercing blue eyes, gorgeous lips, perfect skin. "You serious? The model?"

"That's what everybody says."

"Whoa. You know, Jeff, you shouldn't feel bad about losing out to that. He's gorgeous!"

"Thanks, Theo. That makes me feel so much better."

The Latin piece was over. Scores were switched out from the music stands, tuning was checked, and Roger looked up.

It was impossible to miss the moment he saw Jeff.

Roger looked like one of those guys who always had some pink in his cheeks, but he went an even darker shade of red. I looked at Jeff. He raised a hand in a small acknowledgment to Roger, and gave an infinitesimal lift of the head. He didn't give anything away, but, from where I was, perched on the stool next to him, I could see his jaw muscles clenching.

The woman on second violin picked up her bow and played the opening solo from Gershwin's *Rhapsody in Blue*—if you don't know it from anything else, you know it from the airline commercials. I glanced at the program and saw it was a whole Gershwin medley. And Jeff's old boyfriend had done the arrangement. Impressive.

The opening is written for a solo clarinet, but it sat fine on the violin. It started with a trill toward the bottom of the range and then went up through this bluesy slide about two-and-a-half-octaves before she knocked out the famous theme from that piece. The other three were the rest of the orchestra. After a few minutes of the "Rhapsody," they moved into "Fascinating Rhythm," led now by the viola. And then it was Roger, playing the ballad "You Can't Take That Away from Me."

I gotta tell you, this incredibly cool thing happened while Roger was playing. Slowly, this room full of self-important lawyer-assholes (yeah, I know that's redundant), one by one these baboons stopped talking and turned their heads—because the music was *that* beautiful, *that* compelling. Not just because it was this Gershwin tune that most people knew, but because of how this guy played it. Like he had listened to every broken heart in the world, and he'd given them voice through those strings. This Roger-guy was no slouch. At the end, he did this little run of eighth-note triplets with a delicate *ritard,* ending on a G way way up there, a note he held and held and let fade, and then—it was gone.

And there was a pause—you could feel the whole room suspended in that silence—and the cello thumped in with "Strike Up the Band." Roger's arrangement was brilliant. Their earlier numbers had gotten a little applause here and there, mostly from me. At the end of "Strike Up the Band" the room erupted into a spontaneous ovation.

It was fantastic. It was an affirmation of everything I believed about music and songs, and the power they can have in a room, no amplification, just the real sound, real music, so that even a bunch of tone-deaf, philistine lawyers had to shut up and listen.

I was *so* glad I'd invited myself to their silly-ass party.

The quartet took a quick bow, and began to collect their things, and everyone returned to their schmoozing and boozing like nothing had happened.

Troglodytes.

"Your boyfriend can really play," I said.

"Not my boyfriend." He nodded toward the tall blond. "*His* boyfriend."

"And it's fantastic that Roger does the arrangements."

"He does?"

"How could you not know that?" He just shrugged. "So, will you introduce me to this other guy's boyfriend?"

"To Roger? As what? My hide-a-bed buddy?"

"If you want. Or you could just introduce me as Theo, dwarfbrain."

"I don't think so."

"Fine." I hopped off my stool and headed toward Roger, who was wiping down his bow. I got the reaction I knew I would: the hand of God came down on my shoulder—or at least the hand of Bornic.

"Stop," he said.

I smiled up at him sideways, giving him a load of the cherubic dimples.

"Just give up, Jeff. Resistance is futile."

He heaved a mighty sigh.

"Okay, c'mon then," and he ushered me off toward the musicians. "Hey Roger," he said as we approached.

"Jeff," said Roger looking up, shoving this mass of curls back from his forehead. "I saw you out there. I'm really glad you heard us play."

"Yeah, me too."

"Hi," I said. Jeff might want to ignore me, but *that* was never going to happen.

"Hi," said Roger.

"I almost forgot," said Jeff. "This is Theo. Theo Dwarfbrain."

I made a face.

"You had to do that, didn't you."

"I did."

"Theo McPherson," I said, turning back to Roger.

"Hi Theo," said Roger, looking from me to Jeff and back. We shook hands. "Roger Prescott."

"Your quartet is fantastic. It was a real thrill to hear you guys."

"Wow. Thanks," said Roger.

"And you do the arrangements? I mean not the Haydn, obviously—"

"Yeah, Haydn did his own charts. But some of the others."

"I am seriously impressed."

"Thank you."

"Jeff. Say something nice."

"It was good. Roger, you know—I don't know anything. But it was good, I thought."

"You were way too good for *this* crowd," I said. "Bunch of idiot lawyers."

"Jeff and I are both idiot lawyers, you know, as are the viola and second violin."

"You know what I mean."

"Theo plays piano," Jeff volunteered.

"Really? Bob—the cellist?—and I have been talking about finding someone to play some trios, just messing around. Any interest?"

"You mean like Brahms, Schubert?"

"We were thinking Ravel to start, actually, but yeah."

"I don't have chops like *that*. I'm actually a songwriter," I said.

"Oh really?" he said, interested, not at all snarky about it.

"Well, struggling."

"Aren't we all?" said Roger.

"Theo had a couple songs in a showcase recently," said Jeff. "They were really good!"

Wow, I hadn't expected that.

"You—actually went?" asked Roger, surprised.

"I did!" said Jeff, smiling. "I know, hard to believe, right?"

I know that back at Don't Tell Mama I maybe wasn't exactly gracious about Jeff's turning up, but all of a sudden I was pretty stoked about it. Jeff Bornic had come to hear my songs, and he'd *liked* them! Of course it didn't really *mean* anything, because Jeff was an idiot. But yeah, somehow it meant something.

"I was pretty surprised, too," I confirmed.

"Really. Now I'm the one who's impressed," said Roger.

"So did you guys change your name?" asked Jeff, looking at the program. "Weren't you the Goodkin Quartet or something?"

"Goodkin Berdann, yeah, but I left the firm—"

"Tommy told me."

"And I thought we shouldn't be *that* tied to Goodkin Berdann & Dunkel. And since it was already GBD…"

"I didn't think of that," I said, looking at the program. "You're the G-Major Quartet!"

"A little obvious," said Roger, "but it was the name we could all agree on."

"G-major?" Jeff was lost

"GBD," said Roger.

"If you say GBD to a musician," I explained, "that's G-major."

"Every pitch has a letter-name assigned to it," Roger tried. "A through G. But—you know—I'm sorry, never mind. I know this stuff doesn't interest you."

"Let's try this," I said. "Roger, hum a G." He did. "I knew your pitch would be better than mine. String players have amazing pitch," I explained to Jeff. "Now listen. *Geeeee.* Now you sing that."

Roger laughed, and Jeff balked.

"What? Here?"

"Yeah. Why not? Sing—*Geeeeeeeeee*."

Jeff—unbelievably—did what he was told.

*"Geeee,"* he sang. Softly, and looking over his shoulder, but he sang it.

"Perfect. Now do that again and this time hold it and we'll join you, don't freak. Go ahead, sing the G."

*"Geeeeeeeeeeeeeeeeeeeeeeeeeeeeeee,"* Jeff sang.

I came in right after him a third higher.

*"Beeeeeeeeeeeeeeeeeeeeeeeeeeeee,"* I sang.

I raised my eyebrows at Roger, who obligingly finished out the triad.

*"Deeeeeeeeeeeeeeeeeeeeeeeeeeeee."*

Okay, this would all be incredibly stupid—not to mention the weirdest bit of cocktail chatter of all time—but for the look on Jeff Bornic's face while he was singing. His befuddled expression became a smile that spread involuntarily. The recognition in his eyes, all the while holding the G, looking at me, at Roger, at me again, *that* was worth it. Jeff Bornic was really hearing music probably for the first time in his life.

All around us heads had turned, but I didn't care. I gave the boys a cutoff, and Jeff just grinned.

"And that," said Roger, "is a G-major chord."

"That was—so—cool!!!" said Jeff.

"And you were the tonic," I said. "The fundamental of a major chord."

"Wow. *Now* I sort of see why you guys do this. It was actually awesome to be in there, a part of that."

*"Now* he gets it!" said Roger.

"You boys starting a doo-wop group?" It was the second violinist, a big blowsy blonde woman, almost as tall as Jeff. "Jeffrey, how have you been?"

"Hi Katrina," said Jeff back in schmooze-mode.

"Lot of rumors around town about you and a partnership over there, and I'm sure they're all true."

"Yeah, we'll see. Fingers crossed."

"Are you on the *Hiromi* case?"

"Maybe, don't know yet."

"Well—good luck!"

"Thanks."

"We haven't met," she said to me suddenly. The way she towered over me, I thought she was going to eat me. "Katrina." She extended her hand.

"Katrina, this is—"

"Theo," I said, before he could dwarfbrain me again.

"You're at Parker O'Neill as well?"

"Temporarily," I said. "I loved your performance this evening!"

"Thank you! It's so nice of you to say so. Jeffrey, have you ever heard us perform? As I recall, you didn't have much of an ear for music."

Jeff glanced at me a second before he answered.

"I'm learning."

I don't know why I was blushing, but I knew that I was. I looked around and there was Roger, eyeing me like I was some interesting new species.

"Hey guys." Fletch had stepped over to us, although I don't think he'd ever been very far away. "Jeff. How's it goin'."

Wowza. He was even better looking up close.

"Hope you're well, Fletch," said Jeff.

"Thanks, I am."

"Good to see you, Jeff," said Katrina, and she went.

I was watching the triangle of guys around me. It was interesting that Fletch didn't feel any need to put his arm around Roger or anything, which anyone else would have done. I guess when you look like Fletch, you can be pretty confident, but still—I admired him for it.

"Hi," I said to Fletch.

"Fletch this is—"

"Theo McPherson," I said firmly.

"Nice to meet you."

I *hated* hanging around in clumps of tall people like this. Which gave me an idea.

"Fletch, could you introduce me to the other musicians?"

"Um, sure. You guys okay?" The last question was addressed entirely to Roger.

"Wait," said Jeffrey, and his hand gripped my arm. Pretty firmly too. Was that panic? "Where are you going?"

"I'm just going to congratulate the others," I said, gently pulling my arm free.

"Yeah, okay," said Roger, answering Fletch's concern.

"We'll be right back," I said.

I figured Jeff and Roger had some issues, and maybe if somebody said I'm-sorry and the other person said I'm-sorry-too, maybe somebody would feel a little better.

But what do I know?

# Chapter 23
## Abandonment Issues

*JEFFREY*

I watched Theo walking away with Fletch. That kid really was a piece of work, wasn't he? First he *insisted* I talk to Roger, which I seriously did *not* want to do, which he *knew* I did not want to do, and then he just ditched me. I stared after him as Fletch introduced him to the other woman from the quartet—what was her name? Viola? No, but something like that.

"Hey," said Roger, pushing his curls back the way he does.

"You look really great, Roger. Not being a lawyer agrees with you."

"Yeah, it's been a lot of changes, obviously, but they've all been really good. I'm doing some graduate work at NYU, and I have a handful of students, my one beginner and a few older kids prepping for their college auditions. I'm playing a lot. I'm pretty happy."

"I'm glad. And you and Fletch finally…"

"And yeah, Fletch and I finally. And you? Seriously, how are you doing?"

"Seriously? I'm great. Everything's great. Never better."

"Really?"

I took a breath.

"Okay, I'll admit you knocked the wind out of me, but—I'm doing better." He just looked at me, like he was expecting more. "I'm not sure why, but I honestly feel like I'm doing better. Okay? That's all you're going to get from me."

"I wasn't trying to get anything, I was just sincerely asking."

"I know. And you sent Tommy over to spy on me, so I'm sure you're up to date."

"No! The move was totally his idea! And I promise you, he hasn't been reporting back to me. For example, he'd told me about Theo, the funny new kid at the firm, but he hadn't said a word about *you* and Theo."

"Me and Theo?"

"Not really your type, but I think he'll be really good for you."

"Theo?! We're not—no, we're—he's just—"

"Really? You guys aren't...?"

"Really. Definitely really. We're not."

"Then is he writing a book about you?" Roger seemed to think this was pretty funny, and I didn't get the joke.

"What are you talking about?"

"The way he watches you."

I had no idea what he was talking about. I glanced over to Theo where he was talking to the guy, the cello player. And yeah, Theo was looking past them back over to me.

"Well, I don't know what that's about, but don't read too much into it. You remember Rebecca McPherson?"

"Of course. How is she?"

"She's great, she's here somewhere. Theo is her little brother."

"Ah. Of course, I can see that now."

"The hair," we said together.

"So no, nothing going on there," I made clear.

"If you say so."

"Dweeb, you about ready?" Fletch always called him that, I never knew why. He had Roger's violin case slung over one shoulder, and his music bag in the other hand. Theo was somewhere behind him.

"Yeah, I am. Take care of yourself Jeff." Roger gave me a quick one-arm hug that I didn't have a chance to return. "Nice meeting you, Theo."

"You too. It was really nice meeting you both."

And they went.

I looked around the room, faces I knew, faces I didn't.

There was Dan Kaminsky, holding forth to a group of associates over by the bar. Funny, from here he looked like a nice guy, but I knew, up close and personal, he was a complete shit-hook. You don't get to bill what he bills an hour by being nice.

That was my world, over there. Business. Making money. Talking about making money. What was I doing, talking about string quartets and major chords? That was my *Hiromi* competition, yukking it up over one of Kaminsky's famous anecdotes. I should be in there, pretending I haven't heard the stories before. Not like me to let those ass-lickers get ahead of me. But for some reason I just couldn't move.

Was it Roger? No. Roger didn't upset me. It's not like I wanted him back or anything. I didn't. Never did. But something...

I looked over at the crowd around Kaminsky again.

I heard myself sigh.

"Hey," said a quiet little voice next to me. Theo's voice. "You okay?"

"Me? Heh. Never better." I shook it off. "You were hoping this was going to be a big scene or something, weren't you?"

"Maybe a little scene anyway. *Or* maybe there'd be a little scuffle and you'd step back and bump into some old broad in a tiara who'd fall into a guy carrying a pie, and the next thing you know..."

"Oh man! You should have told me! I'm sure we could have managed that, and that would have been fabulous!"

"Just a *little* effort on your part, Jeff."

"Nothing like a dash of the Three Stooges to make a party really click." I was still surveying the crowd, but now I was picking out a few faces that I'd love to hit with a pie. That one, and that one, and what's her name, that jerk from corporate...and oh! Victoria! Most definitely Victoria, *kerpow,* right in the kisser. Theo was a genius.

"Honestly, Jeff? I'm sorry." Did I really hear that?

"Did you just—apologize?"

"Only a little bit, and don't get used to it. But you owe me some stories, I think. You and Roger, how it all went wrong, da-da-dee da-da-da."

"You think so?"

"Oh for sure." He grabbed an hors d'oeuvres off the tray of a passing waiter. "This is sooooo good," he said with a mouthful of stuffed mushroom.

"Newsflash. I don't owe you zip."

He snagged two glasses of champagne off another waiter and handed me one.

"I got half the story from Rebecca already anyway."

"Remind me to speak to Rebecca about that."

"I just figured you'd want to give me your side of things. She said she was never really sure how serious it was for you. Roger, the break-up."

"She said that? Not sure I was serious?'

"Yeah, something like that. So, were you?"

"What?" I looked down at him. He had that mocking grin on his face, as usual. Those taunting dimples on those pretty cheeks. I just wanted to slap that jeer from his face. I'd have done anything to stop that mouth from laughing at me.

"Serious," he said.

"I'm sorry—what are we talking about?"

"Roger?" he prompted.

Oh, yeah.

I looked at this glass of champagne that had gotten into my hand somehow, and I tossed it back in one big swallow.

"C'mon," I said, stifled the little burp that followed, and plopped the glass down on a table next to a couple of first-year associates—who looked offended.

"Boo!" I said, just to watch them jump. I grabbed Theo's hand and started for the ballroom door with him following.

"Where we going?" For absolutely the first time ever, he wasn't fighting me, just following.

"I want to show you something."

"Hey Jeff," said Theo behind me, "what you got to show me, I don't wanna see."

*Great, keep taunting me.* At least he was still following. I led him out through the front lobby and onto Fifth.

"Taxi, please," I said to the doorman.

"Are you kidnapping me?"

"Could be. Just get in the cab." He was still holding a glass of champagne. I took it from him and gulped what was left. "Here," I handed the glass and a twenty to the doorman.

The cab pulled away.

"I am going to regret this, I know it," said Theo.

"I definitely will."

# Text to Rebecca

*Your party is a snore-fest.*

*Where are you? Are we at the same table for dinner?*

*Actually, your plus-one is subtracting himself.*

*Traitor!*

*Ha.*

*Wait.*

*I'll go with you.*

*Too late.*

# Chapter 24
## Caution: Hard Hats Must be Worn

*THEO*

You know how people say things like 'I'm here against my better judgment'? I finally knew what they meant.

Every instinct told me, do *not* get into a cab with this guy.

Okay, it wasn't like I was crawling into the backseat of a taxi with a total stranger. It was Jeff. I was not going to wake up, trussed like a turkey in a leather sling, or in a bathtub missing some internal organ or other. It was Jeff, my sister's best friend. I'd been sharing a hide-a-bed with him for a week, and if you can't trust your sleeper-couch comrades, then who? But still. He was being really weird. And don't forget, Jeffrey Dahmer was nice-looking, too.

All this was rattling through my brain as I scooted across the backseat of a taxi and Jeff climbed in next to me.

But no, I reassured myself, ol' Jeff was way too square to be a serial killer. That at least would be *interesting.* And Jeff wasn't very interesting, was he?

In any case, I had gotten in a cab—against my better judgment. Jeff gave the driver an address on the Upper East Side, which I figured was his apartment. Why were we going to his apartment? He obviously wasn't taking me there for the usual reason guys take you to their apartment.

He pulled his tie loose and undid his top button.

Maybe Jeff just wanted to get stoned. Did super-square lawyers—who wanted to be partners someday—get stoned?

At his building, we walked across a lobby of polished terrazzo past a weaselly-looking doorman who was sneaking a cigarette under the desk.

"Good evening, Mr. Bornic," said the weasel. Jeff gave a tiny wave without actually looking at the guy. Come to think of it, he hadn't looked at *me* since he'd pulled me across the ballroom of the Pierre in front of half of the New York legal community.

We got in the elevator, and he pressed 24. Then he changed his mind and pressed 23. Hmmmm. What, did he forget where he lived? Neither of us spoke until he had stopped in front of a door and put his key in the lock.

"Just to warn you—it's a construction site. Watch your step."

He pushed open the door to a dark apartment, reached inside and flipped a light switch. A small light over the door came on, just enough so you could see—a really big, mostly empty, room. There was a stack of drywall to one side, some orange power cords coiled and piled up, plaster dust everywhere. Bare walls of plasterboard, with white tape covering the seams. Rough-cut holes with wires hanging out. But the dominant feature of the space was a really big expanse of glass on the opposite wall, and the city beyond. Along the right wall, a staircase came down from the floor above.

Christ-on-a-crescent-roll, this was going to be a hella nice apartment.

"C'mon in."

I followed him, tentatively.

"Why are we here again?"

"I told you—I want to show you something."

"Okaaaaaaay. What exactly?"

"This!" He made a big, sweeping gesture to the empty room. "The first thing I want you to see is the large open space here in the living room and the grand piano in front of these windows."

"The grand piano?"

"The architect and I, we planned this, so you'd come in and see the huge windows and the view, and the gorgeous piano in front of it."

"I know you don't play."

"Not even the radio." An hour ago he didn't know what a major chord was.

"Then—why?"

"Well, I used to know this guy—he plays violin in a string quartet, if you can believe it. He has a little console piano in his apartment, so I figured he must use it for *something.* And even *I* can hear the difference between a console and a grand."

"The piano was for Roger?"

"Bought and paid for, and sitting in a warehouse somewhere. The Steinway people are just waiting for a delivery date. They're very accommodating, the Steinway people."

"Yeah, I'll bet."

I stood in front of the windows—and the view to the East River and beyond. The glass was so big, it actually made me a little nervous standing next to it.

"Notice the staircase," said my tour guide. I turned and looked back to the stairs coming down. "Generally in duplex apartments in the city the staircase is super steep. Or a spiral. Staircases are really expensive things because they eat a lot of square footage and square footage on a crowded island is, well, really expensive. And a staircase eats the square footage on both floors. Most people want to minimize that—hence the steep spiral staircase. But I said, noooooo, make it a shallow, gracious descent. Know why?"

"I bet you'll tell me."

"For little tiny Scottish terrier legs. They can't go down steps that are too steep because their little legs are so short, they tumble right over."

"Let me guess who has a Scotty."

"Ding ding ding!" He touched his nose with his index finger. "So I designed this really expensive staircase—the custom work alone, and then the loss on the resale value of the property because of the lost square footage? Don't want to guess. And I don't even like the dog. There's a lot more apartment that direction," he gestured off toward a hallway, "and the new kitchen's going in along there," he gestured in the opposite direction, "but it's all just bare drywall. C'mon." He took my hand again, like it was the most natural thing in the world to do, and he led me over to the stairs. "Careful, there's no railing."

At the top, the opening into the other apartment was closed off with a plastic tarp. He had to rip up the tape that held it in place, and he was able to get an opening big enough to climb up out onto the next floor. He helped me up, and turned on a table lamp.

This was clearly his current apartment—everything here was finished, although furniture was pushed up against the wall and covered in plastic drop cloths.

He pulled off his jacket and tossed it at a chair—which was covered in plastic, and the jacket just slid to the floor. He didn't seem to notice.

"I want to show you something down here," and he led me toward the kitchen at one end, a counter separating it from the rest. He turned on the overhead kitchen light, but stopped just outside. "With the new kitchen going in downstairs, I'm taking this out, and the wall will be moved out to here." He pulled me into the kitchen. "So imagine that wall pushed out a couple feet beyond the counter. The space will be closed in, and soundproofed, floors, walls, ceilings. So someone could practice in here anytime, day or night, and never worry. It's big enough that a quartet could rehearse in here even. With his little piano against this wall for whatever he does with his little piano. Room enough even for a bed for that goddamned dog. And there's a handy powder room next door." He flipped off the bright overhead light, and we just had the softer light from the table lamp by the stairs.

"No terrace?" I said. Jeff's head snapped up to see if I meant it. I didn't.

"No," he said laughing quietly. "No terrace. Leave it to you—I show you all of *this,* and you ask me about a terrace."

"Why *are* you showing me all this?"

"Because you asked me."

"I asked you?!"

"If I had been serious."

Ohfuck. What was I supposed to say to that? Yeah, I'd been provoking him, but I had no idea. I didn't mean to put him through all this. The evening had started out to be such fun, listening to music, teasing Jeff, but now—now I felt like last year's pond scum. I stepped over to the couch, pulled up one end of a drop cloth, and sat.

"Did Roger know you were doing any of this?"

He shook his head.

"Here's a joke for you—I wanted it to be a surprise!" And he laughed a little. "Instead, it turned out to be a really big surprise for me when Roger told me we were done."

"Jeff, you don't have to—"

"Another surprise? Almost as soon as he dumped me, I realized—how do I put this?—I was okay with that. I mean, I was pissed about it. I was really angry he'd dumped me, I was angry I'd been outmaneuvered by Fletch—by Fletch of all people. But pissed off isn't the same thing as brokenhearted. I guess that's what confuses Rebecca."

"Runs in the family."

"I'm just figuring it out myself as I'm standing here. I wasn't in love, architect's bills to the contrary. Roger had a lot of things I wanted in a partner. And he was a lawyer, and I thought how cool is that? Two go-getter young attorneys pursuing their careers side-by-side. And I kept trying to coax him in that direction, shape him into the life-partner I wanted him to be, ambitious, driven. We'd be this perfect couple, two young legal stars conquering New York together, we'd do the cocktail parties and we'd be this fabulous power couple with a fabulous life and a fabulous apartment and two fabulous incomes, giving fabulous parties and taking fabulous vacations. We'd be envied by everybody. But of course that's not who Roger is at all."

"So…why did you go ahead with all this?"

"By the time Roger dropped the axe on me, I was already into the architect for a ton. Everybody who needed to sign off on the plans had signed off, custom risers for the staircase had already been ordered. Even the piano was bought and paid for and, it turns out, the Steinway people aren't *that* understanding. There was no going back."

"And nobody knows you did all this?"

"Nobody knows. Not Roger, not Rebecca, nobody."

"Just me."

He looked over to me.

"Huh. Yeah. Just you." He was by the window, leaning against the wall and looking down into the street below. "Why you?"

"Jeff, I'm sorry. I didn't mean to—I don't know. All this."

I was trying to figure out how he was doing, but his face showed nothing. I didn't have a clue if he was going to start throwing things, or howl at the moon.

"Jeff, are you okay?"

"Never better."

I got up and walked over to him by the window.

"You sure?"

"Theo," he said, still looking out, "you have been laughing at me since we met. And here I have just shown you this—the Roger W. Prescott Memorial Construction Project—my biggest stupidity, my greatest humiliation. You should be eating this up." He turned to me finally. "And you're not laughing."

"Somehow it's not very funny."

He was still looking at me. Was he going to kill me now?

Or try to kiss me.

He was nice enough looking. More than that. Not like a model, not like Fletch, but more boy-next-door-ish. If the boy next door was thirty. But somehow he didn't really seem to be all that much older just now. In fact he looked like he was my age. He looked just as unsure and insecure as I felt.

And he was definitely more than nice looking. Maybe not gaw-jus but…

Would I *let* him kiss me if he tried?

Would I have a choice? He was a lot bigger than me and way stronger. Under the tailored shirt I could see how built he was, his shoulders, his chest. Still, was it possible for one guy to rape another?

Of course it isn't rape if you—

I was distracted by his eyes. Really beautiful. Nice nose. Lips. Lips.

The door was behind me. I could still make a run for it, but that would mean turning my back on him. And if I turned my back—

Oh hell, who was I kidding? I wasn't going anywhere.

He was looking out the window again.

"I've been thinking about your song," Jeff said finally.

That was about the *last* thing I expected to hear at that moment.

"My song?"

"The one about the typist—they'll whisper and they'll wonder—that one."

"Yeah."

"And you know how she's afraid no one knows she's special?"

He turned back to me, and he seemed to study my face. Why had I never noticed those eyes before?

"Yeah."

He was standing so close. Why was he so close?

"No one ever looked at you," he whispered, "and didn't know."

"What?" I said without a sound.

"That you were something very special."

I heard a gasp, and realized it was mine. If he'd punched me in the gut, it couldn't have landed harder than that quiet sentence. I was surprised to feel the sudden burn of tears in my eyes.

I had no idea anyone knew me like that, saw that about me. But he did. This arrogant—awful—lawyer-person—he knew. He could see me with those soft blue eyes.

I was scared of him.

I hated him.

I couldn't look at him.

I needed to get out of there.

I turned—and I felt his arm slip around me, warm, and so amazingly strong.

No, I was definitely not going anywhere.

# Chapter 25
## And the Dawn Comes up Like Thunder...

*JEFFREY*

The first bit of light was coming through the windows in the living room, as I did my stretches on the floor. I didn't want to wake you-know-who. I had no idea how he was going to react this morning to what happened last night. He definitely seemed to be having a good time and then the pizza, and then—

But that was last night. Who knew what he'd think this morning. This was Theo, after all.

And Theo was insane.

Fortunately I didn't have a lot of clutter so there wasn't much stuff to throw.

Anyway. Time to go. I'd written him a note, in case he was gone when I got back.

I stepped as quietly as possible into the bedroom. I picked up my keys and phone from the bureau and glanced over to the bed. I could see a sliver of sparkle from one eye.

"What's the story, morning glory?" he mumbled. That was a good sign. Made a nice change from 'douchebag,' anyway.

He hadn't picked his head up from the pillow, he just lay there half wrapped up in my sheets.

I sat on the side of the bed, pushed his fantastic hair back from his face. "Hey, handsome."

"Where are you going?"

"For a run. Wanna come?" I stretched a little more from where I was sitting.

"No, but if you run past Bellevue—check yourself in. I think you have lost your mind."

"I think you are right." I leaned over and kissed him on the side of the head.

"Running away?"

"Just running."

"Good," he said, turning his face into the pillow.

"I set out a new toothbrush on the sink. Help yourself to whatever you need. If you have to go, just make sure the door closes all the way behind you, and I'll see you at the office." One more kiss, and I snatched up the empty box from the pizza we'd ordered late, and I headed out to drop it in the trash chute.

More stretching in the elevator, and then out into the street.

Thamp thamp thamp thamp.

All the usual characters. There's the garbage truck.

"Hey guys," I called, waving.

They looked up and waved. I smiled back and kept running.

I smiled?

I stopped at the corner for some traffic and there was that enormous, cream-colored poodle next to me. His head was at my waist. I held out my hand and he sniffed it, and I even ruffled up the silly-ass pile of curls on top of his head. Couldn't believe how soft it was. That dog was actually pretty cool. Even the ridiculous haircut looked—I don't know—kinda sharp.

Then the poodle surprised me—he reached over with his nose and jostled my balls in my nylon shorts, sniffing. He looked up at me quizzically.

"You can ask, but I'm not telling."

"Excuse me?" said the fat guy on the leash.

"Sorry," I explained. "It was just between us," and I gestured to the dog and me—and jogged across the intersection. I could see why somebody might want to keep a dog around. Not me, but, you know, somebody.

I realized I wasn't in a shitty mood for once. In fact, I was in a good mood. I was being playful with a poodle. How did *that* happen?

Thamp thamp.

All I needed was to get laid? That didn't make sense, there had been probably—I didn't even want to *think* about how many there'd been.

As I thamped my way past the little 24-hour market, I paused, looking in and jogging in place for a few seconds. And then I kept running.

I got all the way to the light at Fifth Avenue and had to stop to wait for it to change, and then, when it did—I turned around and jogged back to the little market. Inside, I found myself in front of the bakery counter with only half an idea what I was doing.

I asked the guy for two bagels, which he tonged into a bag. I tossed some cream cheese into a red plastic shopping basket I'd picked up. Did Theo like bagels? *I* didn't even like bagels. I had the guy put two croissants in the bag as well. But he's such a little kid. And two chocolate croissants. But then I thought—he's from Iowa. And two cherry Danish. And two apricot, in case he likes those better. And I grabbed a quart of juice. Are those bear claws? Yes, two please. And I checked out.

When I got back to the apartment, I snagged two plates, and went straight to the bedroom with my white paper bags full of breakfast for seventeen. Theo cracked an eye.

"That was quick."

"My heart wasn't in it." I pulled my phone out of its holster and told it to call my secretary.

"Darlene, when you get in, would you please go through my calendar and let whoever needs to know that I'm calling in. Not sure what's wrong with me, I think it's something I picked up at the Pierre last night," I said looking at Theo, who looked wonderful in nothing but a sheet. He was already digging through the bags to see what I'd brought him. "I can't possibly make it in today. I'm going straight back to bed. Thanks. I'll try to check in later."

"Wow, is that cherry?" he said, looking up from his foraging.

I picked up his pants from the floor, fished his phone out and tossed it to him.

"Your turn," I said.

"I've only worked there for a week. I can't call in sick."

"Oh yes you can," I said, pulling my shirt up over my head.

# Chapter 26
## Who Was at the Zoo? The Monkeys and Who?

*THEO*

He bought me some overpriced popcorn, which was really nice. It was late morning, cool and overcast, but he'd loaned me a gigantic Princeton sweatshirt of his, and we were walking through Central Park Zoo. He'd also paid for the tickets. Okay, he was an attorney making gazillions, and I was a temp secretary who hadn't even had a payday yet, so I didn't feel *too* bad about mooching off him here and there.

"This was crazy, calling in today," said Jeff.

"Seriously? That's what you want to say to me? Because forty-five minutes ago you were all like *yeah, keep doing that, don't stop.*"

"Shut up, you nitwit," he laughed, and he actually blushed. I was figuring out that he got really embarrassed whenever I talked about sex—it was cute.

We had stopped to lean on a railing at the snow monkey enclosure. The monkeys weren't up to terribly much. They sat on rocks, they diddled around in the water around their rocks. To break up the boredom, they occasionally annoyed each other. I could totally relate.

"I didn't mean that I was *sorry* about calling in sick. This morning was fabulous! *And* last night. No, I was just thinking about work piling up, the usual crap. But seriously, Theo—I'm really glad to be here with you, I mean that. I just wish the job didn't keep nipping at my brain."

"Making the world safe for fast-acting antacids. It's a tough job, but...."

"It could be worse. I don't have any cases involving laxatives or hemorrhoid medications. But don't *you* start making fun of me about it."

"You say that to me, of all people."

"Yeah, pretty stupid, I guess."

"And of course you need to pound in the hours to keep your name at the top of the famous *Hiromi* list."

He turned and looked down at me a few seconds. I couldn't read his face at all.

"I think—I got this idea last night—I think I'm taking myself *off* the *Hiromi* list."

That was news.

"I thought *Hiromi* was the Holy Grail, the Triwizard Cup, the Golden Ticket to the really *big* bucks."

"Well, yeah, it is, but I don't really—I don't know, I just—I should talk to Victoria about it."

You'll remember that Victoria was my boss, and she sort of dictated the lives of the lower orders, even Jeff, who was the upper crust of the lower orders.

"Want me to put you on her calendar?" I joked.

"No, don't," he said a little distracted. "I'll—send her an e-mail or something."

What was that about? But he seemed sort of done with the subject. Fine. Last thing I wanted to talk about was the law firm.

I watched his face. It's funny that I hadn't really noticed how good-looking he was, but he was. I'd been so focused on what an asshole he was—he was *still* an asshole—that I'd overlooked the perfect nose. All of a sudden dirty blond hair seemed way sexy. And of course those eyes.

"We need to sit down. You're too tall." I pulled him to the side and we sat on a bench. I was still a little cold, even with the sweatshirt, and I snuggled up against Jeff. Okay, maybe I *wanted* to snuggle up against Jeff. Just a tiny bit. Maybe. I pulled his arm around—purely for warmth.

"So were you planning something like this when you pushed me into that cab last night?"

"No! No, I didn't really know what I was doing. I just wanted you to see the apartment—that was suddenly important. Not sure why. Why? Is this what *you* were thinking when I shoved you into the cab?"

"No, I was thinking you were probably a serial killer just getting started in your career. So you wanted me to see the apartment—because you'd bumped into Roger?"

"I guess. I don't know. It doesn't really make any sense."

"Certainly *this* doesn't." I snuggled a little closer.

"Clearly not." He pulled me tighter.

"So speaking of Roger, and all that. Rebecca told me some of the story. Fletch was Roger's ex?"

"It's not much of a story. Roger and I were together, and one day we were out in Chelsea Park with Roger's dog—"

"The Scotty."

"The hated Scotty. And we bumped into Fletch."

"Who looked like that."

"Who looked like that. I knew he was Roger's old boyfriend, but I wasn't really worried about it."

"Jeff, why wouldn't you feel threatened by a guy who looks like Fletch? I mean really, who *wouldn't* leave you for him?"

"Remind me again which one of us is the asshole? Because I get confused sometimes."

"You know what I mean."

"And of course you're right. Seven weeks later, I was out."

"And Fletch was in?"

"Not sure of the timing of their getting back together, but—I don't know—around Christmas?—I went to get coffee and heard some bitchy little first-year associate telling some other bitchy little first-year associate all about how hysterical it was that my boyfriend had dumped me and immediately taken up with this guy who was 'totes hot'."

"Well, I think *you* are totes hot, Jeff."

"Why thank you, Theo."

"You're welcome."

"And of course that was one more damned thing that ticked me off about the whole experience—between my firm and Roger's firm and everybody in between, half the lawyers in New York knew all about it. First-years who'd been scared to death of me were now giggling about me behind my back."

"Flog them."

"I wish."

"Worked out for the best, though, don't you think?"

"Yeah, probably. I mean yes, obviously."

"Otherwise you might never have met me!"

"The thorn in my side?"

"Actually, I was thinking more along the lines of the grain of sand that causes the oyster to produce the pearl—but your metaphor works too."

He looked at me for a second.

His phone vibrated for about the sixteenth time that morning. He glanced at the text, and moaned.

"My dad."

"What's up?"

"He's in the city today—"

There was another text.

"He wants to meet for drinks before he catches the train this afternoon. I'm already having dinner with them Sunday, so I don't know what this is about."

"Friendly little get-together?"

"Not likely. He'll want something. Usually he just wants to tell me what's wrong with my life and exactly what I need to do to fix it."

"Some fun."

"Yeah, tell me." His thumbs were typing. "Out of the blue like this? He's up to something."

"Doesn't sound all warm and cozy."

"Not even a little bit."

"When can I meet him?"

"Don't joke. And trust me, you don't want to meet him."

"You guys fight a lot or something?"

"We don't fight—nobody fights with my dad. He just gets his way. Like this. He says meet me at such and such, and I will meet him there." He looked down at me. "Sorry."

"Oh. Time for me to head on home then?"

"No. We've got hours still." He stood up.

"Where to now?"

"Back to the apartment."

"You naughty boy, you," I said.

He stretched a hand out behind, which I took, and he tugged me along after him.

The snow monkeys would have to carry on without us.

Actually, now that I looked, I realized a couple of them were way ahead of us.

# Chapter 27
## Mea Oh-So Maxima Culpa

*JEFFREY*

I have to come clean. I did something bad, really really bad. And I don't know what to do about it. Before this whole thing with Theo started, back when I was still in my permanently crappy mood, I did something that nobody, and I mean nobody, is going to look at and *not* think I'm the biggest prick on the planet. Except my dad. My dad would be so proud.

Here's the story.

Rebecca and I go back to when we were first hired at Parker O'Neill. Baby lawyers tend to start together in a clump—in the fall—and we started in the same clump. What's more, as first-year lawyers we didn't get our own offices—first-years had to share. Rebecca and I were officemates. Me and the farm girl, we had absolutely nothing in common, and—I'm not exaggerating—by lunchtime we were best friends. Just like that.

Now. Once upon a time in a far-off land known as Delaware, we were working on this terrible trial together—the *Mayerhoffer* case, for future reference. I should point out that this was not one of my pointless advertising claims cases, it was a pretty complicated breach-of-fiduciary-duty case. We were there in lovely Wilmington along with a slew of other bright, young, bleary-eyed attorneys. We were all knocking in huge hours, barely sleeping, and during one of those late nights Rebecca screwed up. I'll skip the technical details, but she made a judgment call about how some evidence should be marked, and she realized a couple days later what she'd done and saw that she'd potentially screwed this case for us. She came to me, trying not to cry, and when I'd heard the story, I saw a solution. I saw a chance, and the only chance, to fix it, and the two of us stayed up all night, off the clock so no one would know—which was enough to get us both fired right there—and we cleaned it up. We saved the case, saved the client, saved Rebecca's career.

And no one was any the wiser.

You're thinking, *Hey, that doesn't sound so bad. This Bornic character is a real mensch.* Yeah well.

Here's Episode Two of Rat-Bastard Theatre. Bear with me.

Rebecca and I are now in direct competition, both hoping to get in on this goddamned *Hiromi* case. Two senior associates, both on the cusp. Within the year we will either be promoted—or not. If it's the latter, it will be a pretty good indication that it's time to polish up the old résumé.

My career thus far: Depending on how you look at it, I got lucky or unlucky early on. I got on one of these stupid advertising claims cases, and out of nowhere one of the more senior attorneys—who was seven months pregnant—was put on complete bed rest. I, inexperienced as I was, was told to pick up the slack. Which I did, and did well. Work that I did contributed directly to our winning the case. People noticed. The head of Litigation noticed. Even Victoria Collins, who never seemed to like me much, noticed.

That was the lucky part.

It was *un*lucky because I was now typed as an advertising-claims guy. Which I so did not want to be. I wanted to be a big-ass financial litigator, doing big-ass financial litigations with really huge corporations suing really huge banks and vice-versa. Cases like that, like *Hiromi.* Like the work Dan Kaminsky does all day and for which he bills $1,060 an hour, and he just closed on his *third* house, with two kids at Yale and an ex-wife. So.

Obviously, I want to be Dan Kaminsky when I grow up.

Getting myself on a case with him—like *Hiromi Industries*—would be a really good start. If I cover myself with glory, as I fully expect to do, it will pretty much solidify my chances of being made partner at the end of the year. From there I would finally be in a position to back myself out of defending the advertising claims of a fabric softener, and do more big-ass financial litigation.

Hence the obsession with the *Hiromi* case you keep hearing about.

By comparison, Rebecca hasn't been so lucky in her career. She hasn't had that one big case where she's been able to stand out and be brilliant and get attention. She's a good attorney, better than I am in some ways. Despite the *Mayerhoffer* case, she's actually way more thorough than I am. If I don't see the solution to a problem in the first three minutes, the problem is unsolvable and I'm not wasting my time on it. Two days later Rebecca will walk in and say 'look at this.' She'll have worked it out. That's the difference between us.

Like I said, it just hasn't happened for Rebecca yet. But—if she could get on a big case like *Hiromi*, and perform well under the nose of Dan Kaminsky—who tends to keep a close eye on attractive female attorneys anyway, albeit for the wrong reasons—it would do a lot for her career, and perhaps get people to see her as partnership material as well.

Now of course the happy ending would be that we *both* get picked for *Hiromi*, and we are *both* brilliant and the appropriate rewards are rained down like ticker tape on *both* of us. It's possible. There will be a veritable cadre of associates on the case.

However—and it's a big however—the competition among the associates, large and small, has been building for months and it's getting pretty nasty, even at a firm that prides itself on its collegial atmosphere. Each one of our smiling colleagues has his/her own motivation for wanting very much to get picked for this trial—and the kids are starting to eyeball each other like it's the Donner family picnic and somebody forgot the hot dogs.

Of course you're still waiting for the rat-bastard part of this story.

Late one night, a few weeks ago, when I was still suffering from chronic crabby-pants and hating the world in general, I got an idea how to get myself a little advantage against my *Hiromi* competition.

I drafted an e-mail to Victoria Collins, Theo's boss, the partner in charge of associate assignments. In that e-mail, I laid out what had happened on the *Mayerhoffer* trial way back when, and how I had stepped in and quietly—not to mention magnificently—saved the day.

Unfortunately, there was no way of telling this story that didn't also make Rebecca look bad. Like the worst attorney ever. But I drafted it anyway. Rat-bastard enough for you?

*But!* I had argued with myself. *But!*

*This is business!*

And really, on the one hand, it was a total no-brainer. I saw an opportunity to give myself a leg up in a business situation, and I was going to take it. Any smart person would, wouldn't they?

On the other hand...well, yeah.

Rebecca = sweet, kind best friend.
Jeffrey = biggest prick on the planet, going to burn in hell.

*But wait,* I hear you—or somebody, probably my dad—ask. *Wouldn't Rebecca do the same thing if she'd had the chance?*

A reasonable question. And the obvious answer: *Not on your life.*

Of course she wouldn't. She's from Iowa. That's practically like being Canadian.

*This isn't personal,* said the voice in my head, which by now definitely sounded like my dad. These were all *his* arguments.

Personally, Rebecca was my friend, but professionally, she was my competition. These were two different, unrelated things.

On the professional side, it was survival of the fittest. You do what you have to. In the end, the game goes to whoever wants it most, right? This is a tough town. Rebecca should have stayed in Iowa if she didn't want to play with the big boys—and let's face it, the big boys play rough, and when necessary, they play dirty. And I was determined, one way or another, to be the biggest of the big boys.

Those are the arguments that I made *(in loco paternis)* at the time.

I thought about the thing from every angle—and I sent that e-mail anyway.

Yup. Biggest prick, going to burn. That's me.

Of course, since that time I'd spent a week living in Rebecca's apartment, sleeping on Rebecca's couch. With Rebecca's little brother. With Theo. Theo, who for some reason was getting better looking every day.

More than anything, I was suddenly aware what brother Theo would think of me, should he ever find out what I had done to his sister. Out of the blue—and this is the real kick in the subpoena—what Theo thought of me had become strangely important. Hugely important.

I don't know why it should be. I don't know why this pipsqueak should matter. But—having finally seen his eyes looking at me without contempt—I didn't want to give him a reason to change his mind. I didn't want to lose the softness I had seen there for the first time. I didn't want him to know that I was the kind of guy who could throw his best friend to the wolves over a shot at a promotion.

And I didn't want to *be* that kind of guy either.

I did once.

No doubt about it. At one time, I definitely wanted to be the ruthless, unscrupulous bastard. Like my dad. But now?

I should fix this. I just don't know how. Victoria acknowledged the e-mail, so she's read it, and I can't make her un-read it.

I could talk to her. I could try to mitigate the damage maybe.

And I could take my name out of consideration for the trial. Whatever else, at least I wouldn't benefit from my betrayal.

Or would that just move me from the category of World's Biggest Prick over into the column marked World's Biggest Chump? When I *don't* get this case, when I *don't* get the partnership, and when I'm stuck with an enormous apartment and correspondingly enormous contractors' bills and matching mortgage payments, and I'm eating cat food out of the can?

What would my dad say if he found out that I took myself off of this case? He would finally have the proof that I was the worthless loser he'd always known I was.

Of course I would never tell him. One more thing to add to the list of lies I tell my parents, another thing I'm not particularly proud of.

Of course if Rebecca and her cute baby brother never found out—and there's really no reason that they should—I could come out of this thing *with* the case, *with* the career, *with* the partnership, and with no downside. Huge return, zero cost.

But what if? If anyone *did* find out, there would definitely be a cost.

It could cost me a best friend.

It would cost me my self-respect.

It would cost me a pair of blue-green eyes.

It also occurred to me that maybe it would be smart to take a step back from the little brother until I'd figured this mess out.

And now I was making myself perfectly miserable thinking about all these things while I was hiking across Midtown to meet my dad for drinks.

Man, I could think of seventeen different things I would *rather* be doing instead of going for drinks so I could be bullied by my dear father. And I was meeting both my parents for dinner in a few days anyway, so why?

But there's no arguing with my dad.

He's a formidable character. My grandfather started a little construction company way back when, building cute little houses in cute little Jersey suburbs. When my dad got into the biz, the suburban houses became apartment buildings, casinos, hotels; and the little construction company became one of the larger contractors in New Jersey.

My father has a will, and he is not used to being contradicted. He is also not above hitting his children, even his grown children. His father hit him, so it all makes sense to him. To be honest, my brother Greg (two years younger than me) gets it even worse than I do.

So. There was no point in my bitching about it, I was halfway there, I was going to meet my dad, I was going to hate it, and I was going to try to get away without getting hit. Low expectations and modest ambitions. These were the safest bets when dealing with my father.

I was relieved that he'd picked a sports bar over by the train station and not closer to my office. I like to keep *my* life, meaning my New York City life, separate from my New Jersey life. It's better that way. It's just not always easy to accomplish and sometimes it's pretty nerve-racking, but it's still better.

I saw him sitting at the bar watching a baseball game on one of the forty-seven big-screen TVs. He's sixty now, my dad, and his hair is still really thick. I had that going for me—thick Serbian hair. But where mine's dark blond, my dad's hair had been deep black, and mostly still was. With a matching salt/pepper moustache.

I glanced at my watch. Exactly on time. My dad hates tardiness.

"Hi, Dad," I said, and patted him on the shoulder. He likes to be called 'Dad' because it sounds more American than 'Papa,' so we call him 'Dad.' Our mother prefers 'Mama,' but our dad would rather that we call her 'Mom'—so we call her 'Mom.' See how that works?

"Good. You're here." He nodded to the bartender, female and blond, who came over. "Honey, bring my handsome son here whatever he wants."

I looked apologetically to the bartender.

I tend to avoid alcohol generally. I like to stay fit—you've seen how I am about running, and if I have even two drinks the night before, I feel it out on the run. And I hate that. I like my run to be perfect. I like my body to be perfect. So I was about to order a glass of tonic water—and then I remembered my father.

"Scotch and soda, please. Double." I could use all the help I was going to get.

"You look good," said my father.

"You, too, Dad. What's up?"

"I just wanted to say hello. And I have a message from your mother. She says you don't call often enough."

"Sorry."

"Anyway, message delivered. I don't have to tell you how women are."

I gave a small, jocular laugh. It's what you do with your dad, isn't it? If he's happy, I'm happy.

"Speaking of women," said my dad, "what was that girl's name, the Caputo girl, you know the one?"

"Jennifer?"

"You dated her a little, didn't you?"

Deep breath.

*This* was why my father wanted to see me?

"I did, yeah."

You're starting to figure out why I keep my New York and New Jersey lives separate.

I'm gay, I'm totally down with it, all my friends are down with it, it's not a big deal—in the city. As far as New Jersey is concerned, I am completely straight. Pathetic, I know, in this day and age, but I would die, I swear. It would kill my mother if she found out, and that would kill me. I just can't. And my dad? I don't even want to think about it. I already mentioned he's not afraid to hit his kids—and he's not afraid to hit them really hard.

So I have twin lives, one in the city and one in New Jersey, and these two circles never ever cross. It's not easy, but I've managed so far.

"Ask her out again, wouldja?"

"Jennifer Caputo. Out of the blue? I can't just call her out of nowhere and ask her out."

"Tell her you lost her number, whatever, I don't care. Just be nice to her."

"What's this about anyway?"

"Her father threw some business my way, and I wouldn't mind if he threw a little more. Ask her out, be nice to her. It's not like she's hideous or anything."

"Dad, I can't—"

"I'm not asking you to marry the girl—although think about it, you could do worse, and my business with her family's business, we would be huge. In the meantime, take the girl to dinner."

"Make Greggy take her out."

He made a face like he had a bad pain somewhere. God, did he make that face when somebody mentioned *my* name to him?

"Your brother can't—he's got no—you know Greggy—anyway I'm askin' you."

I took a sip of the drink in front of me. I took another, much bigger sip.

"I'm kinda seeing somebody, Dad," which was almost true, "so it isn't really an—"

"Don't be seeing somebody, not serious. Too distracting. You need to focus on work. Get that partnership. And keep your options open." Then he remembered. "Except for the Caputo girl. See her."

Of course I could tell him the truth—that I was maybe seeing this fiery redhead, a real spitfire in bed. That would impress him. And just leave out some pertinent details.

Also of course: I could easily imagine the scene that would follow if my fiery redhead found out I was dating Jenifer Caputo, a New Jersey bimbo who thinks of the Kardashians as role models.

Do you think Theo would be understanding when I explained that I was only shagging the Italian chick to help out my dad's construction business?

Who would? But where most people would just dump you for something like that, Theo would have an epic, violent, screaming hissy-fit—the kind that leaves bruises and that the folks back home in Iowa would be able to hear. And *then* he'd dump me.

"I bet a pretty Italian wife wouldn't hurt you when you're up for that partnership."

Fuckaduck.

"Dad, I'm not going to—"

"Hey! Any news on the *Hiromi* case?" he asked checking his watch. As far as he was concerned, Jennifer and I were a done deal.

"Not yet."

"Stay on top of it."

"I'm thinking of taking myself out of consideration for it."

"You crazy? I thought you needed that case!"

"I don't *need* it, other lawyers *need* it, and my caseload is heavy enough and—"

"Don't be *gloop.*" A good old Serbian word. It means stupid. "Now I have to get my train." He stood up and tossed back the last of his bourbon.

My old man. What amazing efficiency. He had allowed exactly enough time to fix me up with Jennifer, with a thirty-second allowance for misc. scolding—and he's right on time to get his train. No need to waste any time making small-talk with his kid. My jaw clenched as he laid a fatherly hand on my shoulder.

"I'll tell your mother you'll call her tomorrow."

"But we're having dinner on Sunday—"

"What did you say?" There it was. That look. The eyebrows pulled together, his forehead like a funnel cloud. With that tiny half-sentence objection I'd stepped over a line. And what did I do?

"Sorry, Dad. I'll call tomorrow."

I buckled.

"Good boy." He patted my shoulder again. "And you get your name on that case. You push those other wannabes out of the way and you take that case for yourself. What have I taught you? No one's giving you anything."

"Yeah, I know, Dad."

"You have to take. Business is business."

Yeah. My dad. What did I tell you?

# Text to Tommy

*Hey.*

*Any interest in Starbucks this morning?*

*Absolutely. You owe me some gossip, I think.*

*Meet you there.*

*I'll be wearing a pink carnation.*

# Chapter 28
## Starbucks Revisited

*Theo*

"I brought you a present," said Tommy as he kissed my cheek.

"A present?"

Tommy reached into his bag and pulled out a tube of—moisturizer? Seriously?

"Gee, thanks, Tommy. Is this a hint? Got any breath mints in there while you're at it?"

"It was free. And hey, you may look fabulous today, but it's *never* too soon to moisturize. Everyone says so. And this stuff is great, I use it every day, and look at me! I look fantastic, and I'm as old as the Hilton. Anyway, it was a free sample, so it's yours."

"Thanks."

"And I mean it's *really* a free sample, unlike Jeff's so-called free *Hamilton* tickets."

"He said they were free! How was I to know?"

We joined the vaguely S-shaped queue for overpriced coffee. No Javi behind the counter today, I noticed.

"So what's up, kiddo?" asked Tommy. "When last I saw you, a blond caveman was dragging you by the hair across the lobby of the Pierre. That certainly wasn't the end of the story. Especially not after you called in sick yesterday. I thought he'd killed you."

"How well do you know Jeff?"

"Not as well as I thought, apparently. And not as well as *some* people I could mention. Who shall remain nameless. But whose *initials* are—"

"I don't know the guy at all!"

"Of course it's none of my business, and you don't have to tell me a single thing, but where the aitch did you go after the benefit, hmm?"

"His apartment," I admitted.

"I'm shocked! Don't tell me another word! And then what?"

"What do you think!"

"And the next day?"

"Mostly his place. And he took me to the zoo."

"To the zoo! Kinda boyfriendy, and romantic. Hand-in-hand with cute little animals."

"It was cold and gray. And Jeff, romantic? I don't know if I've ever thought of him as 'romantic.'"

"Aaaaaaaaaaaaaand? What *do* we think of him?"

"I'm not sure *what* I think. I mean, on the one hand, I'm not done punishing Madison who is still out there somewhere—"

"And Jeffrey Bornic is right here."

"Yeah, so he gets a point for convenience. Not much of an argument for going to bed with somebody, is it?"

"There are lots worse reasons, trust me. And I can't believe you're even thinking about Madison. But. There are bigger questions to consider, Padawan. So—setting Madison to one side for now, far far to one side—how do we feel about this Jeffrey guy?"

"Conflicted."

Tommy nodded, considering.

"Conflicted is good. Keeps life interesting."

"Seriously. I don't even like the guy."

"I'll bet you dollars to doughboys that's not how you felt the other night."

"No."

"And yesterday morning?"

"Yesterday morning—he was almost—bearable." Tommy's eyebrows weren't buying it. "Oooooo-kay, to be honest, he seemed pretty—great."

"I can't quite believe I'm going to say this about Jeffrey Bornic, but—he has lots of good qualities."

"Name one."

"He's seriously nice to look at."

"Hate to admit it, but yeah, he's not bad."

"I've always suspected he had a great body too."

"Yeah. No complaints there."

"Check. He's wicked smart."

"He's smart about all the wrong things, though. He knows a lot about business and making money, stupid crap like that, sure, but nothing that matters!"

In front of us two guys in suits that didn't fit turned and gave me the weirdest look. *Yeah yeah, go back to your Wall Street Journals, capitalist pigs. Come the revolution—*

"And when you say important stuff," said Tommy, pulling me back from happy thoughts of blood running in the gutters, "you mean stuff like music, art, theatre, opera...?"

"Exactly!"

"Golly, Theo, do you know anyone who might be able to teach him about those things? Because maybe all he needs is a little exposure and guidance and the opportunity to learn. Pity we don't know *anyone* who could possibly lead him gently—"

"Okay shut up."

"Theo, here's what I know. Roger tried to get Jeffrey to open his ears and listen—and then he quit. Roger, I mean. Almost immediately."

"I got Jeff to sing part of a G-major chord at the benefit."

"You what?"

"He, Roger and I sang a G-major chord together."

"Seriously. You got Jeff to sing. At Dan Kaminsky's benefit. With all those lawyers around?"

"I did."

"So tell me—are you a hypnotist? Rasputin's great-great-grandson? Because he would never have done anything remotely like that for Roger. I've seen Jeffrey do things in the last couple weeks that I wouldn't have believed possible. He makes jokes now. I never heard him be funny before. And what was he doing at your showcase? *And* he stayed for the whole thing. And he listened—I watched him. And he even behaved himself—"

"Until he was a dick."

"Even then—it was funny and charming—"

"Charming," I huffed.

"And what did he do that was so awful? He kissed you. It was harmless—and damned cute."

"He was being a dick."

"He was staking a claim, bucko, even if neither of you knew it at the time. Did you also notice his reaction to Madison was a little O.T.T., hmm? And the whole *Hamilton* thing?"

"He was a turd after, though."

"Excuse me, *who* was a turd?"

Fuck, I'd already told Tommy most of the whole *Hamilton* story, which meant I'd already told Tommy too much.

"Fine. It was a draw in the turd department."

"Stop trying to talk yourself out of this. It's okay to like him."

"He's a suit!"

"Good news is—suits come off. As you've discovered. Now maybe all these new aspects of Jeffrey's character were always there. Or maybe this personality development is the result of his heartbreaking experience with Roger. Or maybe he's actually learned something from his mistakes, and he's trying not to screw up the next time. Or *maybe,* just *maybe,* this new depth of character has something to do with someone he only recently met. I can't say."

"What do you mean?"

"Draw your own conclusions, kiddo. You're a bright boy. And then answer me this."

"What?"

"Could this effing line *be* any slower? You can tell Javi isn't working today."

# Chapter 29
## Whose Office Is This, Anyway?

*JEFFREY*

My plan was to get to work early, thinking I'd get a head start dealing with everything I'd let slide the day before while I was out doing—what I was out doing. Call it a mental health day, which I obviously very much needed. Theo was right—I *was* ready for Bellevue. Because this was pure madness.

My best friend's little brother. That was weird enough.

A secretary at the firm? Really?

Almost six years younger, not to mention eight inches shorter. And artsy-fartsy. After Roger and his damned violin, I was definitely *done* with artsy-fucking-fartsy.

I had a game plan here, didn't I? I was supposed to find some bright, ambitious (and gorgeous, of course) guy, and be part of a fabulous power couple, remember?

And instead I was messing around with this—this Theo-thing. I couldn't begin to imagine Theo doing the cocktail parties with me. Picture Theo McPherson in a tux. I know, I can't either!

And think of the optics. We'd look ridiculous together. People would laugh. He'd look like my ventriloquist dummy.

My dad was right—I needed to focus on work. I couldn't afford to get involved with anybody, not seriously. (Unless maybe he fit the above description, *e.g.,* fabulous—in which case I would make time.)

A boyfriend could be a huge time suck. Did Theo look like low-maintenance to you? Exactly.

Theo had been nothing but an irritant since I met him. He complained all the time, and God knows he jeered at me constantly, and who needs that?

And he was disruptive. I couldn't think straight when he was around, and it was worse when he wasn't.

What would he think of *this*, would he like *that*, what would Theo say if he were here now. *Ad* fucking *nauseam*. All day in my head, it's *this* happened and this *other* thing happened, and *I need to tell Theo about it.* Why??? He was just this little speck from Iowa.

I needed to buckle down and focus on work, and Theo was nothing but a constant distraction. I'd worked too hard to let it all slip away because of a pretty guy in worn-out gym shoes.

I walked in past Darlene's desk—empty now but for her vast collection of little beanbag animals—aaaaaand apparently, I hadn't come in quite early enough.

There he was, my distraction, my own personal shoe-pebble, sitting in *my* office, in *my* chair, with his beat-up sneakers (a clear violation of the firm dress code, by the way) on *my* desk. He was sipping his Starbucks and mousing through something on the computer.

I know! I couldn't believe it either!

Theo was like a monument to *cajones*. I was sure if I looked up audacity in the dictionary—I'd never know *what* the picture was because Theo would slam the book shut on my nose, just to spite me.

"Take your feet off my desk," I said, closing the door behind me and dropping my briefcase on a guest chair. The only thing that moved was his index finger on the mouse—which led me to the observation: "You're left-handed?"

"Yes, indeedy, Sherlock. I'd have thought you mighta noticed that yesterday when I was—" He made the appropriate, totally inappropriate gesture.

"Okay! Okay! The feet please?"

The feet on my desk—those shoes. In addition to the duct tape on the right one, I could see a good-sized hole in the bottom of the left. They were the shoes of a homeless person. And soooo tiny. I guess he was too, so it shouldn't surprise me, really. Except for that thing about guys with small feet. Theo obviously disproved that one pretty thoroughly.

And boy, I did *not* need to be thinking about Theo's hoo-ha right now.

"What size are those things anyway?" I had to ask.

"Six-and-a-halfs, and don't be throwin' shade on my shoes." They weren't a brand you'd recognize. With fake-Adidas stripes on the side, the shoes had been white and red once, but not recently. "I like my shoes."

"And you've liked them for a long, long time, I can tell."

"Funny, but when you pay thirteen bucks for a pair of shoes, they don't last as long as you'd think." He waved with the right one. "Didn't take long for this one to come unglued."

"I know just how it feels."

"And they don't come with red laces, you know. That's *my* touch. Nice, huh? It's the details that pull an outfit together, don't you think?"

"Dazzling. Now get your damned details off my desk, would you?"

"Nice chair, by the way," he said. "Much nicer than the shit-ones they give us peons."

"Difference is—you peons sit in your chairs until five o'clock, and I could be sitting in *that* chair until ten thirty tonight. That is if you ever get your skinny ass out of it. I'm dead serious—get out of my chair. I've got a ton of stuff to catch up on, after yesterday."

"Which you now totally regret."

"Now that you've decided to camp out in my office, yeah, I'm starting to."

"See?" He looked at me—man those mocking eyes of his. "This is what happens when you mess with the staff. Lines get blurred, social order breaks down, discipline crumbles, morals decay, there's no respect for authority, just a growing impertinence from a discontented rabble. I'm pretty sure it was diddling with secretaries that got ancient Rome in all that trouble."

"Diddling. Is that what you kids call it these days?"

"Among other things. And don't think I haven't noticed that so far all the diddling has been going one way. It's definitely my turn to diddle you back."

"Oh for crying—" I know I come across as pretty self-confident, but there are things I just cannot talk about. "I am *not* having this conversation in my office."

"Although my very favorite is flip-diddling."

"Stop!" Not quite thirty years old, and I could so easily become a victim of a stroke. "Theo. Seriously. You've got to give me my office back."

He reluctantly, and with a heavy sigh, put his feet down. I stepped around behind him and there on my computer screen was—my calendar.

"How did you get into my calendar?"

"I didn't tell you? I'm one of those scary hacker guys you see in the movies, no system is safe. No? I didn't mention that?"

"No."

"Well, I'm not. But your secretary Darlene keeps a list of passwords conveniently taped on the side of her CPU where it's always handy." I just groaned. "Right behind the little beanbag beaver." Of course she would. That's just what Darlene would do. "So—dinner with the parents on Sunday, I see. Can I come?"

"Just –" I stopped myself before I screamed or hit him or both. "Just—move." He finally got out of my chair. "Thank you." As he stepped past me, he let his hand glide over my backside.

*Why me?*

"Okay," I said. "Some boundaries, please. This is my workplace. *Our* workplace. Don't make me get you fired."

"You could really do that?"

"I'm golden here. They will do anything I say."

He tossed my briefcase to the floor and plopped down on the guest chair.

"That's so nice for you. I'm glad." And his feet went *back* on my desk. Grrrrrrrrr. "Of course if you *do* try to get me fired, I might not go without making a little bit of noise. After what has transpired, you know, you, me—oh, and don't forget what we did with the cream cheese! It's clearly—what's it called again?"

"I'll deny it."

"You could. One of those he-said/he-said things. Of course you weren't exactly discreet at the benefit, dragging me across the room to the exit. People saw us get into a cab together. And then there's the mysterious coincidence of our matching sick days. I have a teeny feeling that when the firm gets served with the summons and complaint—is that the right term for it?—you might not be so goddamned golden around here after all."

"You louse."

"You were just about to fire me because I had my feet on your desk, and then admitted you were willing to lie to do it, so I'm not totally sure *I'm* the louse here. Put your hackles down, big guy. I have no intention of blackmailing you. Just of teasing you a little, so chillax."

"You're still a louse."

"I suppose I am. What are you doing tonight?"

"Busy."

"There's nothing in your calendar."

Really???!!!

I closed my eyes. Deep breath.

"Listen, Theo. Don't have a mess of expectations here, okay? Look," I said, softening my tone of voice and leaning in a little, "you're clearly a great guy, fabulous really, but I've just come off this terrible—"

"I swear, I'm dying."

"What?"

"Christ-on-a-hot-cross-bun, you forget that you've already given me that break-it-to-him-gently speech before we'd even met, remember? Do *not* try to horseshit me now."

"Okay! Theo, honestly, it was great, the *whole* thing, and I don't regret it in the least, but—"

"It was just a hook-up."

"No! It wasn't just a hook-up. It was a really *hot* hook-up. It was like a twenty-four-hour hook-up, for chrissakes. For me, that's huge. But it was a one-off."

"It was hardly a one-off." He held up five fingers, and then four fingers.

"What's that supposed to mean?" I asked.

"It was five for me, four for you, but you're older, and I can make allowances."

If I threw him against the window hard enough, would it break do you think?

"I'm just saying, don't expect a repetition, okay?"

"Got it."

"No second date."

"There was no *first* date."

"We had *Star Wars.* Dinner and a movie. Sounds like a date to me."

"It was, but it was somebody else's date, remember? For me it was—what? A hand-me-down."

"Look. I'm trying to be perfectly clear here. We're *not* dating, okay?"

"You're serious."

"I'm serious."

"Just one of those things."

"Pretty much."

"No interest."

"No interest."

"Because that's not how it sounded yesterday when you were all like—" And he made gagging noises. Not like a retching cat, but like—yeah, you get it.

"For the love of God, Theo—"

"Fine. Be that way. Don't cry for *me,* Argentina."

"Look, Theo, don't be mad—"

"I'm not! You're not raining on *my* parade."

"Good. No reason we can't be friends—"

"I'm fine! The sun'll come out tomorrow. You menopausal fart."

"Glad you're not mad, then," I said, with*out* rolling my eyes even.

He got up, walked to the door, and I breathed a sigh of relief. He'd go without me killing him first.

"It's your loss, Jeffie. But anyway, Madison and I are trying to work things out."

"Really?" I tried not to laugh. "Good. I'm happy for you both. Is that what you were doing the last couple days, working things out with Madison?"

"Madison is crazy about my body, you know. I know he doesn't look like much, but in bed? Madison, he gets down there and he just *worships* my—what'd you call it—my hoo-ha?"

"Hey!"

"Too much information?" The little bastard.

"Just—just—just go, okay?"

The brief thought of that slob with Theo and his—hoo-ha—rattled me beyond words. I was repulsed and horrified. And furious. And jealous. Viciously, viciously jealous.

Theo had done that deliberately.

Yeah, I admit it. My first reaction was jealousy. I've always been easily jealous. I can be jealous about things I don't even want. Maybe I didn't want Theo as a full-time thing, but I didn't want him back with that overgrown, overripe Brooklyn slacker either. Or anybody else.

He was leaving. Should I say something?

Theo opened the door, stood in the doorway, and turned back to me.

"Enjoy the rest of your morning." The smile he gave me was half-seductive, and the other half—was straight from hell. "Later."

And he went.

Deep breath.

I tried to calm down. *Don't think about him. This is exactly the reason this guy can't be even a small part of your life. Too distracting. Huge waste of time and energy. Focus on work. Do not think about Theo. Or Madison. Fuck.*

I turned to my computer to dig through the pile of I hadn't dealt with the day before. Which I would do without thinking about Theo. No Theo. No thought of Theo. Totally Theo-free.

I started clicking through my e-mail, and—fuckaduck—nothing on the computer was working right. It took me a few tries to solve the mystery.

My mouse was backward. Of course it was.

Theo.

That little left-handed lemur had switched the buttons on my mouse, something I suppose, when you're left-handed, you know how to do; and when you're right-handed—you don't. I had no frigging clue how to change the damned thing back. I looked all over the mouse for some kind of lefty/righty switch but there wasn't one, not that I could find. I was ready to scream.

And I realized—this too Theo had done deliberately. He didn't even have to be in the same room to drive me crazy.

I didn't have time for this. I simply did not have time to ponder the sheer maliciousness of that satanic little vandal, and I most definitely didn't have time to futz around with a fucking computer mouse!!!

I'd figure it out later. I'd find time later to google the fix and until then—muddle through. Most of this was just read/delete anyway. Shouldn't be that hard.

Of course, half an hour later I was tearing my hair out, trying to remember to use my middle finger for everything—but only after my index finger had already gotten in the way and opened some frigging menu or other. Everything was taking me forever.

I had been in a bad mood when Theo left and since then that bad mood had tripped over a skate and gone crashing down a flight of stairs—what with Theo and the backward mouse, my frustration with said mouse, my frustration with said Theo about whom I was *not* going to think, remember? Theo, who had pissed me off so much I'd almost forgotten to think about fuckingfuckingfucking Madison, all fat and naked and hoo-ha worshipping—

I was interrupted in this peaceful reverie because some moron had made the mistake of knocking on my office door.

"Yes!" I yelled.

The door pushed open a few inches.

"*¡Hola!*" It was the hottie from IT, the guy from the cafeteria. "Wassup?" he wanted to know, and he came in a step.

Funny, just a few days ago I'd have been all smiles for this guy, and now I'd be all smiles throwing him down an elevator shaft.

"You need some help?" He gestured to the computer.

"Why?" I spat it out like an accusation.

He held up his hands in surrender.

"Hey, I'm only here because Theo said your mouse got switched around to left-handed and you didn't know how to change it back. Need help or no?"

"Theo said."

"He did," said Enrique. "So?" He looked at me like he was expecting something. It took me a second, and then I hopped up to get out of his way.

"Have at it."

The hottie sat down and started minimizing stuff I had open, most of which I'd opened by accident because of that damned mouse and that damned Theo.

Theo.

And a dark, warty, venomous thought came slithering into my brain.

"So—like—when did you talk to Theo?"

"Just now," he said casually. "I check in on him every morning, make sure he's doing okay."

"Just part of your job, right?" I asked, all friendly, even as I was thinking of ways I might get this scumbag fired.

"Yeah. That and," at this point he paused in his work to look over his shoulder at me with a roguish smile, "just between you and me, that kid is hot."

"Hadn't noticed."

*Okay,* I reminded myself. *I* had made the decision that I didn't want anything steady with Theo, so why did I care? Even if this guy was so obviously a total player—it was Theo's problem, it had absolutely nothing to do with me. There was no need for me to twist myself into a knot over this, if Theo wanted to do...whatever.

Enrique winked at me. Whoever thought winking was sexy? It's not. It's just slimy.

"Cute little Theo just needs a little convincing," he assured me. "He'll come 'round."

Enrique was between me and the letter opener or things might have gone very differently.

"Yeah? Think he's all that into you, do you?"

"You know I didn't at first, but dude—check this out!" This grinning hormone case pushed up his sleeve to show me the sexy underside of his sexy forearm. There, some twerp—and you didn't have to work too hard to figure out who, because the twerp had put his twerpy little name right there in big block letters—some twerp had written something along the sinews of Mr. Testosterone's beautifully developed arm.

"Theo" it said. Followed by a cell phone number.

The hot Latino underscored the significance of this revelation by bouncing his eyebrows at me a couple times. Enrique should have been able to *hear* my teeth grinding.

"Are you—*done* yet?" I asked, still thinking about that letter opener.

"Oh, yeah, sorry. It's taking me a little longer than it should because— you know—the mouse is messed up."

"Hadn't noticed."

"Finished." And with that, the guy, whom I suddenly hated way more than his life was worth, stood up and went to the door. "I told Theo to put his number in my phone, but he insisted on writing on my arm, all old school like that."

"Almost like a billboard."

"I know, right? He was pretty cute about it, too. Couldn't stop giggling the whole time."

"I'll bet."

"Open?" he asked as he stood in the door.

"Closed. Definitely closed."

*"¡Hasta la vista!"*

I stared at the closed door.

"Not if I *vista* you first."

I sat down at my desk to ponder what had just happened.

Theo.

Deep breath. And again. And again.

I wasn't going to think about Theo today, remember? And what had I done so far? And what was I going to do for the rest of the day?

I stared at my screen full of e-mails.

I stared at my mouse that that nice Enrique had just fixed for me. I was clenching my teeth 'til my head hurt. Words—and images—floated through my head.

Theo. Enrique. Madison. Worshipping. Diddling.

Flip-diddling.

I reached down with one hand and calmly untied my right shoelace. I pulled the shoe off, held it up by the toe and—*with three good thwacks*—bits of computer mouse were flying in all directions.

A little later, both shoes on, I passed my secretary's desk on my way out.

"Darlene," I said. "Call IT and tell them I need a new mouse. Something happened to mine."

# Chapter 30
## One More Stab at a Blind Date

*THEO*

I'm not sure how much I'm willing to admit to, but I'll go this far: I was maybe a teensy bit more put out by Jeff's dismissing me—correction: his attempt at dismissing me, his pathetic and utterly ineffectual attempt at dismissing me—this morning, than I may have immediately let on. Hence that little telegram I sent him by way of poor Enrique.

Now it was evening, I found myself with nothing to do. Footloose and fancy free. And those loose feet found themselves fancying a walk.

Across Central Park.

You know what happens if you're on the Upper West Side, and you walk across Central Park long enough? You get to the Upper *East* Side. And the next thing you know, you're standing in front of Jeff Bornic's building. Or, more accurately, across the street from it anyway, so you can get a better look.

Jeff had said he was busy. Too busy for me. Fine. Somebody *else* might have been daunted by that. To me, it just meant that if I interrupted him, it would be even *more* irritating.

Even so, I wasn't completely sure what I was going to do. I could ring the bell—but there actually *was* no bell, just the weaselly doorman. Okay, I could go ask the weasel to interrupt his illicit cigarette to call upstairs. I could just imagine how that would go.

Weasel: "Your name, sir?"

Me: "Theo McPherson."

Weasel (speaking into the phone—for some reason, in my imagination, the weasel has an accent straight out of *My Fair Lady*): There's someone here to see you, sir. Claims his name is Theo McPherson." (He listens, then he hangs up.) "Mr. Bornic says he never heard of you, and that I should, to use his words, 'throw the baggage out.'" (That's actually a *line* from *My Fair Lady*. At this point, the Weasel starts to get up, scraping his chair loudly on the terrazzo.)

Okay, so forget that plan.

I could give him a fake name.

Seymour Wieners.

Warren Piece—I always thought that would be a great porn-star name if I were ever going to be a porn star. I was so disappointed when I found out a porn star had actually used it.

Helena Handbasket?

It was almost worth it just to hear the weasel say one of those names on the phone. But Jeff would know right away it was me. Same result.

If this were TV, I'd create a diversion, slip past the weasel and knock on Jeff's door, thereby successfully interrupting his no-doubt well-planned evening, whatever it was. As I was calculating the possibilities of success (slim) with this diversion scheme with no accomplice to do the actual diverting—I saw something that made me stop, mid-scheming.

He was about six feet tall, dark curls, with blue eyes—always a killer combination—and he was totally built. Not a full-on body builder, but super fit and bulgy in a really sexy way. He was either wearing a very tight blue polo shirt or he had one painted on. With a perfect lock of black hair pulled artfully down onto his forehead. One of *those* guys.

Please understand, this little sex-puppy didn't catch my eye because I was thinking I wanted to git me summa *that*. Nosiree, he caught my eye because he looked exactly like the kind of sex-puppy who might catch the eye of a certain douchebag lawyer.

I hadn't really tried to imagine what Jeff would be doing that he was going to be too busy to see me, but it definitely hadn't occurred to me that he'd be busy doing some gym-bunny pick-up.

Then I thought to myself—*be fair. This guy could be going anywhere, he could even live here, you never know*. It didn't necessarily mean anything. I didn't even know if Jeff was home. He'd said he was busy, he was probably out somewhere, not waiting at home for this hot gayboy. The city was full of hot gayboys. I shouldn't jump to any conclusions about this particular hot gayboy.

And then this particular hot gayboy looked at his phone. I would have bet my Steve Sondheim autograph that the little skankster was double-checking the address. In his Grindr app, I was sure. The guy had "internet hook-up" stamped on his gorgeous forehead, and I was pretty certain I knew exactly where the guy was going.

As he headed for the door, I scrambled across the street to get in not too far behind him—and not too close either. He stopped at the weasel's desk just as I stepped inside.

"Jeffrey in 24H please." I knew it. IknewitIknewitIknewit. Jeff Bornic: Attorney at law and part-time whore-ball. He was too busy to see me, because he was going to be too busy banging *that*.

Fine.

He'd made it clear we weren't going steady—who wanted that anyway? So fine!

Calm, easygoing, laid-back guy that I am, you can imagine just how well I was taking this.

"Ya' name?" the weasel asked the gym-slut. In reality, the weasel's accent was more Passaic than Mayfair.

"Name's Chip," he said.

Of course it was. And I was Warren Piece.

My first impulse was to throw something. Starting with Chip. But I stopped myself.

The weasel called upstairs, then he waved Chip in, and Chip strolled off toward the elevator bank.

I still didn't have a plan, but I went in after him anyway. I'd wing it.

"Hey, how's it goin'?" I waved to my old buddy the Weasel-Boy as I strode past.

"Hey! Whehja' think *yer* goin'?" he yelled after me.

"I'm with Chip," I called back.

Of course I had caught the attention of my new best friend, Chip-Chip the Chelsea Boy. As we waited for the elevator, he looked me up, he looked me down, he even leaned back a little to check out the rear elevation. Subtle, dude, real subtle.

He smiled, slyly.

"Jeffrey didn't say anything about a three-way, but I'm down for anything." He smiled. "*Or*," he added, lowering his voice seductively, "if you just wanna get outta here, I'm sure we could have a good time, just us. You're *way* hotter than Jeff's picture." Ding, the elevator doors opened, and two nattering old ladies stepped out past us. Chip waited until they were gone before he added, as further inducement, "I go cuh-razy for redheads."

"I bet you do," I flirted back. "I'm gonna pass this time, but c'mon up." He followed me into the elevator. "Jeff and I hooked up not that long ago. And just so's you know, that picture he's using? Ten years old, at least. Just sayin'." The elevator door had closed. "I'm only here to drop something off." I reached into my pocket and pulled out the tube of Tommy's moisturizer. "I just got this stuff from the drugstore. The old guy said to shampoo down there really well with this—and wash *all* the bedding in *hot*—and that should take care of 'em." The elevator door opened and I stepped out.

"You're kidding me," he said, but he didn't follow me.

"You ever had this problem?" I asked, shoving one hand into my jeans to scratch my pubes for effect.

The effect was effective.

His index finger jabbed frantically at the button for the lobby until the doors started to close on our Chip. I gave him a little wave.

"Bye, Felicia."

And I whistled a happy tune as I went down the hall to Jeff's door, which opened right about then.

"Hey, sexy," I said, and pushed in past him.

"What the—" He leaned out to look down the hall. "Theo, you can't stay. I'm expecting somebody."

"You're looking for Chip?"

"How do you…?" he said turning back to me.

"We met in the elevator. Nice guy, and hot? Hoo-*ee*!!!" I waved my right hand—bent at the wrist, the way guys do when someone is hot, don't ask me why.

I wandered into Jeff's apartment, now with fewer drop cloths—and I carefully skirted the gigantic hole in the floor for the stairs. "But the old Chipster must have suddenly remembered another appointment." I opened the fridge, and helped myself to a bottle of water. "Or maybe Chip got a better offer, I don't know." I started flipping through Jeff's envelopes and catalogs. "Man, you get a *lot* of bills. Anyway, the guy seemed a little feckless to me. I should tell you, he even hit on *me* in the elevator. Complete absence of feck."

"What are you talking about?"

"Chip! Keep up!" Poor guy. "Jeff, you look downright discombobulated. Do they say that out here? We say that in Iowa anyway. Discombobulated." Jeff stuck his head back out into the hallway again, hoping. "In the end," I said, calling him back, "and what a very nice end it was! I just wanted to reach out and—well, anyway. In the end, he simply skedaddled."

"Just like that."

"Just like that. Good-bye, Mr. Chip."

I flopped down on Jeff's couch and set the water bottle down on the coffee table, just so I could watch Jeff scramble for a coaster. I picked up the remote control and turned on the TV. I was a little surprised by what the TV was paused on.

"Seriously? *Dancing with the Stars*?"

"I wasn't watching that."

"Yeah. Right. Then you won't mind if I—" I started flipping through channels.

"You messed up my date."

"Ah, c'mon. Calling a Grindr hook-up a date? Get real—let's call a spade a damned shovel and get on with it."

"You really chased him off?"

I interrupted my channel-flipping to turn to him with a face dripping with wronged astonishment.

"How *could* you think this was somehow *my* fault? Really. I didn't do a thing!"

"It's just a coincidence, I suppose, that you turn up and my—whatever—disappears? Hardly."

"It's possible."

"Theo, everything, absolutely everything that's wrong in my life these days, can be traced in a direct line back to you."

"Wow. Really?"

"Really."

"Cool!"

"And what happened to Edwardo, or Alejandro or—"

"Enrique?"

"Whatever."

"I don't know. Guy's been calling me all day for some reason."

"Maybe because you tattooed your name and number on his arm in letters three feet high."

"Oh, yeah, I did, didn't I. Dja like that?"

"What are you doing here?"

"Me? I just came by to give you this," and I tossed him the tube from Tommy. "Moisturizer. Tommy swears by it, and he insists it's never too soon to start, although in your case..." and I made a little face. "Awesome flat screen by the way, much nicer than Rebecca's. Anyway, those crinkles around the eyes give you character *now* maybe, but in a couple years you've got character like Maggie Smith, and you don't want *that*." I went back to flipping channels. "Did you know that Robert Redford used to be hot? Hard to imagine."

"I don't need moisturizer!"

"At least I *think* it's moisturizer. Yeah, I'm sure that's what it is. Chip seemed to have the silly idea it had something to do with body lice, but whatever put *that* crazy notion into his head, I'll never know."

I gave him my most cherubic smile, which people tell me is pretty goddamned cherubic.

"If you weren't so puny—"

"Hey! I'm short. I am not small. I am not little. I am not— Oh, fantastic! Found it!"

"What?"

"The old movie channel. And look, it's a silent! I love silent movies, don't you?" I plopped my feet up on the coffee table. "Is that Mary Astor? So young!"

I can't tell you how awesome it was to know that I had this condescending, conceited, whore-chasing lawyer-boy totally knocked off balance. He stood there looking down at me for a couple seconds trying to figure out what to do with me, before he finally gave up and dropped on the couch next to me in surrender.

"You—you really chased off my date?"

"Hook-up."

"Why?"

"Not sure, but—and I'm not gonna lie—it was strangely very satisfying. Do you have any popcorn? Microwave is fine."

"I could just smack you, you know."

"Of course you could probably find a replacement, but honestly at your age? Maybe you should give it a rest. And just out of curiosity, how much does a guy like Chip charge? I mean, for the—you know—the whole shebang? Or is it hebang in this case?"

"I'm not— He's not— Why you little—"

"Anyway, save your money, and your back. After the exertions of the last couple days, you're lucky you didn't pull something. No cracks, please." I reached over and smoothed out the crow's feet on his left eye with my thumb. "Oooh, speaking of cracks." I tsked my tongue a couple times. "*Definitely* not too soon for the moisturizer." I pinched his cheek and he yanked his head away.

I turned back and watched Mary A. getting downright girlish with John Barrymore.

He glanced at the screen.

"I don't even like *black* and *white* movies, let alone silents."

"Reading skills not up to it?"

"I should just—"

"Yeah, but you won't."

And then there was a distinct shift in gears. He scooched a little closer.

"You are so bad, you know that?"

I swear I could *hear* his boner starting up. I turned from the TV to him.

"Hey," I said gently, touching his jaw with one hand, looking deeply into his eyes. "You're clearly a great guy, fabulous really—"

"You bastard," and he pulled away.

"—but don't have a bunch of expectations, okay?"

"Fucker."

"Just don't expect a repetition. And besides."

"Besides?"

"I'll bet *anything* you use a moisturizer already, don't you. I bet your medicine cabinet is stuffed with skin-care crap."

His face. He went from frustrated to surprised to a half-laugh and he looked at me a long time. I always had the idea he was trying to figure something out. Right at that moment I was pretty sure he was trying to figure out if he should shove me down the garbage chute, or try again.

"Hey, Theo?" he purred, his voice all low and seductive-like. He was obviously taking the second option.

"Yeah?"

"You *do* sort of owe me, after all." He was moving in again.

"Do I?" I purred back. We were getting closer. "You think I should make it up to you?"

"Uh-huh," he said, meaning yes.

"Because I've been bad?" I moved forward and brushed his lips with mine.

"So bad."

"Am I?" Another brush with the lips.

"Uh-huh."

"Know what else I am?" I said, and I leaned in and oh-so gently took his lower lip between my teeth for a second, before I pulled away.

"What?" he said, hoarse.

I answered, still all soft and kittenish.

"I'm nobody's fucking second choice." And I hopped up from the couch. "I'm gonna run," I said, all perky. In my head I was thinking, *you poor bastard, you've been a good two beats behind since I walked in here.* I headed to the door, stopped and turned back. There he sat, mouth open. His khakis looked like the circus was in town. *What a sap.* I gestured to the TV screen, where Barrymore was giving us his profile for all he was worth. "Tell me how it ends."

I let the door pull itself closed behind me.

And if anybody saw me skipping down the hall toward the elevator—I wouldn't be a bit surprised.

# Chapter 31
## Pound Puppies

*JEFFREY*

Late morning on a Saturday. If I were smart, I'd be in the office, racking up the billable hours. Never enough billable hours in the day. But instead, I was here. At an animal shelter with a hundred and thirty-seven barking dogs in a building made of cement blocks. The noise was seriously unbelievable. Ten minutes of this and I'd be running for the exit.

I was at the animal shelter where Theo volunteered. I figured he'd been blindsiding me for a while now. It was my turn to ambush *him* for a change, throw *him* off balance and see how he liked it. So I wandered, adoption brochure in hand, through room after room of kennels—first cats and then dogs—with a bunch of other people. The dogs all seemed to have something to say about the whole thing.

As I came into the second room full of dogs, I saw him. Not who you're thinking. There, sticking out of a dog cage, was a skinny little ass in a pair of skinny little black jeans.

"Swithin?"

He backed out of the cage carefully, a soapy sponge in hand, straightened up and turned.

"Hey!" He was as surprised as I was.

"Hey yourself. What are *you* doing here?"

"I was about to say the same thing. I volunteer with Theo. He didn't tell you?"

"No, he hadn't mentioned it, but we haven't really talked about" and I gestured around me "this."

"I'm just like him. I want a dog, but I can't really have one at this point in my life, so I come here to play with *these* dogs."

"Looks like fun," I said, pointing to the sponge. There was still something brown clinging to it.

"Oh—yeah," he said, remembering the sponge, and he tossed it at a bucket of soapy water. "I need to finish that, too. Don't let me forget. Theo know you're coming?"

"No, it was sort of—spontaneous."

"I think he's just in the next kennel," and he pointed to an open doorway to the next room.

"Thanks. Nice to see you."

"Nice to see you not in a suit—you look good," he said, fishing the sponge out of the bucket.

When I came into the next big kennel room, there was Theo in the middle of some milling visitors. He and a woman were squatting down to a dog whose neck the woman was scratching. I stepped back a little. I wanted to watch him for a second. Could this woman really be thinking about adopting that dog?

The dog in question, I have to tell you, was no prize winner. Almost no hair, ribs sticking out, and large purplish spots on its skin. And at just that moment, this hideous animal went into a squat and took a truly stupendous piss. Like gallons.

Nice doggy.

Both the woman and Theo sprang up—but the piss-pond had already flooded as far as Theo's shoes and he was now tracking it on the concrete floor.

I thought of that hole in the bottom of Theo's sneaker—ewwwwww!!!

I waited. What would little Theo do? Theo, the poster-boy for bad tempers. Theo, whose bark was so nasty, he didn't *have* to bite. From my experience with Roger's Scottish terrier, I'd figured out that sarcasm didn't really work on dogs—lord knows I'd tried—but I certainly expected to hear an explosion of ironic invective to be heaped upon this poor beast.

Like so much in my life lately, in this I was disappointed.

Theo just went to a closet—and came back wheeling a janitor's bucket and a mop, and set to work, patiently cleaning it up, all the while still trying to sell this poor woman on the virtues of this complete loser of a dog.

*N.b.,* I just used the words 'Theo' and 'patiently' in a sentence, which I would have never thought possible.

"She's generally pretty house-broken, but she's been in a cage all morning, and so as soon as she came out, whoosh, Johnstown. You really shouldn't hold it against her. It's my fault for not taking her out to the exercise pen right away. I'll be right back."

He wheeled the bucket and mop away.

When he came back, he went straight down to the little tail-wagging monster, scratched the thing around the ears with both hands, and scrunched his face while this—creature—went to town, licking, licking.

"Ooooooooooooh, yes," he said cooing between the licks in the most ridiculous baby-talk voice, "who's the prettiest girl? Hmm? That's you! That's you!" This of course spurred the mutt into even more frantic licking.

Was this really Theo, the Snark King of the Great Middle West? Or was this just his job? Maybe he was working on a commission? I didn't know, but he seemed dead-set on selling this poor dupe this grotesque animal. It was, at best, ethically questionable—and at worst, fraud. Roger's Scottish terrier Haggis had annoyed me no end, but at least that dog *looked* sharp. This little atrocity on a leash was just an embarrassment.

"If you want to take Clarice out into the exercise yard for a bit, you guys can get to know each other a little. Maybe she wants to pee some more—although hard to imagine. I'll be around if you have any questions." And he turned away from the pair—who seemed pretty smitten with each other—and he saw me.

"Heyyyyyyyy," he said smiling. "What the hell?"

"I just happened to be in the neighborhood, thought I might pick up a dog, maybe two."

"Yeah, we don't do adoptions like that, sorry. But I'll be happy to show you some candidates that might suit you."

"I can't have *that* one," I gestured in the direction of the dog he'd just sent out into the yard. "The whizzing wonder? He's so pretty!"

"I think *she* may be going to her new home today. Isn't that fantastic?"

"Really?"

"I admit she's not the prettiest, but she looks much better than she did when she came in. She's gaining weight, and she's on some drugs for the skin thing, and her coat will come back in full in a few weeks. *And* she's so sweet. That's why it would be awesome if she found a forever home today."

"I'm not really here to adopt."

"I figured. Why *are* you here exactly?"

"Beats me. I just wanted to see...you know...hey, you get a lunch break?"

"Are you asking me out? Like on a date? Because you shouldn't really have a lot of expectations—"

"—expectations, yeah yeah, silly me."

"Anyway, I just came back from my break. Sorry."

"Next time."

"I'd suggest tomorrow, but you have dinner with your parents."

Gotta say one thing for Theo. He certainly didn't make it easy.

"I changed my password!"

"You think I don't know that?"

"Hey—be nice to me. It's my birth week."

"I know that, too."

"There's a party."

"Old news."

"Wanna come?"

"Well, you hadn't invited me, and you know how I *am*. I figured—"

"—you were just going to show up anyway."

"Absolutely. And I intended to be very embarrassing."

"Which you're so good at."

"I try, I *do* try. I hadn't quite decided, but I was thinking I might just ring the bell and tell them I was the hired stripper, see where that gets me."

"Well, I'm inviting you, so now you can't crash. And I'd much prefer it if you didn't strip for my friends."

"Really?"

"Really."

"Doesn't mean I won't behave badly."

"Too bad about lunch."

"Ask me again sometime. I enjoyed saying 'no.'" He grinned at me with that impish smile he can do. In my annoyance with him, I generally forgot how pretty he was, but he was. And a good thing too, or someone would have killed him long ago.

"Theo, can I ask you something kind of personal?"

"Mayyyyy-be."

"Are you standing there with a sock soaked in dog piddle?"

He seemed to think about it and looked down at his miserable shoes, wiggling his toes in them.

"On the advice of counsel..." Not sure how long we stood there smiling at each other before—

"Hey Theo!" It was Swithin coming in from the other kennel room. "Did you just get a text from Jessica? She says LCT is looking for an office assistant."

"LCT?" I said. Not a firm I'd ever heard of.

"Lincoln Center Theatre," Theo explained. "Seriously?" He was digging his phone out of his pocket. "Oh my God!"

"You said the people are horrible where you work," said Swithin.

"The pits," Theo agreed.

"Hey!"

"Oh shit, you work there too?" asked Swithin

"I've made my point," said Theo.

"Isn't he just the sweetest thing?" I appealed to Swithin.

"Anyway, Theo," said Swithin, holding up his phone. "You should call them. You can actually do word processing and stuff. Aside from *Finale,* my only computer skill is Facebook."

"You're forgetting *Call of Duty.*"

"True that. Maybe I should put that on my résumé? Anyway, bro. Call them."

"Yeah—you got this while I step outside?"

"Sure."

"Hey." I stopped him before he abandoned me. "I'm going to go. Let me know how it—you know. And, you know—what is it you guys say? Break a leg?"

"Thanks."

Wow—he smiled at me, and it wasn't snarky at all.

"I'll talk to you later then," I said.

"Sure."

And I did the weirdest, totally dumb thing.

Without thinking, I leaned down and I kissed him good-bye. On the lips, but really quick. Nothing going on, no tongues, no smooching or anything, just a quick, chaste, good-bye kiss.

Like you'd kiss your boyfriend.

That's what it felt like. A casual, thoughtless kiss you can give somebody when you're together. Not the kind of kiss you give somebody when you're *not* together.

And we, according to me anyway, weren't even dating.

Were we?

Theo seemed a bit surprised by it too.

So was Swithin. First time I'd ever seen him actually push his hair back out of his face.

"I'm sorry," I said. "I don't know why I did that."

"It's—it's okay," said Theo.

"Dude," said Swithin, smiling. "Never apologize. Not for that."

He probably was right.

"I'll let you go. I'm sure you've got somebody more important to mop up after."

# Chapter 32
## Tell Me On a Sunday, Please

*THEO*

I was in the middle of Rebecca's living room, working at the keyboard, as always. I had headphones on, but I was mostly staring at a legal pad. The tune was in my head. See, I had these two lines –

> *You don't have to hold my hand—*
> *I don't believe in broken hearts.*

And I really liked them. I thought that would be a pretty kick-ass way to end a song for this girl who doesn't want sympathy. But if those lines were going at the end, they had to rhyme with the line that came before the couplet. Best effort so far:

> *Please tell me when your train departs.*
> *You don't have to…etc.*

Not particularly good.
Or there was:

> *How long before the dancing starts?*

Dicks don't get much limper than that. Or pick one of these lovelies —

> *This marzipan is off the charts.*

*The actors hardly knew their parts.*
*Please bring me lots of lemon tarts.*
*Rebecca's Spock grip really smarts.*

These are but a small sample of the excrescent lines that littered my legal pad, none of which was remotely usable or anything you could shoehorn into a song about broken hearts. That's how my afternoon went until I found myself actually writing down the line –

*What makes you think I give two farts?*

At that point I decided that I was maybe done for the day.

But even before this, it had been a weird day. I'd spent a good chunk of it with Madison of all people, and now, well, I just couldn't concentrate.

It was like this. I had carefully and rationally turned over the issue in my head—did I or did I not want something with Madison? All indicators pointed to one outcome—a great whopping Not.

You will be asking yourself—*what took him so long*? Well, ya got me there. I can only say that sometimes I'm slow.

The most notable among all those indicators was that even the boring, stuffed-shirt lawyer, whether he had any interest in anything or not, had still been much more fun (and was way better looking) than the creative, artistic type in the form of Madison. In fact it occurred to me that the most fun I'd ever had with Madison was lately, writing him bitchy texts. *That* had amused me no end.

So. Since he was still occasionally bugging me to get together, I suggested Madison train down from ye olde Goodspeed and meet me for lunch. Which he did, since they (meaning his show) had Sunday off.

"So, Mads, how's the show going?" I asked because, after all, I'm the nice one.

"Oh God."

"That good?"

We were in a noisy little place on the Upper West.

But, as I said, it was Sunday, and lunch on Sunday in Manhattan meant—brunch. I hate brunch. I hate brunch, and I hate noisy Manhattan restaurants that serve brunch, with their tables shoved impossibly close together so you're practically eating your eggs Benedict with complete strangers.

Not that I would ever order anything as chi-chi as eggs Benedict, even if Mads was paying. And Mads was definitely paying.

Another observation: Madison was a devoted brunch eater. One more reason to dump him. Clearly the kindest thing to do would be to set him free to wander happily among his own kind.

And, as mentioned, this brunch place was really noisy, so everyone had to talk really loud, making it even noisier. If that weren't enough, somewhere under all those decibels they actually had some kind of background music playing, so every now and then, when there was an accidental moment less loud than the others, you could catch a bar or two of eighties pop.

Wake me up before you go-go. Not exactly a Sondheim lyric.

So why had I agreed to this little *tête-à-tête* over much-despised brunch in a much-despised brunch-place? Because I knew if I dumped old Mads in a text—which was my first thought—I'd feel rotten about it. Seemed sort of a gutless way of avoiding something unpleasant.

I will tell you that I had actually toyed with a particularly brilliant solution to the whole problem wrapped up in one neat text message.

*Hey Mads, wassup.*

*Say, I was wondering — if you were to going to get dumped, purely hypothetically of course, how would you (hypothetically) like it to happen?*

*Face to face?* ☐

*By phone?* ☐

*Text?* ☐

*E-mail?* ☐

*Other (specify) _____?* ☐

*(Pick one.)*

A thing of beauty, isn't it? Seemed to me that that would pretty much just take care of the whole deal. I'd be spared the guilt of having broken up with somebody in a text because technically I hadn't—and yet Mads would still get the important have-a-nice-life subtext. Madison wouldn't have to go through the hassle of the change-trains-in-New-Haven exercise (twice). And I wouldn't have to sit through frigging brunch.

All that with one seemingly guileless text. It was almost elegant in its simplicity.

But it still seemed a bit craven, so I had agreed and here I was. Brunch had been Madison's idea. I had acquiesced, since I felt bad that I was making him take a two-hour train ride in anticipation, no doubt, of a grand reconciliation, complete with wild and raucous make-up sex—and the only thing the poor son of a bitch was going to get were some *huevos rancheros* and a big fat kiss-off.

So in the name of being a stand-up guy and doing the right thing, I found myself at a deuce (that's restaurant lingo for a table for two) squished between two other deuces, and since I'm left-handed, I was literally rubbing elbows.

Specifically, I was literally rubbing elbows with Billy—thirty-something and sort of swish. He was trying to go gluten-free but was clearly not happy with his quinoa French toast.

You thought I was exaggerating about how close the tables were, didn't you. And seriously, who *would* be happy with quinoa French toast???

Opposite him was—get this—William. How does that happen? Billy and William? If I met a guy named Theobald or even Theodor, I don't care how hot he was, I'd spit in his eye and be so out of there.

Anyway, William was maybe a bit older, and very straight-acting.

I looked at Madison, gestured discreetly to the guys, pointed at my ring finger, and then looked back toward the pair. They sported matching goatees—and wedding rings.

"It's the little things you do together," I said. *That's* Sondheim.

And of course Madison fed the next line of the song right back to me. See, that was the thing with Madison. We had musical theatre in common, and he knew so much more than I did because he grew up out here, and until two years ago I was still out in Iowa stepping over cow pies. I had so much catching up to do. And that was the bond we had. I had thought, anyway. But now...?

On my *right* was a middle-aged woman in an expensive suit that was just the teensiest bit snug. Her daughter Joan was getting married to John in June, and yes, I was already working on a song in my head. That was much too good to waste.

Judging from the fit of her suit, and the egg white omelet she'd ordered, I guessed she was shooting to lose a few ell-bees before the happy event.

Opposite her, next to Mads, was Louisa, another middle-aged woman in another expensive suit. Thin, and ramrod straight.

The ladies seemed to be headed to a matinee, I wasn't sure what. Perhaps a piece of Mahler's.

Brunch. Unlike everyone else in my corner of the sky, I was not eating light. Brunch had been Madison's bright idea, and, dumped or not, he was going to pay for his bright idea, so I was having everything—eggs, toast, sausage, two orders of bacon, another kind of sausage—everything.

But I noticed there was a problem. No ketchup.

I had a mountain of fried potatoes, and no ketchup. There, on the table on my left, smack between William and Billy—a bottle of the precious stuff, beckoning, and going to waste. Obviously nobody wanted ketchup on quinoa French toast.

"Excuse me, William?" I said, with a quick, apologetic smile to Billy for the intrusion. William was, of course, totally surprised.

See, there's a rule about these things. Because New York is so impossibly crowded, you have to go through your day pretending that none of the other people actually exist. Because otherwise you'd go crazy. If you acknowledged the people who were pressed up against you from all sides on a rush-hour subway ride—the woman whose boobs were squished against your shoulder, or the guy whose junk was riding on your left hip—it would be too much. All the faces around you, the snatches of conversations—they belong to human beings, sure, but if you took the time to recognize that, you'd blow your brains out before nightfall.

People who are sitting at a table separated from yours by two inches? They fall into the category of the nonexistent. That was the rule, part of the New York social contract. And I had just reached across that unseen but sacred barrier and shattered it.

So naturally William was surprised.

"I'm—sorry?"

"It is William, right?" I said. "Theo," I introduced myself and smiled. "Are you guys through with the ketchup?" Of course I could have reached right over and snagged the bottle, but my mom raised me better.

"Oh. Sure."

"Thanks."

William and Billy exchanged looks as I reached and got the stuff.

"So, tell me about your show, Mads," I said, thumping the bottom of the ketchup bottle.

"Well, we tried several things Tanner's way, but it wasn't always working out, and Jason—he's playing Jack—he started to get seriously pissed because Allison's part kept growing and his kept shrinking, you know, Tanner's ideas, and—"

"Excuse me, Louisa?" I interrupted the woes of my soon-to-be ex-boyfriend to address the other table.

"I beg your pardon?"

"I'm sorry, I'm Theo."

"Young man, if you're selling something or collecting for a charity or some religion, I'm not—"

"Oh hell, no," I smiled. "I was just wondering if either of you would like some ketchup?" I turned from one to the other.

"No, thank you," said Louisa, clearly the alpha-dog of her table. She made it pretty clear where she stood on ketchup, not to mention how she felt about reckless lunatics who went around violating the laws regulating personal space.

"Might perk up those egg whites," I said of Joan's mom's omelet, fomenting a small rebellion at the next table. "No fat in ketchup, I don't think."

"You know, it couldn't hurt," said Joan's mom, taking the bottle from me. She finally found the courage to look back to Louisa. "At least they would taste like *some*-thing! Thank you." This last was addressed very quietly to me.

"Don't mention it. It actually belongs to William over there," I gestured, and William of course stopped mid-sentence hearing his name. "William and Billy," I started the introductions. Various small hi's were exchanged here and there, embarrassed nods, tiny waves, not to mention wide-eyed looks. "Louisa," I continued. "And—I'm sorry, but I..." I couldn't really introduce her as Joan's mom, could I?

"Fern," said Joan's mom. Did she really say "Fern"? Fern. The woman's name was Fern. Coolest name *ever*.

"Theo and Madison," I finished up. More nods, and a how-do-you-do from Fern.

Madison had watched this little exchange first with mild horror, like any New Yorker would, and then with an impatient annoyance. One of those stupid Theo things.

Of course from his point of view, here it was: The total breakdown of civilization was happening right before his bloodshot eyes. The only possible result was chaos. And it was all my fault.

Wanna know a secret? I *adore* chaos.

"Well. You were totally right about Tanner, by the way," said Madison.

"What? That you had the hots for him?"

"I didn't have the hots for him."

"Who are you kidding? That was all you talked about!"

"He's directing my show! His name's going to come up!"

"You had a raging hard-on for the guy."

Louisa glanced at me and cleared her throat in such a way to make it clear that she didn't approve. Okay, I was the one who'd torn the rift in the fabric of time and space. In return, I was going to have to behave or get throats cleared at me. The price I'd have to pay. Fine.

"My God, Theo, " Madison sputtered. "You are such a—I didn't— I don't—"

"I apologize for the language," I appealed to Louisa directly, "but consider this. I went all the way up to Chester, Connecticut—"

"That's such a lovely town," said Joan's mom, hereinafter Fern. "Some wonderful antique shops in Chester."

"I bet you're right, but I wouldn't know because, after going all the way up there, to see my boyfriend—"

"I have a new musical in development up there, and I was extremely busy," Madison defended himself.

"You do?" asked Louisa, intrigued.

"That's right. He has a musical up there, isn't that great?"

"How lovely for you," said Fern.

"You're in the theatre?" It was time for Billy to charge in. "What do you do?"

"I write, usually book and lyrics."

"Have you done anything we might have seen?"

"I had *Time Flies* at Manhattan Theatre Club a couple years ago."

"Five years ago." Just to be clear, I figured.

"Funny how time flies," said Madison, giving me the dirtiest dirty look.

"The title sounds familiar," said Louisa.

"Sorry, I missed that one," Billy apologized.

"There's just no end to the people who missed that one," I pointed out. And then I added, because I knew it would totally irk Madison—"If you ever want a laugh, google *New York Magazine*'s review of that show. Unbelievably mean." Not that I would ever gloat over somebody's bad review or anything. Much.

"*Time Flies*," mused Fern. "Which one was that again, Louisa?" One by one, each member of the quartet had shifted in their chairs so they could talk to us a little more easily.

"It was about this time traveler—" Madison explained.

"The time travel show! We saw that, you remember, Fern?"

"We did, didn't we! *Time Flies!* Oh, I had such a hard time following that one." Poor Fern.

"Ignore her," said Louisa. "I really liked that show!"

"You should see what *New York Magazine*—"

*"And* a little before that" Madison really hated hearing about *New York Magazine*—"I did just the book, not the lyrics, for *Mutant Prom Queen Bingo.*"

"You wrote that? In that little dive over on Ninth Avenue?" This time it was Billy. "That show was a scream!"

"Did I see that?" William wanted to know.

"Sorry, doll. Before your time."

"Oh. So you saw that with—"

"Don't start. There is no need to speak ill of the dead."

"Oh!" said Fern. "Was your former partner..."

"Tragically struck down by a double-decker bus full of boy scouts? Sadly, no. But he's as good as dead to me, so it's quite unnecessary for certain people to—"

"I didn't say a word," said William, holding his hands in the air as proof of his innocence.

*"Mutant Prom Queen* was a scream, that's all I'm saying." Billy wanted to make clear to Madison. "Just a scream."

"Thanks."

"When she came out with that thing on her head, thought I'd die, I swear to heaven, thought I'd die."

"Madison didn't actually write the hat," I felt compelled to make clear. Let's give credit.

"You know what I mean. The show was a scream!"

"Thanks! It's nice to hear that."

Having been repeatedly reassured that this show from a bygone era had been nothing short of a scream—Madison was *now* digging the great fissure that I'd slashed in the whole personal-space dress code, which I was starting to regret having done.

I mean, honestly, what are the odds you strike up a conversation with total strangers, even at brunch on the Upper West Side, and you find yourself in the middle of some bizarre coven of Madison fan-girls.

Just you wait, Henry Higgins. I would put a stop to this.

I was about to make very clear to them just what a total douche-nozzle their new sweetheart really was.

"What's the new one called?" Louisa was clearly an avid theatre-goer. "The one you're working on?"

*"You Again."*

"I hope you make this one easier to follow." Fern, of course.

"I'll try."

"So," I charged in while I had my chance. "Chester, Connecticut. I went all the way up there to see him and he had zero time for me."

"Well, Theo," said Louisa, "if he's working on a new musical, you can't really expect him to drop everything…"

"But," wondered William, "if you knew you were going to be so busy, why would you ask Theo to go up there?"

I was just about to reconsider my impression of William, when Mads interrupted him.

"That's just it! I *didn't* ask him to come up!"

"You did too!"

"I did not! You invited yourself!"

"Is that true?" Louisa looked at me like a barn cat hearing a rustle in the straw.

"Well, sort of, maybe, but he said it was okay!"

"Ohhhhhh," said the Mormon Tabernacle Choir.

"That's not quite the same thing, now is it, Theo." Louisa could be a little judgmental, if you asked me.

"But Louisa, think about it," said William. "It's just good manners, if you have a guest…"

"That's true, Louisa." *You tell her, Joan.* "It's just rude."

"But the question you guys should be asking is why *didn't* he have time to see me, his ostensible boyfriend? I'll tell you. Because he was too busy pining over this total no-talent pretty-boy director, named dubiously-enough Tanner."

"I wouldn't make fun of people's names," said Madison. *"Theo."*

"If one more person says that to me—"

"Oh, I'm so disappointed in you, Madison. Really?" Fern was completely on my side. "Just look at that boy's face—" I let them see my big-eyed-waif face. "And you wanted to slip around with some floozy named Tanner? How could you do that?"

Now that's more like it. I wanted to lean my head on her motherly shoulder—but I had more to tell.

"You haven't heard the best part. After an entire day of watching his show—and trust me, it's not that good—and watching him swooning over sexy Tanner, Madison turned to me and told me that he literally couldn't bear to have me in the same state, and he insisted I get the next train back to the city." The quartet looked at Madison, unified in their horror that this viper had somehow crawled under the edge of the tent among decent people.

"Now really, Madison," tsked Fern. "How could you?" One more gesture to my sad little face.

Billy patted my forearm, comfortingly. I guess with all the elbow-bumps, we'd sort of bonded.

"I'll tell you this, Madison," said Louisa, sternly delivering her final words on the subject. "I, for one, will not be seeing your new musical, I don't care *what* the *Times* says."

"Sing out, Louisa."

"You know? I'm just going to eat my eggs," said Madison.

"And," I added, "he's never even apologized."

"Okay, now that's just a lie. I've done nothing *but* apologize ever since!"

"You've pestered me with a million texts because you want to get back together. That's not the same thing."

"Well, Madison—" Louisa started.

"I don't want to get back together!"

"No?" My disbelief was apparent in the arch of my right eyebrow.

"No!"

"Then why have you been bugging me to meet you somewhere, hmm?"

"Because I didn't want to break up with you in a text!"

"Ohhhh." It was like the chorus in *Oedipus Rex*. Four heads turned slowly to me.

"No...way," I said. "No way in hell are *you* breaking up with *me*. The only reason I came here today was so *I* could break up with *you*!"

"Serves you right, too," said Billy, giving Madison the stink eye.

"No one likes a cheater, Madison." William and Billy were a united front.

"But I never touched the guy!"

"Of course you never touched the guy!" It was my turn again. "That was obvious. You never had a chance!"

"Why do you say that?"

"Tanner's way out of your league, Madison."

"Oh gee, thanks."

"You should see this guy," I explained to the gayboys. "Unbelievably pretty, and totally into himself."

"One of those," Billy nodded, knowingly.

"But wait," said Louisa, a firm voice of reason. "Doesn't that sort of solve everything?"

"What do you mean?"

"You want to break up and you want to break up. You finally agree on something."

"True."

"So break up! Walk away! Get on with your lives!"

At this point, Fern let out a small shriek. We all jumped. The passing busboy jumped. People out on 73rd Street probably jumped.

"Louisa! Look at the time!"

"We have to run or we will never make curtain. Check please!"

They were scooping up their things.

"We should get going too, doll," said Billy.

"It was so charming to meet you all," said Fern. "And best of luck to you Theo." And she pinched my cheek. What *is* it about my face, women of a certain age just *have* to pinch it?

"What are you seeing?" William asked.

"What's it called, Louisa?"

"*American Psycho*. The musical."

"I've heard it's funny," said Fern. "I do hope it's funny. I so love it when they're romantic and funny."

I looked at Madison, and then at the boys next door.

"I'm not telling her," said Billy.

Credit cards were flashed, checks sorted.

"Oh, Louisa, do you think we have time for one of those selfies?"

"No!"

The women were gone and the boys waited for their charge slip to come back.

"I have to say," said William, "I'm so glad you guys worked this out."

"Doll, they're splitting up."

"That's what I mean. I never saw two people who didn't belong together as much as you two guys don't."

"Gee, thanks," Madison said.

Billy pulled on a leather jacket with a very genuine fur collar.

"Best of luck to you, Theo. The right guy is out there, you'll see." He looked adoringly at William.

After another round of exit lines, they headed for the door, hand-in-hand. Nothing will make you appreciate your boyfriend quite so much as brunch with me and Madison.

I turned my attention back to my sausage. On my plate, you perv.

"So we're done, right?" I said cheerily, digging in.

"Theo," said Madison leaning back in his chair and shaking his head. "Now that *that* little circus has finally headed out of town—and thank you so much for starting that by the way—"

"Don't even, Mads, you were eating it up—"

"Yeah, yeah, sure—but we should talk."

"About what? What's left to say?"

"For your own good, Theo," he answered, "and, I'll admit, for my own personal satisfaction, I'd like to set a few things straight."

"Oh good." Total sarcasm, by the way.

"Theo, you know what your problem is?"

"Me?!" was my devastating retort. "You were the world's worst boyfriend, Mads!"

"I know, I know, because I couldn't satisfy this enormous hunger you have to be the center of attention at all times."

"That's ridiculous. I'm not like that."

"No—you're right. You need to be the center of attention at all times—until you don't. And woe to the poor chump who doesn't intuit the mood swing."

"What are you talking about?"

"But I understand. I may be the only one who does, which is why I held out as long as I did."

"Understands what?"

"You! Or at least I understand a little bit."

"Oh great, tell me all about *me* then."

And he did, pissing me off more and more as he went, and ending with an anecdote.

"See, when I was a kid," he said, "we had this little mutt terrier dog, cutest thing in the world, but he was terrified of everything, scared all the time, and occasionally he'd bite somebody."

"Fear-biter," I said. I know about dogs. I was much more comfortable talking about dogs. "Very difficult to correct."

"Exactly, Theo. That's you. You let people close, but when they get too close—chomp. I just haven't figured out—what are you afraid of, Theo?"

* * * *

So that had been my farewell brunch with Madison. Some fun, huh. And it was obviously still in my head. Leastwise that last bit.

I was so upset, I realized later, that I hadn't even eaten all my bacon. Can you imagine!

So.

Fine.

So yeah, sometimes I said harsh things to people.

And yeah, I'd made a guy cry in the songwriters' workshop. *Once.* Hadn't been my *intention* to make him cry. I was totally surprised when he did.

And the second time it happened, it was absolutely not my fault.

But did that mean that *I* needed to change? Or that these people just needed to man up some?

And I wasn't afraid of anything. Okay, I'm not crazy about snakes, but other than that...

In any case, none of this was helping me when it came to finding the perfect rhyme for a girl who didn't give two farts about broken hearts.

And then—the weird bloopy noise of the door buzzer.

"Who is it?" I asked at the box on the wall.

Someone said something, two syllables, but it was otherwise unintelligible. Sounded like 'oil can.' Too funny. Should I buzz the Tin Woodsman in? Maybe not—he *does* carry an axe. Then it occurred to me. Two syllables, sounds like: 'mail man.' Made considerably more sense than 'oil can.' I hit the magic button to buzz him in and went to the door, waiting. Waiting. Staring down the hall at the elevators. Arrrgh. How long can it take to get an elevator up four flights? You might never guess this about me, but patience is not really my thing. *Any day now!* I thought. Finally there was the elevator door opening. The mail-guy looked down the hall, and saw me.

"Five-oh-five? McPherson?" he said, reading off the package.

"My sister."

"Your sister's name is Theo?"

"Wait, no, that's me!"

It was for me??!! *That* had never occurred to me. I just figured I was doing Beccs a favor and getting her package for her. Who would send *me* a package? Our mom maybe? Care package from home? Brownies imported from Iowa?

No, it was obviously Amazon—who actually delivers on Sundays for some reason.

I signed, the mail guy headed back to the elevator and I closed the door.

I ran to the kitchen to get a knife to cut the box open. Inside the box, another box. Adidas. I pulled it open. Sneakers. Real Adidas, not fake ones. Size six-and-a-halfs, too. White, and the stripes were red.

Wow. They were—perfect.

There was a gift note.

"In case of Clarice. I hope these are watertight. Jeffrey."

Ohmygod. He sent me shoes. The perfect shoes. He'd actually been—like—paying attention. Too bad about the laces, but I knew a place where I could get red ones, because it's so much sharper to have red laces.

Then I realized there was something loose sliding around in the bottom of the box.

I looked.

One pair of red shoelaces.

*I can't even.*

Some guys send flowers. With some guys, it's probably jewelry. I got gym shoes.

What kind of guy gives you gym shoes?

And you know what? I was really glad nobody else was around, because the smile on my face was so absurdly, preposterously, colossally stupid, and I couldn't stop it. I'd shake myself, and make myself stop smiling like a baboon and in ten seconds or less—Baboon City. Half an hour later I was *still* staring at my feet in my dazzling new shoes, and

grinning,

grinning,

grinning.

# Chapter 33
## The Parents

*JEFFREY*

Dinner had gone fairly smoothly. No one had been hit, anyway, and I always booked that as a win.

I'd picked an Italian place just off West End Ave., far away from my office and hopefully far away enough from any potential complications.

"I know you have plans for your birthday, honey," said my mother over her espresso and tiramisu, "but it would be really nice if you could figure out a time we might do something together? Maybe some friends over? I bumped into that nice girl you used to like, Aurora? Such a beauty. She was asking after you, and I'm sure she'd love to see you again. You two got along really well, didn't you?"

"She's fine, Mom," I said. "I'll see how work goes."

"The boy needs to concentrate on his job," pointed out my father.

"Yes, I know, but he should also think about settling down. You know you want him to settle down."

"Yeah, sure, but he's seeing Jennifer Caputo right now."

"Actually, Dad, I thought—"

"Jennifer who?" asked my mother. "These Italian names!"

"It doesn't matter Jennifer who," said my father, "but he's not going to mess it up by seeing the Ferrari girl."

I figured it was smarter to let them bounce it back and forth between themselves, than step in and try to clarify things I couldn't clarify.

So I sat there with cold coffee, while my parents traded views on the various candidates for the job of Mrs. Jeffrey, when I saw Theo come into the dining room, looking around.

Icy fear shot through me.

I swear, if Freddy Krueger had walked in snapping his fingers, it wouldn't have scared me *half* as much as seeing this five-foot-six Iowa farm-boy glancing around the dining room.

He saw me, and his face—and those eyes—lit up in greeting.

*Beam me up, Scotty.*

I gulped my coffee on the off chance someone had tossed in a shot of something—like Jameson's. Or strychnine. They hadn't.

"Hey, Jeff! So these must be your parents?" said Theo coming up to the table. And I thought—*This time I really will kill him. I won't have a choice.* "I'm Theo," he said extending his hand.

My father looked at him like he was from Alpha Centauri. Which he obviously was. My dad was not accustomed to this great Midwestern hello-ness, and he didn't trust it. My mother was just a bit overwhelmed.

"Theo," I said, improvising and gently pushing his hand down. "Did you finish those edits I left you?"

"I'm sorry?"

"Theo is my new assistant," I explained to my parents. And to Theo.

*Just go with it, Theo.*

"What happened to Darlene?" asked my mother. "She seemed so nice."

"She's still there, still nice, but I've been so overworked. I'm desperate and I really need Theo's help right now. Awful, isn't it Theo?"

"Soooooooooooo awful," he said looking at me. "I can't keep up."

"I know being my assistant is still really new, and I can't tell you how I appreciate your pitching in and helping me out like this."

"No problem?"

"It's late, Theo. Go home."

"What did you just—"

"But you know what you could do for me that would be a huge help," and I pulled a receipt out of my wallet. "If you could pick up my dry cleaning on your way in in the morning, that would be fantastic." I handed him the receipt, which he stared at, open-mouthed.

It was a first.

I had stunned Theo into speechlessness instead of the other way around. Somehow I didn't feel much like celebrating the milestone. I knew I was being a shit.

"Are you kid—"

"Excuse us a second," I said getting up in a hurry, grabbing Theo by the elbow and walking him toward the door.

"Ow," he said about the tight grip on his arm.

"Theo, please, I'm begging you, just go. Please, they're my parents. This isn't funny. Don't make a thing."

"What is all this about?"

"They want to think I'm—successful—"

"I thought you *were* successful, isn't that what you're always telling me?"

"Yeah, I am. Please, just go along. Please? Just go and I'll talk to you in the morning. Okay?"

"You're like Madison all over again! Am I that embarrassing that nobody can introduce me?"

"No! Of course not! It's nothing to do with you." I knew my dad's back was to us, but I also knew my mother could still see us if she wanted, and she would definitely want. I should have done this out on the sidewalk. "Please please please, Theo, I'll make it up to you, I swear it. I'll take you to lunch someplace really nice. Or dinner, you name the place."

He looked at me for a second, one of those horrible, humiliating, sneering Theo-looks.

"I'd starve first."

I stood there and watched him walk away, and I felt like the world's biggest heel. I suppose I probably was. I stared after him, and then at the door he'd gone through. What? Like I was hoping he'd come rushing back, saying "I understand! It's all okay!" ????

Of course he wasn't going to understand—and I couldn't explain it to him. He was just going to be pissed.

Fuck.

I went back to my parents.

"Nice looking boy," said my mother.

"Is he? I hadn't noticed." What a lie.

"Where'd you find him?" asked my dad. "Wouldn't last two minutes in my office. Not very bright, that one."

"No, he's not," I said. Another lie. "But he means well." Ha! Maybe the biggest lie. I never met anyone as malevolent as Theo McPherson.

"I thought he was nice," said my mother. "I think you should hang on to him."

"Don't think I can, Mama. Don't see how I can."

Finally, a bit of truth.

# Chapter 34
## ...and into the Streets!

*THEO*

I was back in his office, in his chair, with my feet—in my beautiful new shoes—on his desk, flipping through the Internet, waiting for Jeff to come in.

I had gone to the restaurant the night before to thank him for the shoes—and when I got home from the restaurant, I had been *this* close to shoving these lovely shoes down the trash chute. Thing was, I had already shoved the *old* shoes down the trash chute, and I wasn't going barefoot, not even to spite what's-his-face.

In my fury, I'd spent half the night looking out the window at Rebecca's street, alternating between contemplating just how much I hated Jeff Bornic; kicking myself for wasting my time hating Jeff Bornic; and trying to figure out what that had been about, that ridiculous thing with his parents. Then it suddenly seemed so obvious what it had been about, that I felt positively dim-witted.

I was also really glad I hadn't thrown my beautiful new shoes away.

Anyway, that's where I was, and that's what I was thinking, when the door to Jeff's office opened.

The look on his face—not exactly combobulated, if you know what I mean. Can't tell you how much I *loved* surprising this guy.

"Theo." He stopped in the doorway.

"Hey, like my shoes?" I said cheerily, waggling my pretty feet at him. He came in, closing the door behind him, and sat down in the guest chair. "I had them on last night, but you didn't seem to notice."

"Theo—if you want to have a tantrum, okay, but please let's do it after work away from here."

"Tantrum? Me?! Never! I'm not really the tantrum-throwing type."

"If only."

"Which is, I'm sure, why you hired me as your new assistant-assistant, remember? I was just getting a head start on our day. You've got a 9:30 with Mr. O'Malley, in case you forgot."

He looked a little relieved. *Yeah, don't get too comfortable, Jeffie.*

"I don't suppose this means that you picked up the dry cleaning," he half-laughed.

"Of course I did. Your fourteen identical gray pinstripe suits are all hanging up. In the closet. Right next to *you*."

He looked up at me, he took a deep breath.

"Theo, if it's at all possible, try to see my side of things?"

"Oh, I understand completely. Honestly, it's pretty damn funny. Because you're totally out here, completely cool about it. But you're not out to your family."

"No one in New Jersey—my dad is really old-fashioned, he could never understand."

"Not going to clasp you in his arms and shout 'darling boy'?"

"He would kill me."

"So—what? Like somewhere in the middle of the Lincoln Tunnel, you turn straight?"

"Something like that."

"Some powerful mojo in that tunnel. Is there anything else I should know about your double life on the other side of the Hudson?"

"What do you mean?"

"Oh, let me see, you got a wife and kids over there maybe?"

"No!"

"Girlfriend?"

He didn't answer so quickly.

"No."

"But you have had."

"I don't do that anymore, I swear. My dad's trying to set me up with somebody, but I can't."

"Such integrity."

"Hey, great, mock me, I don't care, I was an idiot to ask you to try to understand—"

"What's *really* funny about all this is that nobody *here* knows you're in the closet, do they?"

"No."

"You're so frigging dishonest, you're in the closet about being in the closet."

"Yeah. I know—it's pathetic."

"You're not only in the closet, you're like in a *shoebox* tucked away in the *back* of the closet. Like my brother's porn collection, now that I think of it."

"Nice metaphor."

"Simile."

"Simile."

"For somebody who looks like he really has his shit together— you're a total mess."

"I'm a complete sham."

"But don't worry. I'm not even going to tell my sister what a craven coward you are. But I *do* reserve the right—without prejudice—to torment you mercilessly about this and other things."

"As if you *ever* needed my permission to torment me."

"So tell me—you were thinking you and Roger were this serious thing? How were you going to explain *him* to the parentals?"

"I had a plan. A fantastically stupid plan, but still."

"What?"

"I can't tell you. You'll laugh."

"That's so not fair. You only say that because I always do."

"I thought Roger would help ease things along. My dad wants nothing more than to be all waspy and shit. And nobody is waspier than Roger Prescott."

"So you figured…"

"Yeah. I knew he still wouldn't like having a gay son, but if his new gay son-in-law was from good Puritan stock, well…I told you it was dumb."

"And you were right. Here, take your chair back. I need to get to work."

I stood up and let him sit.

"I don't suppose you actually picked up my dry cleaning, did you?"

"Are you kidding?"

"Can I at least have the receipt back, so I can send Darlene out?"

"Ehhhh—the thing is, there was a trash bin right there on the corner at Columbus Ave., and it was calling out, 'Theo! Theo!' in a strangely alluring and plaintive way—"

"Great."

"But," I added, glancing at my wrist because I never wear a watch, "I'm sure if you hurry, hmmmm, you'll still be too late. Sorry!"

"Fair enough, I suppose."

"Let me know if I'm uninvited to your birthday party."

"Will it make a difference?"

"I'm far more likely to come if you tell me not to."

"Then definitely don't come."

"Cool. It's a date."

"Need the address?"

"I'll just get it out of your contacts."

He slumped in his chair, capitulating. My work here was done. I started to go but then—

"Hey," I said, pointing out the window. "Is that a great big gorilla climbing up the side of that building?"

For half a second he actually looked out the window—which was long enough to kiss him on the cheek.

"Thanks for the shoes, by the way." He smiled, and he maybe even looked embarrassed for a second.

Like I said, I really liked keeping this guy off-balance.

Speaking of off-balance, I left Jeff's office just as Darlene was sitting down to her desk. She too seemed a teensy bit discombobulated to see me, a temp, coming out of a closed-door confab with an attorney. *Her* attorney.

In fact, she stood there with her cardboard coffee cup in her hand, and gaped.

"Love your hair like that, Darlene. So cute."

Yeah, well, let her think.

# Chapter 35
## The Birthday Party

*JEFFREY*

I hadn't really been looking forward to this. I was turning thirty.

I had planned to host this little clambake myself, but the contractor's change in scheduling—which included cutting a large hole in my living room floor three weeks earlier than originally planned—left me with an apartment that was essentially little more than a gigantic liability claim waiting to happen.

Then Dave—an old frat brother and occasional FWB—called and asked what was up with the party, and I told him about the hole-in-the-floor thing and my vision of watching one lawyer after the other stepping into the void like so many over-educated lemmings, and Dave volunteered to spare me the embarrassment and subsequent litigation and said he would host. Or more accurately, he volunteered his boyfriend Michael's place for the party. They're actually married with flower girls and cake and the whole nine-and-a-half yards. I had been one of two best men at the ceremony. He even referred to Michael as his 'husband' and everything, a word I couldn't really wrap my brain around.

As I said, Dave and I knew each other from college, the two closeted gayboys in the fraternity. It didn't take either of us long to suss out the other's secret and, well, boys will be boys.

Dave's hubby, Michael, whom Dave acquired subsequently, was loaded. I assumed it was family money. He did something in publishing, which notoriously pays crap, but he seemed to have piles of the stuff and a fantastic apartment. And a sailboat.

In any case, the party was at their huge apartment only a few blocks from mine. And that's where I found myself in the middle of a group of noisy well-wishing friends and acquaintances, nodding, smiling and thanking. Who *were* these people? And for reasons I wasn't really comfortable exploring, I was constantly on the lookout for you-know-who. I mean, I had invited him, so naturally I should look after him, etc. He wouldn't know anybody here, etc. That's why I had my eye on the door. That's what I told myself anyway, and that it had nothing to do with wanting to see him or that ridiculous hair.

That ridiculous hair, which I *didn't* see, and as the evening wore on, that was bumming me out even more than turning thirty. Where *was* he, the little squirt? It would be just like him to stand me up after all, birthday or no.

I needed to be nice to the hosts—they had really gone all out to do this. Dave was bustling around while Michael smiled graciously—but there was a hired bartender, a waiter shifting trays of food whom Dave would *not* stop bossing, and at least one other person in the kitchen. All for me!

"Dave," I said, catching him in the midst of fussing, and nagging at the poor waiter-guy, "I can't thank you guys enough."

"How often do you turn thirty?" said Dave, giving me a hug.

"Probably not as many times as you will."

"Of course with *my* looks, I can get away with lying about my age so much better than you."

"Thanks."

"Any time."

"But seriously, you saved the party I was ready to cancel, and it's terrific. I owe you one."

"Absolutely."

He went back to bossing the poor little cater-waiter, and I went back to staring at the apartment door—just in time to see Michael letting Theo in.

I had to stop myself from pushing through people to get to Theo, just to say hello. I went on with the small talk, and only occasionally let myself peer through the crowd of blathering lawyers to see if I could find him in the sea of shoulders and heads. He was so short, he was easy to lose. I thanked people for their happy-birthdays and I absentmindedly talked shop, while now and then straining to see another glimpse of red hair. He finally tore himself away from the buffet table to meander over to me, like I was the last thing on his mind, instead of the reason he was here.

"Hey, birthday guy," he said.

"Hey, cutes. Glad you came."

"Really?"

"Yeah, I know, crazy, right?"

"Come here," he said, and he grabbed me by the hand and pulled me off into a hallway—almost private.

"Hey." I looked at him for a bit. "Talk to me about something that has nothing to do with law."

"Sure—but what do you mean?"

"I've come to the realization that the only thing lawyers can talk about is work—and I'm just as bad as any of them."

"Well, let me see. The food here's really good."

"Is it? Good, I'm glad."

"There's even a great big bowl of caviar over there. I've never been to a party before where they had a great big bowl of caviar."

"You like caviar?"

"You kidding? Me? Caviar?" He shrugged, and laughed an I-eat-it-all-day laugh—then he leaned up toward me and whispered, "There isn't enough money in the world to make me put that stuff in my mouth."

"That's what I figured, Iowa farm-boy."

"Iowa farm-boy and proud of it. So read any good books lately?"

"I read cases and briefs and drafts of briefs."

"Opera? Theatre?"

"How about golf?"

"You're pathetic. Tommy says I should give you a break, that you just need training, but I have my doubts."

"Tommy said that? I thought he hated me."

"Could be. Could be he just hates Madison more."

"Understandable."

"I don't have a present for you."

"How about a truce. That'll do."

"Yeah, I can do that. How about no teasing—just for today though."

"I'd like that."

"And I can give you this," and he leaned up on his toes and kissed me on the cheek.

"Hey, it's not just my birthday, you know, it's my *thirtieth* birthday."

"I'm trying not to think about it."

"What I'm hinting at is—it's a *big* birthday. You can do a little better than a peck on the cheek, I think."

His eyes looked up at mine. I could see he was weighing this in his head, trying to read behind it. Of course I didn't know myself what I really meant other than kissing him seemed like a good idea. He finally went up on his toes again and kissed me on the lips. My arms pulled him in.

And after about a second and a half—he pulled away.

"Many happy returns," he said, with that sort of wicked, teasing, sideways look he gets. And he walked away and left me there. Not quite the outcome I was hoping for—definitely not what *part* of me was hoping for. Before I could rejoin the party, I had to rearrange things in my expensively worn-out-looking jeans.

Michael found me first. I was always a little uneasy around Michael, given my past with Dave. Michael was a great guy, he seemed nothing but generous and warm. He was older. Probably forty. And honestly—he deserved better than Dave.

He'd probably tossed out a couple thousand on a birthday party for me, and now he had an apartment full of people he'd never met in his life. Who does that? And these weren't even people—they were lawyers. Guy deserved a medal.

"Hey, old man," said Michael.

"Hey, Michael," I shook his hand. "Can't thank you guys enough for this fantastic party."

"It's nothing, and this apartment is really made for parties."

"Send me the caterer's bill, anyway. I'll take care of it."

"Don't even think about it. Happy birthday, Jeffrey."

"Wow. Thank you. You know, this is far nicer than the party I was going to throw myself."

"As it should be, as it should be. We're happy to host. Which reminds me—doing anything tomorrow?"

"Not sure. Why?"

"Dave and I are taking the boat out." I mentioned before that Michael had money. He had a sailboat he kept out on Long Island. "Want to tag along? We'd love the company."

I was a little reluctant. Sailing could be fun, but then after a while it was just sitting and looking out at water. And more looking, more water. The last time I'd gone out with them, I'd found myself yawning and thinking of a dozen other things I could have been doing instead.

"I'll check my calendar, okay?"

"Do try! It'll be lots more fun with you along!"

"Happy birthday!" said another lawyer, throwing herself around my neck.

"Thanks, Allison," I said, looking apologetically across to Michael. He nodded and smiled and went off to play the host for someone else, and I was relieved to be out from under.

After another eternity of best wishes and lawyer-talk, with me trying to catch a glimpse of Theo to see where he'd got off to, he sneaked up on me from behind and tapped me on the shoulder.

"Hey there, you with the stars in your eyes," he said.

"Stars in my eyes?"

"Never mind."

"Having fun?"

"It's starting to wear thin. You?"

"Not gonna lie. You were right about lawyers talking about lawyering—although at least one friend of yours has something else on his mind. Seems to think I'm cute. Or maybe he's blind and he's trying to read me, I don't know."

"Touchy-feely?"

"And persistent."

"If I hear cries for help, I'll come running."

"If you hear cries for help, they'll be his, as I carefully break one finger after the other."

"Who is it? I'll straighten him out."

"Some guy, he told me his name but I wasn't listening," he said. "He actually pushed his way into the bathroom with me. I pushed him back out so hard he bonked the back of his head against the wall behind him. I think he got the point, finally. My God, the guy is like your age!"

"Oh, thanks!"

"But better looking."

"I thought we had a truce!"

"You're right, I forgot. Sorry. Old habits. Definitely not better looking."

"Thank you. You look pretty nice, too."

"Hey, I know it's your party and all, but—you want to get out of here?"

"What are you thinking?"

"Just a walk."

Bail on my own party? I thought about it, and then thought *why the hell not?*

"Sure."

We grabbed our jackets, and I kissed Rebecca on the cheek as we passed her.

"Where are you two going?"

"For a walk," I answered, like it was the most obvious thing in the world.

I'd been a little shy with Rebecca about whatever it was I was doing or not doing with her little brother. My guess was that Theo had been just as reticent. Now she looked from me to him and back a few times before she finally leaned closer.

"Do not kill him."

I wasn't sure which of us she was talking to.

Theo seemed to have somewhere in mind, and soon we were crossing Fifth Avenue. He was taking us to the park.

You'd think the kid from the farm would be intimidated by the city, but he seemed to have no fear. By comparison, growing up in New Jersey, with horror stories of the big city looming just *over there*—I was certain that Central Park at night was a no man's land of chaos and crime, where drugs were dealt, gangs warred, tourists disappeared, and bodies were scooped up in the morning.

But the ever-intrepid Theo took us straight to a hill he seemed to know, where we sat together on a large rock. It was nice.

"Hey, Jeff," he said finally, still looking out at the park.

"Hey."

"Happy birthday."

"Yeah. It's my birthday. Thanks."

"Did you call your mother?"

"I did, thank you. She asked after you, by the way."

"She didn't either."

"I know it's weird, but she actually did. Just how she is."

"So whose apartment was that?"

"It's Michael and Dave's."

"They have an actual library. I never knew anybody who had an actual library before."

"I'd have introduced you around, but you scooted off on me. Dave is an old fraternity brother of mine."

"Of course. I knew you had to be a frat boy."

"What have you got against frat boys?"

"Frat boys—bunch of middle-class straight guys interested in just one thing—hanging out with other middle-class straight guys exactly like themselves. Girls come a distant second."

"Bros before hos."

"In a nutshell. Their only interest is in hanging out with others of their kind, and to allow them to do that, they've developed these elaborate structures to make sure they never have to deal with anyone who doesn't fit in, winnowing out the unsuitable through the whole rush thing."

"Oh that's what rush-week is. Someone should have told me."

"Like you didn't know. Think about it." And then he dropped his voice to sound really butch. "Jim's a nice guy and all, but he's not really an Upsilon now is he?"

"It's not like that."

"It's exactly like that. Even your interest in sports is just an excuse to have a common subject to talk about with other guys like you, and so you have a code by which you can recognize each other when you meet—and identify the outsider, who doesn't know his hockey scores—definitely *not* an Upsilon."

"It has nothing to do with liking hockey?"

"Absolutely nothing. And you guys do all this because deep down you know you're a bunch of insignificant, scared little boys—but if you're surrounded by a group of similarly inconsequential and untalented guys, it gives you this comfortable sense of your own self-worth. Even if it's totally false."

"Damn. Don't hold anything back, just because it's my birthday."

"You know I'm right."

"But you said 'a bunch of middle-class *straight* boys'—and obviously I'm not straight."

"Were you out in college?"

"Well...."

"I knew it. You were there in disguise. I bet you and your friend were messing around furtively in the attic."

"Basement," I had to admit, laughing.

"So how was your birthday? Feel old yet?"

"Only since I sat down on this rock."

"I got a phone call today from the animal shelter," Theo said after a bit.

"Puggle on a pay phone?"

"No, although almost as startling. It was from the director of development, thanking me for introducing you to the shelter."

"Oh, her. She wrote me a nice letter, too."

"You sent them a check?"

"Maybe."

"You didn't need to do that."

"It's deductible."

He looked up at me out of the corner of his eye. I felt that about half the time I was around him, I didn't begin to understand him, or know what to do with him. In that moment it looked like it was the other way around. For once.

"Do you even *like* dogs?"

I shrugged. I didn't really have an answer.

"You do," I said finally.

And I could feel the heat rush into my cheeks, as I stared down at my hands. Oh good lord, I was blushing?! I felt like I was turning thirteen instead of thirty.

His hand slid across the rock until it was on top of mine.

"So," he said. "How's it feel to be thirty years old?"

"Right at this moment, sitting on a rock in Central Park, holding hands with a cute guy? Not so bad."

I looked out at the empty park.

"But *generally*?" I went on. "I don't know. I mostly feel like the same jerk I was yesterday, the one trying to bluff the world into thinking he's got it together and knows what he wants—the same insecure fraud I've always been, as you so kindly pointed out about me and my frat brothers. The career thing is really good. I'd love to get out of ad claims, sure, but I'm good at what I do, and I'm seen as being good at what I do. Which is all good. I still get a charge out of doing a good job. And I get a bunch of money for it. Also good."

"Sounds like there's a 'but' in there."

"I suppose there is. But. In a way, I'm still waiting for it all to start, you know? I remember being a little kid, thinking, someday my life will start and then stuff will happen, I'll do this thing, I'll own that car, I'll go there and there, I'll have this big adventure, I'll meet this special person and it will all happen. And I still feel like that."

"What are you waiting for? What do you think's going to happen?"

"No clue," I laughed, and looked down at his face. He was smiling a little, and really beautiful with the light from the street lamp on his upturned face. "Maybe it's starting now finally."

He leaned up and kissed me on the cheek.

"What was that for?" I asked.

"It's your birthday," he shrugged.

"*Maricón*," said somebody.

*Ahhhhhh fuck*. I don't speak Spanish, but I certainly know the word for faggot. I also knew this was not going to go well.

In the shadows, just a bit down the hill from us, stood this guy. Probably homeless. Probably drunk. Probably about my age, which, in light of the conversation we were just having, gave me something to think about. I mean, how's *this* guy feel about the way his life's going at this point?

The guy started rattling in Spanish until Theo interrupted him—in Spanish. Who knew? I was impressed.

But it was weird. It was like watching a movie you've seen before, that had been dubbed in a foreign language. Without understanding a word, I still knew what they were saying. The mocking contempt in Theo's voice was rising in a familiar way, and then the homeless guy said something about *maricón* again, and then Theo said *sí* something, and something *maricón.* And then—

"*Besame,*" he said, smiling. "*Justo aquí, amigo.*" And, with a sneering air-kiss, he pointed to his left butt cheek.

This was apparently an insult too far, and the guy started lumbering in our direction. I stood up to intervene. I would be the hero, and with luck I'd do it without having to put Theo in a fireman's carry to get him home, since he hadn't really appreciated that the last time.

"Hey, my friend," I said to the homeless guy frankensteining toward us. "There's no need for a big thing," and I reached for my wallet. "Here, why don't you get yourself something to—"

Before I could give him the twenty—or finish my sentence—a meteor came hurtling out of the sky and slammed into my head. I was blind, I was lying on wet grass, my head and left eye were screaming with hurt, and I was holding my face, moaning and rocking back and forth, oblivious to everything in the universe but the pain.

Then I was sort of aware enough to hear Theo. I felt his hands holding my face, and I tried to open my eyes enough to look at him.

"Theo," I asked, "are you okay?"

"I'm fine!" he said, laughing. "He didn't hit me, just you."

"Why is that, do you think?"

"You pissed him off, dude."

"Why didn't he hit you?"

"I never get hit."

"That makes no sense to me," I said feeling the flood of tears—at least I hoped it was tears—running into my hand. "Is my eye okay?" I tried to open it a little.

"Here, let me see. Yeah, you're okay, but I bet that hurt."

"Yyyyyeah. It did. Does. Fuck."

"So—nine-one-one? Or walk home?"

"Walk home, for sure."

"You don't want to call the cops."

"Did he take my wallet?"

"No, just the twenty you dropped. And then he staggered off."

"No doubt with a profound sense of satisfaction. I can't blame the guy. After all, he'd just bumped into Theo McPherson. It's totally justifiable. Not sure why he hit *me,* though. Here, help me get up."

Which he did.

"Your place?" Theo asked, watching me to see if I was going to fall over.

"Yeah. My place."

He looked at me again under the brighter street lights of Fifth Avenue—which my left eye did not like at all.

"Dizzy? Blurred vision? Nausea?" asked Dr. Theo.

"No, I'm good, I think. Humiliated, but okay."

"Wait 'til Monday when you're explaining that eye for the seventy-third time."

"How *will* I explain this? This ijit I know tormented a homeless person, so naturally the homeless person slugged *me*."

"You should probably lie. Less demeaning."

"You are a hazard, you know that?"

"The red hair is supposed to be like nature's warning. You should have known it wasn't going to be easy." He gestured to the little twenty-four-hour market we were just passing. "We should get you something for that eye."

"Okay."

He was hoping for a steak—he'd seen that in a movie somewhere—but he settled for a bag of frozen peas. And some Dr Pepper.

I had some aspirin at home, so we were good to go.

We hobbled into my building past Buddy, the ferrety door guy, and Theo got me into my apartment. We split a Dr Pepper and I got into the shower, which I wanted more than anything. When I got out—in fresh underwear, and cautiously toweling my head—Theo was still there, sitting on my bed, flipping through a golf magazine.

"There are no cute golf players. Not one." He tossed the magazine on the floor. "Got any tennis magazines? Cuz some of *those* guys…"

"Sorry."

"So. You okay, you think?"

"Yeah. Just bruised."

"Happy birthday."

"Seriously! Happy fucking birthday!"

"You want me to go?"

"No. No, I do not want you to go."

"Okay," he said, "but understand—there will be no repetition." With a sigh, I flopped down on the bed, leaning against pillows and the headboard.

"You have the meanest way of training me."

"What are you talking about?" he laughed, carefully untying his new shoes before pulling them off.

"Whenever I say something stupid, I hear it parroted back to me for the next several days so I realize just how stupid it was." He settled himself in under my arm.

"Yeah, I guess I do do that."

"You said do-do," I said.

"Yeah, I did-did."

"I don't think I'm quite in the condition for a repetition anyway, okay?"

"Fair enough."

"But you'll stay?"

"Of course."

"Hey, Iowa," I said after a second. "Ever go sailing?"

"No, why?"

"Want to? I got invited. Tomorrow—wanna come?"

"Is it fun?"

"Yeah, kinda. And it can get kinda boring, too, staring at the water."

"And you can't just stick your hand out and call a cab."

"No. Which is why I was going to pass, but it would be fun if you came along."

"Okay, sure."

"Good." I kissed the top of his head, and sent a quick text message to Dave.

"I'm sorry you got clobbered," he said, once we were settled under bedcovers.

"Me, too."

"It's funny, I do this shit all the time, and I never get hit. I think you must be doing something wrong."

I wanted to pinch him so bad. And I wanted to pull him still closer to me. Guess which one I did. And before you judge me too harshly because I was getting all sentimental over somebody who could easily be mistaken for a Chucky doll—I would just like to point out that I had had a severe blow to the head, so cut me some slack.

And thus I saw the thirtieth year of my life come to a close—with this stupidly pretty boy's head on my chest. When I woke up on the first day of my thirty-first year, he was still there.

There are worse ways to get a year older.

# Chapter 36
## Sunday, by the Blue, Purple, Yellow, Red Water…

*THEO*

"Wow, Jeff. Your eye turned a really impressive color. Not sure what you're going to wear that'll go with that particular shade of violet."

"Sunglasses."

Jeff booked one of those Zipcars, which we found easily enough, and his phone worked like a GPS. I hadn't been in a car in a while, being a poor farm-boy transformed into a poor city-boy, and I thought the GPS thing was pretty cool.

It looked like a fantastic day for my first time sailing on the ocean (or anywhere). The sky was almost completely clear, and it was warm and sunny. Oh, what a beautiful morning!

We rolled the windows partly down to enjoy the rush of air. That's how it started anyway. By the time we got out on Long Island, the sun was gone, we'd closed the windows, and I'd even discovered that the heater in Jeff's cheap little rental didn't seem to work.

It was less than an hour getting to the harbor. As Jeff parked, a couple guys started waving from the deck of a boat that was at the dock.

"There they are," said Jeff.

*No no no no no no no.*

"Those are the friends we're sailing with?" I asked, my stomach sinking.

"Yeah—why? The roly-poly one is Michael, and the younger one is Dave, my old frat brother. They hosted my birthday party. That was their apartment."

"You remember I told you about the guy pestering me at the party?"

"Dave?"

"You can probably get his fingerprints off the bruise on my thigh."

"If he touches you again..." said Jeff, and he yanked the emergency brake lever so hard, I thought he'd rip it out.

"Whoa. Easy, Tarzan."

"It's not funny," he said.

Maybe not funny, but I had to say it was pretty cute. Not Dave, of course. Dave was revolting, and he didn't get any *more* charming when I understood he had been reaching for my ass in the posh apartment he shared with his partner.

Jeff, on the other hand. Getting all ferocious, defending *me* of all people. That was pretty damned cute.

"Hey there!" shouted the chubby one. "Good lord, what happened to you?"

The black eye.

"I told you it was too much eye shadow, Jeff," I said.

"You didn't have that last night—did *you* do that?" he asked me.

"Hey Michael, have you met Theo?"

"At the party last night, of course," he remembered after a second. "Glad you could come along today."

The other one—the icky one—jumped down onto the dock.

"Ooooh, that's pretty," he said, pulling Jeff's sunglasses off. "How'd you do that?"

"I bit it," said Jeff, gingerly putting the sunglasses back in place.

And the asshole turned to me—and for once I don't mean Jeff.

"We met at the party, too, didn't we, Theo?" he slimed at me, rubbed the back of his head and smiled.

"We did. I'm glad I made an impression on you."

Was the whole day going to be like this, trapped on a teeny boat with this letch making handsy-handsy the whole time? And right under the nose of his boyfriend?! What a turdball. I was just about to tell him what would happen if he touched me again, but there was suddenly a big strong arm around me, pulling me close.

"Pretend you're my boyfriend," Jeff whispered as he nuzzled against my ear. I immediately slipped my arm around Jeff's waist, and gave good ol' Dave my most vicious smile.

*Take the hint, peckerwad.*

"Ever been sailing, Theo?" said Michael, reaching down to me and pulling me up onto the boat.

"No, I haven't! Thank you so much for inviting me."

"A virgin!" That was Dave, of course, and no doubt staring at my ass as I climbed up.

"Hey!" That was Jeff's voice. I turned, and I could see where Jeff had spun Dave around to him, and Dave was doing one of those asshole I-don't-know-what-you're-talking-about faces. I thought they might get into it right then and there, but —

"Let's get started, shall we?" said Capt. Michael, blithely clueless.

Michael and Dave got the boat away from the dock and steered carefully out of the harbor using a tiny motor—while Jeff and I did our best to stay out of the way. Once the boat was out in the clear, Dave switched off the motor, and we were enlisted in helping get the sail up—which immediately caught the breeze and pushed the boat forward. This little farm-boy had to admit—it was awesomely cool. It was so quiet! I loved that.

There was a little seating area in the back of the boat and Jeff pulled me down next to him, with Michael just to our right, steering. Dave was futzing around getting us sandwiches—poached chicken sandwiches if you can believe it. La-di-fucking-da! I gave Jeff a look—my pinky cocked as high as possible—at the sheer gayness of poached chicken sandwiches. No crusts of course.

"What's the green stuff?" I asked. It tasted like something you pulled out of the bottom of a lawn mower.

"Watercress," said Dave.

"Of course it is," said Jeff, trying not to laugh, but not trying very hard.

"Go ahead," said Dave, all martyr-y. "I try to do something nice…"

The best thing about the watercress was that it was easy to pull out. I cast my greens upon the water and hoped they never came back.

As we got farther out, the wind really picked up and the whole boat leaned sharply over to the side where Jeff and I were (the port side, someone said, which is 'left' to you and me). The boat leaned and it kept leaning, and I thought –

*Ohmygodthisthingisgoingrightoverandwe'reallgoingtodrown.*

I grabbed the side of the boat, petrified. I thought for sure this was it.

Nobody else seemed worried, so I resisted the impulse to scream at the top of my lungs. Could be embarrassing.

I tried to smile, while my grip on the railing was like steel. The water was like *Right! There!* Just inches away. Did nobody else see this???

I tried to keep calm. I tried humming something from *Unsinkable Molly Brown,* but all I could think was that that ocean looked like it would be really cold. Really cold, while we clung to the wreckage, drifting, waiting for a rescue that wasn't coming, saying brave and funny things to each other until our hands grew so numb from the icy waters that we would, one by one, slip quietly under the surface, just like Leo Di—

"You okay?" Jeff whispered in my ear, and put his arm around me. "You don't look very happy. Seasick?"

"No, I'm good. It's just—" My whole body was a knot. Jeff didn't seem worried. Was I being a big baby? I didn't want to be a big baby.

"You should have told me you were afraid of the water!"

"I'm not!" I said, still whispering. "I'm not afraid of anything! Okay, I'm not crazy about snakes, but aside from that..."

Had I known I was going to die on this boat today, I'd probably have done a couple things differently.

Like not gotten on this boat.

"What's wrong then?"

"It's a little tilty, is all," I whispered back. "Is it supposed to be all tilty like this?"

He pulled me closer.

"Yeah, it's okay. Sailboats lean, but they have really deep keels. The boat is built for this—all tilty."

"Okay. Good to know." That helped. I tried breathing again.

"You can't swim?"

"No I can swim. I swim great. In a pool. In a lake, that you'd probably call a pond, yeah I can swim. Maybe not in the Atlantic Ocean though."

"It's Long Island Sound."

"I'll keep that in mind."

"Hey Michael," he said. "Don't capsize today, okay?"

"Promise," said our stalwart captain, without taking his eyes from the horizon.

"See?" said Jeff.

"So Theo," said Dave. "We all know Jeffrey is this incredibly boring lawyer defending laxatives or tampons or whatever, but what about you? What do *you* do?"

"I'm a songwriter," I said. *Like it's any of your business, slime-licker.*

"Really?" said Michael, eyes still looking out ahead of us. "That's *way* more interesting than being a lawyer. What kind of songs do you write?"

"Musical theatre."

"Even *more* interesting!" He actually looked at me. "Are you serious? I *adore* musicals!"

"Oh of course! It was *your* vinyl collection I was pawing through last night!"

"You found the library, I take it. I'm so glad. So tell me, what's your favorite show of all time."

No hesitation.

*"Sunday in the Park."*

"Brilliant, isn't it?"

And we were off, swapping names of shows, songwriters, hits, flops, and our mutual admiration for all things Sondheim. I'd only been in New York a couple years, but Michael had seen a *lot*. I totally forgot to be scared. I even forgot about awful Dave for a while.

"There was actually a musical *Dracula*?" asked Jeff, when he heard Michael mention it.

"Godawful as it was, yes!"

"There were three vampire musicals that season," I pointed out.

"Each one worse than the last. Although my all-time favorite terrible-idea-for-a-musical has to be *Anna Karenina*," said Michael.

"You didn't see it, did you?"

"Are you kidding? Of course I did! It was the *worst*! I wouldn't have missed it for the world."

Poor Jeff and Dave, I thought. And I looked across at Dave, sitting on the bench opposite us. He didn't look bored at all. He was staring back at me, and you know how you hear about somebody undressing you with his eyes? Dave was way past that.

I gave Jeff an elbow.

"If you don't make him stop," I whispered, "I will."

Jeff leaned forward.

"Dave—a word?" and he gestured with his head toward the front of the boat. "I'll be right back," he said, giving me a kiss on the side of the head. I'll admit it, I was kinda digging this whole fake-boyfriend thing, and I missed that big warm arm as soon as he pulled it away.

I watched the two of them clamber up and around toward the front of the boat. I'll tell you something else about Jeff—he wears a nice pair of jeans.

"So my pick was *Sunday*," I said, as I realized that I wasn't scared about the boat any more. "What's *your* favorite then?" I asked Michael.

"*Chorus Line*. It was also my first. I was fifteen years old, it was a rainy Saturday, it was a matinee—and I never wanted to leave."

I'll spare you the rest of the musical-theatre-queen stuff.

# Chapter 37
## You Know that Road-to-Damascus Thing You're Always Hearing About…?

*JEFFREY*

Listening to Michael and Theo go on and on about musicals, something I knew absolutely zip about, should have been annoying as holy hell, but it wasn't. They were so *excited* about it. Listening to them was one of those times when I wondered if I was really gay after all. These two were rabid. Passionate! Can you imagine? What was *I* passionate about, I asked myself. The Knicks? Not even.

In the middle of listening to their raptures, and starting to think that I should really get to the theatre more often than I did, which was never, Theo sort of nudged me. I glanced across to my old frat brother sitting opposite us—and I'll be damned if he wasn't still staring at Theo like a cartoon wolf.

"If you don't make him stop," said Theo, "I will."

I had to do something. Like break his nose.

"Dave—a word?" and I nodded toward the bow. "I'll be right back," I said, and quickly pressed my lips against his curls.

Dave and I climbed up around the cabin to the front of the boat, leaving Michael and Theo still swapping stories.

"'Sup, bro?"

"So Dave," I said quietly, as we were in the front of the sailboat. "What the fuck?"

"What?"

"Did you invite us out on the orgy cruise or something? Because if I'd known that's what you had in mind, I'd have said no."

"Hey, it's potluck. I thought you'd brought a dish to pass." He looked back toward the stern. "And Theo is definitely a dish!"

"Shut the fuck up."

"What?"

"Look, if that's what you guys have planned, turn this thing right around and drop us back on the dock. I did not bring Theo to be your dessert."

"Chill, dude. We didn't plan anything. I just thought—when you brought the pretty little pastry along...and after all, you do owe me one."

"Let me put it this way, Dave. You will get your eyes off of Theo, or I will rip your dick off, just for the fun of watching the gulls fight over it. Is that clear enough?"

"Hey! Since when did you get so uptight? You never had a problem sharing before!"

"This is different!"

"What?" He was laughing. "Are you and the little redhead really a thing?"

"Yeah!" I said. "Yeah, we are!"

What.

The.

Fuck.

Until that second, I absolutely *knew* that we *weren't* 'a thing,' as my articulate asshole friend had put it. Theo was just this guy, my best friend's kid brother. He was mostly a total pain in the backside who could, I'll admit, sometimes be kinda fun to hang around with. And then I had to ask myself, when was the last time I'd actually had fun—before Theo I mean. But that didn't necessarily *mean* anything, did it?

And you're probably thinking: *Well duh!*

So, yeah, maybe I should have figured out that the ringing in my ears was the clue phone, and I should probably pick up—but I hadn't. I hadn't articulated any of this in my head. In my version of things, we were still just a couple guys. Anyway that's what I'd thought, right up until that totally unexpected Yeah-We-Are had come bounding out of its hiding place like a great big mutt puppy with oversized paws. And once it was spoken, I had to wonder.

Were we really—maybe—becoming something? I looked back to Theo. He had pushed his sunglasses up onto his head, his hair ruffling in the wind, the sun was shining for a bit and he was laughing at something Michael had said. He looked—dazzling. Fabulous. Transformed somehow from the oh-so snotty boy I'd met at lunch one day into this preposterously good-looking guy, this thing, this Theo.

So I answered Dave again, a little more thoughtfully.

"Yeah," I said finally. "I think maybe we are becoming something. And I'd really appreciate it if you'd stop trying to lick my boyfriend, okay?"

"Sorry. I didn't know."

"Just—go sit with your husband." Yeah, I know. Husband. But I used it deliberately here to remind him of his status. "Forsaking all others, remember?"

"Yeah, yeah," said Dave, as we climbed back around the cabin. "You forget, we left that bit out."

As soon as I sat down next to Theo, he worked his way back under my arm. Maybe he liked me a little too.

"So Theo," said Michael. "How did an interesting person like you ever get hooked up with this old stuffed shirt?"

"We slept together," said Theo dead serious.

"Like so many couples we know," said Dave.

"I was staying at Rebecca's," I clarified, "because of my apartment—"

"And I was too," said Theo.

"Theo is Rebecca's little brother."

"Oh," said our hosts in unison.

"And we had to share the fold-out couch," Theo finished.

"That must have been all cozy—and convenient," said Dave.

"Wasn't at all like what you're thinking," I said.

"We fought every night," said Theo.

"Cold feet? Blanket hog?" said Michael.

"Somebody eating crackers?"

"I don't even remember what the fights were about," said Theo. "Do you?"

"No, but it was something, every night—"

"And sometimes more than one fight per night—"

"And Rebecca would always come stumbling out in the most ridiculous pajamas, and she would break us up—"

"Or we'd still be yelling."

"So," said Dave. "Rebecca's little brother. Have you two known each other for years then?"

"No," I said.

"Only since I was meeting my sister for lunch one day and instead..." said Theo, looking over his shoulder to me. "Not very long at all, when you think about it."

"No, not long at all," I agreed, looking back at him.

"That's so sweet," said Michael. "Must have been love at first sight."

Theo and I burst into laughter.

"Two minutes into our first conversation, Theo threatened to castrate me. In the middle of *Café Un Deux Trois*. With a table knife."

"Ouch," said Michael.

"He totally had it coming."

"I'm sure he did," said Michael.

"And you've been together since…?" Dave trailed off.

I looked at Theo and he looked back to me. What should we say? When did our pretend relationship start?

"It's very new." It was the best answer I could think of.

"Ah," said Michael. "Explains everything."

Theo was still looking at me. His eyes were so close, I could see the different colors in the irises—the blues, the greens, even flecks of amber. It's a stupid cliché to describe somebody's eyes by saying they're blue as the sea or some such crap. I wasn't poetic, I wasn't all that sensitive or artistic or anything. I only knew this—Theo's eyes were suddenly the most beautiful thing I'd ever seen. No ocean even came close.

We were still staring at each other when Dave finally spoke up.

"Hey, you two. You guys want to go sit up on the bow? It's fun up there in the wind."

I looked at Theo, who nodded.

"You sure?" I asked.

"Yeah, let's do it."

"And if you don't like it, we can come back here, okay?"

"Okay."

I led him along the cabin—with him holding the arm I held out behind me—and he followed me out to the deck in front of the sail.

"Here," I said, and I settled down and leaned back against the front of the cabin, and spread my legs. "Sit here." And he carefully lowered himself until he finally just had to plop down in front of me between my knees. Dave's text that morning had said it might get cool out on the water, so I'd worn a windbreaker and Theo had grabbed a sweater. Both of these were miserably inadequate for the day, and I knew Theo had to be freezing. I pulled him to me, unzipped my jacket so he could lean against me a little closer for warmth, and I put my arms around him tightly.

"You okay?" I asked.

"Yeah."

"Not scared?"

"No, not a bit. I feel stupid now."

"It's okay."

Dave clambered out to us.

"Here," and he handed us each a glass of wine. "Enjoy!" And he climbed back to Michael.

"What did you say to him to make him behave?"

"I told him if he didn't, I'd rip his arm out and beat him with it."

"Can I watch?"

"Absolutely."

"Seriously, what did you guys talk about?"

"Seriously? Aside from the threats of physical violence?" I looked at him. I could have told him—but I was a coward and I totally chickened out. "It's a secret."

"Wow, you're no fun."

"Tell you later, maybe."

We looked out at the waves for a while, quiet, close.

"Hey, speaking of telling things," said Theo, "I didn't tell you—I had a job interview yesterday."

"Seriously?"

"I told you I was sending my resume in for an office job at Lincoln Center Theatre. Nothing will come of it, but I was totally surprised when they called."

"So, are you excited?"

"You kidding me? I mean it's just office work, but at least it's in the theatre. It would be hugely helpful making some professional connections."

"And bags and bags of money, I hope?"

"Ha! Welcome to not-for-profits. If I get the job, I'll probably have to apply for food stamps. But I'm sure there were mobs of applicants. I'll never get it."

"But you got the interview."

"True. I got the interview. Who knows how many others they talked to."

"I'll miss you 'round the office."

"Nothing'll come of it."

I looked down at his face a bit, as much as I could see from behind and above—just the outline, really, as he stared out at the water. Some freckles, the eyelashes.

"Hey, pretend boyfriend," I said finally.

"Hey," he said, nestling a little closer in my arms. "This is nice."

"It is. Even just pretend."

"Because we can't be real boyfriends."

"Nooooo," I said.

"Nooooo," Theo agreed.

"There's still Madison, after all."

"Actually...I may have given Madison the boot," he said. "Or he me. I'm not sure which."

I pulled myself around so I could look at his face a little better.

"You guys are..."

"Totally splitsville, man."

"Since when?"

"I don't know. Week ago."

"And you didn't say anything?"

He shrugged.

"Madison's a jerk," I said.

"True. He didn't like you much either."

"Screw him."

"Funny thing is—I don't think he liked *me* much either."

"He didn't really know you."

"No?"

"Too self-absorbed to know anybody."

"Probably. Same could be said of me though."

"True."

He pinched me really hard.

"But you're much better looking!" I howled.

"That's better."

And so we sat, pretend boyfriends, smiling and content, cuddled together and looking out at the sea, the Connecticut shore, the gulls, the white caps. I leaned my cheek against his ear on the windy side, to shield it. The sea was getting pretty rough, and Theo clung to my arms even tighter.

And I wanted nothing more in life than that, to hold him, to take care of him.

Why? I wondered. Why this impulse to look after him? Because he was young? He was twenty-four, he just looked younger. And innocent? Don't make me laugh. Judging from his skill and deportment in the bedroom?— Theo had clearly been playing sword-in-the-stone for a while now.

He might seem small and frail, but I knew what an illusion *that* was. He was about as delicate and fragile as a lynx.

Still, under all the snarl and the snark, I'd also heard some carefully hidden soft spots. That night when he was so angry because I'd picked him up—like he was nothing. He was terrified of that, of being dismissed, overlooked, discounted. And lord knows, Theo was definitely *something*.

And the frigging weirdest thing happened. I suddenly had this huge lump in my throat, I could hardly breathe. I had no idea where it came from, but all of a sudden it took everything I had not to shake with crying—I didn't want Theo to see this. And why? You'd think somebody had died. And then I knew.

I knew in that instant that I was in love, stupid in love with Theo.

I squeezed him tighter, pressed my head against his and closed my eyes.

I'd clearly never been in love before, and now, without a doubt, I was. God help me, I had fallen in love with this little fiend, this hell-puppy, this wolverine cub.

He was like a feral kitten, you wanted to take care of him, but he could explode in all directions, a fierce ball of hissing and claws. And this was what I had picked to fall in love with.

There he was, leaning up against me, and I couldn't get him close enough. I was tempted to whisper something to him, to tell him what I'd just realized, to say the famous three little words, but how would he react? To be honest—Theo sometimes scared the piss out of me, and this little epiphany I'd just had on a boat deck left me that much more vulnerable. Vulnerable—not a word I normally used to describe myself. But if I told Theo how I felt, and he laughed at me? I'd die. And of course he'd laugh at me. So instead, I squeezed him again, and I kissed his cold ear, and he pressed his head against mine, and I said what I had to say silently. Maybe he was telepathic.

It was about then that Dave called up to us, telling us we were nearly back to the harbor.

I was freezing, and Dave's prissy little sandwiches hadn't begun to make a dent in my hunger—but I was still sad to hear we were turning back. Would we ever have this closeness again? Or would we immediately revert to the sparring, the teasing, the yelling, just as soon as we were back on the dock and this strange magic was broken?

I fished in my jacket pocket for my phone, held it out and did something I hardly ever do anymore—I took a selfie. Of us, his face so close to mine. He looked genuinely happy to be where he was. At least for this moment, yeah, maybe he was a tiny bit in love too?

"What was the selfie for?" he asked.

"Just—felt like it."

"Do one on Snapchat, with the dog ears," he said, sitting up. "I love those."

"No," I said, closing the camera on my phone.

"Oh c'mon. I did one of those with Tommy last week—thought I'd bust a seam, it was so funny."

"No." I slipped the phone back into my jacket pocket.

"You're no fun," he said, smiling, squeezing my arm, and leaning back against me like a cat, getting comfortable.

"Nope, not the tiniest bit."

He leaned his head back, his temple against my cheek and I thought, yeah, maybe he was a little bit in love, too. And just thinking about the possibility of that, I was afraid I might blubber like a baby.

Or just bust a seam.

Back at the dock, Michael and Theo swapped plans about seeing some show, and we said our thank-yous and good-byes, and walked to the car. Theo scrambled in, still really cold and shivering and I hadn't realized how wet he'd gotten from the spray when the waves had kicked up. Now it was starting to drizzle. I heard deck shoes running on the wet asphalt behind me. I turned and it was Dave. He glanced in at Theo through the car window, and then turned to me.

"I'm glad I caught you. I just wanted to say—I'm really sorry about before. You still mad?"

Was I? No. No, I couldn't be mad.

"We're good, bro."

"Good." I thought we were done, but he had something else to say, so I waited, both of us squinting a little in the light rain. "I gotta tell ya. Watching you guys out on the bow this afternoon? I was so jealous."

"Jealous?" I chuckled. "Of what? Me? Or Theo?"

"Of you both. You guys—you're so obviously head over heels for each other. And I sat there wondering if I'd ever in my life been that much in love, like you two." I had no idea what to say. He looked back toward the boat. "If I ever was, I don't remember."

I glanced at Theo, who had his sweater pulled up over his nose, trying to get warmer, completely oblivious to how adorable it was.

"Dave, I—"

"Hey. Hang on to him. He's special."

"Yeah. He is." He tapped me on the upper arm, and turned to go. "Hey," I said. "So's Michael. Don't forget."

"Yeah. You're right." He turned and jogged back to the boat.

I got in the driver's seat.

"What'd *he* want?"

"Your phone number."

"Shut up."

"I didn't want to give it to him, but I do owe him for throwing me the birthday party and all—" He looked like he was about to vesuvius any second, so I jumped in quick before he could. "He said he thought we made a cute couple. Or something like that."

"Oh. Really?"

"More or less."

I couldn't believe I was blushing, and I tried to cover my embarrassment by starting the car. I reached and turned the heater on. The broken heater.

"No," said Theo.

"No heat!"

"Christ-on-a-cross-dressed-nun, we'll *die* before we get back."

I pulled out of the parking lot, drove straight across the road into another lot in front of a small souvenir store, and opened the car door.

"Where are you going?"

"They have homemade ice cream. Want some? I sure hope they have butter brickle."

"Shut up." He shivered even harder.

"Stay here, I'll be right back."

And within a couple minutes, I was. I tossed the plastic shopping bag in his lap and climbed back in the car.

He opened the bag and pulled out the jumbo white sweatshirt, a souvenir of beautiful—Sag Harbor.

"Is this Sag Harbor?"

"Not even close, but that was the sweatshirt they were selling. Don't ask me."

Theo wasted no time and quickly pulled his damp sweater off and he tugged the XXL sweatshirt down over his head. I watched as the red curls appeared in the neck hole, and then his head popped through.

Even at our first terrible meeting when he was such a scowling brat, I'd still recognized how pretty he was, the almost girlish features, delicate, and of course the whitest skin. But now, as his head appeared suddenly out of the sweatshirt, the straight, narrow nose, the freckles, the soft, teasing lips, and of course those mocking eyes—he was heartbreakingly beautiful. I had literally stopped breathing, watching him. There was no way he'd been this good-looking a week ago. I'd have remembered that.

He turned to me, obviously wondering why I was staring at him like an idiot.

"What?" he said laughing. "What?" And he ruffled his hands through the curls, in case maybe that was it. Every word, every gesture, every nuance that played across his face, every glance from those laughing eyes seemed perfection, seemed designed to make me want to hold him still closer. "What's wrong with you?" he asked finally.

"Nothing," I lied.

# Chapter 38
## April Showers

*THEO*

Fortunately the drop-off for the car was close to Rebecca's, and we raced back to the apartment. Jeff and I were both desperate to try to get warm again, if that was even still possible.

"I got dibs on the shower," I said, fumbling frantically with keys and frozen fingers at the apartment door.

"No way, Jose!"

*"Mais oui, Henri!"*

*"I* got the car, *I* drove, it's *my* friend's boat—"

*"Your* friend's hand on my knee."

"And I defended your knee valiantly. *I* get first shower."

By now we were kicking off our shoes and pulling shirts over our heads and pushing each other as we fought in front of the bathroom door—and then we stopped and looked at each other. There was an obvious solution that occurred to us both in the same instant. Without a word, we went back to pulling off clothes, and in no time we were standing together under the steaming shower. Merciful heavens.

And of course, after a while, once I'd stopped shivering, there we were. Two naked guys, close proximity, and—biology being what it is—one thing led to another, and the next thing you know...

Shower-sex is, I think, generally over-rated. Far better in concept than in execution. It *sounds* like this incredibly romantic, sensuous experience. In practice, there's never enough room, nothing lines up right, and you could seriously break your neck in the wet tub. When you factored in my five-foot-six and his six-foot-something, certain options were struck right off the menu. But, after some considerable trial and error and *lots* of laughing, we found a couple or three things that worked. Then we just stood together under the water, talking a little, kissing a little, holding each other until the ceiling was dripping with condensation from the steam and our fingers were long-since pruned. For the longest time I just let the warm water run over me while I pressed my face against his collar bone and neck, one arm around him and one hand on his chest.

As a rule, I didn't go out with big guys. I had sort of a knee-jerk prejudice against them. Big guys who thought I was cute invariably thought I was cute because they could pick me up and throw me down on the bed. Enrique, the trainer guy everybody was so hot about? I could tell—one of those guys. That guy had 'he-man' written all over him. I don't know about you, but I can't tell you how much I *hate* being picked up and thrown down on the bed. The last guy who tried that won't try it again soon. For all I know he still can't straighten up. I have no use for he-men.

Got a caveman fetish? Go hump a mammoth.

So that's where I stand on guys who are a lot bigger than me. Like Jeff. And I suppose, if I'm going to get all revelatory here, I would maybe admit that I didn't go out with big guys because big guys—okay, I don't want to say they scared me, but let's face it, the big ones could hurt you, and they probably *would,* just because they could. That's what I'd thought anyway, and I'd just stayed away from them.

But now, with Jeff? Feeling all of this in my arms, the size of him, the shoulders, the breadth of his chest, the muscle, this bit of coarse chest hair under my hand, and his amazing arm around me—I wasn't scared. I felt somehow safer than ever.

I knew I could be a little overly wary with people—hence my general spikiness. Like Madison said, I guess.

But I was starting to think I could trust this guy, this suit, this— shudder—*lawyer.* Jeff wasn't going to hurt me. I was sure of that.

And somehow just saying that to myself, I felt like I'd set down a weight or something. Like I could finally relax. I pulled him even closer and he held me tighter too, almost as if he knew.

We hadn't really been planning ahead when we started this whole shower adventure, and when we finally turned off the taps, we realized that there was only one small towel on the towel rack. We tried drying each other off with it, giggling. I should mention that Jeff had a fantastic body, which I was only just starting to appreciate. I don't know why I hadn't been sneaking peeks at him earlier. I was about to go out and get another towel when we realized, between giggles and fighting over the towel, that we could hear someone else in the apartment.

"Theo! I'm home," yelled Rebecca all sing-songy.

"Shitballs!"

"Ooops," said Jeff.

"Quick—climb out the window!" I said. Remember, we were on the fifth floor, and this sent us into a further wallow of giggles.

"Tell her it's the plumber," suggested Jeff. "Checking your pipes." Funniest thing on earth.

"Shhhhh!"

"We didn't bring the robes," Jeff pointed out. I glanced around. Fuuuuuck! "Go get them."

"Okay, hang on," I said taking a breath. "Ready?"

I wrapped myself in the one very wet towel and opened the bathroom door *juuuust* far enough to stick my head out. There was my sister, sitting expectantly in a chair in the middle of the room, facing the bathroom door.

"Hey, Becca."

"Heeeeeeeey, Thee-o." Then she added, still sing-songy. "Whatcha doooo-in'?" Like she didn't know.

Obviously she had heard us—God knows how long she'd been in the apartment—and now she was sitting there, hands folded in her lap, looking like the cat who just swallowed the Canary Islands.

# Chapter 39
## *Quelle suprise!*

REBECCA

I'd expected to be in the office until six or seven, but I just couldn't do it. At three I'd finally bagged it and grabbed a car service home. After a quick stop at Whole Foods, I staggered in, dropped the groceries on the kitchen counter—and noticed a pile of wet clothes on the floor in front of the bathroom. Obviously Theo needed a little talking to. It was then, as I seethed, that I heard something that made me forget all about Theo's lazy carelessness. I heard laughter. Male laughter. From the bathroom.

More accurately, male *laughters.*

Okay, it was Theo. But there was another voice in there, and it took me a bit to recognize it. Of course I'd have recognized it sooner, if it hadn't been so impossible. It almost sounded like Jeffrey Bornic. If I didn't know better, I'd swear that was…you get the picture. Because unless they were re-enacting a scene from *Psycho* in there, complete with real blood, the *last* person I expected to hear laughing in the shower with my little brother was my best friend Jeffrey. WTF, as they say.

The water turned off.

Voices. Giggles. Jeffrey could giggle? I'd known him how long? And I'd never heard him giggle. Was this a miracle ? Or a harbinger of the end times?

I decided I really needed to watch and see how this played out. The boys would have to come out sooner or later, wouldn't they?

"Theo! I'm home!" I called. I wanted to give them a little warning, if only to spare myself the spectacle of one of them prancing out here with a dangling participle.

Did Theo just say 'shitballs'?

"Ooops," said Jeff.

And then there was some whispering and muttering and more giggles.

I decided to pull up a chair in the middle of the room facing the bathroom door. This should be fun.

Finally the door opened a smidge and Theo stuck his face out.

"Hey, Becca." He had the best case of beard-burn I'd ever seen.

"Heeeeeeeey, Theo. Whatcha' doin'?" I asked, all childish innocence.

"Ehhhhhhhhhhh—could you do me a huge favor, and hand me my robe from over there?" It was on a hook with some other things.

I got up.

"This one?" I said, holding up the green robe that Jeffrey had bought him.

"Yeah. And the other one—it's still right there?"

"Oh. You mean this one? Jeffrey's robe? You need Jeffrey's robe, too?"

"Hey, Rebecca," said Jeffrey, sticking his head out over Theo's.

"Wow, nice shiner!"

"Oh yeah I'd almost forgotten about that," he said.

"Have a good day?" Theo asked.

"Maybe not quite so good as yours, but yeah, it was okay." I handed over the robes.

"Thanks," said Theo, and the bathroom door closed. There was more whispering, some more giggling, and finally they appeared. Theo seemed a little sheepish, which was totally out of character; but Jeffrey had apparently decided he was going to gut this out. He plopped down on the couch, and pulled Theo down next to him, both arms around him, and he grinned at me. I'd never really seen Jeffrey grin before when it wasn't downright menacing. There were associates in the office who were terrified of his smile. But now—he looked positively gleeful. And something else. Proud? Yeah, that was it. He was holding on to Theo and proud about it.

"So hey, boys," I said. "What's new?"

"Not much," tried Theo. "What's new with you?" And they burst into sputtering laughter.

"First," I said, turning to look out the windows, "if you're going to sit around in robes, you need to sit like ladies, okay?" Knees slapped together and those beautiful robes were tugged in place. "Thank you. So. How'd you get the black eye, Jeffrey?"

"Theo."

"Hey!" objected Theo. "You promised not to tell!"

"The kid has a vicious right hook," Jeffrey explained to me.

"Seriously?" I asked.

"No, of course not," he laughed. "He can't reach that high. Owwwwwwww!" Theo had reached around behind him and was pinching Jeff where he'd have a spare tire if he didn't run umpteen miles every stinking day. "Damn!" said Jeff scowling seriously. "That is going to leave a *huge* bruise!"

"You'd been warned. You should have known better."

No remorse there.

"The black eye?" I asked.

"It's a long story," said Jeff, still rubbing his side.

I waited.

"Somebody got—understandably—pissed off at Theo, so he, the somebody—not so understandably—punched me in the head."

"That's the truth, isn't it," I said, recognizing what had been more or less Theo's life story.

"Yup," confirmed Jeff.

"Yup," added Theo.

"So did you guys go sailing today after all?"

"Oh yeah. Sailing!" said Theo.

"We did!" said Jeffrey.

They looked at each other, grinning again.

"It was fun," said Jeffrey.

"But cold," said Theo.

"So cold. Really cold."

"And there was no heat in Jeff's crappy rental car."

"True. And Theo was wet—"

"The waves kept splashing up—"

"And we were both freezing. That's why we needed a hot shower."

"Like pronto."

"Naturally," I pitched in.

"But we couldn't agree on who got the shower first, so..."

"Naturally," I nodded. "Makes perfect sense."

"Does it really?" said Jeffrey sputtering a little.

"You guys *did* clean up after yourselves, I hope. I don't want to go to take a shower and find it all Jackson Pollock in there."

Theo's eyes got huge and he jumped up and bolted to the bathroom while Jeffrey laughed.

"So, just tell me. Are you guys—together now?"

"I don't know," said Jeffrey. "I haven't—we haven't talked about it. Hey, Theo?" he called.

"Yeah," said Theo from the bathroom, and we heard water running.

"Rebecca wants to know—are we together now?"

Theo stuck his head out.

"I don't know," said Theo. "Are we?"

"Maybe? Would you hate that?"

"I don't know about 'hate'."

"So—maybe?"

"Maybe." Theo turned to me. "Yeah. A definite maybe." He ran over, kissed Jeffrey's cheek, and ran back to the bathroom.

"So it's more than just the one time," I tried, hoping for clarification of how things stood.

"Today?" said Jeffrey.

"Just the once, today," said Theo from the bathroom.

This was not helping.

"So it's on-going?" Theo came back and flopped down on the couch, leaning against Jeffrey again.

"All clear!" he grinned.

"Like a lady," I reminded him.

"Sorry!"

"Thank you."

"Rebecca wants to know if we're on-going."

"I don't know about on-going," tried Theo. "It's been more on-and-off, wouldn't you say? Static, really."

"Static's about right," said Jeffrey. "Static's a good word."

"Thanks. I'm a writer, you know," said Theo. "Important to have the right word. Good writing—good nouns and good verbs."

"Static is neither of those."

"Well, if you're going to get all technical about it, static *can* be a noun, as in 'stop giving me static, you quibbling little prig'!"

"That's not how you were—"

"And why do you have to be such a pedant? At *every* opportunity?"

"Me? *I'm* not the one—"

"Hey hey hey!" I stopped them. "May I point out that about two minutes ago you guys came out of the bathroom wrapped in robes and afterglow, and now you're bickering about parts of speech."

"Yeah," said Theo. "Pretty funny, huh?" He grinned at Jeffrey.

"You two hated each other," I pointed out the obvious.

"Still do," said Theo. "Don't we?"

"Definitely," said Jeffrey, and he pulled Theo closer and rubbed his face in the red curls.

I looked from one to the other—my best friend, my baby brother. With grins that could light up a black hole.

"Hey," said Jeff. "Can we revisit 'static' for a second?"

"I *know*!" said Theo. "It's an adjective!"

"That's not what I meant."

"What then?"

"Do we want to try something—less static, maybe?"

The look on Jeffrey's face. He was about ten years younger at least. And scared and unsure of himself. So *not* like the hungry lawyer on the fast track that I worked with every day, the one who could sniff out weakness like a cheetah. Jeffrey Bornic, the born killer, famous among the associates for his threatening glare, was suddenly a nervous teenager in front of Theo.

"You mean, you think we should maybe try being more on than off?" asked Theo, eyes glued to Jeffrey's. His face mirrored Jeff's expression perfectly.

"Yeah. Or we could try—just—on."

"Yeah, okay. If you want."

"Would you? Like that?"

Theo just nodded.

"I think you're both insane," I said after a second, just to remind them I was still in the room. "The way you two squabble. I hope you're not doing anything stupid."

"Me too," said Jeffrey.

"Me three," chimed Theo.

"But I have to say something here, seriously. Theo, he's my best friend. Be nice to him, okay?"

"I'll try, but you never know," said Theo looking sideways at Jeffrey with a teasing smile.

"Jeffrey. He's my little brother. If you hurt him? I will—I will—I will get on the phone and call our brother Gilbert, the one who played for the Hawkeyes? And Gilbert will not hesitate, he will happily hop on a plane, come here, and break your back."

"No joke," said Theo, nodding seriously to Jeff. "He will."

Jeff looked down at Theo.

"Well then," he said softly. "I guess I better promise."

"Promise what?" said Theo looking back up at Jeffrey.

"Never to break your heart."

*Wow,* I thought. *If anybody ever looked at me like that...*

I picked up my keys from the counter and went out. I don't imagine they even noticed.

# Chapter 40
## And Then One Day the World Came Quietly to an End

*THEO*

So we'd had this fantastic weekend, with the sailing and everything, and deciding we'd try being—you know—a couple for a while and see if we could do that without killing each other, which was okay because I hardly felt like killing him at all now. And then the week started and it was Monday, and we were back at the office, trying to be cool about the whole thing, which was way harder than you'd think, because we both kept smiling too much, and then one of us would say, "Stop smiling at me like that," and the other would say, "I'm not the one smiling, you are," "no, you are," "no, you are," and then we'd try *not* smiling until one of us would start giggling and after that you could just forget about it.

I'm sure we were enough to make any normal person urp.

We were starting to get looks and the second time Victoria caught him leaning on my desk she straight-up told him to stop wasting my time and to go bill some of his own—so Jeff decided to stay away from me (at work anyway) as much as possible.

With that in mind, we knew we couldn't eat lunch together in the firm cafeteria, so I had lunch with Tommy instead.

Tommy is easily the nosiest person I have ever met, so of course he started pestering me with questions about the birthday party, so I told him about the party and about Dave, the gropey creep, and how much I hated gropey creeps and who doesn't? And the homeless guy in Central Park who called me a *maricón,* and how I *hated* being called a *maricón* and who doesn't? And how Jeff stepped in to protect me, which was ridiculous because the guy was so drunk and if Jeff had only ducked, the guy would have fallen over and we could have pissed on his unconscious gay-basher body and gone on our merry way. (I know, I should have greater empathy for our homeless brothers and sisters, and generally I do, but when they call me a *maricón*—game over.) Anyway, I explained to Tommy how Jeff *hadn't* ducked because he was too busy pulling out his wallet, as usual, and then—*pow*. Tommy seemed strangely impressed that Jeff had taken a punch for me. I mean, yeah, doesn't happen every day, but he shoulda ducked. Anyway.

Now Jeff was going around telling people either that he walked into a door or that it was a strange food allergy, by turns. And then I told Tommy about going sailing with the gropey creep from the birthday party and how Jeff and I pretended to snuggle to keep the gropey creep at bay and now we were like really going steady, just like high school. Only with heaps more sex.

And you know, I was actually thinking that this last bit of my story would leave Tommy speechless—okay, a ridiculous idea, but that's what I'd honestly expected—and instead? Instead he said he knew it was coming, and that it was about time we figured it out.

Turned out *I* was the speechless one.

I left work early because it was Monday, and I went to workshop— where, wonder of wonders, miracle of miracles, there was no Madison. I skipped the usual coffee-klatch after so I could spend more time with Jeff, now that I had a key to his apartment, and we ordered Mexican food and watched *Seven Brides for Seven Brothers* because Jeff had never seen it. Can you imagine?

His education begins. Poor sap has no idea what he's in for. (He made me promise to go to a hockey game with him, but he didn't say when. A terrible oversight for an attorney, don't you think? I'm spared watching a bunch of toothless goons with sticks who...yeah, don't get me started.)

And that's pretty much how the week went, with me stopping by Rebecca's after work to pick up fresh clothes and then sprinting across the park over to Jeff's. (A bicycle would have made life so much easier. Or a pony.)

The point is, we really *were* boyfriends after all.

Imagine. Me and a lawyer? Me and a really *tall* lawyer?! Me and Jeff *Bornic*???

And then on Thursday, Victoria had asked me to organize her e-mails on the *Hiromi* case, just pull it all into a new folder, which is what I was doing, when the subject line of one caught my eye. It was: R. McPherson.

Okay, this e-mail was clearly not meant for me to read. It was from Victoria, addressed to Tommy's boss, the Kaminsky guy. About my sister. It was forwarding an e-mail from Bornic, Jeffrey A.

I should have stopped. I knew I should. But of course, being the jerk that I am, I didn't. I kept right on reading.

**To:** Kaminsky, Daniel
**From:** Collins, Victoria
**Sent:** Tues., Jan 19, 2:32 pm
**Subject:** R. McPherson

Dan—
Jeffrey Bornic sent me the attached, detailing something that happened on the *Mayerhoffer* case. Perhaps you remember it -- if I had ever known about it, I'd forgotten it. His narrative does point up a serious lapse in judgment on the part of Rebecca McPherson, and probably warrants at least speaking to her about it, and getting her side of the story.
Quite frankly, I wish this had come from anyone besides Jeffrey. Perhaps someone needs to speak to him about the culture here, and that while this sort of cutthroat approach to internal competition might be commonplace at other firms, etc.? I also thought he and Rebecca were friends, or did I miss something?
In any case, as much as I don't like it, I don't think we can ignore Jeffrey's revelations. With that in mind, I have to recommend that you take Jeffrey onto your *Hiromi* team and leave Rebecca where she is.
I will, however, remember this, should anyone ever bring up Jeffrey's name as a potential partner.
Let's discuss.
V.

Attached was an e-mail from Jeff to Victoria, laying out something I didn't really understand that happened on this case, where Becca apparently screwed up big time and Jeff covered her ass.

Until now.

I'm sure I just sat there and stared into space for a good long time. Everything seemed to hurt. I pulled out my phone and tried to send him a text.

I could barely see.

# Text to Jeff

*I need to talk to you.*

*Hey, cutie! I'd love to see you too, but can't it wait til after work? LOL*

*I'm not being funny. I need to see you. Front of the library, by the lions.*

*Hey—you ok?*

*When can you get there?*

*I'm in a meeting. Half an hour? If I can get out sooner, I will.*

*R u ok?*

*?*

*I'm coming now.*

# Chapter 41
## The Smoking Gun...Pointed at My Head

*JEFFREY*

He saw me before I saw him—he'd obviously been waiting for me, and if I didn't know something was up from the strange text, I certainly knew as soon as I saw him.

"Theo, what's wrong?"

"This!" he said, and he punched a couple of pieces of paper against my chest. "This is wrong! So un-fucking-believably wrong!"

I read through the first few lines of Victoria's e-mail. Ohgod. I glanced at the page stapled to it, and saw my e-mail to her about Rebecca.

I was apparently getting the *Hiromi* case, but Victoria hated me anyway, and my chances of a partnership at Parker O'Neill were exactly zip—and I didn't care. I just didn't care.

The only thing that mattered was the angry, red face in front me. Angry and hurt.

There was no coming back from this. He would loathe me now. *I* loathed me.

"Say something. Explain this. Make this okay." He thumped me in the chest with each sentence.

"Please don't hate me."

"How can I *not* hate you?" It was a warm spring day, sunny, there were tourists everywhere, and Theo was getting loud. "You threw my sister under a bus!"

"You don't understand," I tried. Maybe if I could make him see.

"Please, explain it to me. Make me see how betraying your best friend isn't as despicable as it looks."

"It wasn't personal! It was business."

There was a big group of French tourists getting a lecture from a fruity-voiced woman only a few feet away from us.

"Oh, that makes it so much better. After sleeping on her couch, not to mention—"

"Sleeping on her couch, that's personal. You—that's personal. But this—this is business. Business is business. It's a tough place."

He hated me for being a bastard. Well, I *was* a bastard—just like my dad.

"And that justifies anything?" he asked.

"No! But—yes! In a way. I need that partnership, Theo. I need to get out of advertising claims. And a partnership? There's a *lot* of money at stake!"

"I'm so glad you were operating from such a lofty motive!"

"You don't understand! This isn't Iowa! This is New York! You have no idea, the pressure— You're just a kid, playing around with your little songwriting buddies, but this is the real world!"

"Fuck you and fuck your real world then."

"You don't know what business is like!"

"Shut-up-shut-up-shut-up-shut-up!"

The guide from the French tour group stopped in her speech about the library lions, and the heads of sixty French tourists turned to us. Theo was oblivious.

"Theo—"

This was the price of getting ahead. The price of getting rich. A price my father paid, I guess. We all hated him. His enemies, his friends, his wife, his sons.

Was that *really* what I wanted?

"Theo, I don't believe any of that crap I just said. Those were the kinds of arguments I used with myself to make it okay—but it was never okay. You're right. I'm so, so sorry. Please."

"You know, Madison asked me why I push people away all the time, why I bite the hands of everyone around me, and I didn't know how to answer him."

"Please—"

"I know now. This is why. *This.* This is why. I knew you were this asshole when I first laid eyes on you, but then I thought—maybe—" In his fury, he was wiping tears from his cheek with the back of his hand even as he was screaming at me. I had made the most precious thing in the world cry. I really *was* despicable.

"I don't want to be that asshole anymore," I tried, softly.

"Well, good luck with that."

"Theo, let me explain, let me fix this somehow."

"Give me one reason why I should ever speak to you!"

"Because I love you, damn it."

He looked at me for a second and bit his lips together. He pressed the heels of his hands against his eyes. When he spoke, all the rage was gone. I could barely hear him.

"That just makes it so—much—worse."

He sounded—I don't know—defeated. And so was I.

His head snapped back in the beginning of a sob and he turned and he ran. He dodged through the tourists, down the steps to Fifth Avenue, and bolted through the traffic until he disappeared around the corner at 40th.

I wanted to run after him. I wanted to stop him, hold him, make him stay until he calmed down, make him cry it out, make him understand how much I loved him. I would force him to listen to me, force him to be reasonable.

But I couldn't force him to stay. This was Theo, after all. The feral kitten. I couldn't force him into anything. I couldn't make him listen. And even if I could get him to be reasonable, it wouldn't help. It was reasonable to hate me.

So I didn't chase after him. I stood there without moving a step for I don't know how long—an hour maybe?

Because I knew, as that last flash of red hair caught the sunlight and then disappeared around the corner at 40th Street, that my life, my hope, and any reason I could think of to go on—slipped around the corner with it.

# Text from Rebecca

*What did you do to him?*

*Didn't he tell you?*

*No. He says everything's hunky-fucking-dory,*
*he's fan-fucking-tastic. His words.*

*Good. I'm glad he's happy.*

*He's not happy, you dickhead.*
*WHAT DID YOU DO?*

*Tell him I'm sorry.*

*Tell him yourself.*

*I can't.*

*?*

*?*

*Don't you dare ignore me!!!*

*Dipshit.*

# Chapter 42
## Running Out

*JEFFREY*

You know how I mentioned that after it was over with Roger, I hadn't really missed him? Hadn't sat around staring into space, reliving every conversation, every moment we'd spent together. I had apparently saved it up for Theo. I was doing all of that now like a pro.

I hadn't slept, I'd been sitting in this chair in the dark, staring out a window at the windows across the street since yesterday afternoon.

It was starting to get light out now. I should clean myself up and get ready to go to work. I should. I just couldn't quite get myself to stand up. I should go shower. Or not.

And then I got an idea.

The one thing that always made me feel better.

No, I wasn't going to jerk off. I was going to run. I always felt better running. Mostly, I suppose, because when I was running, I didn't feel at all.

I could use some numbness today.

I managed to will myself to stand up. I got to the bathroom and peed for about ten minutes. *Man* did I need that. And I stripped and pulled on some running gear. I stretched, did some warming.

This will be good, I thought.

This will work. If I run, I'll forget. Just run and don't stop.

Out the door, stretching in the elevator.

I was later than usual. No garbage guys, no poodle. There was sunlight and there were people out and about. There was traffic in the street. A dickhead in a Mercedes. Ever notice guys with those cars all drive like

Nazis? Yeah, yeah, you can wait two frigging seconds, Adolf. Great, blow your horn. You can blow me while you're at it.

I made my way over to Fifth Ave., ran in place at the light, and then decided—screw it—and I ducked across the street without waiting for the light to change. A horn blared as I dashed across. *Okay, that wasn't the smartest thing I've ever done in my life,* I thought, as a delivery van braked and swerved, still laying on the horn the whole time. *Yeah, well. Bite me, pal. So sorry to be an inconvenience. Dumbfuck.*

I jogged along on the path around behind the museum, made the sharp right onto the running path, and I let it happen. I let my legs reach out in their long strides.

Thamp thamp thamp thamp.

Now it would happen. Now I'd be able to turn my brain off.

I glanced down for a second to see my legs working, the blond hair on my legs in the sunlight, the muscles underneath. I had good legs. Theo said my legs were hot.

*Shut up. Just run.*

Thamp thamp.

Could I just pretend this didn't happen? Pretend that I'd never felt anything? See him around the office? Nod in the elevator? Could I bear that? Could I really go to work every day with him there?

I couldn't quit. I had sixteen subcontractors depending on me to put their kids through college.

And I couldn't get Theo fired. I couldn't do anything to hurt him. More than I already had, I mean. Fuck.

*Run. Just shut up and run.*

I would just go to work, avoid him as much as possible—and then if we did bump into each other, just let it be as miserable as it was going to be. Just gut it out, Bornic. You made your bed.

He'd be okay, I figured. I had never been sure how involved he was anyway.

Of course I'd made him cry yesterday.

Thamp thamp.

So he must feel *some*thing.

Thamp thamp.

I was such an unbelievable fucking bastard.

I normally ran earlier, so the sunlight shining across onto the buildings to the West Side was new to me. I'd never noticed these things. I was running along with the Reservoir on my left.

I'd made that beautiful boy cry. My God, I was the absolute dregs. Even fat, awful Madison had probably never made him cry. Other way around maybe.

Thamp thamp.

And I couldn't see a way forward.

I couldn't undo what I'd done. I couldn't make it better.

I didn't want to be the asshole he thought I was. And that I *was*. I wanted to be the guy he saw when he looked at me in my apartment that night. I wanted to be the guy he smiled at in that selfie, that selfie that I'd spent half the night staring at until I had to plug my phone in.

By now I was past the Reservoir. I would just turn left up ahead and bend back downtown to start down the other side of the park, like every other day.

I could do that. But what would I be running back to?

*Just shut up. Stop thinking.*

This so wasn't working, was it. Nothing was working. My head was supposed to be empty when I was running and instead it was full of this. I was supposed to feel numb. I felt like shit. I *was* shit. Of course he'd dumped me, he deserved so much better.

Now he knew me, knew what I was capable of. He knew what a dick I was, what my dick-father had made me, what I'd *let* my dick-father make me.

I was running, and my head was still stuffed, stuffed with Theo and those eyes and his freckled little hands pressing back tears. And this incredible horrible coldness in my chest.

Thamp thamp.

I got to the turn—and I did what I *never* do. I veered off my path, I went right instead of left. I wasn't ready to turn back, I couldn't. I had to go on.

Thamp thamp.

*Just run, you bastard.*

I picked up my pace. I was really moving now. I didn't know how long I could sustain this, but I wanted to feel my calves hurt, my thighs, I wanted my lungs to burn. I pushed on.

*I hate this fucking park. How the hell do you get out of here anyway?*

As I went past the—what?—the Harlem Meer maybe?—I saw a sign for 124th Street, and I followed it.

There had to be a way. There must be something I could do, some way that I could make him see, so he'd know that I was trying. It wouldn't fix anything, but he'd at least know I tried. At least he would know that I wasn't somebody who didn't *try*.

I bolted out the park gate and crossed the street—whatever it was—against the light. Was this 124th?

I'd never been up here above the park in my life. I was on the sidewalk, running past people. This was Harlem, I was pretty sure. I just kept going.

*Run farther,* I thought.

I wasn't running away from anything, I wasn't running *toward* anything either. I was just running.

Thamp thamp thamp thamp.

The rhythm in my head started talking or maybe it was the rhythm in my feet.

Done something awful.

Done something awful.

The light was against me, but I couldn't stop, didn't dare stop. I turned right instead. Scared to stop. I knew if I stopped, *I'd* stop. I'd literally stop. Crushed under this. So I had to keep moving, no matter.

*Just fucking run.*

Long crosstown block. Stretch out the legs. At the corner—traffic. I had to turn left, pushing farther uptown. I was really moving out now. Practically a sprint. No idea where this was coming from, I should be dying by now at this pace. I was only aware of the sound of my shoes on the pavement, the sound in my head.

No way to fix it.

No way to fix it.

No way to fix it.

No way to—

And on I went. Red light—turn. Get to the corner and turn again.

Red light. Screw it. Across the street against traffic. Just keep going, they'll stop.

Another red light. Run faster. Listen to your feet, the burn in your chest.

Can't make it right.

Can't make it right.

Can't make it right.

Can't make it—

I had no idea where I was, I couldn't see the street signs anymore, I couldn't see much of anything anymore, it was all blurred for some reason. My eyes burned. My face was wet.

Nothing you can do.

Nothing you can do.

Another red light.

Nothing you can do.

Go for it, go for it, go for it. They'll stop.

There was a scream of a brake and a car horn. Someone on the sidewalk yelled. I turned to see this smear of yellow coming at me, stopping in time—almost. I held out my right hand to fend it off, and managed to sort of vault myself off the hood of the taxi and up and over onto the far side of the street. I fell forward and crashed against the pole of the traffic light, which I grabbed and held myself up. Someone was yelling. Maybe it was even English. Maybe it was Bangla. No idea. People were talking, talking, and more yelling.

There was a face in front of me—dark, pockmarked skin, jaundiced eyes, he was asking me something. I blinked to clear my eyes and tried to focus. I wiped the sweat from my forehead with my forearm—there was blood on it.

"Are you okay, buddy?" asked the old face. "Are you okay?"

I nodded. I needed to breathe. I couldn't breathe.

I nodded that I was okay. My lungs were like torches in my chest.

"You don't look okay, buddy," he said. "You sure you're okay?"

"Yes," I said although nothing came out. If only I could breathe, I'd be fine. I felt my grip on the lamppost slipping. "Yes—yes," I managed to croak between the sobs that convulsed me, that I couldn't stop. I was pretty sure I was going to fall down. "Yes," I said louder. "Never better—I'm perfect. Fan. Fucking. Tastic."

## Text to Rebecca

You still speaking to me?

Probably not.

I promise I'll fix it.

That's a start.

But I need a favor. Big time.

Huge.

?

Can you come pick me up?

??

Columbia Presbyterian—
emergency room entrance.

Did Theo put you in the hospital???

No! And I can't believe you
actually made me laugh.

Ouch.

What happened?

*Stupid accident. I'll explain. But they won't let me go unless somebody comes to take me home.*

*WTF?*

*I'll explain. Don't say anything to Theo.*

*Please.*

# Chapter 43
## Rescue

*JEFFREY*

"I really appreciate this."

It took me forever to get the forms and releases signed, and that was without reading them. Who knows what rights I was throwing away. Goddamn lawyers. I was doing my best to keep the poor cab driver out of trouble—it wasn't his fault, and he hadn't actually hit me, I'd run into a lamppost, as I'd explained to the two cops they'd sent to interview me.

"With that bandage, you look like you're back from the wars," said Rebecca. Aside from some bruises and the scrapes on my hands, my only real injury was where I'd banged my head on the traffic light. The whole thing was incredibly stupid and embarrassing. But because I was bleeding—and apparently couldn't stop crying—they had plopped me in here, shoved a couple bottles of saline solution and God knows what else into me, and I'd slept for a day—except that they kept coming around to wake me up and shine little flashlights in my eyes, which got to be seriously annoying.

"Home, James," I said, hoping for humor.

Rebecca called a car service, and now, after a quick consult from the doctor discharging me, she was helping me get in the backseat like I was ninety or something. I had a bump on my head, not a shattered pelvis!

"You're coming back to my place," said Rebecca.

"No."

"You've had a concussion. You shouldn't be alone. You're coming back to my place."

"Theo."

"What about him?"

"I can't. And he can't either. We—just can't." I gave the guy my address.

"What the hell happened?" she asked as she climbed in the other side. She told the driver to ignore me and gave him *her* address on the Upper West before she turned back to me. "Look, nobody knows better than I do that Theo is not the easiest person in the world, and neither are you. But not very long ago you two were stupid goofy about each other, and now you're—you're this! He's manically pretending that nothing's wrong, and you're—what?—suicidal, apparently—"

"I'm not suicidal."

"You ran out in front of a taxi."

"I didn't *mean* to get hit. Look. I'm much better now. I've had all day in that bed to think about it. I'll be okay."

"What *happened*?"

"I did something a while back. And I meant to try to undo it, but I didn't because—because I'm an awful person. I did something bad."

"To Theo?"

"To you, Rebecca."

"Oh."

"I'm really really sorry, and I'm going to try to make it up. I'm going to try to fix it. But Theo was reading Victoria's e-mails, and he caught on to what I'd done and now he hates me, and he's totally right, and you'll hate me too when I tell you."

She looked out at the Hudson River for a few very long seconds.

"Then don't," she said finally.

"What?!"

"Don't tell me. I don't want to hate you."

"Serious?"

"Yes. Tell me about it when you've fixed it, how's that for a deal. And for heaven's sake don't look at me like that! You start crying and I'm taking you straight back to your bedpan."

Turns out, Iowans are even nicer than Canadians.

"I so don't deserve you," I said quietly.

"You got that right."

"Or Theo."

"Ehhhhhhhh—I don't know about *that* one. If you two don't deserve each other, who does?"

"You think so?"

"You're both really smart and at the same time total idiots. And you both occasionally feel compelled to be mind-boggling assholes. Match made in heaven."

We rode together quietly for a bit.

"I am so in love with your little brother, Rebecca."

"Yeah, I'd sorta picked up on that."

"I've never felt like this before."

"I sorta picked up on that as well. You were pissed off after Roger, but you never chucked yourself in front of oncoming traffic."

"God, I feel so stupid."

"You got that right too," she said, and leaned forward. "Change of plans—looks like we're going to the Upper East Side instead."

# Chapter 44
## A Broken Heart, Soldiering On

*REBECCA*

So that night I shared a bed with Jeffrey Bornic. He had a whole guest room, but I didn't really think he should be alone—because of his head, and, well, because of his head. So without either of us saying a word about it, we just bunked in together—me, in a borrowed track suit. Not as comfortable as my flannel nightgowns, but you make sacrifices.

I didn't see Theo again until I got home after work. He was hunched over his keyboard, earphones on. I gave him a big wave to let him know I was there—but he still didn't see me, so I just went on into the bedroom to change.

"Whoa!" He threw the headphones off and jumped up as I walked past him. "Oh man, you scared me!"

"Sorry. I tried to get your attention." And I went on into the bedroom. "Did you eat?" I called out.

"I'm good." That meant no.

"Hungry?" I asked, poking my head out, knowing what the answer would be.

"Not really."

As far as I knew, Theo had never had a big love thing. He'd dated, he'd had boyfriends, and I'm sure there were more than I knew about. Madison had been a little drama, but then he'd sort of fizzled out to nothing. I knew Theo got a lot of attention from guys, and I think more than a couple people had shattered their hearts over him. But the other way around? Not until now. And this one, as much as Theo wanted to pretend it was nothing, was hitting him hard. It was a misery for me to have to watch, especially since I was convinced that there was nothing broken here that couldn't be mended with just a little effort from one side or the other.

"Want to go out and get something to eat, anyway? Just to keep me company?".

"Not really, sorry."

"Want to spend another evening sitting around the house and being miserable?"

"I'm not miserable, I'm busy," he said, working something out on the keyboard, although there was no sound. "Where did *you* spend the night, by the way?"

"Jeffrey's." I knew that would get his nose up off the plastic ivories.

He stared at me for a couple seconds, deciding if he was going to be furious with me or not.

"Did he tell you everything?" he said finally.

"No. I wouldn't let him."

"Why the hell not? No, wait." His focus was back on the keyboard. "I don't even want to know. It's got nothing to do with me." Looking up again. "But why did you sleep at Jeff's?"

"I promised not to tell."

"Fine." Keyboard. "None of my business. Don't tell me. Not like I care anyway."

"That's what I thought. Hey, I bought some ice cream. It's cherry."

Both hands slammed down on a chord I was glad I couldn't hear.

"Stop doing that."

"What?"

"You think you're being this great sympathetic big sister, going to cheer me up. Little Theo has an owie and you'll joke him out of it and get his favorite ice cream, the poor thing, and make it all better. Well stop. It's really totally unnecessary."

"I see."

"It's true! There is no owie! I know you're thinking this—whatever— with Jeff was some kind of a big deal, and it wasn't."

"He thinks it was."

"That's his mistake then. It wasn't anything. *He* was the one who told *me* it was just a hook-up. And it was. It was fun and then it wasn't. I thought he was different, and that was *my* mistake, and he is the way he is, which is a complete rectum—you might have warned me by the way and I don't know how you can be friends with him—but that's that. Just as well I found out how big a pustule he is *now*, don't you think? Before it could get serious?" His voice was a little quavery at the end there. "And I'm totally fine."

"Good. Thrilled to hear it. So why aren't you eating?"

"Don't feel like it."

"Did you sleep last night?"

"I need to get this song finished."

"How's it going?"

"Stop it! Just stop it!"

I threw my hands up. His phone rang. He pulled it out of his jeans pocket, glanced at it as if eager to push it off—but then his face changed and he took the call.

"Hullo?" Listening. "Yes." Listening. "Oh wow, that's great." Listening listening. "Sure I can come in." He scrambled for a pencil, snatched up a piece of crumpled manuscript paper from the floor, and he scribbled something. "That sounds great." Listening. "No, thank *you!* I'm really looking forward to it." Listening. "Yeah, me too. Bye." He looked almost happy as he hit the disconnect.

He finished whatever note he was writing on the paper, and looked up finally. He seemed—a little lost.

"Want to tell me something?" I asked.

"Oh, yeah. That was the woman from Lincoln Center. They offered me the job. Great, huh?"

"That's fabulous, Theo! Really!" I gave him a quick hug. "Poor Victoria is going to be brokenhearted, of course."

"Victoria will get over it. They want me to start in a couple weeks. I'm going to be working for a real Broadway production company! Isn't that amazing?"

"You must be thrilled!"

"I am!" he said. "I really am! I'm—ecstatic even. It's everything I've ever—" The first thing I noticed was a little tension around one side of his mouth, and then high on the cheek and his upper lip started—and then his whole face was transformed, contorted, into one enormous, gasping sob.

I pulled him to me, and let him bawl on my shoulder. Finally.

"Do you want me to call Gilbert? Have him come out here and break Jeffrey over his knee?"

He sobbed even harder—and he gave a very definite nod.

# Chapter 45
## And the Runner Is Out at Home

*JEFFREY*

It wasn't just my hands that were shaking. I was shaking everywhere. I think my *intestines* were shaking. Felt like my balls had retreated to somewhere around my navel. I only hoped this dread didn't show in my face. My mother could spot the smallest things. A fading black eye and a bandage on my head—smaller now, but a bandage nonetheless—were more than enough to send her into full-on mother-mode. Not to mention the fact that I'd invited myself to dinner with both of them, so obviously something was up. And now I sat on her couch in its plastic slipcover, with a mug of her truly vile herbal tea in my hands.

I had decided to do this at home with them, just us. Of course it had occurred to me that if we'd gone to a restaurant, they wouldn't be able to make a big scene. Then again, with my father, anything was possible.

In the end, taking them out in public to duck a potential confrontation seemed sort of cowardly, and I was through with cowardly. And it wasn't really fair to them. Whether I liked it or not, I figured I should give them their chance to have a big scene if that's what they needed.

It would be easy to see this conversation as being all about me, but I realized it was also about them.

My God, listen to how grown-up and responsible I sound. Scary.

I was also thinking I needed to be done with selfish for a while too. Selfish and cowardly had played way too big a part in my life up to now.

So I had opted for this—dinner at home with the parents. I also figured I should get this over with early, if only to put me and my mother out of our misery. I didn't dare eat first or I'd be hurling my mother's *podvarak* all over her dining room parquet, which would be a terrible waste of some really good Serbian cooking.

"So, Dad, Mom," I said. "I have something I want to talk to you about first."

"I'm starving, you can talk while we eat."

"No, Dad, just this once. Please?"

My mother had this expectant look she gets. I knew she wanted grandchildren more than anything, and for the first time in my life I was going to disappoint her.

*I can't do it,* I thought. I couldn't possibly do what I'd come here to do. There was no way. But just when I decided to bail on the whole thing—

"All right then, out with it."

—my father forced my hand.

I should wait until after he's eaten. The old man was always really crabby when he was hungry. *You're making excuses.* The old man was always really crabby, period. *Just do it. Stop being so spineless.*

I looked at them.

What do I say?

I should have rehearsed this. I should have written it out or something. But it had been so awful to contemplate telling them, that I hadn't thought about what I'd actually say. I'd been too busy thinking about what they'd say back—meaning what my father would be screaming at me, purple-faced.

But now here I was, two blue eyes and two brown eyes were staring at me, waiting, and I had no idea what to do next. I mean, I knew what I needed to tell them, but what was I actually going to say? The words, I mean. Or more to the point—word. I'm—

Gay—?

Homosexual—?

Queer—?

Fudge-packer—?

*Peder*—? That's Serbian for pretty much all of the above.

Mom, Dad, I like to do this thing with another guy's hoo-ha—?

Yeah, probably not that one.

*Man up, Jeffrey. You can stare down an on-coming taxi. You can do this. Take a breath.*

"Something big happened to me recently," I started, "and you're my parents. I want to be able to talk to you about it."

"You got the partnership?" asked Dad.

"No, that won't happen until the end of the year, *if* it happens, and it's not likely it'll happen."

"Why not likely? What did you do?"

"You met someone?" said my mother. Oh, you sly girl, if only you knew.

"Yeah," I said, trying not to slip into panic. I could feel my face muscles tighten with fear. "I did."

"Hey, that's great, son," said my proud father, getting up, with an eye on the dining room. "When do we meet her? Or do we know her already?" He started to pat me on the back. "Of course if you tell me it's the Caputo girl—"

"No, Dad. Wait. It's just—" Well, you know what's coming, only I still couldn't get it out. I stalled. "I don't know. I may have screwed things up already. I doubt anything will come of it."

"*Idiot*!" said my father. It's the same word in Serbian. "How could you mess it up?"

"I did something dumb."

"*Gloop*!" he yelled. You might remember that means stupid.

"What! So you never did anything *gloop*?" I yelled back. Both my parents were shocked. *I* was shocked. No one ever snapped at my father. I certainly hadn't thought about it before it came out, because if I had, I'd have kept my yap shut. Or ducked. But out it had come.

I guess my psyche was thinking—*he's going to disown you anyway, you might as well at least stick up for yourself for once. Go out with a bang.*

The bang would probably be upside my head.

But he didn't hit me—yet. And I was obviously stalling. It wasn't just the elephant in the room, it was this weird invisible elephant that only I could see.

"So yeah," I continued. "I did something stupid." Deep breath. "But that's not the part you're going to hate, believe me."

I have only a handful of words in Serbian, so I can't translate what my father was grumbling to himself. Might have been about me—might have been the *podvarak*.

"It's that boy, isn't it?" asked my mother, softly.

!!!

I couldn't believe she said that.

I only *thought* I was scared before. *Now,* faced with my mother's eerie, intuitive guess, I was gripped with an absolutely paralyzing terror.

Wherever my balls were before, they had now packed their things and moved out.

My first impulse was to deny everything. Yeah, I know, I had come here to 'fess up to exactly this, but now that I was presented with it, accused of it, I was totally ready to be my usual cowardly self and lie lie lie.

"You know," my mother went on quietly, "the assistant who isn't your assistant, is he. The one with the hair?" She made a swirling gesture toward the top of her head. "What was his name?"

"Theo," I said, hardly more than a whisper. Her voice was so kind, and her eyes were so soft and so beautiful. I was completely in her power.

"Your assistant screwed this thing up with the girl?" my father asked incredulously.

I sat down on the couch next to my mom. And I nodded.

"Yes, Mama. Theo, Mama," I said. "His name is Theo."

"Who cares about your lousy assistant? I told you to fire that kid. If you had half a brain—"

"He's not my assistant, Dad. He's my—I don't know what he is." I thought about him, and saw his face in my thoughts. "I have a terrible feeling—he's the love of my life."

My father looked at me. Disbelief battled with slow recognition.

"What?" he said very sharp, and very quietly.

When he was angry, his face would get really dark, but now—I'd never seen him so pale. The silence lasted a long, long time before I found enough backbone to speak again. And once it was there, I knew what I needed to say.

"I'm gay, Dad."

"But—I don't understand. You always—"

"I've *always* been gay. Always."

"But all those girls you dated, the girls you...?"

"They were for you, Papa. Never for me." A tear ran down my mother's cheek. "Mama, I'm so sorry."

She shook her head.

"No, it's—I always—wondered. Guessed maybe. But when I saw that boy, I thought—and when I saw you watching him leave—no one looks at an assistant like that."

I wanted to say something but there was such a huge lump in my throat I couldn't possibly.

"My son," said my father. "You're—*peder*?"

I knew I'd hear that word before we were done.

"Yup, Dad. I am. Always have been. I knew when I was fourteen but I was so scared. Still am. I'm gay. I'm queer. *Peder.* And whatever other terrible words you have for it, that's me, your son."

"And you've...?"

"Sure have. Lots."

I thought for sure, *now,* he would hit me. I almost wanted him to.

He got up—but he didn't hit me. He just walked off into the kitchen. I hugged my mother, while I listened to the clatter in the next room. My father was fixing himself a plate. Naturally.

My dad. He had done so much for me. He'd paid for my education at one ridiculously expensive school after another, without a word of complaint. For which I was hugely grateful. And I had rewarded him by graduating top of my class at Princeton Law, something he accepted as though it were his due, as though anything else would have been a disappointment.

For years—my entire life—I had tried to please this man, and now, because of this, I probably never would.

And I had tried so hard to *be* like him. Why???

My dad had taken a small contracting business and made it into a huge contracting business, and made us all rich. He was feared. He was hated. He was ruthless, maybe heartless, and occasionally violent.

Why would I want to be like him? If I had a son, would I want our relationship to be like *this*? Full of anger, fear, resentment? And God knows whatever he felt for me, which at the moment was apparently contempt.

No, I did not want to emulate this man.

It was emulating my father that had brought me to betray my best friend. And had cost me Theo.

I deserved to lose Theo. I'd been a complete bastard to get where I was. Believe me, the kid at the top of his class at Princeton Law is *not* a nice guy. I'd never been popular or well-liked. I'd bullied my way through too much of my life, or brown-nosed, or used money to solve problems instead of dealing with them, I'd ducked responsibility whenever I could, and taken credit for other people's work. These were all things I'd learned from this man who now sat alone in the kitchen, eating bacon and sauerkraut (that's *podvarak*—now you know), instead of dealing with his wife and son. His gay son.

I'd taken a step. I'd told my parents. For once I'd taken the hard way instead of the easy way. No matter what happened, no matter if my father ever came to terms with it, I knew I wouldn't regret this.

I also knew I wasn't done. I wasn't at all sure I could ever fix all the things I'd screwed up, but this was a start.

I meant it earlier. I was through with cowardly.

And if maybe someday a pair of blue-green eyes could look at me again with a little less derision in them—that would be good, too.

# Chapter 46
## The One with the Waggly Tail

*TOMMY*

I have done some crazy-ass shit in my time, just to sort of put myself in front of some cute guy or other. Anything to get his attention. I have listened to no end of music I couldn't care less about. In London I once got up at the wisecrack of dawn to sit through a seventeen-hour Hindu drama, just so I could sit next to a boy with the dreamiest eyes. After seventeen hours of the *Mahabharata* (not a lot of laughs in the *Mahabharata*) and one amazeballs night in dreamy-eyes' bedroom while his family slept down the hall, I was ready to convert. I made the mistake of mentioning this to dreamy-eyes, which unfortunately led to this incredibly tedious discussion of how that word was loaded with imperial history and how it wasn't really a concept in Hinduism, and he didn't even notice I was pulling my pants on and calling for one of those funky black London taxis while he talked.

I have marched in marches (Protect the Whosits! Free What's-His-Name!) and I once sat through an evening where Newt Gingrich was the keynote speaker. Lesson learned: Do not try holding hands with your date at a meeting of Young Republicans. That guy was also probably the worst sex I've ever had—draw your own conclusions.

But I digress.

My point is—to find myself standing in the middle of an animal shelter with a veritable host of barking dogs probably wasn't even the craziest crazy-ass thing I'd ever done to get a guy's attention. But it was right up there in the top five anyway.

I had decided to tag along with Theo at the animal shelter. Why? You guessed it. Because a certain very cute young man with the ridiculously adorable name of Swithin also volunteered at the animal shelter—so now *I* volunteered at the animal shelter. And omfjesus, the noise.

I have no idea how many dogs there were, but every single one of them was barking. Not quietly barking, not barking and then giving it a rest. No, they were just barking non-effing-stop, relentlessly and without pause. I know that's redundantly redundant, but I can't stress that enough—there was never the teensiest millisecond when they communally took a breath. Nope. Just barking.

The other thing about this place—which I had not quite anticipated— the dogs were in kennels, and they had to be let out to pee and poop, and they were really stressed out, and sometimes things didn't go according to plan, if you get my drift—and if you do, I'm sorry, just move upwind.

And who takes care of all this? The volunteers! The happy, cheerful volunteers who rush to the rescue with happy mops and cheerful Lysol. That's the part I hadn't anticipated. I guess I thought I was volunteering to come in and *play* with the dogs, and I figured I could handle that. I'm no end of fun. And I would, of course, simultaneously, impress the cute guy.

I'd dressed for the day, too. For the impress-the-cute-guy part, I mean— not for the clean-up-dog-ooky part. I had a new pair of tight rocker-boy jeans, black, like the ones Swith wore. And sexy? Oh hells yes. And a pale blue v-neck sweater (nothing underneath) made of a cashmere/silk blend that just screamed to be touched. And the color made my eyes huge. I was scrumptious. At least that was the plan. Even my sneakers—from Italy and *so* expensive—were cute.

"I'm on the adoption desk today," said Theo, whose idea this was. "So you can help Swith in here with the dogs."

That was fairly subtle, pairing us up like that. Or maybe he just wanted to avoid us because he knew I'd ask him about his bust-up with Jeffrey.

To be honest, I was a little worried about young Theo. He'd told me that he and Jeff weren't happening after all.

"Hey, Theo—you okay?"

"Of course. Why shouldn't I be?"

"You know—"

"It's no big deal. Really."

"Seriously?"

"Seriously. People only get hurt when they have expectations. I always thought Jeff was an asshole. You told me Jeff was an asshole. Turns out—Jeff's an asshole. No big let-down there." Sound like denial to you? "Hey, Swith?"

"Yeah?" said Swithin, coming back in from the exercise yard with a couple of puppies. OMG. Like he wasn't cute enough!

"Show Tommy what he needs to do."

"Sure thing. Hey, Tommy."

"Well Theo—if you need to talk about it…" I offered.

"I definitely do *not* need to talk about it."

And Theo went off into adoptionland.

"You think he's okay?" I asked the cutie.

"No, but there's nothing you can do—unless you like having things thrown at your head, because that's what you'll get."

"Yeah, I guess."

So. Swithin and I—alone at last. With thirty-seven barking dogs.

"Hi," I said, suddenly shy.

Why do I put myself in these situations? I know I might come off as totally self-confident, completely comfortable with myself, and mostly I am, but sometimes, when the guy is a little too good-looking—like Swithin, alas—or probably straight—like Swithin, alas alack—all of a sudden I don't know where to look.

"I didn't know you were helping out today. Cool. First time here?"

"Very first."

"You must be as crazy about dogs as the rest of us."

"Must be!"

"C'mon, I'll introduce you around."

Which, of course, I thought meant that I was going to go meet the staff. Instead he took me around from cage to cage and gave me the skinny on each of the inmates in an excited voice. He was really nuts about these dogs. Of course I missed most of his lectures, what with the never-ending barkfest, and trying to catch Swithin's amazing face as it was occasionally revealed from behind the veil of bangs. It was like a blond burka that only intermittently allowed glimpses of the sparkle in those dazzling eyes, eyes that promised so much—

"So Tommy." What was he saying? I needed to pay attention. "Why don't you start with taking dogs out to the exercise pens?" Swithin suggested. "Ideally everybody gets a quick pee-break before it gets too busy with visitors. If anybody's interested in a dog, let them take the dog out into the yard. You don't have to do anything. The dogs pretty much sell themselves."

"O-kay!" I said cheerfully. I *was* the cheerful volunteer, after all. Swith handed me a leash, smiling.

"I'll start on the next room."

Oh. And he went off into that next room. Not this room, the next room. Where there were yet more dogs, if you can believe it.

I had kinda thought he'd be here with me, but no, first chance he got... I was cheerful no more.

Sigh.

But I was here, I had stuff to do. I turned bravely to my first client.

It was a large cage with a large and mostly black dog, about whom Swithin had no doubt told me everything I needed to know—none of which I could remember. The card on the front said Charlie. Cute. Charlie looked at me, a bundle of tail-wagging oh-joy-oh-rapture. With very expressive brown eyebrows. This wouldn't be so bad.

I clipped the leash onto his collar and we headed out. There was a courtyard in back with a couple large-ish pens of chain link fence, each pen strewn with wood shavings. It was nice. The sun was shining and the seven thousand barking dogs were just a bit less immediate. It was so nice, I got a brilliant idea.

I pulled out my phone and squatted down to Charlie. I figured I could brag on Facebook a little about my charitable endeavors. Show what a great and selfless human being I was. I held out the phone at arm's length, and Charlie, instead of smiling for his close-up like a professional, decided that I needed to be licked.

Cute, right? Except I was already squatting, and eighty-five pounds of black and brown mutt, not to mention dog breath, was more than enough to knock me off my equilibrium and onto my assets.

I managed to get Charlie off me long enough to get up, I wiped the slime off my face, dusted off my brand-new jeans, and I managed to take a couple more pictures—this time with a strict no-tongues rule, thank you, Charlie—before I let the dog loose in the exercise pen to do whatever he came here to do. I carefully closed the gate (I am nothing, if not conscientious), while he sniffed, hither, thither and yon. I flipped through my phone to post the best selfie. Funny thing was, the one with Charlie licking me and me looking surprised and falling over was actually super-cute. Spontaneous and candid. Like me. That obviously was the one. I captioned it "Volunteering with my new friend Charlie," and posted it. I smiled in happy anticipation, waiting for the likes to tsunami in.

As I stared at the phone, hearing the satisfying sound of those happy little dings begin—I felt something warm on my leg. What the hells? I glanced down. Charlie, of course, was a boy-dog, and we all know boy-dogs kick up a hind leg to pee, and Charlie, it seems, had decided to kick his leg up on the post next to the gate of the pen. Unfortunately I was standing just on the other side of that post, and Charlie's aim wasn't all that great.

The dog was having a wee on my calf. On my new super-tight jeans.

I screamed (in a very masculine way, of course) and jumped back from the gate. Charlie was profoundly oblivious and went off sniffing around the pen, completely ignoring my displeasure and distress, to say nothing of disgust.

Did I mention these jeans were *brand* new? Specifically bought to impress yon swain, Swithin? And my cute Italian sneakers, which had cost me like a week's paycheck? Even my sock was wet! With pee!!!

Swithin came around the corner.

"Hey! You okay?"

"Fabulous!" I said, startled. "Copacetic! *No problemo!* I'm just getting to know Charlie is all." Charlie came over to the gate, wagging his tail to say hello to Swithin. "See how happy he is?"

"Okay," said Swith. "Let me know if you need any help."

"Will do." *You can help me kill this effing dog, for starters,* I thought. "C'mon Charlie. It's back to the slammer for you, big guy." I put Charlie away, went back out into the courtyard, pulled off my shoe and sock (the wet ones), and did my best to rinse my pant leg under the hose before I delicately rinsed off my fancy-schmancy, slightly ruined gym shoe. I buried the sock deep in the trash where it wouldn't be found. Too embarrassing.

Back to work. With one sock.

The Charlie Incident was a mistake you make only once. The rest of the trips to the exercise pens went without any big events. Aside from a few big events that required the pooper-scooper. I often walked Roger's dog—but his cute little Scottish terrier couldn't *touch* what some of these brutes could leave behind. No wonder nobody wanted to adopt them. I was appreciating Roger's dog more by the minute.

Among my large charges was a teeny little dog cage with the leetlest dog I'd ever seen. I've had bigger margaritas. The dog was also hideous.

"Well c'mon, gorgeous," I said, as I bent over and snapped this tiny string of a leash on this tiny ogre's tiny collar.

"My, aren't *you* cute!" said someone behind me. I smiled. It didn't sound like Swith, but a boy could hope. I straightened up and turned—it wasn't Swithin admiring my hinterlands after all. It was a middle-aged woman, and she wasn't even *looking* at me *or* my butt. She was beaming at the little repugnance at the end of the leash.

Did I mention this dog-ette was ugly? It had teeth sticking out in all directions, and a tongue that seemed to hang permanently out the left side of its mouth. Bulgey eyes. It was practically, but not quite, bald. And if that wasn't enough, the little mini-mutt shivered non-stop. If ever there was a dog that didn't need to be rescued, this was it.

"You're looking to adopt a dog?" I asked. This *was* why I was in this dreadful place, supposedly—not *just* to pick up guys.

"I don't know," she sighed wistfully. "Ever since my Dollsy died..." And she sighed again. "What kind of a dog is he?"

"This one?" I said, looking down at the bug-eyed thing. I made a stab in the dark. "Part—Chihuahua?"

"Cute! And what's the other part, do you think?"

I considered.

"Chupacabra?"

"What a beauty!"

Eye of the beholder, clearly. I was starting to think I'd seen this dog somewhere before. Maybe on the side of Notre Dame, spewing rainwater.

"I was just about to take it outside to the exercise pens. But if you'd like to do the honors? You could—you know—hang?"

"What's his name?"

"Whatever you want it to be," I said, handing over the leash.

And with that she waddled chirpily out into the courtyard.

"Reinforcements," said Swithin, and he came in with Theo.

"I'm done with adoptions, if you guys want to take a break," said Theo.

"I just have the one dog left," I said, "and one's out with somebody doing his you know." I gestured to the tiny—empty—dog crate behind me.

"Sidney?" said Swithin and Theo *ensemble.*

"Tommy," I corrected.

"Dude, the little Chihuahua-mix," said Swithin. "His name's Sidney."

"It has a name? *Why*???"

"Sidney's been here for years," said Theo.

"And somebody's thinking about adopting him?"

"I don't know about that, but she at least seems pretty tickled, watching the little tyke tinkle."

We went to the door and looked out to watch the woman basking in the presence of the teeny-tiny dog, who, in that moment, was busy taking a teeny-tiny crap.

"Well I'll be," said Theo. "Nobody has *ever* been interested in Sidney before."

"So other than Sidney, *if* that's his real name, I just have—" I stopped. I couldn't go on.

"Oh God," said Swithin.

"That has to be Mona," said Theo.

They were talking about this incredibly rank sewer-smell that had just run over us like a train.

We all three turned—and there was my last dog, a big, gray furry thing, turned around facing away from us—and shooting diarrhea a good couple feet out through the door of his cage Her cage. I had learned so *much* today. She missed me by mere inches.

"I think your last dog started without you," said Theo.

"Oh my God that's bad," said Swithin, with the neck of his Ramones tee-shirt pulled up over his nose.

It was really really incredibly bad. If a rotting corpse ate caca and puked in a cattle truck. I could not speak. It was that bad.

"You want to take Mona out and give her a bath?" asked Swithin. "Or wash out the cage?"

"Me? I'll— I'll—" I tried to answer. "I don't think—"

My situation was apparently obvious.

"You need some air," said Theo.

"Let's go let's go, quick!" said Swithin, and he grabbed me by the arm and rushed me out into the courtyard. I leaned against the wall.

"Breathe deep," said Swithin, "nice fresh air, breathe nice and slow and deep."

This day was not really going at all how I'd hoped. I'd hardly spent any time with Swithin and now, when he *was* around, one deliciously sexy hand on my shoulder even—I was pale, sweating, panting, and threatening to barf. And I smelled like a diaper.

Serious boner material, right? All I needed to do now was burst into tears—and I was about one unsteady step away from it—and I'd be irresistible.

"Dollsy!" someone hooted.

My first impulse was to flip the bird over my shoulder at who-the-eff-ever it was calling me names at this point in my life.

But I forbore.

I turned and looked up and saw the little fat woman, holding the quasi-Chihuahua/Quasi-modo *thing* in the air to admire it some more. "I'm going to call him Dollsy!" She was thoroughly pleased with herself—and her complete lack of imagination. For a flicker of a second, I wondered if this was Dollsy II or maybe merely the last in a long line of Dollsies who'd come before, part of a Dollsy dynasty, and I further wondered if all the previous Dollsies had been such perfect little googly-eyed gargoyles as this one was, but then—I was once again overwhelmed by my vast indifference.

"That's wonderful!" said Theo appearing in the door. He was holding a leash with the big gray furry dog, d/b/a Mona, still dripping from a hasty bath to her hindquarters. "If you want to go inside and visit Joanne at the adoption desk, she can walk you through the process."

"I'm so excited! He's perfect!"

"Isn't he?" How Theo McPherson could look at himself in the mirror, knowing he was capable of uttering such a balls-out lie, I'll never know.

She tucked the little dog-ling under her arm like a clutch that panted, and she toddled off inside, looking like any minute she could break out in a rash.

"Can you believe somebody is going to adopt Sidney?" said Swithin.

"That dog's been here longer than I have," said Theo. "I might even miss him."

"Really?"

"Okay, maybe not, too."

"Hey," said Swith to me. "How we doin'?"

"Better," I said. "Thanks."

"I'm going to put poor Mona here in the ex-pen," said Theo. "If you guys want to bolt, I got this."

"You're sure? I mean—her cage...?" said Swithin.

"I grew up on a farm. Nothing grosses me out. And I think Tommy's done for the day, don't you?"

"I think you're right. C'mon, Tommy. Let's step across the street."

Swithin grabbed our jackets and shepherded me outside.

The thing that struck me right away—like a rainbow or the face of Jesus in a cloud?—was the astonishing quiet, the stillness, the abrupt and beautiful absence of barking. Was this the miracle that was the world that, until now, I had never appreciated in all its wondrous, non-barking glory?

And, as we jaywalked, an MTA bus came hurtling down at us, horn blaring. So much for the peaceful wonder that is the world. Welcome to Brooklyn.

In desperation, we had to run for our lives. Okay, scamper. We scampered for our lives until we were safe on the sidewalk sanctuary behind a bulwark of parked cars.

I had no idea where Swith was taking me until he guided me through a door from the sunny Brooklyn street into a dark—and distinctly beery—Brooklyn interior. Lots of wood.

As my eyes adjusted, I could see it was one of those old, working-class taverns, where a couple of old, working-class guys sat on stools at the bar. Each had a glass of beer in front of him, either half-empty or half-full, depending. Probably one of each. They were watching a baseball game on

TV—was it baseball season already?—and there were some old wooden booths along the wall, into one of which Swith plopped me.

"What are you down for?"

"Euthanasia?"

"Coming right up."

He came back with the handles of two beer mugs in one hand, and two shot glasses carefully balanced in the palm of the other.

"Help."

I reached up and took the shot glasses without spilling too much, and he set the beers down.

"Don't drink it if you don't want it," he said, nodding at the shot he pushed over in front of me.

"Wow. A beer and a shot. How manly!"

"That's me," he said smiling at me from beyond the veil, one blue eye twinkling.

A shot and a beer is such a butch thing—and you may have noticed that I am not exactly—ahem—butch. But I figured, under the circs, it was probably just what I needed to straighten me out. So to speak.

"To Betty White," said Swithin raising his glass.

"Long may she wave," I agreed, and I tossed back the shot like the brave little boy that I was.

Whoa.

My eyes started to tear up. A shuddering spasm ran up through my entire body, ending with a violent shake of the head.

"You okay?"

"I'm—good," I said, checking my status as I spoke. "Yeah, I'm actually better. Thanks."

"Good. I don't think you had much fun today."

"It wasn't quite what I—honestly, I don't know what I expected, but it was not big ugly dogs shooting flaming diarrhea out their back ends at me."

"That was pretty special."

"I could have handled some moderate squirtage, but what Mona was doing, that was like six, seven feet! And obviously toxic."

"Look at this way, though. I think that woman is actually going to adopt little Sidney today. That's huge."

"I think little Sidney is going to be stuck with 'Dollsy' for the rest of his lap-sitting life. Whether he likes it or not."

"Are you kidding? That dog is so lucky. He's going to live out his days in spoiled comfort and he'll love that woman fiercely. And that's fantastic. You should be so proud! You had an awesome first day!"

"Who knew?"

"It's not your thing, is it."

"I guess not. I walk my friend Roger's dog when they need it, and Haggis and I get along pretty well, but this..."

"So, why did you volunteer?"

"You don't know."

"I have a guess."

"Hmmmm. Can I ask *you* something? Personal?"

"Uh-oh."

"You—got a girlfriend?"

"Nope."

"You—got a boyfriend?"

"Nope."

I waited, thinking he might volunteer *something* here. He tilted his head to show his face and a little smile like the sphinx. But with a nose. And he tilted his head back again.

"You're enjoying this, aren't you?"

"Maybe a little." Tilt. There were those smiling eyes again.

"So if you *had* a boyfriend or a girlfriend, which flavor do you think it would be?"

"You know, you're blowing my whole mystery vibe here. For two years my songwriting workshop has been whispering."

"America needs to know."

"Okay. I've had girlfriends. I've never had a boyfriend. I have messed around with guys."

"And if you were looking for something now...?"

"I haven't been. Looking, I mean."

"But if you were..." I pressed. I'd watched Barbara Walters. I knew how this was done.

"I suppose...I'd probably be looking for someone a little shorter than me, sandy brown hair, blue eyes, with a keen fashion style and a wicked sense of humor, who makes me smile absolutely every single time he opens his mouth." He tilted his head, and he was grinning at me. And blushing.

It may not have come up before, so I should mention that *I* have sandy brown hair and blue eyes. And, at least in that moment, a face the color of a stop sign—only I didn't mean stop. And he didn't.

"Someone," Swith went on to say, "who might volunteer at a dog shelter, even though he's not really into it, just so he could hang out with me. Can you recommend anybody?"

"If you're free, my best friend's string quartet is playing tonight. If you like string quartets."

"I love string quartets. What are they playing?" The blue eyes were unveiled again.

"Ravel and Bartok."

"I love Ravel and Bartok."

I could still see just enough face under there to know that he was beaming.

"Liar," I said. "Nobody loves Bartok."

Under the table, my Italian sneaker—the one *not* peed upon—found Swithin's black canvas Converse.

Footsy. Those eyes had reduced me to playing footsy.

It *must* be the real thing.

# E-mail from Jeffrey

**To:** Kaminsky, Daniel
Collins, Victoria
**From:** Bornic, Jeffrey A.
**Sent:** Monday, May 2, 6:45 a.m.
**cc:** McPherson, Rebecca
**Subject:** *Hiromi Industries*

I regret that I feel I must withdraw my name from consideration for the litigation team for this important case. If you would like to discuss my reasons for doing so, I will be happy to meet with you at your convenience.
I don't know how much weight it carries, but, contrary to anything I may have written in the past, I would like to give my strong recommendation to Rebecca McPherson, whose work has always proven exemplary and professional. If selected, she will bring a sharp insight and intelligence to the case.

I deeply regret that I have ever given the impression that I considered her to be anything less than one of the finest and most talented lawyers I've worked with in my time at Parker O'Neill.

Thank you.
J.A.B.

# Chapter 47
## And Boy Were My Arms Tired

*JEFF*

I had been schlepping a pile of stuff for the last three hours, and I was beat. It was also May now and really warm for the first time this spring—which would normally be lovely, if I hadn't been running around trying to get all this stuff together. In a hooded sweatshirt.

Of course I had no reason to think that any of this would work, but I had to try.

I had done everything I could think of to fix this, at least so far as this thing could be fixed, so here I was, standing in front of Rebecca's door with an armload of things I'd picked up. Beccs had assured me that Theo was home. Thank God, after everything, I at least still had Rebecca on my side.

I plopped the armload of precious booty down to one side of the door, pulled the sweatshirt off and toweled my face with it. I leaned against the wall, and gave myself a chance to think and to cool off a little. Red-faced and pitted out was not what I'd have picked for this—confrontation—when I so desperately needed all the charm I could muster.

Deep breaths.

Of course this was New York, and the thing about New York? There's always somebody. So frigging crowded. All you want is a moment to yourself, and there's *somebody*. This particular somebody was a neighbor with his little shih-tzu-whatever on the end of a leash. Looked like an old gay guy. The neighbor, I mean, not the shih tzu. Although, come to think of it...

The guy eyed me suspiciously—yeah, like I'm a mugger with a great big pile of stuff on the floor here.

*Just keep moving, Dorothy,* I thought. *And little Toto too.*

Only now did he take in my pile of props. His turn to smile.

*I'm so glad you find me amusing, gramps.*

The shih tzu was finally bored with my shoes and waddled on, taking the gay geezer with him.

"Good luck," the old guy said.

"Thanks," I said after them, a little surprised.

I've said how I had resolved to stop being a selfish coward—it occurred to me I should also really try to stop being quite such a cynical, crabby-assed dick while I'm at it.

Deep breath.

Truth was, I was here and I was scared to death. My whole life could go down in flames right here—and probably would. If I couldn't get Theo to talk to me again, I had no idea what I would do. Sell my apartment and join the Peace Corps. I'm sure they could use me. I could teach. I could teach starving children in Ethiopia how to write a really kick-ass brief. Useful stuff like that.

Or I could enlist in the CIA and disappear into a secret life. Or maybe move to Tibet and become a monk. So many options. Is there still a French Foreign Legion, do you think?

But I could do this, right? I pep-talked myself. I had faced down Dan Kaminsky and Victoria Collins. I had vaulted over a New York taxi. I had stared Death in the eye and laughed a bitter and ironic laugh. I could do this.

Of course none of that meant squat. Theo McPherson was *way* scarier than Death ever *hoped* to be.

I reminded myself that I had made my resolution and I was sticking to it. Gut it out, Bornic.

Which reminded me of something that had occurred to me in my brooding, during these long, dark, Theo-less days: whatever happened today, I was stronger now. I was so much braver than I was before beautiful Theo came along and threatened to take my balls off in the middle of a Midtown bistro.

I pulled myself up straight. Deep breath. It was now-or-never time. I tapped on the door. No answer. Fuckaduck, could *nothing* be easy here? Did absolutely *everything* have to be an ordeal. I took another deep breath, and knocked again, louder. After a bit, it opened. Rebecca.

"Theo," she called over her shoulder and stepped off to the side, holding the door open for me. "There's someone to see you."

I stood out of the doorway, and extended one hand in the open doorframe with my first peace offering—a dozen red roses.

"Go away, we don't want any!" said the man of my dreams, the prince of my heart. He was out of my line of sight—I don't know if he even looked up.

Rebecca took the roses, shrugged a little and gave me an encouraging nod.

I stuck my hand in the doorway again, this time holding a big ol' heart-shaped box of chocolates. I had no idea what might work, so I was covering all the bases.

"Get lost! Go home! Get a life!" yelled the water in my desert, the sunlight of my days.

Rebecca took the chocolates, and gave me a thumbs-up. Yeah, like this was going soooo well.

Okay, I hadn't really expected that either of those was going to work. I was betting everything on my next shot. I picked up this enormous teddy bear—sitting, he was probably close to three feet tall. I held him in front of me and stepped into the doorframe.

"Theee-oh!" I said in a funny very un-bearlike voice. At least I hoped it was funny and not just stupid. I wagged one of the paws in a teddy-bear wave. "Hey Theeeeee-oh!"

"Will you—" he started. And my precious treasure, the center of my universe, the key to my happiness—reached over and grabbed a jumbo eraser from the top of his keyboard and he flung it at the doorway.

I ducked behind the bear, my Kevlar vest in a bow tie. The eraser bounced off the teddy's tummy and fell to the floor.

"Theo!" said Rebecca, reprimanding.

"Ouch!" said the silly bear voice.

"Oh wow," said the guy I loved more than anything on earth. He had finally looked over.

I had figured this much out—if you want to get around Theo McPherson, just remember: he's only seven years old. I took a step inside, and poked my head carefully around the bear, making sure it was safe.

"Theo?" I said in my own voice. He didn't throw anything. "Please talk to me? I'm sooooooo sorry. I screwed up, but I'm trying. Please?"

"Where did you get him?" He had no interest in me, he wanted to talk about the bear. My heart's desire, my darling, my all. I sure can pick 'em.

*Why you?* I wondered, watching his animated face. Why did this strange alien have such power over me, that it absolutely hurt not to be with him. I didn't have an answer—I only knew that he was it. He was everything.

At least he'd spoken to me.

"Saks," I answered. "And just for your amusement, please picture me carrying this thing around the store trying to find a cashier to ring him up. And lugging him around Rockefeller Plaza while I found a florist *and* a chocolate shop. And then carrying him up Fifth Avenue, *with* the chocolates *and* the roses, while trying to get a cab to stop. Tourists were taking pictures. The indignities I put myself through. A German couple wanted to take a selfie with me and would not take *nein* for an answer. There are people checking their Facebook feed in Düsseldorf right now, laughing their schnitzels off."

"You dope," he said, finally glancing at me. It was the most beautiful thing anyone had ever said to me in my entire life.

He hid behind the bear.

"I was just hanging around, in case someone was needed to call nine-one-one," said Rebecca. I'd forgotten she was still there. She was fluffing the roses, which she'd put in water. "But I think you boys got this." She picked up her keys from the counter.

"Wait," I said. "Before you go—I had a talk with Dan Kaminsky—*and* the lovely Victoria."

"I saw your strange e-mail taking yourself off the *Hiromi* case. What's *that* about?"

"I told you I'd try to fix my mess, and I think I have. *Hiromi* is almost certainly going to trial, and you should plan on making yourself available for it."

"I'm in?"

"You're definitely in."

"Wow. That's fantastic. I didn't expect to hear *that* today."

"Keep it under your hat, as they say."

"Wait," said Theo, looking up from the bear finally. "What did you do?"

"I had to make it right, if I could, and I did."

"Thank you, Jeffrey," said Rebecca.

"Don't thank me."

"Yeah, really," said Theo. "You shouldn't."

He had taken the bear from me and was making him dance on the couch.

"I'm going to—um—" and she kissed me on the cheek. "Text me when you're ready for me to come home." And she kissed Theo on the cheek. I guess she slipped out the door. I could only see Theo; and Theo could only see—the bear.

Now that we were alone, we were both a little shy.

"What'd you do to your head?" he asked after a bit. The bandage.

"Lost it, apparently." He glanced at me, and then back to the bear. "There's a card."

I had punched a hole in the corner of a 3x5 card so I could lace a piece of red satin ribbon through it—and I'd tied it to the bear's wrist with the best bow this clumsy lawyer-boy could manage.

He looked at the card for lots longer than it took to read it.

I suppose I should tell you what it said. It wasn't a big thing. I'd *wanted* to tell him how special he was, how I'd recognized that he wasn't 'nothing,' that he was clearly an absolutely magnificent something, and that I wanted as much of that magnificent something in my life as he could allow me. But I kept it simpler. All the card said was, "Please. I love you so much." And I'd signed it "Jeff." Not Jeffrey. For him, I could be Jeff.

"Thanks," was all he said. That would have to do. "Are those for me too?" he asked, nodding to the flowers and chocolate piled on the kitchen counter.

"Of course."

"Cool. Anything else? If I were still not speaking to you, is there like a Fiat downstairs? Or a Shetland pony, at least?"

"No, 'fraid not. I thought about a puppy, but then if it didn't work, I'd be stuck with him, and I wasn't sure the Foreign Legion would take me with a puppy. The bear was my best offer."

"The bear's pretty good—oh, wow!" He had opened the heart-shaped box and eaten one of the little chocolates. "Man! These things are life!" He held one out for me, and I ate it from his fingers, still looking at his lovely freckled face.

"I did buy you a bunch of underwear, but I was too embarrassed to bring them."

"You should have. Should have started with the underwear, you'd have had me right there."

"Good to know."

We traded blushes.

"My mom wants to meet you," I said finally.

"I've met your mom."

"Well, now that she knows you're not my assistant, she wants to meet you again. I told her. I told them."

"You outed yourself?" He looked at me a bit.

"You shamed me into it."

"Cool." He looked away again. "What did you say?"

"I told them that you weren't my assistant. And that you were very probably the love of my life."

"How'd they take it?"

"My mom wants to meet you for real. That is, if you're still my boyfriend."

"I don't know. You want me to be your boyfriend?"

"That's all I want in the world."

"Shut up. And your dad? What'd he say?"

"He doesn't care if you're my boyfriend or not."

"Idiot."

"That's exactly what *he* said. To be honest, I think he liked you better when you were the lousy assistant I should have fired."

"That's just because he doesn't know me yet," said Theo, propping the bear up on the couch and trying to get him to cross his legs. "But wait til he gets to know me, and sees how sweet I am. How does he feel about professional football?"

My head spun at the thought of Theo giving my father his football speech.

Having found the pose that he wanted for the bear, Theo stepped over to me, and, without another word and without looking at me, he slipped his arms around me and pressed his face against my chest. I pulled him to me as tightly as I could.

I thought the lump in my throat might be fatal.

"So. I'm the love of your life?"

I nodded, and cleared my throat.

"Seems like," I said finally.

"Too bad about you."

"I know, but what can I do? And just so you know," I added, "I took myself *off* the *Hiromi* case."

He looked up at me finally.

"That's good. That was the right thing to do. But doesn't that hurt your promotion thing?"

"Actually I offered to resign, if that's what they wanted."

"You did that?"

"There isn't anything I wouldn't give up, Theo, to prove to you—"

"Shut uuuup and just give me the underwear already!" he said blushing, grinning, and he buried his face against my shirt. I put my arms around him and squeezed, and pressed my face against his curls. "You really quit your job?" he asked.

"Well, no. I explained everything, and I offered to resign, if that's what they wanted. They didn't want. In fact, Mr. K. wants me next to him on the *Hiromi* case."

"Really?"

"Yeah. I guess I must actually *be* the hotshot lawyer I make myself out to be."

"That's good. Hey—I got a job too!"

"Oh wow! The thing at Lincoln Center?"

"You know how I said it wouldn't happen? I was wrong. I start on Monday."

"That's awesome! I'm so glad for you!" And I really was thrilled for him and I hugged him still tighter. And I thought—*Please, Theo, please don't ever let go.*

"I'm in show business!" he went on. "The only bad part is—they pay total crap. So—unless I can find another incredibly cheap apartment situation, I'm going to be sleeping on Rebecca's couch for the rest of my life."

"At least until you get your first Broadway show."

He looked up at me for a long time. I think maybe I'd finally said the right thing.

"Yeah," he said, smiling a little sideways. "Until my first Broadway show."

It seems to me about then that I was struck with a bizarre case of acute dementia, because an absolutely mad idea came into my head, and without a moment's consideration, I was talking.

"You know, if you're looking for a flat-share, I just *happen* to know somebody who has a gigantic apartment that he just knocks around in."

"Great! Where?"

"Upper East."

"Not my favorite neighborhood, but at least it's Manhattan. Close to your place?"

"Not far."

"Can I afford it?"

"Probably. It's a bit of a construction mess right now, but when it's done…"

He pushed me out to arm's length and looked at me.

"You insane?"

"Obviously. There's lots of space. Of course the bedroom at the end—that's really a practice room. The guestroom downstairs—well, I was going to use that for my gym equipment. There's another bedroom—but I was going to use that for my office."

"Does that still leave room?"

"If you don't mind sharing."

He put his face against my shoulder again, and I held him tight. Man, I loved him like this.

Then he pushed himself back up.

"Hey!" he said, a light bulb glowing above the red curls. "Your building takes dogs, doesn't it!"

I shook my head.

"Of course you would go there."

He smiled at me a little shyly.

"Hi," he said, suddenly quiet.

"Hi, Theo." I pulled him back to me.

"I love you, too, by the way," he muffled into my shoulder.

"Good to know."

I kissed the side of his head. How I had missed this, missed him.

When I opened my eyes, I saw that three-foot teddy bear sitting on the couch behind him, looking goofy.

"You know, I didn't really think this through," I said.

"What do you mean?" and he pulled back, scowling.

"I could spend the rest of my life with that stupid bear sitting in a corner of my bedroom, couldn't I?"

He looked at me a good long while, taking in what I'd just said. I needed to think about it, too. It had just slipped out. Certainly hadn't planned on that.

"I'm going to give you the chance to rephrase that, if you want."

"You mean that bit about 'the rest of my life'?"

I knew what he meant It was way too soon, wasn't it? And was that what I even wanted? This completely impossible, uncontrollable Tasmanian devil to be my partner in life and in my bedroom, for forever and always?

"What about your plan?" he asked.

"My plan?"

"You know—you and some other hotshot lawyer, fabulous power couple, hand-in-hand litigating your way through life, the envy of everyone? That plan."

"Good lord, Theo," I said looking down at the talented, funny, brilliant and breathtakingly beautiful guy in my arms. "Who wouldn't envy me?"

"So, you're really thinking," he kissed my chin, "you, me, the bear—the rest of your life?"

I nodded.

He gave me one of those tormenting, sideways smiles of his.

"If you're lucky," said my dreamboat, my angel, my sun, moon and stars.

"Yeah," I said. "If I'm very, very lucky."

# Special Thanks

Travis J. Sherrod, Neil Montiel, Ophelia Julien and Timothy Brown, who all cast their critical eyes over earlier versions of this novel and offered invaluable advice.

Sonya Lashua Fagan, who took brilliant photos of my feet and my dog.

And of course the dog, my writing partner and my companion—Watson. He puts up with a lot.

# About the Author

**Chase Taylor Hackett** was raised on a farm in the Midwest among hogs, ponies, corn and soybeans—far from his current home in New York City. His first novel—*Where Do I Start?*—was recently published by Kensington Books.

While working on that book, he realized he had a character who was a total jerk, and he wondered what would happen if the jerk met someone with zero tolerance for jerks.

*And the Next Thing You Know...* he'd written another novel.

Chase lives in upper Manhattan with his partner Travis, and a Scottish terrier named Watson.

www.ingramcontent.com/pod-product-compliance
Lightning Source LLC
Chambersburg PA
CBHW020733250626
47155CB00003B/741